Valley of Thracians

ELLIS SHUMAN

Valley of Thracians

A Novel of Bulgaria

By Ellis Shuman

Cover Design by Shiran Waldman

The characters and events portrayed in this book are fictitious. Any similarity to real persons, living or dead, is coincidental and not intended by the author.

ISBN: 1482552442
ISBN-13: 978-1482552447

For Jodie, who lived the Bulgarian adventure with me.

Part One: The Unintentional Tourist

CHAPTER 1

"Is this your first visit to Bulgaria?" asked the passport control clerk at Sofia International Airport.

"Yes." He looked through the smudged glass at the woman as she flipped the pages of his passport. She glanced up to compare the weary-looking, gray-haired man standing in front of her with the much younger version that smiled reservedly from the faded photograph. Today he had little in common with that self-assured academic who had enthusiastically traveled the world giving lectures and attending international conferences. It was almost as if they weren't even related.

"Welcome, Simon Matthews," she said, stamping his passport with Sofia Airport's inky signature before sliding it back under the glass.

He smiled at her, but she was already beckoning the next traveler to the booth. As he placed his passport into his travel bag, his shoulders drooped with the weight of what he planned to do in the days ahead. Executing his self-appointed mission in a foreign country would not be easy.

Waiting for the baggage carousel to spring to life, he reminisced with surprise that he had managed to come this far. "Maybe this is all a mistake," he murmured to himself for the hundredth time since leaving Chicago. Hadn't his son warned him against traveling to

Bulgaria on his own, arguing that due to his advanced years, Simon was no longer capable of coping with strange situations and unfamiliar environment? Perhaps that was part of the reason he had come—to prove Daniel wrong. Couldn't his son see the importance of this trip?

Simon fidgeted nervously, hoping that he would be able to recognize his suitcase before it passed from view on the moving belt—and not feeling fully confident that he would be able to retrieve it by himself if he did. His leg was aching again, his muscles contracting painfully after the long hours of cramped flight. He should sit down, he told himself, but he didn't want to lose his place near the carousel. The other passengers, speaking amongst themselves in their foreign-sounding language, nonchalantly passed the time as if delays in airports were the most common thing in the world. Well, actually they were.

Getting to Bulgaria hadn't been a simple task. Maybe someone was trying to tell him something.

Minutes later, with his suitcase dragging behind him on its shaky plastic wheels, he limped past customs to the small arrivals hall. As local residents greeted family members and friends, he went over to an ATM to withdraw local currency with his credit card. The blue-tinted bills were freshly printed; he had to work at them with his thumbs to make sure that he hadn't been shortchanged. How much was a twenty leva bill worth in dollars, anyway? He had done some calculations in the days preceding his hastily arranged departure, but like so many other things recently, the details slipped his mind.

"You want ride into Sofia?"

He turned to face a short, stocky man wearing a bulky leather jacket that appeared inappropriate on the warm June afternoon. "Do you know where the Hilton is?"

"Hilton hotel?" the man asked, pronouncing each 'h' with a harsh, grating tone.

"Yes, the Hilton."

"Sure, I take you. My taxi outside."

The taxi sped toward the city, traveling on a bumpy divided

roadway shadowed by colorful billboards advertising luxury shopping and computer products. The slogans reminded him that, like Russian, Bulgarian was a language that used the Cyrillic alphabet. Much of the information he saw posted was totally incomprehensible. A telecomm company's banner, which used English to welcome arriving tourists with promises of constant connectivity, made him feel a bit more secure. Advertisements announcing Internet deals and mobile phone service were signs of Bulgaria's modernity, dispelling his preconceived notion that he was traveling to an isolated third-world country.

The weathered tenements he passed on the road looked just like those he had imagined Eastern Europe would have, with laundry drooping from metal-railed balconies and faded, chipped paint barely concealing the aging cement bricks of the structures. Graffiti sketched in oversized letters and psychedelic hues shouted at him from the concrete walls, as unintelligible here as such statements of protest were in any urban setting. Simon assumed not much had changed since the country's communist era, but he really knew nothing about this city, its history, or its people. He stared out the window, taking in the passing scenery with wonder, like the unintentional tourist that he was.

"How much?" he asked with a sigh of relief when they pulled to a stop in front of the very modern Hilton in its park-like setting.

"Eighty leva," the driver said, flashing an array of golden fillings.

"Eighty levs?" Simon replied, trying to calculate the cost in his mind. That was more than fifty dollars for what had been barely a twenty-five minute ride. Nothing had prepared him for such an expense.

"Standard cost," the driver shrugged as he pocketed the four blue bills.

Simon immediately realized he had been tricked. The taxi driver had taken advantage of him, seeing easy prey in an elderly foreigner. Frustrated, he went into the hotel to check into his room.

Set up in his seventh-floor room a short while later, Simon eagerly switched on his laptop, connected the retractable mouse, and followed the hotel's instructions to log on to the Internet. Perhaps there was a message from Daniel. He half hoped that there would be other important emails demanding his attention, although since his retirement nothing urgent came looking for him anymore.

He waded through the unexciting messages. *"You're missed at the university,"* wrote one former colleague. *"Have you started on that book project?"* asked another. *"Wishing you a wonderful time in Bulgaria,"* said a third.

A *wonderful* time in Bulgaria? He wasn't exactly here on a vacation!

Before signing off, he opened up his Skype program and glimpsed at the list of his contacts. The names of some friends and family members around the world appeared online while others were not. Daniel was offline, which was expected because Bulgaria was ten hours ahead of Los Angeles, where his son lived. What time would his son be getting up? Had he perhaps misjudged and missed his son's early-morning computer time? He couldn't keep track of time differences.

Near the bottom of the program window, one moniker drew his attention more than the others, despite being marked with a faded status icon. He moved his laptop mouse, hovering over the name for many seconds, but the gray failed to switch to active green. Simon closed his eyes, took a deep breath, and then quickly returned his gaze to the screen. The contact was still offline, and there was no indication when this particular Skype user would be available.

"I will find him," Simon vowed under his breath. "I will find him," he whispered again, the power of the mantra growing with each repetition.

CHAPTER 2

"Your grandson is dead."

Those words never failed to strike at his core, cutting into him as sharply now as they had when he heard them for the first time. He held his head in his hands for a moment, trying to ease his emotions, and then he lifted his tear-filled eyes to face the embassy's deputy consul sitting across the table.

"I am not sure," he started, wondering where to begin. "I'm not sure that this is really true."

"The case has been closed for three years," the official stated in a manner that precluded possible arguments.

"I know," Simon sighed, his hands shaking as he spoke. "But it's not closed for me."

"Look at all the evidence we have," the official continued, glancing for a moment at his associate, a young female employee of the United States Consular Service. "The wallet and passport of twenty-three-year-old Scott Matthews were discovered on a beach at a resort north of Varna three years ago. The Bulgarian police investigated, and your grandson was never found. Possibly he was washed out to sea; it's not clear."

"But you never found his body," Simon said, his voice almost pleading for the officials to give him something that he knew they could not provide.

"We never found the body," the female associate admitted.

"They searched up and down the coast," the deputy consul continued, stating the basic facts, things that Simon already knew. "We were in constant liaison with our counterparts in the Bulgarian National Police. In addition, we contacted the police forces in Romania and Turkey. They searched for him everywhere along the Black Sea coast. The beaches in Varna and at Golden Sands, well, they were combed very thoroughly. No body was recovered; no unidentified body was ever found matching the description of your grandson."

"Was there money in his wallet?" Simon asked.

"Yes, there was money in the wallet. There was no evidence of foul play, Mr. Matthews," the woman pitched in. "No suspicion of a kidnapping or anything of that nature."

"It's Professor. Professor Matthews." He had avoided using the title during his years of academia, but ever since his retirement he had latched onto it as a vainglorious reminder of his former standing.

"Professor Matthews," she apologized.

"And what about his laptop? Did you ever find his laptop computer?"

"No, his laptop was never found," the woman said quietly.

"We all know why your grandson came to Bulgaria," the deputy consul stated, clearing his throat as if to indicate that he wanted to change the direction of this discussion. "We know all about that, but the circumstances leading to his arrival in the Varna area are unclear to us."

Yes, Simon thought to himself, he also knew why Scott had traveled to Bulgaria, but what had occurred during his grandson's sojourn in the country remained a mystery. According to the American officials, there was no connection between Scott's original purpose in visiting Bulgaria and his later disappearance. Unfamiliar with what his grandson had experienced during his stay, where he had traveled, and whom he had befriended, Simon lacked the evidence that would lead to a similar conclusion.

"Your son, Daniel Matthews, came here shortly after your grandson's, um, disappearance," the deputy consul continued. "He concurred with our findings. There is no reason to doubt the fact that your grandson is dead," he concluded.

Simon winced at that statement. The Americans, along with their Bulgarian counterparts, had tried to find Scott's body but had failed. Perhaps that was because there was no body to be found. In their failure, Simon felt hope; hope that Scott was alive. Why couldn't the embassy staff share some of this hope?

"What brought you to Bulgaria at this time, Professor?" the female official asked.

Why had he come now? That was the very question his son had raised during their heated long-distance arguments in the days before the flight.

"Don't go to Bulgaria," Daniel said over the phone line. "There is nothing for you there."

Daniel had come to terms with the fact that his only child was dead, that his body had gone missing somewhere on a Bulgarian beach. Scott's mother, Susan, had been heartbroken, more devastated than any of them. She was unable to bear the pain and suffered from overwhelming outbursts of grief even three years later. But Daniel kept his sorrow buried deep inside, as he had from the very first when he bore the devastating news as if he was immune from expressing his feelings. Daniel had returned to Los Angeles with no coffin or ability to conduct a real Jewish funeral. They held their memorial service, mourned the loss of the young adult who had departed from their lives, and then Daniel moved on, distancing himself from other family members and their effusive emotions.

"Dad, don't you see what you're doing?" Daniel pleaded, his voice rising. "You're reopening all the wounds, bringing back the pain. Why do you want to hurt Susan and me more than necessary? Why are you doing this to yourself? Don't you see it's useless—that anything you uncover in Bulgaria will only result in more bad memories? Scott is gone, and we can't change that fact. Nothing you can do in Bulgaria will ever bring Scott back."

Why had Simon come to Bulgaria, a country he had never visited and of which he had absolutely no knowledge? He could not respond to Daniel with clarity any more than he could now explain his reasoning and determination to the American embassy officials. It was a feeling he had—a gut feeling that was burning inside him and growing in intensity from day to day.

But there was more, and this he could barely explain to himself. There had been a sign recently, a nearly physical sign, and he truly believed that this proved his grandson was not dead. What he had witnessed suggested that Scott was living somewhere in Bulgaria, where he had last been seen three years before. It was not an illusion that Simon had seen, but something quite clear that commanded his attention and dictated his actions. The sign had been there, he repeatedly told himself, convinced that it was real.

He couldn't bring himself to tell Daniel what he had seen nor could he offer proof that it had been something real and not imagined. He couldn't explain what he felt deep in his heart because Daniel would argue that his convictions were but prayers for what could never be. Simon had faith that Scott was still alive, and that was what had brought him to undertake this trip.

He had hoped for Daniel's blessing for this trip, some indication that his son approved of his mission—or at least gave it the benefit of the doubt. Despite Daniel's dismissals, he had booked his flights. He had flown to Bulgaria not for Daniel's sake, for Daniel's heart had already cemented the pains of the past. He had come to Bulgaria for his own sake, to find closure for something that he believed should not be closed.

More importantly, he had come to Bulgaria for Scott's sake, to find him and to save him if at all possible. That of course meant proving, somehow—and against all odds—that it was not too late to find his grandson.

"Why are you in Bulgaria now?" the deputy consul said, repeating his associate's question.

"You have no proof, no absolute proof that my grandson is dead. I believe him to be alive. I intend to find him. I really do."

"We want to help you," the woman official said, reaching forward with her hand as if she could comfort him with her touch. "But, realistically, Professor Matthews, it's been three years, and there is little more that we can do."

"I know, I know," he sighed. "Thank you for your time."

The deputy consul gave Simon his business card, the name Brett Thompson printed on it next to the U.S. embassy logo, assuring him that he would be available if the professor came up with any new information, anything that would warrant reopening a closed investigation.

I will find him. For Simon, the case was anything but closed.

CHAPTER 3

Dear Grandpa,

Hi! How are you? I bet you're a bit surprised to hear from me so soon after my visit last week. It was great staying with you and Grandma over Christmas vacation. I bet you enjoyed beating me in gin rummy just as much as I enjoyed teaching you how to use email and surf the World Wide Web. Grandpa, you've got to catch up with the rest of the world; you need to learn all this Internet stuff. I'm writing you now to make sure that you're capable of opening your incoming messages.

If you received this email, write back and let me know. And if you didn't receive it, write back and let me know. Ha!

I always like coming to visit you in the wintertime. In Chicago you see snow on the ground, and it really feels like winter. Isn't that how December and January are supposed to be? Here in Los Angeles you can't really call what we have winter. The temperature drops a bit, and there's some rain, but it's not the real thing. I wish I was growing up in a place where there was snowfall every year. I really like the white stuff!

I enjoyed hanging out with you and Grandma. You guys treat me well, don't pressure me too much, let me sleep late. That's the kind of vacation I prefer. I can do what I want, when I want.

At home, Dad and Mom, well, especially Dad, pressure me all the time. Even on school vacations they want me to get up early, do chores around the house, and whatever else they can think of. I mean, come on! On a vacation you're supposed to have a bit of free time, wouldn't you say?

They're putting a lot of pressure on me to do well in school, but can't they see that this is having the opposite effect? The more they say "devote more time to your studies," the less I want to hit the books. If they would just lay off me for a while, things would be better for everyone.

School is a bore. Come on, who needs to study the American Revolution? How's that going to help me in life? I know basic arithmetic, so what's the point in studying trig? My teachers are complete idiots, and there are times when I can't take them anymore. Sometimes I just skip classes. I'd rather smoke under the football-field bleachers than sit half asleep in a classroom. I can't take that kind of pressure. That's not me. I mean, why should I work so hard to pass a test if what I'm studying has no real value? I'm sorry, but I think tests are a bourgeois attempt to corrupt the minds of America's youth!

Didn't I tell you these things when I visited? Why is it that I can share these frustrations with you when my parents won't even listen to me?

Hey, something else. I wonder if you remember this. This is kind of strange, but it's one of my earliest memories.

I recall one of my birthday parties held in our backyard here in LA. I must have been something like five years old. The party had a costume theme with balloons, streamers, and party favors. Mom and Dad went all out. Some of my friends dressed up like cowboys and Indians. Others were policemen and ballerinas. I was a pirate, I remember that clearly. I had a red bandanna around my neck and a black patch over one of my eyes. Mom had penciled a beard and moustache on my face, and my costume came complete with a plastic sword.

And then an unexpected visitor showed up. It was a tall, thin clown, wearing baggy pants, ridiculous floppy shoes, a huge orange nose, and a shocking display of dreadlocked hair the same color.

The clown laughed, declaring "Birthday greetings, young Scott!" He honked a rubber horn, and all the kids gathered around, pulling at his clothing, kicking his legs. But the clown kept talking directly to me.

I was speechless. To tell the truth, I was scared out of my wits. Here was this unfamiliar person—well, not exactly a person—overwhelming me with his orange hair and makeup. I started crying hysterically, and nothing Mom or Dad said could calm me down.

Do you remember any of this? I distinctly recall how the clown took off his fake nose and wiped some of the makeup from his face, and then I saw that it was you, Grandpa. I was shocked! You and Grandma had flown out to LA, and I didn't know that you would be there, at my party. You showed up unannounced, well, unannounced to me anyway, and you came dressed as a clown. I wish I had known in advance! Only when I recognized that it was truly you did I stop bawling like a baby.

I was so proud that you had come to my party, thinking you had flown all the way from Chicago just to make me happy. What you did meant so much to me.

Hey, why did I even remember this now? Kind of strange what the mind remembers, no? So, did you get this email? Let me know!

I guess that's all for now. Love to Grandma.

Scott

CHAPTER 4

Simon sat on a tall stool at the bar off the Hilton lobby, reminiscing about his grandson. Scott's emails, which arrived over the years at an irregular pace and appeared to be hastily written, detailed difficulties in his studies and an inability to get along with classmates and teachers, as well as the friction Scott felt at home. It was clear to Simon that the boy had problems handling homework assignments and classroom disciplinary requirements. Scott wrote openly of his plans to drop out of high school, to leave LA and travel around the world. Scott desperately sought to escape the sort of future his parents envisioned for him, one in which not only would he pursue a college education, but he would follow that with a graduate degree before settling into a high-paying career as either a lawyer or a doctor. Simon's responses, never critical or dictating about what his grandson should do, expressed understanding and sympathy—alongside his constant, patient request for Scott to reconsider, to stick it out and graduate from high school.

Somehow, Simon's message had gotten through—or at least he credited himself with contributing to Scott's change of heart. After instances of truancy and under threat of expulsion, his grandson had reluctantly resumed his high school studies. Scott postponed his world travels indefinitely and instead was determined to first graduate from high school, a goal that he fulfilled with above-average grades, if not with distinction.

Just before his graduation, Scott confided something to his grandfather that neither of his parents yet knew. Daniel and Susan, having raised their hands to acknowledge their parental failures during Scott's rebellious streak, had given up any hope of seeing their son to apply to a prestigious university. Scott's academic record and SAT scores were far from stellar, making acceptance to Princeton, where Daniel had studied, or at another Ivy League school, nothing more than a vain pipe dream. But Scott had other plans. Unbeknownst to his parents, Scott had sent off an application to a community college not far from where the family lived. He informed Simon first, seeking his grandfather's stamp of approval, and only then let his parents know that he would be pursuing a liberal arts degree while living at home.

Simon had been hopeful that Scott's problem years were at last behind him. That just goes to show what the boy was capable of accomplishing when he set his mind to it, Simon thought. Scott's college years flew by without incident, as far as he knew. He wished that his grandson's emails would arrive at a more frequent pace so that he could fully be part of what the boy was experiencing as he matured into an adult. Even so, every time the two of them got together, their familial connection and closeness were as strong as ever.

Simon beamed with pride at his good rapport with Scott. It was this powerful bond between them that made Scott's disappearance just a year after his college graduation so much harder to bear.

He looked at the Artists' Bar menu, trying to decide what to order.

"Is this a Bulgarian wine?" he asked the waitress, pointing to the line listing a 2008 Sakar Merlot and Pinot Noir.

When the waitress went to pour his glass, he turned to look down the counter. A finely dressed woman with copper-colored hair and dark brown eyes was sitting two stools away, gazing at him with a questioning look.

"Do you know our Bulgarian wines?" she asked, her words touched with local accent.

"Not really," he replied. "Actually, this will be my first taste."

"Oh, but they are very good!" she said, as if he had suggested otherwise. "Do you mind if I join you?"

He hesitated for a moment and then indicated the empty seat between them.

"I hope you don't think I'm too, what's the word, immodest? Someone just stood me up, and I'm a bit upset," the woman said. She set down her own glass of burgundy-colored wine on the counter in front of the seat next to Simon. "Oh, don't get me wrong. It wasn't a date or anything. I had a business meeting, an appointment with an associate actually, and he just called to say that he won't be coming. I think one of his children has come down with something. Are you here on business?"

"Yes," he replied, charmed by her articulation of Bulgarian-flavored English. "Well, business of a personal nature, actually," he added quickly, and then he immediately regretted it. Were all Bulgarian women as forward as this, approaching old, single men at bars?

"You're new to our country, aren't you?"

"How could you tell?"

"You look a little lost, if you don't mind my saying so," she said coquettishly.

Did he look so foreign, so out of touch with his surroundings? His meeting at the embassy had been brief, yet it had drained him with its lack of results. Having dozed afterwards in his hotel room, and still jet-lagged from the flights, he was sure he looked somewhat disheveled. Unconsciously, he sat up straighter on the stool.

He glanced over at her momentarily, afraid to stare for too long. She was a slim woman, wearing a fashionable black dress clasped at the waist with a gold belt. She had more gold on her wrists and in the rings on her fingers; her earrings, though, were simple studs. Her shoulder-length hair framed a pleasing, thin face. Simon assumed she must be in her fifties, but he really wasn't much of a judge of women.

"Bulgaria has many fine wines," she said, backing away from the personal question that had left him feeling a bit uncomfortable. "We have had a wine-making tradition since ancient days, since the days of the Thracians."

"The Thracians? I don't know much about them. Was that a culture here in Bulgaria during the Roman era?" he asked.

She laughed, tapping her hand against the bar counter a few times. "Actually, they came before the Romans! Thrace was a country in this part of the world before the rise of the Greeks and the Romans. Its territory included Bulgaria, parts of Greece, and parts of Turkey. With our love for connecting to the past, we label many of our wines as Thracian. Today, our Thracian wines are produced all over Bulgaria and marketed throughout the world."

"Maybe that's what makes them taste so good," he said, raising his glass to hers.

"*Nazdrave*," she said, clinking his glass.

"*Le'chaim*," he responded, using the Hebrew term, causing the woman to cast a curious glance in his direction.

The wine he was drinking was ruby in color, its aroma somewhat heavy. He found the taste fairly conventional, pleasing but with no outstanding qualities. But then, what did he know about wines? He was not a connoisseur who could intelligently distinguish the subtle differences between varieties. Drinking wine was a social necessity, something he did not for the specific pleasures it released but rather to allow him to fit in with the requirements of his professional standing at university functions, faculty parties, and the conference cocktail parties that he otherwise would have avoided. Even so, from his first sip at the Hilton bar, a sense of relaxation engulfed him, making it easy to converse with the attractive woman at his side.

"The Thracians were subjugated by Alexander the Great and later were conquered by the Romans," she continued, staring not at him but at the bottles displayed behind the bar. "As a people, the Thracians eventually became Hellenized and later yet, they were subjects of the Roman Empire until finally their culture and language disappeared—a forgotten chapter in history.

"But enough about that. We haven't been properly introduced," she apologized. "My name is Sophia, Sophia Ivanova."

"Sophia?" he asked. "Sophia from Sofia, Bulgaria?"

"Yes, I know it's a bit odd. My mother was Italian, and she adored the name, probably because of her affection for Sophia Loren's films. My father was Bulgarian and insisted on giving me a true Bulgarian name, so my official birth name is Svetlana. But Sophia was what my mother called me as a child, and it just stuck."

"Nice to meet you, Sophia from Sofia. I'm Simon Matthews from Chicago. I'm a professor, well actually a retired professor, from the University of Chicago."

"Really? That's interesting. What did you teach?"

"English literature, which I assume is not the most popular of topics here in Bulgaria."

"Oh, you never know!" she said, laughing, her eyes focused on his. "I am also in academia. I teach at our local St. Clement of Ohrid University. In the history department, specializing in Thracian culture."

"So that's why you know so much about these Thracian wines?"

"Hardly! I prefer beer, really," she said, the twinkle in her eye dazzling him and leaving him thirsty for further conversation.

After a few awkward moments during which they both sipped at their wine, she asked him a new, ice-breaking question. "Professor, tell me something. What is the perception of Bulgaria among average Americans?"

"I'm not sure there is a perception of Bulgaria among average Americans. I think there's quite a substantial Bulgarian community in Chicago, where I'm from. At least I've come across some former Bulgarians in the city, and there were many Bulgarian students at the university. But the average American, well, I don't think they could even find Bulgaria on the map."

"Yet, you've come here. Surely you heard something about Bulgaria before coming to Sofia on your business trip," she challenged.

"I know it's a former communist country, now part of the

European Union, and you use the incomprehensible Cyrillic language," he said, realizing that this basically constituted his entire knowledge of Bulgarian politics and culture. "Okay, I admit it, I really don't know anything. I checked ahead on the Internet for the weather conditions, and I booked my stay here at the Hilton online, but I guess I didn't do my homework about anything else."

"No need to apologize. I'm sure most of the businessmen who come to Sofia are in the same boat. And that's a shame because my country is a very pretty place. You should see the country, the mountains, the seashore. Will you be doing any sightseeing while you're here?"

"No, I doubt I'll have the time. I'm traveling to Varna for the weekend, and then I have some meetings back here in Sofia."

"Well, if you need a tour guide, just let me know," she said, placing her hand on his arm and then hurriedly removing it as if it had been an accident.

The simple, momentarily touch of her hand made him wonder if she was flirting with him. When was the last time he had been touched, intimately or otherwise, by a woman? It was a strange yet pleasant feeling, reigniting nerve endings that he feared had died long ago.

He quickly dismissed these unfamiliar thoughts, assuming instead that Sophia was just trying to promote good-natured international relations on behalf of the Bulgarian Foreign Ministry.

"Thank you," he said politely. "But as I said, I'm here on business, not pleasure. Who knows, maybe I will have a chance to see some of the country while going back and forth to my meetings."

"Let me give you my card," she said impulsively, reaching into her shiny black handbag. "Perhaps when you get back to Sofia you will give me a call. It's not every day that you can see Sofia with Sophia."

"Yes, perhaps I will," he replied, smiling at the offer.

CHAPTER 5

Dear Grandpa,

When I got back to campus, I couldn't stop thinking about the fact that we never got to talk, really talk, at the funeral. I hurried to the library computers to shoot you off an email. I am still in shock, unable to comprehend or accept the cruelties of this world. And if I am feeling this bad, I can't imagine what it's like for you.

I am so, so sorry. I loved Grandma dearly. You know that, but it's something I needed to say. I have all these emotions inside of me—memories and warm feelings that surprise me with their intensity. I can't go back to my studies as if nothing has happened. Right now, as hard as everything is, and as powerful as the loss is, I feel I'm very close to Grandma. I don't want to lose this closeness.

I remember a few months ago when you first informed me that Grandma was seriously ill, that the breast cancer had spread, and that the prognosis was not good. I couldn't believe it, couldn't accept it. I mean, Grandma had been part of my life since the very day I was born, so how could she get sick? How could she die?

I've never before lost anyone so close to me. Since Mom's mother died when I was just an infant, I have no memories of her, and Mom's father died well before I was born. A classmate of mine here at the college was killed in an automobile accident last semester, but I was never that close to him. Death is so final, so permanent, leaving us only with memories.

I've always relished my visits to Chicago, especially the ones when I came on my own during school vacations. Grandma baked my favorite oatmeal cookies, cooked that fabulous Spanish tongue dish I craved but could never get anywhere else. She pampered me so much. I can only imagine how she pampered you!

I know Grandma's death was hard for Dad as well, although he is not one to openly express his emotions. I watched him closely during the funeral. I am almost certain I saw a tear form in his eye as the rabbi said the final blessings at the gravesite. That's just the way Dad is. Someone dies; life goes on.

Ok, here's something I remember about Grandma. Well, it's actually about the both of you. This is something from long ago. Anyway, I remember when the two of you came out to Los Angeles for my bar mitzvah. You were decked out in a fancy Brooks Brothers Fitzgerald suit. Not used to the heat in California, you were perspiring like crazy. Grandma was wearing this beautiful floral dress. She looked so elegant, like one of those British royals going to watch the horse races at Ascot.

You seemed a bit nervous sitting in your pew in the synagogue; I don't know why. I went up to the pulpit and recited the haftorah. *My father didn't show any emotions, as usual, but you were quite teary and emotional, and, of course, ever so proud of me. I stood on the pulpit with my head bent, listening to the rabbi's lengthy sermon, and that was that.*

Anyway, the point of all these reminiscences is what Grandma said to me at the party in the reception hall after the service. Grandma said that my haftorah *reading proved that I was capable of accomplishing anything I set out to do.*

That's a statement that's stuck with me a long time. Being capable of accomplishing anything I set out to do. Along with your encouragement, it was also Grandma's statement that got me through my troublesome high school years. I set myself a goal, to graduate from high school, and I proved that I was capable of accomplishing that, just like Grandma had said long before while at my bar mitzvah.

It was at my bar mitzvah that you and Grandma gave me something so special that I still cherish it to this very day. Do you remember? You gave me a silver chain with a Magen David pendant. The Hebrew letters het yod, *forming the word for life, were carved on this special Jewish symbol.*

Maybe at the time, as a thirteen-year-old with greasy hair and a face full of acne, I didn't see myself wearing the chain, thinking that such jewelry was better suited for girls. But now, Grandpa, I wear the Magen David chain all the time. Especially here at college. I am proud of it. It is a link to my grandparents whom I will always love so very much.

Your loss is so much greater than mine, but I wanted to share my feelings. I know how wonderful she was. Marcia, my grandmother and your wife. She will remain in my loving memories always.

I guess that's all for now,

Scott

CHAPTER 6

He kicked at the rough gravel, grimacing when the action sent a wave of pain up his cramped leg. What kind of beach was this anyway? The shoreline lacked any traces of smooth, comforting sand, yet the locals didn't appear to mind. It seemed as if the entire population of Varna had flocked to the Black Sea to enjoy the weekend heat. All along the crowded beachfront, he observed, they were exposing as much skin to the summer elements as possible. Lying on their recliners and drinking beer under their colorful umbrellas, they talked happily amongst themselves. Yet, except for a lonesome windsurfer and a few exuberant toddlers, few residents were actually braving the rough waters, preferring the sun to the Saturday waves.

He was a bit shocked with the audacity of the younger Bulgarian women, but then again, this was Europe, where breast baring was par for the course. Bikini tops hung haphazardly on the support beams of the umbrellas and the backs of chaise lounge chairs, liberating their owners and delighting unashamed gawkers. Slim teenage girls and curvy mature women gallivanted up and down the beach, flaunting their assets and attracting the hungry stares of bare-chested young men. He noticed, however, that some of the older women, including a few who were seriously overweight, had removed the tops of their bathing suits as well. They would have better served the public if they had kept their private parts private.

Ah, but none of this could excite him any more at his age, he mused. When he was younger, seeing the breasts of unfamiliar women in whatever context—at a public beach, in the cinema, on stage, or anywhere outside the privacy of his bedroom—would have resulted in an immediate physical reaction. Now the only thing he was feeling physically as he made his way slowly along the shore was the recurrent pains in his legs. He would have to check that out when he returned to the States.

Walking among the half-naked Saturday sunbathers, Simon felt uncomfortably overdressed. He was wearing brown slacks and a long-sleeved blue checkered shirt. His white Reebok sneakers were filling with sand from the beach; one of them was spotted with smudges of black tar. A Chicago Cubs baseball cap, tilted slightly on his unruly gray hair, completed his beach costume. Despite the warm weather and resultant tanning opportunities, he wasn't willing to risk getting skin cancer as a Bulgarian souvenir.

His repeated kicks at the sand as he walked were due to the frustration he felt, especially after his talk with the English-speaking press officer from the Varna police force, with whom he had met the previous afternoon at the local station. If he had imagined he would come out of the conversation with any new information, he was totally mistaken. The officer, who had introduced himself as Borislav Stoyanov, revealed little more than what Simon already knew about the discovery of Scott's wallet and passport.

"They were found in Zlatni Pyasutsi, commonly known as Golden Sands," Stoyanov told Simon, consulting some papers in an orange folder. "It's a popular resort area, just north of Varna. One morning the cleaning staff discovered them on a lounge chair on the hotel's beachfront. Both the wallet and the passport were on the chair, as if someone had carelessly left them there. But there was no sign of your son, I mean grandson. That's what this report says."

"How did they get there? Was my grandson staying at that resort?" Simon asked, although he already knew the answers to the questions.

"No, there was no guest registered under the name Scott Matthews. The hotel staff was shown his picture, and no one could identify him as having stayed at the hotel."

"So, one morning, out of the clear blue, the documents just appeared at a resort hotel, and no one knows how they got there?" He was becoming impatient with these routine, uninformative answers.

"Listen, Professor Matthews, you are referring to a closed case already three years old. I did not deal with this case. One of my colleagues wrote this report. I can only tell you what is written. I cannot give you other information because I do not have other information. I'm terribly sorry, but there is nothing further I can tell you about the disappearance of your grandson."

Simon kicked at the sand one last time before sitting down at an outdoor café to consider his options. From his plastic chair, as he waited for someone to offer him a menu (hopefully one printed in English), he took in the shore activity. He stared at the sunbathers whose exposed Slavic skin was starting to redden in the sunlight. He grinned at the sight of vendors hawking ears of hot corn on the cob and at the realization that this offer was more appealing to the beachgoers than cold drinks or ice cream. He smiled at the huge quantities of beer being consumed by the locals without any visible effects of inebriation. He strained his ears to make some sense of the strange and unfamiliar language being spoken. And he wondered what his next step in this quest would bring.

The young, freckled waitress didn't speak any English. Although he repeated the word "water" a number of times, she failed to understand his request. He turned toward a nearby table, where three noisy teenagers were drinking what appeared to be bottles of the mineral water he sought, so he pointed at them and used sign language to convey his order. The waitress nodded, reassuring him that he could manage in this foreign setting, but when she returned two minutes later, she was carrying a green, perspiring bottle of Zagorka beer. He shook his head, indicating his disapproval. To his surprise, the waitress smiled for the first time and walked away. He didn't understand what had happened, but instead of complaining any further, he took the bottle and sipped at it reluctantly.

After he finished his beer and paid the bill with the unfamiliar currency embedded in his wallet, he flagged down a taxi to transport him to Golden Sands. His meeting at the Happy Sunshine Resort Hotel was scheduled for noon. Although it was Saturday, the general manager had agreed to see him. Even if he provided Simon with nothing else, Officer Stoyanov from the Varna police force at least had been helpful setting up the connection. Simon was hopeful that the meeting would provide him with new information about his grandson's activities, but when he walked inside the hotel, he learned that the general manager was not present. The woman at the front desk informed him that she was unaware of any set appointment. Simon patiently explained to her that everything had been arranged the day before. The woman kept nodding but seemed reluctant to offer additional assistance.

"Who looks for manager?"

Simon spun around to face an enormous block of a man with a shiny shaven head and a frown as wide as his round face. An immense, wide-shouldered build barely contained by dark pants and a white T-shirt suggested that the man was either a professional weightlifter or a Chicago Bears linebacker. His earlobes were huge; one of them sported a diamond stud. The man's narrow eyes darted back and forth nervously. This man appeared capable of knocking out an opponent with one powerful punch. What damage could he do to someone old and weak like a visiting American grandfather?

Simon stepped back, partially in fear of the man's size but also to get away from the stench of his alcoholic breath. "I have an appointment," he said.

"Manager not here. You here not now. Outside you." The sentences were fragmented, missing both verbs and any sort of civility.

The woman at the desk shot out a burst of heated Bulgarian that temporarily eased the man's concerns, and he stepped back. Simon assumed he was the hotel's security officer, although he lacked the minimum hospitality skills necessary for dealing with the public.

"I will call the manager," the front desk clerk said, turning to the professor. "Maybe he can come in today after all."

"Today Saturday," the man said gruffly as he turned to leave. "Manager no business on Saturday."

The man's appearance was so outlandishly goony, almost cartoonish, that Simon covered his mouth to suppress a smile. If the sinister-looking guard hadn't been so serious about his security duties, Simon would have laughed openly at his broken English. He thanked the receptionist and waited impatiently for the hotel manager.

Happy Sunshine Resort Hotel. The name was comical and not particularly conducive to relaxation, he thought. Yet the glitzy lobby was full of tourists, mostly elderly Germans and Russians from the looks of them. They strolled through the public areas wearing bathing suits and wrapped in towels as they headed to the swimming pool and the beachfront just beyond. Some of the visitors were more elegantly attired, despite the fact that it was noontime. Distinguished-looking men sported black suits, cuffed white shirts, and ties, while bejeweled women at their sides dazzled the eyes in silky evening gowns. These fancily dressed guests puffed at Cuban cigars and thin cigarettes and reclined contentedly on uncomfortable-looking leather sofas and armchairs. Apparently they were on short breaks from gambling frays in the Happy Sunshine Casino, a twenty-four-hour-a-day establishment of buzzing activity situated at the end of a long line of designer clothing and accessories shops. White-jacketed waiters circulated with trays of alcohol and stood back subserviently as the foreigners fumbled through wads of local bills to pay for their extravagances. The click of high heels and the distant jangles of slot machines mixed with the slightly nauseating elevator music being pumped through the lobby.

Simon walked aimlessly among this crowd, his baseball cap in his hands, feeling as out of place here as he had earlier that morning on the Varna beach. He almost collided with a harried waitress as she carried club sandwiches to the hungry gamblers relaxing outside the casino. Finally, he stood at the far end of the lobby, looking out through the curtained picture windows at the hotel pool.

"Were you looking for me?"

He turned to face the hotel manager. Alexander Nikolov held out his hand in introduction, and Simon was surprised to find him as finely attired as some of the gambling guests.

"You'll have to excuse my lateness, but I was preparing to attend a wedding," Nikolov said, brushing a piece of lint off his suit jacket. "It is the brother-in-law of my wife's sister who is getting married today. We often have our marriage ceremonies on Saturdays."

"Thank you for coming in. I thought Officer Stoyanov had arranged our meeting."

"Yes, he called, but I'm afraid I didn't understand anything he said. He certainly didn't explain the purpose of your visit."

"He didn't?" Simon had been sitting with the police officer when he made the call, but maybe he had been mistaken as to what had been discussed over the phone.

Nikolov casually ran a hand through the greasy strands of his slicked-back hair and regarded Simon silently for a moment. "Can I get you a drink? Some coffee perhaps?"

"No, that won't be necessary. But I would appreciate it if we could talk, possibly somewhere a little quieter."

"Certainly. Please come with me to my office."

A few minutes later Simon was seated in a deep-cushioned chair in the manager's office, a half floor up from the lobby level. The room was dark and shabby, in stark contrast to the bright lights and glitter of the rest of the hotel. Nikolov went around his cluttered desk to sit below a huge colorful poster highlighting the wonders of the Black Sea coast. He reached into his suit pocket and pulled something out.

"Cigarette?" he offered.

"No, thanks."

"Why have you come here?" the manager asked, lighting up a Marlboro. He puffed a few moments and then regarded his visitor pleasantly.

Simon realized that his Varna police contact hadn't explained anything at all. He would have to begin his story from the very beginning. He told the hotel manager briefly of his grandson's stay in Bulgaria, his subsequent disappearance, and of the eventual discovery of his passport and wallet on a beach chair at the Happy Sunshine Resort Hotel in Golden Sands.

"This was three years ago, you say. I see. And what was your grandson's name?" Nikolov asked, puffing a cloud of thick smoke in the professor's direction.

"Scott Matthews."

At the mention of the name, Nikolov frowned, and the change in his attitude was palpable and immediate. Scott's name had triggered a very visible response in the man, a sign that it was recognized and remembered—even after all this time. The manager stubbed out his half-smoked cigarette in a glass ashtray only to light another one.

"You're also asking about that American?"

"What? Someone else was asking about him?"

"No, of course not," Nikolov said, backtracking from what had slipped off his tongue.

"What do you know of my grandson?"

"Nothing!"

The loudness of the response was unexpected, but Simon urged him to continue.

"No, I don't know anything at all," the manager insisted, making efforts to calm his voice and forcing a thin smile. "It was three years ago, and that is a long time, quite a long time. We know nothing, I mean, I know nothing at all about this. There is nothing to know."

"Who else was asking about him?"

"You must be mistaken. Nobody has asked about him, and there is nothing to tell about him. That is all."

The hotel manager stood up, indicating that the meeting was over and the professor was expected to leave. Simon was shocked at the abrupt change in the man's attitude. He was certain Nikolov had recognized his grandson's name. The repeated denials only convinced him further.

"Please, what can you tell me about Scott's disappearance?" he asked, almost pleading for the manager to reveal what had caused this reaction. "Was he a guest here at your hotel? Was he possibly a member of your staff? Why were his belongings discovered here, of all places?"

"You must leave now," Nikolov said forcefully, ignoring the questions. "I have a wedding to attend. You must go." And that was the end of their conversation.

A few minutes later, Simon stood outside the resort hotel's entrance, waiting for a taxi to transport him back to Varna. There was something wrong; he was quite sure of that. He would contact Stoyanov from the police again, although he really didn't have anything more than a gut feeling to indicate that the hotel manager knew something that he refused to disclose. Perhaps Stoyanov could look into Nikolov's whereabouts at the time of Scott's disappearance. Or was that too much to ask, too far of a leap in connecting the dots in the mystery of his grandson's final days in Golden Sands?

"Varna?" he asked the taxi driver as he opened up the car door.

"*Dobre*, *dobre*," the driver responded with a toothy grin.

The taxi lurched forward through the hotel's parking lot, shoving Simon back in his seat as it picked up speed. Lost in thought, he barely glanced at the passing scenery.

A shiny black sedan with tinted windows pulled into the street shortly after the taxi and followed it at an inconspicuous distance all the way back to the city.

CHAPTER 7

"There are some very shady people around, but Bulgaria is a beautiful country and that's why I live here."

The English gentleman was drinking a mug of ruby-colored Kilkenny ale at the Irish pub on Varna's Slivnitsa Street, part of a pedestrian zone that stretched from Sea Garden Park to the shops on Knyaz Boris I Street and onward to Nezavisimost Square. Sitting across the outdoor picnic table from the Englishman, Simon wiped the froth of dark Irish stout from his own lips, and then stabbed his fork into a tasty dish of fish and chips, deep-fried to finger-licking perfection.

"What do you mean, shady?" Simon asked the man warily, thinking of his own experiences the previous day in Golden Sands.

"You aren't from around here, so I warn you to be extra careful with whom you do business," the Englishman said quietly, as if taking Simon into his confidence. "Some of my friends have gotten the shaft in their dealings in Bulgaria, so you just need to watch out."

Simon had stopped at the pub for the convenience of its familiar menu and the comfort of dealing with an English-speaking staff. Sitting outside on the porch on the Sunday afternoon and overlooking the passersby on the street, he had willingly offered the seat across the table to the middle-aged Londoner, who had introduced himself as Dave Harris as he made his own order of a mid-afternoon pint. Simon hadn't expected his companion at the table to be so talkative. For a short while, he was able to forget about his own worries.

"Many of us Brits have invested in Bulgaria," Dave began. "Back in the days before Bulgaria joined the EU, it seemed like a property market on the up, where a minimal outlay guaranteed you good capital appreciation. My word, you wouldn't normally consider Bulgaria as the ideal location for your second home overseas, but at the time, it seemed like the best investment. It's a shame that this hasn't been the case for all of us. Some of my friends, eager for a good deal to safeguard their economic future, were wiped clean by discreditable dealers, dishonest contractors, and shoddy builders. It's a wonder there are any Brits left in this country at all, but, as I said, I love it here."

Dave told Simon that he had moved to Bulgaria in the summer of 2006. He had invested in a small rural property not far from Varna where it was but a short drive to the seashore. In his mid-fifties, Dave still worked for an international export company based in Britain, but most of his time was spent in his new home, which he was already preparing for his retirement.

"We were smart, my wife and I. Like many, we didn't have the funds to buy some plush villa in the countryside, fully renovated with a backyard swimming pool. We heard about a property in this village, but before we handed over any money, we came out to see the house, to assess its condition and the restoration work required. Only then did we make our down payment. We were smart to have a reliable English-speaking solicitor review the contract. Never buy something sight unseen, that's my word of advice. But, unbelievably, many of my compatriots were not so intelligent."

Dave told of British couples who had been carried away by the hype and promise of real estate advertisements they had seen in Britain, promising off-plan overseas properties in Bulgaria as a worry-free, highly profitable investment. Dealing with real estate agents, often remotely, the couples had purchased flats in as-yet-uncompleted developments, some of them in Bulgarian spa resort towns or near the ski slopes, only to hear repeated reports of delays, excuses for unforeseen expenses, and demands for additional funding. There was a world of difference between initial price quotes and the final cost of purchase and restoration. An enormous amount of bureaucratic paperwork was required to gain permission to buy property in Bulgaria, and sometimes papers and contracts inexplicably went missing. A number of the projects went bankrupt, and the Brits lost entire investments without ever having set foot in Bulgaria. Cases had gone to court, but dealing with the Bulgarian legal system was yet another unpredictable process.

"Do not believe a word they say," Dave said, thinking of the unscrupulous agents who had tricked his friends. "They will basically tell you anything they think you want to hear, give you the world until they have your money. Once they have your money, you're in deep shit. It becomes extremely difficult to get them to fulfill their promises."

Dave nodded in greeting to other English-speaking clientele drinking at the nearby tables. And then he continued to relate stories about foreigners uprooting their lives and moving to Bulgaria.

Simon was surprised to learn that despite the nightmarish hardships Dave described, there were tens of thousands of British and Irish expatriates living in the country. Many of them, like Dave and his wife, lived in villages and enjoyed the quiet, relatively inexpensive rural life. Other expats preferred living in Sofia, Varna, or the other cities where a richer cultural and urban environment made it easy to overlook the occasional shortcomings of a former communist country desperate to catch up with the rest of the world. For many, Bulgaria was a second home, while others had bravely relocated, leaving Britain for good. All of them apparently enjoyed the fact that there was so much on offer in a relatively small country—mountains, beaches, ski slopes, picturesque historic villages, and Roman ruins. In many cases, as Dave freely shared with Simon, what united the expats—despite an unwavering devotion to their adopted surroundings—were the common frustrations they encountered when dealing with the Bulgarians themselves.

"As for Bulgarian builders, don't even get me started!" Dave exclaimed, enjoying the sounding board he had in the visiting American. "My neighbors, an elderly couple from Kent, have spent the last two months cleaning up the mess left behind by their hired crew of builders. It seems the local workers have never heard of masking tape. They spray painted my neighbors' restored farmhouse, leaving paint all over the frames and speckles on the glass. The work they did left a lot to be desired. Some interiors were painted in entirely different shades of color, and other areas were not finished at all.

"Quite frankly, the level of workmanship here is utterly appalling," Dave concluded. "So shoddy, with no attention to detail and everything done on the cheap. I highly recommend doing your own restoration work."

Simon nodded, thanking Dave silently for the unsolicited advice about Bulgarian house repairs. "Yet, you said you love it here," he said, hoping the Brit would steer clear of the negative aspects of life in Bulgaria for a change.

"Yes, I do," Dave said, setting down his empty beer mug and indicating to the waitress his desire for another round, which Simon politely refused. "Bulgaria has a very interesting history; there is much to see and explore. I hope you'll have a chance to tour the sights, to see more than just the shore here in Varna, because this is not typical of what this country is all about. What did you say you're doing here in Bulgaria, Professor?"

Feeling a bit lightheaded from the Guinness, Simon had no hesitation in sharing the reason he had come to Bulgaria. He told Dave about Scott, how his grandson had come to be in the country and how he had disappeared. He informed his British acquaintance of his talks with the U.S. embassy staff, the Varna police officer, and finally, the unsettling and unexpectedly rude conclusion of his meeting with the hotel manager in Golden Sands. He couldn't explain to Dave why he was so determined in his quest at this specific time, preferring to leave that to himself at this point.

"What did you say the manager's name was?" Dave asked.

"Alexander Nikolov."

"Hmm, the name is not familiar, but I'll ask around. I have good connections among the expats, and I also know some of the who's who in Varna high society. Maybe someone knows something about him or about the Happy Sunshine Resort. Very strange—and quite suspicious—how he reacted to your conversation about your grandson. Give me your contact details, and I'll give you a call if I learn anything about this fellow. My word, you're not doing anything illegal, are you, Professor?"

"No, why would you suggest anything like that?" Simon asked in surprise.

"Well, ever since you mentioned your bad experience at the hotel, I've noticed this pair of Bulgarian men sitting at that café across the street. I think they've been there since the moment I sat down with you, but I didn't realize who they were observing until now."

Simon slowly turned in his seat, looking beyond the strolling families, teenagers, and young couples on the tree-lined pedestrian mall that constituted Slivnitsa Street. Sure enough, in the café across the way, parallel to the Irish pub, there were two men sitting at a round table, gazing at him from the distance. As Simon stared at them, one of the men quickly turned his head, but his companion never took his eyes off of Simon as he smoked casually on a long, thin cigarette.

No, they couldn't possibly be watching him, Simon told himself. Dave must be mistaken. Those men were simply enjoying the fine June weather like the rest of Varna's residents. There was no reason in the world that they would take an interest in a retired American professor. Simon turned back to glance at the excesses of an unfinished Guinness on the table. He thanked Dave for the interesting conversation and informed him that he would be returning to Sofia on a Bulgarian Air flight in the morning.

"If you ever come back to Varna, be sure to give me a call," Dave said, rising to leave. "And I'll definitely make some inquiries about that rude manager, Alexander Nikolov. Something about your confrontation with him just doesn't sound right. I'll let you know if I come up with anything."

CHAPTER 8

"Dad, are you all right?"

"Of course I'm okay."

"I didn't see you online all weekend," Daniel typed.

"I was in Varna. Just got back to Sofia this morning," Simon responded, his fingers warming to the Skype conversation. Something was wrong with Daniel's camera and microphone setup, so they communicated in text.

"You need to tell me when you go away like that," his son typed back. "I was very worried."

"No need to worry. What time is it there?"

"Dad, I'm very worried about you traveling around Bulgaria by yourself. I don't understand what you're doing, why you're doing it, and why now?"

That was quite a long sentence for a text message, Simon thought. He hadn't been able to provide his son the precise answer in a phone conversation, so how could he ever give him anything more now over the Internet from halfway across the world?

After Daniel made his father promise to contact him on a daily basis and to keep him apprised of any additional travels, they bid farewell and the chat box closed.

As he did every time he logged onto Skype, Simon went down his list of contacts to see who else was online. His interest centered on a specific listing at the bottom of the program. But as before, that contact was not available at this time. This didn't surprise him, yet he was hoping that one day, just one day, there would be a green icon promising him the chance to communicate with that person. It was yet to be.

Simon had an agenda, a plan of whom to meet and where to go. Everything had been meticulously arranged in advance—contacts made and meetings scheduled from overseas. He wasn't sure what the results of this quest would be, whether he would be any closer to his missing grandson, but he was certain that he was taking the necessary first steps to find Scott.

After the lack of results from the trip to Varna, he was hopeful that his next meeting would be more productive. It was scheduled for that afternoon in downtown Sofia, leaving him with nearly a full day to take in some of his surroundings, to see a bit of the city. As long as he was here, he might as well get a feel for the Bulgarian capital.

"Can you point me in the direction of the center?" he asked the clerk at the front desk. "And please tell me how long will it take to walk there?"

"It's about a twenty-minute walk," the young man replied, indicating the appropriate direction.

The intensity of the bright June sunshine surprised him. He adjusted his baseball cap to keep the sun out of his eyes. The hotel was located near a major intersection filled with electric trams, delivery trucks, and cars jockeying for position at the traffic lights. A wide pedestrian bridge sloped upwards over the main traffic artery; this was the path he wanted. He walked slowly up the incline, pausing for breath at the top.

He grinned when he saw the familiar yellow arches of a McDonald's franchise located on a traffic island below the bridge. The international fast-food corporation certainly hadn't wasted any time before entrenching itself in the opening markets of Eastern Europe, he thought. Even though it was the middle of a Bulgarian workday, the drive-through lane of the restaurant was backed up and the picnic tables were filled to capacity. He watched the traffic for a moment and then continued over the bridge.

A colorful poster on a metal stand caught his attention. It was labeled "Thracian Treasures of Bulgaria," but the rest of the explanatory text was in Bulgarian. The poster pictured what appeared to be the entranceway of an ancient tomb, with female figures carved in high relief on its stone walls. He couldn't determine what he was seeing from the Cyrillic explanations, so he continued walking.

That poster, to his surprise, was the first of many as part of an outdoor exhibition on the pedestrian bridge. One row of poster stands faced him at intervals of every few feet, while another row ran in parallel on the other side. All of the high-relief images pictured ancient treasures, discovered over the years in various locations around Bulgaria.

There were pictures of tombs and pictures of the icons and relics found in those tombs: ancient urns, murals of half-human figures, small and large nude statues, intricately cut jewelry, and well-preserved sarcophagi. A remarkable gold mask with full facial features stood out from the other images, its striking beauty incredibly brilliant after so many millennia of being buried and hidden from view.

Thracian treasures. He had just been talking about Thrace. He remembered drinking the Thracian Valley wine and his conversation with the Bulgarian woman who lectured on Thracian culture. Her spirited explanations of Thrace's role in Bulgaria's history had left him eager to learn more. He took one last look at a poster depicting a ceremonial drinking horn of some kind and then continued toward the center.

On the far side of the bridge the walkway sloped downwards, leading him to a wide, stone-slab plaza surrounding a huge auditorium. Having consulted a free copy of *Sofia Insider* tourist magazine at the Hilton, Simon realized that this must be NDK, the National Palace of Culture. This was Sofia's major convention center—a complex of theater halls, meeting rooms, and exhibition areas. The building was immense and ultra-modern. It looked like an alien spaceship had landed in the midst of the Bulgarian city.

The plaza was a hub of activity, with people of all ages walking down sidewalks flanked by colorful flowerbeds and around fountains and cascading flows of water. Elderly residents sat on wooden benches, quietly observing the scenes, while young mothers pushed baby carriages toward metal tables at outdoor coffee shops. Teenagers skirted past him on their skateboards, executing fearless leaps down the stairs as if performing to an appreciative audience. A woman wearing tall high heels hurried ahead, trying desperately to keep pace with her pair of leashed pug dogs. The hubbub of city traffic was easily forgotten by those relaxing and enjoying the June sun in the plaza.

His leg was troubling him again. He hadn't planned on this much walking; apparently the center of the city was more than a twenty-minute walk from the Hilton. He looked around, searching for a bench where he could sit down and rest, but at this side of the plaza, among the trees and flowerbeds, there was nothing. Suddenly a glimpse of a familiar sign in the distance caught his eye and beckoned him forward. He hurried through thc park and across the street.

The familiar aroma of Starbucks coffee made him forget the discomfort in his leg, and he felt right at home ordering a vanilla latte. This had been his daily vice back on campus, where he would stop by a Starbucks between classes and leisurely review the literary submissions of his students. He loved inhaling the scent of freshly brewed coffee more than drinking the hot lattes themselves. Often he would linger in the campus cafés, enamored by the comforting atmosphere he found within, distracted from the demands of his teaching if only for a short while.

"Professor, is that you?"

He turned to greet the woman he had met at the Hilton bar. "Sophia," he said, surprised at seeing her. "Sophia from Sofia!"

"What a coincidence running into you again. How are you?"

"I'm fine. What happened, did someone again stand you up?" he asked, remembering the circumstances of their first meeting.

"Oh, no, nothing like that at all," she said, smiling at him. "I taught an early class today and am on my way back to my apartment, which is not far from here. Do you mind if I join you?"

Sophia sat down with her own unsweetened latte, which she stirred constantly as it cooled. She was dressed more casually today, in light-colored slacks and a blue sleeveless blouse. "So, Professor, you never told me why you've come to Bulgaria."

He hesitated, wondering how much of his personal circumstances he should reveal to the inquisitive woman. But then he remembered talking about his trip with Dave Harris in Varna. The English expat had offered to check for information about the Golden Sands hotel manager. So, why not?

Over the next few minutes, between sips of his vanilla latte, he told Sophia of his grandson's disappearance and of his own mission to learn what had happened to Scott.

"I am meeting someone downtown shortly. He may have discovered more information. I have other meetings scheduled as well. I'm trying to fully understand everything that occurred from the moment Scott arrived in Bulgaria until he went missing."

"You keep saying disappeared, but the police, they say he is dead?"

"I have this gut feeling that Scott is still alive, but no one believes me. The police certainly don't. The embassy staff isn't open to other possibilities. Neither are Scott's parents. But I need to check everything. Scott could be anywhere, and most likely he's still here in Bulgaria. He may be in need of help, and no one else seems to care. I can't let him go, I can't drop this," he said with conviction.

"Where is your meeting?" she asked.

"On the steps of some downtown church. I think it's called the Alexander Nevski Cathedral."

"Ah, yes, the most famous place in all of Sofia. I'll take you there now, if you'd like."

"I don't think I can walk any farther," he said, running a hand over the sore muscles of his leg.

"Oh, don't worry. We'll take a taxi."

"Are you sure it's not out of your way?"

"It would be my pleasure to go with you," she said, reaching across the table to touch his arm.

CHAPTER 9

Dear Grandpa,

I'm sure you've heard by now from Dad and Mom that I've applied to serve in the Peace Corps. I submitted my application, and I'm anxiously waiting to hear if they'll accept me. I hope they send me to some exotic tropical island, like Fiji or Guam. But I know that if they do take me, I'll go wherever I'm needed.

I'm kind of worried because I don't speak any foreign languages. If you remember, I flunked Spanish back in high school. I wasn't too good with the grammar and my accent, well, it was quite atrocious. The Peace Corps' website says that knowing another language is not a prerequisite for being accepted, so we'll see what happens.

Does it come as a surprise to you that I would want to do this? Dad and Mom, well, they were shocked, to say the least. Maybe it would be a shocker after some of the wild things I did in college, especially since no one, not Dad and Mom or anyone, believed I would ever graduate. But I did it! I have my degree (thank you again for that generous graduation check by the way), and now my college years are behind me.

No, I don't want to continue studying for another degree. A bachelor's degree is quite sufficient, I can tell you. Dad keeps hounding me about this, saying that I would have better chances in the job market if I had a master's degree under my belt. But what would I master in? I barely got through these studies as it was, and I don't particularly know at this point in my life what I want to be doing when I grow up.

Yeah, you read that right. I may be twenty-two years old, but I still need to come to terms with what I want to do. I have done some things of which I'm not very proud, things that you don't need to know or worry about, but hopefully I'm past all that. Now I want to get out and see the world.

It wouldn't hurt anyone, not even me, if I managed to do good things for once in my life. I guess that along with the bad things I do sometimes, there's a positive side of me as well, hiding deep inside and waiting to prove itself. Maybe that's the reason I've applied to the Peace Corps. Maybe I'll be able to show Dad and Mom, and you, that I'm really a good kid after all. If they take me, I'll do anything they want. If I'm smart enough to speak English, I assume I'm also smart enough to teach it.

So, now I'm waiting for them to accept me.

Grandpa, I hope you're ok and managing on your own. You've announced your retirement, so what happens next? Maybe you should apply to join the Peace Corps as well, and then we can volunteer together in Fiji.

Grandpa, don't worry about losing touch with me. No matter where I end up in the world, we'll still be able to talk, I promise you. I'll write to you all the time and Skype you so we can chat and see each other. Just remember to get dressed beforehand because I don't want to see your pajamas again. LOL!

(Do you remember what that means?)

I guess that's all for now.

Scott

CHAPTER 10

"Alexander Nevski Cathedral," Sophia announced with a flamboyant wave at the lavish gold domes towering above as they took to the shade outside the church. "Sofia's most important landmark. It's named after a Russian tsar who came to our assistance back in the Middle Ages. The Russians have often helped us Bulgarians, and this church is dedicated to them. The church's construction started in the 1880s, I think, and continued for quite some time. We in Sofia are very proud of our cathedral, even though we're unlikely to ever pray inside."

Simon followed his guide up a short set of steps to a weathered plaque that informed visitors of the church's completion in 1912, honoring the Russian and Ukrainian casualties of the 1877 War of Liberation from Ottoman rule. Simon took off his baseball cap but refused to go inside.

"Don't you want to see the interior?"

"No, I'm supposed to meet this man outside, on the steps."

"Do you know what he looks like?"

"No, but I'm sure he'll recognize me. I stand out from the crowd, easily recognized as an American tourist," he said.

The name of the man he was due to meet was Bogdan Kamenov. Simon was thankful to Sophia for escorting him to the church, but he wondered whether he should talk with Kamenov in private. Remembering the interest Sophia had taken when he explained why he had come to Bulgaria, he dismissed that thought. He was glad that she was with him.

A bent-over old woman approached Simon, one hand shakily offering a bouquet of colored flowers and the other extended in a plea for charity. Attired in a gray, ankle-length smock that had seemingly been worn for time immemorial, the woman's face was wrinkled to an extreme and her gaping mouth was cankerous and toothless. She mumbled words in a tongue that could have been Bulgarian but may just as likely have been a long-forgotten Slavic tongue. Simon shook his head as an indication that he had no desire to give the hag any money.

The woman smiled and moved steadily closer, her open hand nearly touching his sleeve. Again he shook his head but the old beggar drew closer still.

Sophia stared at Simon and then at the woman and broke out laughing.

"What's so funny?" Simon asked.

"You're just encouraging her!"

"What do you mean?"

"In Bulgaria, we shake our heads from side to side, just like you've done, to indicate a 'yes' answer. To say 'no,' we nod our heads up and down."

"What? You mean, exactly the opposite from the rest of the world?"

"Yes, the head gestures here are inverted," she told him. "You thought you were telling the woman to go away, but in reality, you led her to believe that you would give her something. In Bulgaria, a nod means no and a shake of the head means yes."

Before Simon had a chance to protest, Sophia dropped a coin in the woman's hand but declined the proffered flowers. He was going to say something else but heard his name being called from the church's entrance.

"Professor Simon Matthews?"

"Yes, that's me."

"Hello, I'm Bogdan Kamenov." The Bulgarian was in his thirties and wore faded blue jeans and a short-sleeved white shirt. The strap of a black briefcase was slung over his head; one of the case's zippers was half undone, exposing sheets of lined paper. He looked harried, as if he was running from one appointment to the next, but he smiled when he saw Sophia at the professor's side and waited anxiously for an introduction.

"Sophia Ivanova," she said in greeting.

"Nice to meet you. I'm sorry, Professor, but I only have a few minutes. Can we talk here?"

"Yes, of course."

Kamenov led them to a shadowed recess where they were not bothered by the stream of pilgrims heading into the cathedral. He held his head low, as if afraid that someone would eavesdrop on their conversation.

"I thank you for hiring me as your private investigator," Kamenov began, handing Simon three typed pages. "I've completed the assignment, but unfortunately I haven't anything significant to report."

Sophia gave Simon a quizzical look, but he didn't offer her any explanations. Instead he asked the investigator, "What exactly have you done? I wired you payment, and I'd like to know what you've accomplished."

"I spoke to the hotel manager in Varna," Kamenov continued, but he was immediately interrupted by Simon.

"You spoke to him? Or did you go see him?"

"I spoke with him on the phone. We had a short conversation, but the man wasn't helpful providing any clues about your grandson."

Simon's face reddened and his hands crumpled the investigator's report into a small wad. "I paid you quite a bit of money, and all that you did was speak with him on the phone? I've been in Bulgaria but a few days, and I've already managed to travel to Varna to confront him in person."

"Well, it's all a matter of priority and time," the investigator said. "If you would like to increase the range of my services, I will take a more active role concerning this case."

"What else have you discovered?"

"Nothing else as of yet. Before we continue, I would like to finalize the payment issue."

"I don't think that will be necessary," Simon said with finality. There was no point paying someone who wasn't providing any assistance at all. "Thank you, but that'll be all."

The private investigator shrugged and retreated down the steps to the cobblestone plaza. As he walked off toward the city center, Sophia turned to Simon and saw that he was seething from the encounter.

"What was that all about?"

"I should have known. I contacted him over the Internet, hired him to investigate Scott's disappearance. I didn't want to miss a single clue. I thought a professional could get to the bottom of this much quicker than me. I paid him in advance, and he's produced absolutely nothing. That was certainly a waste of time and money."

"You must be very disappointed."

"I'm too angry to be disappointed. I was very hopeful for the information he would provide me, and in the end our meeting lasted less than five minutes. Well, live and learn. I will just have to continue on my own."

Seeing that Simon was still upset, she suggested something to change the subject.

"What are you doing for dinner tonight?"

"What? I don't know." His mind was still reeling from having wasted money needlessly.

"Some of my colleagues are coming over to my apartment. They all speak English, and I think it would be an interesting experience for you to meet them. I will be cooking traditional Bulgarian food. Would you like to join us?"

CHAPTER 11

"*Nazdrave!*"

"*Nazdrave!*" Simon said in return, clinking his own small glass of the Bulgarian *rakia* liquor with those of the others seated around the dinner table. He was getting used to the word, pleased to see that there was a "*Le'chaim*" in every language. Somehow, the spirited expression made the alcohol easier to swallow.

"*Rakia* is our national drink," Sophia said to him as she continued pouring glasses for each of her guests. He had intended to refuse the drink, but he didn't want to offend his hostess, so he had reluctantly accepted the shot she held out to him.

"Do you know about *rakia*?" she asked.

"*Rakia* is an alcoholic drink produced by the distillation of fermented fruits and is popular all across the Balkans." The explanation was coming from Dimitar Damianov, a lecturer in chemistry at Sophia's university. "It can be made from plums, apricots, grapes, even pears in some cases. Or it can be a mixed-fruit drink."

"There are different names for *rakia*," contributed Stanislav Petrov, another lecturer. "You've probably heard about grappa in Italy. Well, this is similar. There is also *pálenka* in the Czech Republic, *pálinka* in Hungary, and *palinca* in Romania."

"No, those aren't *rakia* at all," Dimitar argued, pushing his glasses farther up his nose with his index finger. "Real *rakia* can only be found in the Balkans. You have *raki* in Turkey, *rakija* in Montenegro and in Serbia, and something else in Macedonia I can't remember."

"What does the name matter?" Stanislav said. "As long as it's home-produced and more than 50 percent!"

"50 percent!" Simon almost had to choke back the tears as the pungent drink torched his mouth, throat, and stomach in turn.

"This *rakia* is from my parents' village," Sophia told them proudly. "I would say that a 50-percent alcohol level is probably a low estimate of what it really contains."

Simon's head was already spinning from the first round when the *rakia* glasses were refilled. Before he had a chance to voice a refusal, a second glass was set before him. "*Nazdrave*!" he piped in as he raised it to join the others.

The moment he had walked into Sophia's third-floor apartment Simon stepped into another culture. He had taken off his shoes in the entrance hall and made his way in stockinged feet to the small living room where he met Sophia's colleagues from St. Clement of Ohrid University. They were delighted to welcome a visiting American professor and made every effort to make him feel right at home. Simon was pleased with this warm welcome. Home-cooked meals and encounters with local academics were not offered on the Hilton restaurant menu.

A wide selection of salads—all of them prepared by Sophia—was displayed on the table, served in colorful ceramic bowls and dishes. As each one was passed from guest to guest, the hostess gave Simon a running account of its name and ingredients.

"This is *shopska salata*, our national salad," she explained.

"Don't let any other country in the Balkans claim *shopska* as its own!" commented Rossi Marinova, a wide-eyed woman who worked with Sophia in the history department.

"*Shopska* is truly Bulgarian," insisted Dimitar, and the others at the table indicated their agreement by raising their glasses of *rakia.*

"So, about the *shopska salata*," Sophia continued. "It's a simple salad really, consisting of cubes of cucumbers and tomatoes, with some onions, parsley, and in this case, grilled red peppers. Over everything, as you see, is *sirene*, our white cheese."

"What is it, a feta cheese?" Simon asked.

"Something similar to feta," she acknowledged.

He couldn't help but notice that the *sirene* blanketed the fresh vegetables in the salad like a layer of freshly fallen snow. There could possibly be more cheese than anything else in the salad, something that would not be good for his cholesterol, but he politely scooped a portion onto his plate.

The next salad to be passed around was something Sophia labeled as *snezhanka*. It was a bowl filled with cucumbers swimming in yogurt and decorated with leaves of parsley. This was followed by a roasted-pepper salad and then a white-bean salad, garnished with green onions, black olives, and radish flowers. His stomach was filling rapidly, but Simon felt obligated to taste each new offering brought to the table.

Dimitar pulled out a pack of cigarettes and offered one to Simon, and then passed the pack to his university colleagues. With the exception of Sophia, all the Bulgarians lit up as they sat back to digest the food.

"That was simply wonderful," Simon said, nodding in satiated fulfillment to his hostess.

"Save room for the main course," she said to him with a twinkle in her eyes.

As they ate, the Bulgarians conversed on a number of topics, politely speaking in English for the sake of their visitor. One of them complained about the state of garbage collection in Sofia. Rossi blamed the situation on the current mayor, while Dimitar argued that it was the previous administration that had reduced the municipality's budget. Stanislav mentioned that the GERB party had yet to fulfill any of its electoral campaign promises, and this resulted in a quick objection by Dimitar. Sophia tried unsuccessfully to get a word in edgewise. The more the university colleagues discussed local politics, the more heated their arguments became.

At first, Simon was able to follow the discussion, but as it continued, he couldn't determine if they were speaking in English or in Bulgarian. After a while, none of it made any sense to him, and his eyes began to water. It was getting hot, very hot. And it was stuffy. Couldn't someone open a window?

The glasses of *rakia* had long been cleared from the table, and now Sophia was pouring glasses of Mavrud wine for her guests. Simon reached his hand forward to cover his glass, but he was too late and the rich red wine was set before him.

He shouldn't be drinking so much, he told himself, his eyes beginning to cloud. He had eaten more than he should have. The veal had been tasty but heavy. The back of his neck was hot, and, in fact, he was beginning to perspire. He took another sip of water.

"More wine?"

"Another portion of veal?"

The room was beginning to spin, or was it his head? Simon took a napkin and dabbed at his forehead, and then he wiped the back of his damp neck. His eyes closed for a split second, and then he forced himself awake and tried again to concentrate on what the others were saying. Something about taxes. Or was it something else they were discussing? It was getting darker in the room. It was hot. There was no air. His eyes began to shut as his vision faded.

"Professor, are you all right?"

Who was asking? Where was he?

And then everything went dark.

CHAPTER 12

"You were mumbling about Scott."

"What?"

"It's okay, Simon. May I call you that?"

He was lying on a bed, staring up at her as she wiped his forehead with a wet washcloth. How long had he been out?

"Oh, well, that was embarrassing," he said, trying to work away the mists of unconsciousness that had overwhelmed him. He attempted to sit up on the bed but lacked the strength to make the move.

"Don't try to get up just yet. You need to rest," she said calmly, as if taking care of retired American professors who fainted in her living room was something she did every day.

"I'm so sorry," he apologized. "I've ruined your dinner party. And it was such a good one. Where is everyone?"

"Everyone has already gone. I think you gave them all a good excuse, as it was getting quite late."

"I'm sorry," he repeated, but she shushed him and kept mopping his face with the damp cloth.

"What was I saying?" he asked her, a few moments later.

"You were saying something about your grandson. Scott, right?"

"Yes, Scott," he sighed. "I will find him, I just know it. The private investigator didn't get to the bottom of this, but I will. Tomorrow I have a meeting that will help me understand what happened to Scott."

"A meeting?"

"Yes, in a small town in the north. Vartsa, I think. No, wait. Vratsa, that's the name."

"You need to go to Vratsa?"

"Yes."

"You're in no shape to go anywhere," she said, patiently wiping his forehead.

"I'm fine, really," he said, forcing himself up on his elbows. His head was still spinning somewhat, and he almost fell back to the mattress.

"How exactly were you planning to get to Vratsa?"

"I asked at the hotel. I could take a bus or the train."

"Oh, really? Simon, I admire your undertaking this mission to find your grandson, but I don't think you're capable of traveling to Vratsa on your own. You should get some bed rest in the hotel for a day or two."

"No, the meeting is scheduled for tomorrow. It took a long time to set it up," he said, rising slowly to his feet in an effort to prove to her—and to himself—that he was up for the journey.

"Let me pour you a cup of coffee to help clear your head," she said. He followed her into the dining room while she put on a pot of water.

As he sipped at the hot instant coffee, not as rich as a Starbucks latte but exactly the caffeine he needed at right now, he realized she was sitting across the table watching him intently, a look of deep concern on her face.

"What?"

"Simon, I have an idea," she said, and he struggled to remember what they had talked about in the bedroom. "I will drive you to Vratsa."

"You can't take me to Vratsa. That's very kind of you, but this doesn't concern you at all. And you have your work at the university to attend to."

"I can't allow you to travel there on your own. Don't you worry about my university work. I will arrange that."

"I wouldn't think of involving you in this," he said, trying to dismiss her offer politely.

"Vratsa is a very interesting town, and there's something quite unique there. I will gladly drive you to your meeting. Who knows? You may need a translator with you, a guide to the sights," she said.

"I'm not exactly on a sightseeing tour," he reminded her.

Nothing he could say would change her insistence on driving him to the town of Vratsa. Why was she making this offer? he wondered. Was it because she felt sorry for him, a visiting retired professor who was beginning to show his age and display a growing number of physical ailments? Did she take pity on him for coming to a foreign country with little hope of finding a missing loved one? Or was it possibly because she felt a need to compensate for her own embarrassment that he had fainted in her home?

He couldn't figure out why Sophia from Sofia was being so friendly to him. He smiled at her and sipped his coffee.

CHAPTER 13

Hi Grandpa,

I made it to Bulgaria! Who would have believed it?!? I'm sitting here on the far side of the world, somewhere in Eastern Europe. I bet you can't find Bulgaria on a map. I certainly couldn't until the Peace Corps accepted me and informed me that this is where I would be volunteering.

I made it all right, but my bags didn't. I had to run to catch the plane in Munich, but I guess my suitcases didn't run fast enough. It looks like I'll need to wait another day until they get delivered. Good thing that I was carrying my laptop in my hand luggage.

One of the trainers in the program met me at the airport, and we traveled together by bus to Vratsa, a town in northern Bulgaria where I'll be doing my initial training. Everything is an adventure for me—even riding the bus. We bought tickets at the central bus station in Sofia and were assigned our seats. We waited quite some time for the bus to arrive, but finally it pulled in. From the outside, it looked like something real ancient, but when we got on, I was surprised to see that the seats actually were quite comfortable. We weren't the first ones to board, but when we did, we discovered that two older women were sitting in our places. We had a huge argument with them, showed them our tickets, we even had to get the driver involved (which was a story in itself because no one spoke any English). Finally, the two women agreed to move to their own seats, which were at the very back of the bus. They kept mumbling the whole time—maybe even cursing us—and we finally sat down for the two-hour trip. Hmm, I guess that could happen anywhere, and it's not necessarily a Bulgarian thing.

We got to Vratsa, and, for some reason, the trainer insisted that I immediately see where our course would take place. It's in one of the local schools, quite a run-down building. They don't have much money for renovations, and the budget for repairs is practically non-existent. In any case, the only memorable thing to say about the school is that the view through the windows is of some high, beautiful mountains in the near distance. It's absolutely gorgeous! I can't wait to go hiking in the countryside. I think I'll like the mountains!

I was shocked to learn that one of the first things I have to do here is learn Bulgarian. Ok, they may have mentioned something about this when I was given details of the Peace Corps program. We're going to start intensive studies right away. Each of us will be assigned a local host family—one that doesn't know any English at all. We'll be spending a lot of time with our families, and I guess it will be a sink-or-swim situation. Either we learn Bulgarian quickly, or we starve.

I guess that's all for now.

Scott

P.S. The Bulgarians are very interested in my Magen David. One of the people I met commented by saying that the Jews are truly respected in Bulgaria. Not exactly sure what that means, but I guess I'll be finding out a lot about this country in the coming months.

CHAPTER 14

"The first Peace Corps volunteers came to Bulgaria in 1991, shortly after the change in the Bulgarian political system. We currently have some 130 volunteers, but over the course of the years, more than 1,100 young Americans have served with the Peace Corps in Bulgaria. We have two groups of volunteers coming a year, although that may change. All of our volunteers work to help Bulgarian youths learn life skills. Even so, English-language instruction remains a key part of our programs. Our volunteers who are focused on youth and community assistance also actively help community members improve their English-language skills."

The woman proudly describing the Peace Corps program in Bulgaria and its accomplishments was Gloria Peters, the organization's program and training officer responsible for the Vratsa operations. Peters, a veteran Peace Corps staffer was originally from New Mexico and she had previously served in Honduras. Having been appointed to lead the training staff in Vratsa six months before Simon's arrival, she hadn't personally known Scott.

The Peace Corps position Peters was now filling had a five-year limit, intended to keep the program's workplace vibrant and fresh. Peters said that she deeply missed her family and friends back in the United States, but her work with the residents of other countries—

teaching them the English language and American values—was so rewarding that she would have difficulties going back to live in the States when her term ended.

"And I've developed a personal connection to Bulgaria as well," she informed Simon and Sophia, who sat across the table from her in the small lounge. She mentioned briefly that she had a Bulgarian boyfriend, and they were planning to get married.

Peters was a friendly woman in her mid-thirties with a pleasant face and a long braid of prematurely gray hair. She was very eager to describe the training program and the service the volunteers did once they had been officially sworn into the Peace Corps.

"We call their initial period with us pre-service training, or PST. PST lasts about eleven weeks, with much of the time devoted to Bulgarian language and culture. We also train our personnel in the technical skills they need to fulfill their assignments. The TEFL volunteers—that's Teaching English as a Foreign Language—receive training in teaching methodology. They are actually training to become teachers and must know how to manage the classroom environment. We have youth-development volunteers, who learn how to work with at-risk youth. They get practical skills, learning how to develop short camping sessions and after-school programs for youth. And our community-development volunteers learn to manage projects, write grant requests, and organize grassroots community initiatives.

"Our volunteers work within the Bulgarian school system, many of them team-teaching with Bulgarian teachers," she explained. "This helps the teachers improve their English competence and learn new language-enrichment activities, both formal and informal. And of course, our volunteers work directly with the students themselves, teaching English through various hands-on projects such as school renovations, English-language summer camps, after-school language workshops, and community or sports activities. The volunteers also help run camps for Roma and other minority children, and help girls and boys develop leadership skills."

"Roma?" Simon asked, not familiar with that term.

"The Roma are an ethnic group spread all over Europe," Sophia volunteered.

"They're commonly known as gypsies, but that's a bit misleading," Peters continued. "Let's just say that they're a minority group here in Bulgaria, one that needs our special attention."

"Everything you've said is quite impressive," Simon admitted. "What I would like to know are details about my grandson's time working with the Peace Corps. Would he have selected Bulgaria on his own?"

"Many of our candidates submit a preference, suggesting a country or a part of the world where they would prefer to work. But the Peace Corps doesn't guarantee anything. We send our volunteers where they are needed the most. Do you know the history of the Peace Corps?"

Without waiting for a reply, Peters told Simon that, contrary to public opinion, it was not actually President John F. Kennedy who had first proposed an American government-led corps of volunteers serving around the world.

"It was Hubert Humphrey, then a democratic senator from Minnesota, who in 1957 first introduced to Congress a bill that would establish an organization of students volunteering overseas. Even so, Humphrey didn't fully support his own initiative, citing in his autobiography that traditional diplomats hesitated at the thought of sending thousands of young Americans to different locations across their world. Many senators, including liberal ones, thought it was a silly and an unworkable idea, Humphrey wrote.

"During the 1960 presidential campaign, then-Senator Kennedy, speaking at the University of Michigan in Ann Arbor, challenged the students to give two years of their lives to help people in developing countries. Later Kennedy would dub his proposed new organization as the Peace Corps. His opponent, Vice President Richard Nixon, reportedly said in response that the Corps would serve as nothing more than a government-sanctioned haven for draft dodgers.

"And of course, we all know of Kennedy's famous inaugural speech, when he stated in clear reference to his proposal, 'Ask not what your country can do for you—ask what you can do for your country.'

"In March 1961, Kennedy signed the executive order that formally established the United States Peace Corps, and he appointed his brother-in-law, Sargent Shriver, to be the program's first director.

"Since that time…," Peters said, preparing to continue relating the organization's history, but Simon interrupted.

"Can you please give me details of what my grandson did here in Bulgaria? Where he volunteered? Whom he helped?"

Peters seemed a bit disturbed with the interruption. "As I told you when you first contacted me by email, Professor, your grandson served in the Peace Corps three years ago. That was before my own arrival in Bulgaria, so I never had the opportunity to meet Scott. What I can see in our records is that he arrived in Bulgaria in 2006 as part of group B19. That name is due to the fact that it was the nineteenth group of Peace Corps volunteers to serve in Bulgaria. I'm sorry, Professor, but I can't tell you anything else that you don't already know about his service in the country."

Simon was disappointed. He had expected someone from the current Peace Corps staff to have personally known Scott from his time in the country. "What about the other volunteers? Maybe someone who knew Scott from that time is still working in Bulgaria?" he asked. "Is there someone I can see to get more information about Scott, his activities and travels during his volunteering stint?"

"You could possibly talk to his host family."

The host family. The mention of that element of the training program shook a memory in Simon's mind. What was it? *Host family*. There was something significant with this, of that he was convinced.

"Just a few days after their arrival in Bulgaria, trainees are assigned a local host family and go to live with them, to become fully immersed in Bulgarian culture," Peters explained. "Trainees eat meals with their families, interacting with them as much as possible. The families are encouraged to reinforce the study of Bulgarian by speaking with the trainees in that language at home. I can assure you that all our host families are carefully selected and trained specially for this role. We inspect their houses in advance to make sure they have a private room for the trainee and that they are located within a short distance of where we conduct our training sessions."

"Yes, I would like to meet them, Scott's host family. That would be very helpful, indeed. Do they live here in Vratsa?"

"They live in Montana," Peters replied, looking up from the file on her desk.

"Montana!" The knowledge that Scott's host family was now living in the western United States made his whole visit to Bulgaria seem pointless.

"Yes, Montana. It's a town about an hour's drive north of Vratsa," Peters said. "It's good that we keep records of these things."

Sophia, who had kept quiet during the entire meeting, sat forward suddenly. She touched Simon's hand and said, "I'll drive you there."

"There's a town in Bulgaria called Montana?" Simon asked incredulously.

CHAPTER 15

The Regional History Museum of Vratsa consisted of nine exhibition halls highlighting Bulgarian history, archaeology, geology, and information about the life and final days of Hristo Botev, the country's beloved revolutionary hero who had been killed by the Ottomans in the nearby mountains. Sophia didn't bother to stop at any of the display cases but hurried Simon along to a climate-controlled room in the back that was the most popular in the entire museum. This was the Treasure Room, home to Bulgaria's largest collection of ancient Thracian artifacts.

In this hall, glass display cases were brightly lit to showcase the silver- and gold-gilded vessels within. Each of the rectangular boxes displayed a number of the items, dated to the first half of the fourth century BC and arranged attractively on top of colored fabric. Descriptions were printed in both Bulgarian and English. Close examination of each piece revealed ornate detail that had survived the centuries.

One gold-gilt pitcher, about thirteen centimeters in height, displayed the barefooted Thracian Virgin Goddess. Her hair was braided and her head was shown full-faced, in what Sophia described as the Thracian manner. A draped *chiton* was flung over her left shoulder and pulled tightly under her right armpit. In one hand the goddess held a bow and arrow, while with the other she was hugging the large cat, possibly a mountain lion or panther, on which she was mounted.

To its side was a second pitcher, two centimeters shorter than the first and crafted entirely of silver. Depicted in its center was another goddess, this one with a disproportionately large head. In each of her hands the goddess held a backward-facing small dog, while winged centaurs galloped at either side. In the lower part of this pitcher, an engraved bull was being attacked by two pairs of enraged dogs.

"The details are absolutely exquisite!" Simon said, looking closely through the glass. He was extremely pleased that Sophia had insisted on a short tour of the museum following their meeting with the Peace Corps training director. The artifacts were stunning, as brilliant today as they had been upon their creation millennia before. "Where were these treasures discovered?"

In 1985, a farmer by the name of Ivan Dimitrov was working on his tractor, preparing to dig a new well for his vegetable garden in the village of Rogozen, some forty-three kilometers north of Vratsa, Sophia explained. Just a short distance below the surface, he encountered an obstruction, and upon investigation, Dimitrov saw that he had unearthed a hoard of silver vessels. More digging revealed a total of forty-two jugs; twenty-two wide, shallow saucers known as *phialai;* and other objects. He brought the artifacts to the staff at the Vratsa museum.

Archaeologists converged on the site and further excavations revealed another pit containing one hundred silver vessels buried just forty centimeters below the surface. In this second location, eighty-six *phialai*, twelve jugs, and two cups were discovered. The archaeologists dated the discoveries to the fourth century BC, conjecturing that the objects belonged to a local noble family that buried its treasures due to extreme circumstances, possibly in fear of a foreign invasion. Some claimed that the treasure was buried to prevent its falling to the conquering forces of Alexander the Great.

"Because most of the Rogozen vessels were made of silver, some will say that the gold treasures discovered by three brothers outside a

Panagyurishte ceramics factory in 1949 were a more important discovery," Sophia said, the excitement apparent in her voice. "But due to the incredible quantity of vessels, I believe the Rogozen collection is much more significant in understanding the ancient Thracian kingdom. On many of the Rogozen vessels you can see inscriptions with the names of the Thracian rulers and even of the silversmiths, goldsmiths, and engravers who made them. The graphic depictions on the Rogozen vessels show a clear connection between Thracian and Greek mythology and culture."

Sophia explained to Simon that ancient treasures were accidentally discovered quite frequently in Bulgaria. Gold and silver vessels were unearthed near the village of Valchitran in 1924, and farmers uncovered treasures while plowing their fields near the town of Borovo in 1974. Other caches of Thracian relics had been dug up by chance at Loukovit and Letnitsa.

"We have unearthed so many treasures, and there are so many more yet to be found. As recently as 2004, Professor Georgi Kitov discovered a unique five-hundred-gram gold human mask near the village of Shipka, in central Bulgaria. It was unearthed in a burial tomb in what we call the Valley of the Thracian Kings. Not as glorious as the Valley of the Kings in Egypt, perhaps, but still, a valley with more than thirty ancient burial tombs of significant value. It is amazing that Kitov was able to discover that mask in pristine condition after it being buried for two millennia. Who knows what other treasures lie just below the surface, waiting for us to find them," Sophia said.

"What was in this one?" Simon was standing by an empty glass case, the largest in the entire Treasures Room hall. "Is this item on temporary loan to another museum?" he asked.

"Hardly," Sophia replied with a sigh. "Unfortunately, that item is no longer in the Rogozen collection, and it was the most stunning Thracian artifact of all! Do you know what a *rhyton* is?"

Simon started to shake his head, but then remembered the local custom. He forced his head to nod up and down. "What's a *rhyton*?"

"A *rhyton* is an ornate drinking vessel, or container, typically shaped like a drinking horn with an animal or animal's head at the bottom. We know they held fluids intended for drinking, however, they may have been used to pour libations in ritual ceremonies.

"In this display case, the museum exhibited the largest, most magnificent *rhyton* ever discovered in Bulgaria. It was absolutely enormous, almost half a meter in length and weighing nearly two kilograms. It was completely silver and covered at its ends in pearls. At the lower part was a finely carved oversized lion's head. As I said, the *rhyton* is a drinking vessel, and as such, its opening was the lion's mouth itself. On the inside of this *rhyton* there was an inscription, and the likely translation from the ancient Thracian meant basically 'Mother Earth.' There is no doubt in anyone's mind that this *rhyton* belonged to a royal family, possibly to the King of Thrace himself. This vessel was very famous. News of its discovery at Rogozen was announced with huge publicity all around the world back in 1985. Of all the items in this collection of treasures, only this one was given a specific name. They called it the Rogozen Drinking Lion."

"What happened to it?"

"It's sad, really. The Rogozen Drinking Lion was hidden underground for two millennia alongside the other treasures that you see here. It was able to escape being captured by the Macedonian kings, including Alexander the Great himself. But it wasn't able to avoid the dangers of modern greed.

"The Rogozen Drinking Lion, perhaps Bulgaria's finest Thracian treasure, was stolen from this museum a few years ago," Sophia said, her eyes never dropping from the empty display case.

CHAPTER 16

That night he had trouble sleeping.

He was too old for this, he told himself. When was the last time he had dined alone with such an attractive woman? In the years since Marcia's death he had never considered starting up again with anyone. The thought had never crossed his mind. Sure, there had been evenings in Chicago when he had gone out to dinner with his female colleagues from the university, but in those cases he was on his home turf—an arena where the topics for discussion were literature and the politics of tenure. He felt on much safer ground dining with a woman in Illinois than he did at a grill house in northwestern Bulgaria.

There was something about Sophia, but he couldn't put his finger on it. She was attractive, single, very educated, and, like him, she came from the world of academia. She had a maturity in her attitude about life in Bulgaria, and her career had elevated her stature above that of most of the women he knew back in Chicago. She was very easygoing, taking readily to her self-appointed role as his tour guide and source of information about Bulgarian history and culture. And, she seemed genuinely interested in helping him find out what had happened to his grandson.

But there could be something more, and this was what was

preventing him from falling asleep. Her interest in him was touching, but he failed to understand what she saw in him. He was a gray-haired American in his late sixties, with aching legs and an inability to hold his alcohol. No, he must be mistaken. Surely her interest in him was solely academic.

The decision to stay overnight in Vratsa had been unexpected, made after Sophia's numerous phone calls had ascertained that Scott's former host family in Montana would only be available to meet with the visiting American the following morning. Traveling all the way back to Sofia was out of the question, so after their visit to the Vratsa museum, they checked into rooms at the gray and uninviting Hemus Hotel off the town square. Simon fell into a deep afternoon nap that lasted much longer than planned. Later, he happily accepted Sophia's offer to explore the town.

Their dinner that evening had been pleasant enough. At the simple grill house, with its stained wood tables and impatient waiters, they shared a platter of mixed meats, which included many pork portions. Although Simon wasn't an observant Jew, eating pork was not something he did frequently. He understood that Bulgaria was a country where pork was plentiful and tasty, and he bit into the white meat with a hearty appetite. As a garnish, he ordered French fries, and he was surprised to receive his side dish sprinkled with white cheese, the same topping that had blanketed Sophia's *shopska salad.* Local beers accompanied the meal. The ice-cold Shumensko was refreshing, completing the picture of a typical Bulgarian meal.

"You know, you keep pronouncing the name incorrectly," she said, and he didn't have a clue what she was talking about.

"The name of our capital city. Sofia. You have been pronouncing it exactly as you do my name—Sophia. But actually, they are different. My name is Sophia, with the accent on the second syllable. And our capital is Sofia, with the accent on the first syllable."

"I didn't notice that!" he said.

"Yes, many of our words carry an accent on the first syllable. The woman we'll be meeting tomorrow, her name is Ralitsa, pronounced with an accent on the 'Ra.' I can't say that this is a general rule for

Bulgarian, as our language has a number of quirks regarding pronunciation."

"Is Bulgarian similar to Russian?"

"Russian is a much more complicated language. I know, I studied it for many years! But we both use the Cyrillic alphabet. Did you know that the Cyrillic alphabet actually originated in Bulgaria?"

"I thought it came from Russia."

"No! There were two brothers, Cyril and Methodius, who were born in Thessaloniki, Greece. They were very instrumental in introducing Christianity to the Slavic peoples back in the ninth century. They also standardized our language, and for this, the church recognizes them as saints. In Bulgaria we commemorate their achievement with a special holiday, Saints Cyril and Methodius Day, or as it is more modernly known, Slavonic Literature and Culture Day. Our national library in Sofia is named after them as well."

"I can't imagine celebrating the creation of an alphabet that is so difficult to read!" he said, laughing, thinking of how she had guided his choices on the Bulgarian-only menu.

They sat silently for some time, enjoying their meal. And then Sophia asked a question that surprised him, sending involuntary shivers up his spine.

"You lost your wife recently?" she asked.

"Yes," he replied quickly, although Marcia's death from breast cancer had been a number of years before. Was the loss still so obvious? For a few minutes he spoke of Marcia, how good and stable their relationship had been, how she had supported his academic career and served as a sounding board to his essay ideas and book proposals. She had let him lead a double life, one private at home with her and the family, and one on his own with his fellow professors and students. She had been a loving wife, a good mother, and a wonderful grandmother.

Without waiting for an invitation, he spoke of his academic years, of the many scholarly papers he had written; of the lectures he had given with no need for notes; and of the constant demand to be familiar with the latest publications in the field of literary criticism.

His few published books were minor volumes that reviewed the works of nineteenth-century American authors, including Melville and Twain. He had longed to write his own fiction but lacked the discipline and stamina to produce anything more than a few half-hearted short stories. He had taken pleasure in reading the papers submitted by his students and encouraged them to seek out original and creative ways to format their ideas. He saw his role as that of a guide, assisting his charges in their creativity as they developed critiques of famous works of literature, which he would afterwards review and grade. It was hard work, he told Sophia, requiring many hours of concentrated effort. For years he had worked well into the night, reading and grading, critiquing in such a way that would encourage and not discourage. Weekends and holidays had been more of the same. There had been literary conferences all over the United States and in Europe as well. He had enjoyed a fruitful career, and having a wonderful and supportive wife like Marcia at his side had made it all possible.

"Do you have any regrets?" she asked.

"No, no regrets. Well, one. I wish my wife was still with me. I miss Marcia, and it's hard to carry on without her."

Sophia put her hand on his. Embarrassed at the touch, he quickly withdrew his hand and hid it in his lap. What was he doing? She was offering sincere sympathy, and he need not fear her kind gestures. A few minutes later, moving it as naturally as possible, his hand was back on the table.

"Simon, why did you come to Bulgaria to look for Scott now? After all, he's been missing for three years," Sophia said, abruptly changing the subject.

The sign—indicating that Scott was still alive. He couldn't keep this piece of information to himself any longer. He needed to confide in someone, but should he be opening up to a Bulgarian woman he had only recently met? She was taking a very keen personal interest in helping him and had invited him to her apartment to meet her colleagues from the university. She had gone entirely out of her way to drive him to Vratsa for his meeting with the Peace Corps instructor, and tomorrow she would take him to meet Scott's host family in Montana. He felt he could explain everything to Sophia, but would she believe his story?

"Okay, I'll tell you what I saw," he said. "Do you know the program Skype?

"Of course. Everyone knows Skype! You talked to your grandson on Skype?" she asked excitedly.

"No," he admitted. "I only wish. It was my grandson who taught me how to use the program. I am pretty much a computer ignoramus, but I can still learn a thing or two. Scott taught me the basics of email, and he taught me how to use Skype. When he first came to Bulgaria, he regularly sent me emails describing his experiences, and he called me at least once a month on Skype to update me.

"The thing is, Scott's laptop was never found, which I thought a bit strange at the time. Even now, this fact continues to irk me. Where is his laptop? Certainly that would be an important clue, valuable information regarding his disappearance. I talked to the police about this, but they apparently never even bothered to search for the laptop. Or if they did, they never found it."

"Simon, I'm not exactly sure what you're saying."

"Just about ten days ago, before I decided to come to Bulgaria, I noticed Scott's laptop online in Skype."

"You mean, you noticed Scott online on Skype?"

"Yes, I guess that's how you'd say it. His username in the program is WildScott1984. I was online on my computer at home and just checking my emails, which I do on a daily basis. All of a sudden, a little green box popped up at the bottom of the screen. It said: 'WildScott1984 is online.' At first I didn't realize what I was looking at. I opened my list of contacts to see who was online. I have friends all over the States, others in Europe. In any case, I went to the bottom of the list of online contacts, and sure enough, WildScott1984 was there, marked with a green icon."

"Did you chat with him?"

"Well, I was in a bit of shock. I couldn't believe what I was seeing. I stared at his name for a moment, but the instant I tried to click it, it faded. He had gone offline."

"It definitely sounds like he was online, but he could have logged into his Skype account from any computer in the world."

"Oh," Simon said, a sinking feeling beginning to engulf him. Seeing the WildScott1984 icon online didn't prove that his grandson was in Bulgaria after all.

"Actually, there are a few possibilities," Sophia said, thinking over what Simon had said. "Scott could have gone online with his laptop or from some other computer. Alternatively, someone may have used his laptop and inadvertently launched the Skype program, automatically logging in with Scott's username and password. In any case, this information is something that no one previously knew. Did you tell anyone about this?"

"No, I didn't think that Daniel or the police would have believed me."

"Have you seen him online since?"

"No. I keep looking. I check Skype every time I turn on my computer, glancing through my list of contacts and hoping—even praying—that I will see WildScott1984 online again. Now I'm a bit confused. From what you're saying, it could be that someone else is using Scott's laptop. If that's true, that person would know something about Scott's disappearance. Perhaps that person is responsible for what happened to Scott. My grandson could be in serious trouble! He could have been kidnapped. Who knows?"

Simon wiped away a tear that threatened to cascade down his face, something that surprised him each time he thought deeply about his beloved grandson even after all this time.

"Looking back, I sometimes think that what I saw may have been a figment of my imagination," he admitted to Sophia. "Maybe I wanted Scott to be alive so intensely that one day that I imagined his name as being lit up in green. If he had responded to me, I would have known for sure. Now, I can't prove anything."

"I think it's good that you've come to Bulgaria to look for Scott," she said, trying to calm him. "You're here now, and together we'll figure out the events that led to his disappearance." Again she put her hand on his, a touch that lasted far longer than he would have expected.

Tossing in his narrow hotel bed later that night, with its rock-hard mattress and lumpy pillow, he couldn't stop thinking about their dinner and her reassuring touch. This shouldn't be affecting him so much, he told himself as he turned over again onto his back. He was too old for this. He hadn't come to Bulgaria to form a friendship with a woman. He had come to the country for a reason, and he needed to fully dedicate himself to that task. Now, if only he could get some sleep.

CHAPTER 17

Dear Grandpa,

Hi, how are you? I'm living with my host family. At first I was doing all right with them, but then something happened, an incident that I don't fully understand. I'm not sure if it's an issue of language or something more.

Ralitsa, my host mother, is great. Even if I wasn't picking up a few words of Bulgarian, I think we'd communicate just fine. She pampers me with her cooking. Every morning she prepares an awesome breakfast, and I'm good for the day. But then she outdoes herself with tasty lunches and sumptuous dinners. Too much food, really!

Radoslav is my kid brother; everyone calls him Rado. He's eight years old and desperately wants to go to America. With Ralitsa I try to speak only Bulgarian, but with Rado, I sneak in words of English. After all, this is why I'm here in Bulgaria—to teach kids how to speak English. Rado loves to play basketball and soccer, which of course the locals call football, but I'm not too good at either game. He has asked me a few times for help with his school work, but it's all in that funny Cyrillic script, so I'm pretty helpless.

Most of the Bulgarian families I've seen around this small town seem to have only one or two children. I don't know if this is by choice or not, because as it was pointed out to us in our orientation, northwestern Bulgaria is the poorest area in the country. The unkempt streets, the broken windows in the school, the shoddy utilities. It's a real shame because the people are so nice.

Boris, the father of the family, works in construction—or so that's what I've been told. I rarely see him, which is probably for the best. He is quite impatient with me, and when I don't understand something, he pointedly ignores me. Not like Ralitsa, who will repeat things dozens of times, making extra efforts to articulate words, helping me in whatever way possible so that I can understand.

Something happened the other night, and I'm not quite sure about what I saw. I was walking alone through the back streets of the town, and everything was so quiet. Someone was standing near my family's home, and I couldn't tell at first who it was. I stepped back when Boris approached me from the shadows. He was panting, and his breath was horrendous. He must have consumed a large quantity of beer that night because he absolutely stank of alcohol. He grabbed me and held a hand to my mouth, so I couldn't shout out. I tried to struggle but realized it was pointless. He is so much stronger than me.

Finally, he let go and spun me around to face him. He indicated something that I immediately understood because it was in a universal language. Boris held one finger up against his lips, signaling for me to keep quiet. I shook my head, assuring him that I wouldn't say a word, and then he left me alone. Someone else showed up, and Boris forgot that I was there.

I really didn't appreciate being rough-handled by my host father. It certainly wasn't a pleasant experience.

If this was just an issue of an inebriated man afraid to admit his drinking habits to his wife, I wouldn't be too concerned. Lots of Bulgarians drink—both beer and hard liquors. But this was not a case of Boris's intoxication.

He's involved in something, and that's what's bothering me. I really can't go into details now or list my suspicions here. Maybe this is nothing, and I'm mistaken about what I saw.

Sorry to trouble you with this story, but I just wanted to update you on what's happening. Don't you worry about it. I'm fine, really.

I guess that's all for now.

Scott

CHAPTER 18

There was something on Sophia's mind as they drove north, but she wouldn't say what, if anything, was bothering her. Simon tried to engage her in conversation, to bring up again some of the subjects that had invoked very passionate discussion between them at dinner the previous night, but these efforts were answered by one-word responses. Simon mentally kicked himself for thinking that this attractive Bulgarian woman had taken any personal interest in him. How could such thoughts have crossed his mind or caused him any loss of sleep?

He turned to look out the window at the beautiful green countryside, a patchwork of fields stretching to a towering mountain range to the west. He recognized the meter-high stalks of summer corn and the green John Deere tractors churning up the soil, but alongside these familiar sights was something quite foreign in the scenery: a farmer ambling across his acreage behind his horse-pulled plow; an old woman weighted down under a tremendous stack of branches; ramshackle hovels with smoke rising from their chimneys; children running barefoot through puddles of muddy rainwater in their yard; horse-drawn carriages and roadside vegetable stands. These were all vivid reminders that he was far from witnessing agriculture in a Midwestern Corn Belt state.

In both Bulgarian and English, black letters on a highway signpost announced their arrival in Montana. Compared to Vratsa, efforts had been made to beautify Montana's public areas, as the town served as the region's administrative center. The streets here had no potholes, and everything seemed clean and well-kept. But the apartment blocks were the same gray, unadorned tenements he had seen elsewhere, and the storefronts were framed with Cyrillic billboards and graffiti.

After stopping only once to ask a passerby on the street for directions, Sophia managed to navigate their way through the narrow roads of the town's laid-back residential neighborhoods. She consulted the address she had written down, and then stopped and parked the car.

"Here we are," she said.

It was a one-story, faded red-brick house, nestled behind a flower garden and surrounded by a green wire-mesh fence. A sidewalk of cracked cement ran from a rusty wrought iron gate to the house's raised porch and alongside the short incline of a ramp that ended at the wooden front door. Large windows with flowerpots flanked either side of the entrance, and a tiled roof sloped away from a brick chimney.

Sophia knocked on the door, and they heard movement inside the house. A moment later, the door eased open, and a tall, thin woman wearing a blue kerchief on her head shyly greeted them. Sophia and the woman exchanged a few words in Bulgarian, and then they followed her down an elongated corridor into a small living room.

Simon shook hands with Ralitsa, not catching her last name as they were introduced. She had a sad face. Her eyes were red and constantly blinking. She motioned for Simon and Sophia to sit on a lumpy sofa and then took her own seat on a kitchen stool. Ralitsa's English was very rudimentary, so Sophia served as translator.

"Ralitsa and her family have been living in Montana for many years," Sophia translated, "but they come originally from a village not far from here, close to the Serbian border. No, excuse me. Her husband's family comes from that village. Ralitsa was born here in Montana."

Sophia and the woman conversed for several moments as Simon's eyes adjusted to the minimal light in the room. The furnishings were simple but practical. A painting of a wooden farmhouse half hidden by a winter blizzard adorned one wall. Short-stemmed red roses in a glass vase served as the centerpiece of a rectangular table that was pushed off to the side. The woman stood up to get something, but Sophia motioned for her to sit back down.

"She wanted to bring us refreshments, coffee and biscuits, but I politely refused," Sophia told Simon. "I asked her to tell us about the time when she and her family hosted Scott during his training program."

The woman glanced nervously at the back of the room, where a door seemed to lead into a bedroom. Then she turned to face her visitors, a half smile forming on her face. She began to speak but took care not to raise her voice.

"I remember Scott very fondly," she began, her words translated into English for Simon's benefit. "He wanted to learn Bulgarian very much. I remember this because my own English is so bad. He was always walking around carrying a dictionary, looking up words. We would help him with his Bulgarian homework every night. It was funny. He was a grown man, much older than our own son, Rado, and here we were helping him with his homework.

"He put these papers, what do you call them? Ah, sticky notes. He put them on objects all around the room so that he could remember the Bulgarian words for them. Table, chair, rug. One of the first sentences he was able to say was 'I like cucumbers.' After he said this, I would prepare salads with cucumbers for him all the time. This was funny because a while later, when his command of the language was better, I learned that he actually hated cucumbers, and what he had been trying to tell me was that he didn't like them!"

"What was his life like when he lived with you?" Simon asked, indicating for Sophia to translate this question.

"Nothing special. He woke up in the mornings, and I made him breakfast. He went to his Bulgarian-language classes and then came home for lunch. I made him lunch, and then he went back to classes."

"Did you and your family get along with Scott?" Simon asked, trying to dig deeper.

"He didn't like that we smoked," came the reply. "We smoke the same as all Bulgarians, I think, but this bothered Scott. There were some times that I went outside to smoke my cigarettes, but my husband refused to do this, saying that this was our house and we could do whatever we pleased in our living room."

"Did Scott get along with your husband?"

At that moment Sophia's cell phone rang, and she excused herself as she took the call. She answered with the Bulgarian "*Alo*" and that brought a grin to Simon's face, but when Sophia realized who was calling, she stood up and walked to the entranceway, out of sight. Simon smiled politely at Ralitsa and waited for his companion to return to the room.

Without trying to eavesdrop at all, Simon realized that Sophia was speaking in English. "Yes, yes," she was saying. "I am here with him now." She was almost whispering as she spoke. Simon couldn't clearly hear any more of the conversation.

When Sophia returned to the living room, Simon began to ask her whether everything was all right, but Sophia ignored him and instead she addressed Ralitsa in Bulgarian.

Ralitsa replied at length, her eyes clouding and her voice becoming quieter and quieter as she spoke. Simon wondered what she was saying and waited impatiently for Sophia's translation. Finally Ralitsa stopped and covered her eyes with her hand.

A noise somewhere in the back startled them, and Ralitsa quickly composed her face. She stood up and excused herself and left the room, giving Sophia time to translate for Simon.

"Her husband and Scott didn't get along—to put it lightly," Sophia said. "They did at the very beginning, when Scott first arrived, but then something happened, something that Ralitsa is not quite sure about. And then, a while later, they were again on friendly terms, as if nothing had ever come between them. In fact, for quite some time they were working together on some project, Ralitsa said. She didn't know any details about this because her husband never spoke about it. But the two of them, Boris and Scott, would go out together late at night, disappear for hours and return home only after Ralitsa was asleep. This went on even after Scott continued with the next stage of his Peace Corps program. And then, everything changed, Ralitsa said, because Scott disappeared. That's what she said."

Before Simon had a chance to respond, Ralitsa re-entered the living room, accompanied by her husband. To Simon's surprise, the man, in his early forties, rolled into the room on a wheelchair. Even though he was sitting in the chair, Simon could see that Boris was a powerful man, with arm muscles that bulged out of a sleeveless green T-shirt. His expression was angry, and he shoved his wife aside as he rolled himself across the wood floor toward the visitors.

Boris shouted at them in heated Bulgarian. Even though Simon couldn't understand a word of it, he could tell that curses were very much a part of the man's verbal attack. Simon stood up and started easing backward towards the entrance corridor, shocked at the intense anger in the man's voice. He looked to Sophia for guidance, but she seemed as startled as he was over the outburst. Ralitsa stood to one side, not making a move to quiet her husband. When it appeared that nothing could be done to calm the man down, Sophia and Simon walked out of the living room and quickly left the house.

As they hurried down the ramp and toward the front gate, Ralitsa shouted something at them. There was no anger in her voice, only embarrassment. Simon assumed she was apologizing for her husband, but he wasn't sure what had just transpired in the family's living room.

"Come on, let's go," Sophia said, urging him toward the car.

It was only later, as they left Montana and headed south, driving alongside the stunning mountain range and the wide expanses of agriculture, that Sophia finally worked up the nerve to tell Simon what Boris had shouted at them.

"He said that Scott had betrayed him," Sophia said, her hands tightly gripping the steering wheel. Her face was ashen as she stared ahead at the narrow country road. It took her a few minutes more before she built up the strength to report one additional thing. "He said that when he sees Scott again, he will kill him."

CHAPTER 19

"Do you know the story of Bulgaria's Jews?"

The bearded man asking the question, wearing a dark suit jacket and sporting a small black yarmulke on his head, stood in the doorway of the Sofia synagogue, eager to welcome the American professor to the central edifice of Judaism in Bulgaria.

"No, I really don't know anything," Simon said.

"Please, come inside, and I will tell you our story," the rabbi said, beckoning Simon to enter the building.

Simon checked his watch and saw that he was early for the unplanned appointment. The strange, unsigned message that had been waiting for him upon his return to the hotel the previous night had not identified the person he was to meet, nor had it provided details about what was to transpire. All that the short message said was: "Meet me at the Sofia synagogue tomorrow morning at 11 for important information regarding your grandson."

The rabbi reached out and guided Simon into the building. "During World War II, Bulgaria sided with Nazi Germany. Tsar Boris III and the Bulgarian parliament enacted the Law for the Protection of the Nation, which introduced numerous legal restrictions on Jews in the country," he said. "But unlike the other European countries that fell under Nazi occupation, Bulgaria was able to save its Jewish population, numbering nearly fifty thousand. That cannot be credited to Tsar Boris III but rather to the Bulgarian Church and the ordinary citizens who rose up against any attempt to deport their Jewish neighbors. In the years after the war, most Bulgarian Jews emigrated to the newly established state of Israel.

"Unfortunately, some ten thousand Jews living in Macedonia and other Bulgarian-administrated territories could not be rescued, and they were transported to the death camps. But Bulgarian Jewry was saved, and for this miracle and for the kindness of the Bulgarian people, we are forever grateful."

"I didn't know that," Simon said, the story distracting him from the reason he had come to the synagogue. "Are there many Jews in Bulgaria today?"

"We number about six thousand in total, with some two thousand living in Sofia itself. I, myself, come from Israel and am serving the Jewish community here at the synagogue. I assume you are Jewish."

"Yes," Simon replied, adjusting his Chicago Cubs cap as he followed the rabbi past a wall of donor plaques into the synagogue's central hall. A guilty thought raced through his mind as he remembered the grilled pork specialties he had enjoyed in Vratsa. "I have to admit, I never knew that Bulgaria was so friendly to the Jews."

"Bulgaria as a whole is a very welcoming country, mostly secular in nature," the rabbi replied. "There is relatively little anti-Semitism here."

The rabbi explained that the Central Sofia Synagogue was the second-largest Sephardic synagogue in Europe, and Simon recognized this term as referring to Jews with origins in Spain and Portugal. The rabbi continued by saying that Friedrich Grunanger, an Austrian architect, designed the building, and construction began in 1905.

"Take a look at the brass chandelier," the rabbi said, pointing proudly upwards at the high ceiling of the main sanctuary. "Manufactured in Vienna and weighing over 2,200 kilograms, it is the largest chandelier in all of Bulgaria."

Simon was stunned at the synagogue's beauty. The rows of hard wooden benches were framed by alcoves marked by colorful columns and archways, painted brightly in magnificent ornamental designs. Above, Simon could see the partially hidden women's section. And at the front of the hall was the raised *bimah*, with its curtained *aron kodesh* safeguarding the holy Torah scrolls within.

"During the bombing of Sofia in 1944, our synagogue was hit several times," the rabbi said. "The balcony was partially destroyed, as were a number of these columns. Most of our Judaic library was lost. Restoration work continued for many years, but I am proud to report that this September we will celebrate the one hundredth anniversary of the Central Sofia Synagogue. The president of Bulgaria and many other high-ranking dignitaries will attend a special ceremony to mark this momentous occasion. The synagogue is the symbol of Bulgarian Jewry and its secure footing in this country."

"Thank you. You've been very informative," Simon said to the rabbi. "By the way, my name is Professor Simon Matthews, from Chicago," he said, wondering if this introduction would result in a response connected to his missing grandson.

"Nice to meet you," the rabbi said, shaking Simon's hand again. "I invite you to attend our *minyan* on Erev Shabbat at eight o'clock. We don't have enough *daveners* to fill the sanctuary, so we use a study hall for our services. We could certainly use you in our *minyan*."

The rabbi turned to greet another visitor. Apparently he wasn't the one who had called the hotel with a hint of information about Scott. Simon wandered around the sanctuary alone for a few minutes and then went back outside to the gated courtyard.

Who was supposed to meet him here? The message had been quite specific about the time, but perhaps the hotel receptionist had made a mistake when transcribing it? He was starting to worry that he had missed the scheduled rendezvous.

"Are you Professor Matthews?"

"Yes," he replied, turning to face the security guard who had originally opened the gate for him at the courtyard entrance.

"This was left for you," the guard said, handing Simon a manila envelope.

Simon's hands shook as he took the envelope. He was barely able to contain his excitement as he opened it, expecting to find a letter inside listing instructions as to where he was to meet his grandson.

There was no note inside the envelope, only a fine silver chain with a Magen David pendant. Simon recognized it immediately. It was the gift he had given to Scott on the occasion of his grandson's bar mitzvah. There was no mistaking it.

"Who gave this to you?" he asked the guard, who had returned to his security booth.

"A woman."

"What was her name? Where did she go?"

"I don't know this woman. It was her first time to our synagogue."

What did this mean? Did this prove that Scott was still alive? Was the chain evidence that Scott was somewhere in Bulgaria? Or had this chain been removed from Scott's body at the time of his death? The Magen David remained silent, offering no clue as to which possibility was true.

He had to find that woman! He again turned to the guard.

"When was she here? What was she wearing? Which way did she go?"

"So many questions. As I said, I don't know this woman. She came here, and then she went."

Simon placed the envelope and its very valuable and sentimental content into the outer pocket of the travel bag he had brought with him. He needed to get back to the hotel to make some phone calls. He was on the trail of his missing grandson at last!

CHAPTER 20

Dear Simon,

You're probably a bit surprised to hear from me. I know that we rarely talked—or more accurately, barely communicated—over the years. I guess that this was primarily my fault, but that's just the way I am. Well, now is as good a time as any to try to mend that error. I apologize for this.

Things haven't been going well for me lately. Ok, I admit it. I've been a total emotional wreck these past three years. You witnessed my sorry state when you last saw me. I could hardly talk to anyone. Please don't think you were being singled out. I avoided contact with many people, including some of my dearest friends.

And that certainly wasn't fair, as you've been through a major loss of your own. I can't imagine how difficult it's been for you without Marcia. I miss her so much.

I know that Daniel argued against your going to Bulgaria, but I don't see the harm in your journey. When you called to tell us that you had retrieved Scott's silver chain, I was beside myself. That Magen David chain also had a chai *symbol, and that's the Jewish symbol of life. Your receiving the chain and its symbol of* chai *must mean that Scott is really ok! You have given me renewed hope!*

There's something else I've wanted to share with you, as this information could help you trace Scott's whereabouts in Bulgaria. Daniel and I have kept something from you all these years, something we've known about our son. You were probably not aware that Scott always had a wild side, a part of his personality that was difficult to control. I'm talking as a parent who strived to rear Scott into becoming a full, compassionate, mature adult. It wasn't an easy task due to the way he was, how he acted.

Ok, there's no simple way to say this. Scott was involved in drugs. I don't know exactly where or how it started. I guess it was during his high school years, when all his friends were smoking weed. He must have felt a need to conform to the norms of his group. But unlike his friends, who smoked marijuana recreationally at parties and on weekends, Scott just couldn't get enough.

There were so many nights when Daniel and I would pass Scott's closed bedroom door, and the stench of pot was overpowering. Daniel tried once or twice to confront Scott, to get him to refrain from smoking drugs in the house, but this led to serious friction between the two. I just couldn't take it.

I wish I could say that Scott's drug habits stopped there, in high school, but when he began college, things got worse. He smoked pot, and I can't even imagine what other stuff he was taking. I know this because he was expelled from school for a number of weeks after he was caught stoned in the university library. Scott was ready to give up everything at that point, to drop out of school, to take the easy way out.

Let's call him what he was. My son was an addict.

Daniel and I tried to help Scott by getting him counseling. The university insisted on this as well, but regrettably, it didn't work. I can tell you that this was a very difficult period for all of us. You didn't know anything about it, but I think Marcia guessed what was going on. She called Daniel on the phone many times to discuss Scott's problems, but Daniel refused to tell her anything negative about her grandson.

Then Scott got his act together. Deep down inside, he was really a good kid, after all. Remember how generous he was donating all his bar mitzvah checks to charity? He could be really considerate and caring when he wanted to, and I guess he wisely came to the conclusion that it would be best in the long run if he got a decent college education. He went back to his books, studied hard, and graduated.

We were so proud of him. I know that you and Marcia were proud of him as well, but you had no clue how far Scott had actually come to achieve this.

Then we were so pleased to learn that Scott intended to volunteer in the Peace Corps. That seemed exactly the right next step for him. We encouraged him. He was accepted and was informed that he would serve in Bulgaria. When he enlisted in the Peace Corps, Daniel and I were certain that Scott's addictive behavior was finally behind him, that he had turned a new page in his life. We truly believed that he had gone to Bulgaria with a clean slate, and this meant being clean of drugs.

This was not the case.

I don't know who he got the drugs from, whether from a fellow volunteer or from local Bulgarians, but Scott began using again. Apparently his addiction got worse, much worse than before. I'm sure he was doing hard drugs as well.

I wonder if Lance, his good friend from the Peace Corps, knew that Scott was doing drugs, but I would assume that he did. If Scott mentioned these things to me, he must have been telling Lance as well. Maybe Lance was just as involved or as addicted as Scott.

So that's how it was. Scott was over there in Bulgaria, doing drugs, and drugs cost money. I doubt Scott took much cash with him when he left the States. Here in LA, his bank account was empty. Where did he get the money to purchase drugs? The allowance you receive from the Peace Corps wouldn't cover this expense, that's for sure.

Scott informed me that he had taken on some odd jobs for his host father. The two of them started some sort of partnership in that town where he initially lived. I don't know exactly what business it was, but thinking back, I tend to believe that it wasn't entirely legal. Scott said the pay was good. I asked Scott if what he was doing was dangerous, and he assured me that I had nothing to worry about. No one would harm him because he was an American, he told me.

What did that mean? Oh, I wish I had discussed this with Daniel at the time! Maybe Daniel could have done something to help Scott? Maybe he would have flown to Bulgaria to bring my son home. Now it's too late!

I stopped for a while after writing those lines because reliving what happened to Scott during those weeks makes me cry. All of this brings back the memories, the pain. I am tired after this outburst of words. I didn't want to tell you everything, Simon, because I didn't want to hurt you. Why should you know what Scott was doing? Why should you be aware of his drug habit, his addiction, his sickness?

I didn't want to ruin your perception of Scott as the perfect grandson.

Maybe if you had known what Scott was like during those trouble-filled years you might have felt less compelled to go to Bulgaria now to try to find out what had happened to him. Even though Daniel won't say it, I'm glad you went.

I hope you will continue your search, no matter what you now know of your grandson, and no matter how hard Daniel will try to convince you to return to the States. Finding Scott's silver chain is a positive sign. I hope and pray you'll be successful. I worry about you, Simon, so please take care!

Love,

Susan

CHAPTER 21

"Don't you see? Retrieving Scott's silver chain is an important step forward," Simon said excitedly.

"Did you tell anyone about it?" his son responded skeptically, his image momentarily freezing due to interference in their Internet connection.

"Yes, of course. I called the police officer in Varna, and I spoke with the deputy consul at the American embassy."

"And what did they say?"

"Well, they were not very helpful. They admitted that the chain was a significant piece of evidence, if it could be proven it had belonged to Scott."

"And what did they offer to do?"

"Nothing, really," Simon admitted, his excitement beginning to wane. "That's why it's essential that I continue on my own. I haven't given up on this yet."

There were so many questions, and Simon didn't have a clue how he could get answers. Who had called the hotel and asked him to come to the synagogue to receive Scott's chain? Who was the woman who delivered it, and what was her connection to Scott's disappearance? Most importantly, did the delivery of the chain prove that his grandson was still alive or rather did it corroborate the assumption that Scott was dead?

After ending his Skype conversation with Daniel, Simon went down to the lobby to wait for Sophia. She had been the first person he called after his trip to the synagogue. While Borislav Stoyanov of the Varna police force and Brett Thompson from the embassy were doubtful about the chain's authenticity, Sophia had been very excited and said she would come to the hotel to meet him and discuss their next steps.

"Who knows that you are staying at the Hilton?" she asked, barely saying hello when she joined him in the lobby.

He looked over at her, a wide grin forming on his face. Her reddish hair was combed back neatly, and she was wearing a fashionable blue dress that accented her figure and made her seem like an impressionable college student. The concern in her voice was touching; he could see that she was as eager as he in considering the options.

"The officials at the United States embassy, the staff at the Peace Corps, that hotel manager in Golden Sands, Dave Harris in Varna, Bogdan Kamenov the private investigator, and of course, Scott's host family in Montana," he said, listing the people with whom he had talked.

"A few more people also know about this," she said, and he regarded her with a puzzled look. "After your unpleasant incident in my home, I told my colleagues at the university the reason why you've come to Bulgaria. I hope you don't mind. Obviously, someone with whom either you or I spoke has a connection to what happened to your grandson. Also, I am wondering something else. Why did they return the chain to you at this time?"

"Well, the answer to that question is obvious to me," Simon said. "They gave me the Magen David chain to encourage me to continue looking for Scott. It's a sign that I'm on the right track. Someone on that list you just mentioned—or someone we're not even thinking about—knows something about Scott, and they've provided us with a clue. They're steering us in his direction."

"And what you've learned from your daughter-in-law doesn't

bother you?" Sophia asked. Simon had mentioned Scott's drug addiction when they spoke earlier on the phone.

"It upsets me that Scott was doing drugs, of course. I didn't realize that he was having such troubles. Learning that Scott was addicted only increases the urgency to search for him. In fact, it makes finding him—or learning what happened to him—more crucial than ever. He could be lying in a bed in some Bulgarian institution, his mind wasted from an overdose. I hate to think about all the possibilities.

"You know, Sophia," he continued. "The more I think of the problems that young Scott faced in his life—problems that until a very short time ago I knew absolutely nothing about—the more I want to help him, if it's not too late. He's my grandson, after all," he said, his voice trailing off into a pained silence.

"That's very sweet," she said. "I just feel so guilty that I haven't been watching over you as I should."

"What do you mean?"

"You shouldn't be doing all this by yourself. Especially when someone like Boris is threatening to kill your grandson on sight! It's frightening to think about that. I should have gone with you to the synagogue. Maybe I could have learned something."

"Would you like to make an order?" a waitress interrupted, her question phrased in English in deference to the American guest at the table. "I can recommend our homemade biscuit cake."

"No, I'm not hungry," Simon said. "But I could do with a cup of tea."

"You know, there's something strange about the threat issued by Scott's host father," Simon said after the waitress left to fill their order. "In his emails, Scott never mentioned that his host father had any physical disabilities. Quite the opposite. Scott wrote to me about the construction work his host father did. I think the wheelchair is something new for Boris. Yet, that was one angry man, wheelchair or no wheelchair. I can't help but wonder if that family is in some way responsible for Scott's disappearance."

"If they were responsible, Scott's host father wouldn't have threatened to kill him," Sophia pointed out. "And certainly he wouldn't have said such a thing if he knew that Scott was already dead."

The waitress served their tea and mumbled something quickly in Bulgarian.

"What did she say?" Simon asked his companion when the waitress left to clear dishes from a nearby table.

"She said, '*Zapoviadete.*' This means, 'Here you are.'"

"Zapovi… what?"

Sophia laughed at his futile attempts to say the Bulgarian word, and then they both waited patiently for their tea to cool. Simon was about to say something when the metallic ring of a cellular phone interrupted them. He looked expectantly to Sophia, waiting for her to retrieve her phone and take the call, but Sophia was looking at him, as if he was responsible for the ringing.

"Isn't that…?" he started to say, and then he realized that the noise was coming from his travel bag. "That's my phone! This is the first time it has rung since I've been in Bulgaria."

He excused himself as he took the call, worried that it might be Daniel again demanding that he cut his Bulgaria stay short and return to the States. But to his surprise, it was Dave Harris phoning from Varna. After exchanging pleasantries, Simon was shocked at what Dave told him.

"So, you're saying that this hotel manager I met, what was his name, oh yes, Alexander Nikolov, is connected to a Bulgarian crime family?"

"Yes, that's exactly what I'm saying," Dave said. "The Nikolov family is well-known in the Varna area. They have been suspected of involvement in drug deals, protection rackets, gambling, prostitution, and even more. And this will interest you. They dabble in the trafficking of stolen goods. I wouldn't be surprised if the stolen goods they move back and forth include illegal antiquities."

"Illegal antiques trafficking?" Simon asked incredulously.

"Yes, that's very big business here in Bulgaria. There are a lot of antiques and ancient ruins in this country. Roman, Byzantine…"

"Thracian," Simon interjected, causing Sophia to look up at him.

"Yes, so you've heard about Bulgaria's treasures?"

"I've heard a bit," Simon admitted.

"There's something else that's possibly even more helpful to you in your search," Dave continued.

"What's that?"

"I've received a report of a group of tourists being led by someone that meets your grandson's description."

Of course this was helpful! Simon thought as he sat forward in his seat. Why hadn't Dave mentioned this from the start?

He listened attentively to what the Brit had to say, and after the call ended, he turned to Sophia.

"He got a tip from one of his contacts," Simon said. "A man—apparently Scott—has been seen on his way to an important monastery south of Sofia."

"The Rila Monastery?"

"Yes, that's it," Simon said.

"That's the most famous tourist destination in all of Bulgaria."

"I'm sure that this is Scott! First I receive Scott's chain and now this lead. I finally know where my grandson is."

"Let's go immediately," she replied. "We'll be there in less than two hours."

CHAPTER 22

Simon's eagerness to reunite with his grandson was almost palpable as they drove south. Was Scott okay? Simon assumed that he must be. If Scott had been spotted leading a group of tourists to a famous monastery, he most certainly was in good health. But why had he not contacted his family in all this time? Why in the world had Scott forsaken his loved ones?

Simon couldn't dismiss from his mind the other thing Dave had told him on the phone. Was Scott's disappearance connected in any way to the Nikolov crime family? No, that just didn't make sense. Simon believed that the harsh reaction of the hotel manager at their meeting in Varna was the result of a misunderstanding. It wasn't possible that Scott was mixed up with that man and his apparent underworld dealings. Illegal antiques trafficking! For heaven's sake, Scott was a Peace Corps volunteer, after all.

This was all very strange and confusing. Within a very short time, Simon would finally know why Scott had disappeared.

"Look at that!" Sophia said to him excitedly, slowing down the car.

They were passing through Kocherinovo, one of the many Bulgarian villages with nearly unpronounceable long names. The village constituted just the one central street, on each side a row of adjoining houses desperately in need of fresh paint and repair. Sophia pointed through the windshield toward the tiled roof of a municipal building. Atop a red-brick chimney, Simon saw a misshapen assortment of twigs and branches. Sitting in the nest was not one but three tall, slim birds, all of them regal and patient as they waited for their meal to arrive by air delivery.

"Storks!" Simon said.

Sophia drove as slowly as she could while yet another stork's home came into view, this one nestled on the roof of a ramshackle house. Here, too, the magnificent birds were visible, even from two stories below at street level. As they watched from the car, the large wingspan of another stork soaring overhead cast a transitory shadow on the ground before coming to roost on its own woody pile atop an electricity pole, rustling its wings and oblivious to the attention it attracted.

Simon chased thoughts of the impending reunion from his mind and regarded the stunning countryside. Past the village, the peaks of the Rila Mountains greeted them. This was the tallest range in Bulgaria. The vista was picturesque and reminded Simon of his vacations in the Rockies. There was something soothing about viewing mountains from afar, as if the capabilities of nature to create such majesty could easily solve the trivial concerns of those who fell captive to its wonders.

The main street of the village of Rila was long and winding, its rows of contiguous shabby houses set on both sides of the road. The pavement narrowed as it inclined into the foothills farther east. Here the road was sandwiched between thick green forests that stretched down the slopes. A stream bubbled somewhere below them, hidden by the trees. Rounding a bend in the road, Sophia pointed out the steam rising from a distant waterfall on the mountainside across the valley.

They reached a plateau, giving pause to their ascent. They passed wooden stands manned by local residents selling amber-colored jars of honey and natural beeswax, as well as what appeared to be homemade jams. Each stand had a pyramidal display taller than the one before.

Sophia slammed her brakes suddenly when three unbridled horses with lustrous black manes wandered aimlessly across the road. For several moments, they watched the carefree horses feeding on the tall grasses at the side of the asphalt until a honking vehicle behind them urged them to move the car forward.

The road climbed higher still, one curve after another. A tour bus came speeding up behind them, followed by a sleek Mercedes-Benz. Sophia eased to the side to allow them to pass. Simon lowered his window, breathing in the sweet aroma of the mountain forest.

As they passed the sign announcing their destination with a colorful montage of pictures, Sophia told him about the important role monasteries played in Bulgarian history. Over five centuries of oppressive Ottoman rule, the country's monasteries—usually situated in the safety of isolated mountain valleys like this one—were guardians of Bulgarian customs and served as teaching centers for the Bulgarian language. In the serene setting, they offered protection to hermits and those seeking religious salvation, as well as to Bulgarian leaders planning their rebellion against the Turks. Bulgarians were not a religious people, Sophia said, but they deeply respected the country's many monasteries.

Simon was silent, barely paying attention to what Sophia was saying. Again his thoughts turned to his grandson, whom he hadn't seen since the college graduation ceremony. How he missed Scott! Sometimes when he thought of Scott he pictured him in his blue bar mitzvah suit. He could still recall giving the young boy, who had just become a man, the Magen David chain, the very one he had retrieved at the Sofia synagogue. A smile lit up his face in anticipation of his imminent embrace with his grandson. How stunned Scott would be when his grandfather presented him with the chain a second time!

An attendant approached them at the entrance of the Rila Monastery's parking lot, his hand outstretched for the four-leva fee. Sophia parked the car in a shady spot alongside the many other cars and buses. Tourists and pilgrims crowded around the entranceway for a photography session before entering the complex.

As they walked through the entranceway, Sophia informed him that the monastery was named after a ninth-century holy man, John of Rila—Ivan Rilski in Bulgarian. Rilski chose this secluded mountain valley, overlooked by peaks covered in snow and surrounded by bubbling mountain streams, as the location where he would spend the recluse years living in a cave. After his death, his students built the first monastery at the site. It would become the most important religious center in all of Bulgaria. The monastery had been burnt to the ground and rebuilt many times over the centuries. The present-day construction dated back to the 1800s.

"Bulgarians come from all over the country on pilgrimages," Sophia informed him. "They call Rila Monastery the Jerusalem of Bulgaria."

Simon pushed past the crowd and entered the wide plaza. Despite his impatience, he couldn't help but stare with wide eyes at the beauty of Bulgaria's most important tourist destination. There was pure harmony here. Graceful arches in bold stripes of black and white surrounded a huge, flagstone courtyard supporting two floors of monastic cells. Wooden railings lined the stairways leading to the upper levels. Beyond the tiled roofs he could see the thick greenery of mountain forests, and in the distance, the rough upper peaks of the Rila range.

But what attracted his attention more than anything else was the church in the center of the plaza. This amazing construction looked too surreal to be an actual house of worship. It was a square edifice, with its courtyard-level porches encased by the same black-and-white striped arches as the surrounding buildings. Below the arches, Simon could depict the brilliant colors of fresco murals that completely covered the outer walls. Atop the arches was a row of gargoyles, their details impossible to discern from a distance. A roof of gray interspersed with layers of red-and-white brick extended upward toward additional decorations. Rising above everything was the church's main dome, one of five topping this unique building.

The inner courtyard was eerily quiet, yet it was filled with worshippers and onlookers—all awed by the holiness of the mountaintop shrine and gazing with reverence at the iconic church. Simon began searching the crowd, wondering if he would be able to spot Scott, hoping he would still be able to recognize him. Dave had suggested that Scott was leading a group of English-speaking tourists, so it shouldn't be that hard to spot foreigners among the local pilgrims. Yet, everywhere he looked, there was no one who vaguely resembled his grandson.

"Let's go inside," Sophia said, grasping his arm and leading him to the church's entrance.

Simon removed his baseball cap and stepped into the gloom of the interior. Why do all Eastern Orthodox churches hide their gold icons and their intricate wood carvings amidst such darkness? he wondered. The shadowy naves didn't seem to bother the faithful, though, who hurried to cross themselves, kneel before the altars, and mouth their silent devotions. The black-robed monks mingled among their flock, swinging incense dispensers in pendulum arcs and guiding the candlelit rituals.

Simon followed Sophia toward the central altar. She mentioned that Ivan Rilski's mummified left hand was kept in a silver casket inside the church and possibly could be brought out for display if they asked. Simon searched everywhere for Scott, pushing past the devout worshippers. He sidestepped a monk who was beckoning him to join the prayers and then circled back, realizing quickly that there were no English-speakers inside the church.

"He's not here!" Simon exclaimed in desperation as he emerged into daylight and joined Sophia on the porch.

Sophia was inspecting one of the apocalyptic frescoes, this one not yet restored to its original brilliance. "Look at all these depictions of the devil," she said, her hand reaching out and nearly touching the faded red-colored figures parading across a surrealistic series of frames like a medieval comic strip.

"Scott is not here," he repeated, sitting down on the patio ledge and barely glancing at the Biblical scenes.

"Wait, there's one more place we can go."

Sophia led him toward the eastern gate, at the far side of the plaza. This passageway cut through the monastery walls to a bridge that spanned a swollen mountain stream. Beyond, a cobbled street sloped steeply downward to another church and a complex of restaurants and souvenir stands. Many of the visitors ended their tour of the Rila Monastery here, buying handmade religious icons and crucifix beads as reminders of the holy shrine. Others wandered along the pathway deeper into the valley toward the original cave where Ivan Rilski lived during his years of hermitage.

It was then that Simon saw them. A man was standing at a small doughnut stand with his back to the monastery, talking to a group of camera-carrying foreigners. The man wore faded blue jeans and a white T-shirt. He held his hand out, and his head was tilted at an angle, a stance that instantly filled Simon with a recollection of his grandson's profile at his graduation ceremony. Simon started down the slope, encouraged by the English he was hearing. Someone was asking about the traditions of Bulgaria's Orthodox church and this question was directed at the man who had led them on the tour, their apparent guide to the Rila Monastery.

It seemed to be, it had to be—it must be Scott!

Simon hurried forward to embrace his grandson after three years of uncertainty, after many eventful days of searching for him in an unfamiliar land that had proven to be more engaging than previously imagined. His mission to find his long-lost grandson was finally reaching the happy ending for which he had prayed.

The slope was slippery. Simon's left foot twisted as he stepped on a smooth stone, leaving him with absolutely no way to catch his balance. He flew forward, his legs giving out totally. He raised his arms to brace for the inevitable fall, his body wincing in advance at the pain of the impact.

He managed to mouth one word before he hit the ground. "Scott!" he tried to call out, his voice failing him in apparent empathy with his twisted legs. The image that registered in Simon's mind was that of the man's face, which turned with curiosity to view the person falling toward him down the steep descent from the monastery's gate.

This man was not his grandson at all, Simon realized, and then he passed out.

CHAPTER 23

"What happened to you?"

"This is nothing," Simon told his son, gently fingering the bruises on his cheek and the scrape across his forehead. "I fell down, that's all. These marks are superficial. I'm fine, really."

Thinking back to the incident at Rila, he almost laughed to himself. Somehow he had misunderstood the information he had received from Dave Harris. His disappointment in not fulfilling his mission was almost as great as the pain he felt from the fall at the monastery gate, yet he couldn't help but be amused at the absurdity of the miscommunication.

Dave's tip had suggested that Scott was leading a group of tourists to the monastery, but Simon had misheard the statement. Dave was not referring to Scott, his grandson, but rather to a Scot, a former resident of Scotland.

The man Simon had literally run into was similar in build to Scott and also an English speaker, but he hailed from Glasgow. Afterward, as Simon was being treated with antiseptic lotions and antibiotic creams, and his pulse was being checked for good measure, he learned that this Scot, whose name escaped him, lived in the town of Kyustendil, west of Sofia, and was married to a Bulgarian woman. As part of his ongoing work in various capacities with firms from his homeland, the Scot was serving as a liaison with a Scottish film studio's production crew. The visitors were scouting out locations for an upcoming venture and had hired the man to take them on tours of authentic Bulgarian villages. They had investigated several possible filming sites, including the Rila Monastery.

"When are you coming home?" Daniel asked, drawing Simon's attention back to the laptop screen.

The smile faded from Simon's face and suddenly the pain of his face abrasions felt stronger than before. It was indeed time to go home. "I'm packing already. I leave first thing in the morning," he said, giving Daniel details of the flights.

"Well, are you satisfied now, seeing that your trip to Bulgaria was in vain?"

"Not everything was a waste of time," Simon said hesitantly, not willing to get into yet another argument with his son. "When Scott was here, he had a deep affection for Bulgaria. He expressed that in his emails to me. I think that by visiting this country, I can appreciate what Scott did when he served in the Peace Corps and how happy he was in these surroundings."

"Whatever," Daniel said, dismissing this statement despondently. "Your trip, well, all I see is the unnecessary damage you've caused."

Simon kept his left wrist below camera level. No need to let Daniel see the bandage there. He was extremely lucky that his leg hadn't been broken or sprained in the fall.

"I'll be waiting for you to contact me the minute you land in Chicago," Daniel said. "No, you know what? I want you to contact me from Heathrow, so I know you've made it that far."

"I'm not sure I'll have an Internet connection in London," Simon said.

"Well, just find one. Let me know when you're there."

The connection was broken and Simon realized that he may have hit the disconnect button by mistake. In any case, he didn't have further patience to talk to his son.

His suitcase lay on the bed, but he made no move to fill it. For a few moments, he reflected on his trip. He had come to Bulgaria with a purpose that had guided his movements and actions. Except for recovering his grandson's bar mitzvah chain, everything else had failed. Hiring the private investigator had been a waste of money. His talks with the Peace Corps hadn't provided any real clues. Traveling around the country with the unfulfilled expectations of seeing Scott had drained his energy. After all that he had done, he had as many unanswered questions today as when he started—and possibly even more. Scott's disappearance remained as much a mystery now as it had been before.

His sadness at failure was compensated—to a small degree—by what he had learned about Bulgaria during his trips to Varna, Vratsa, and Montana. He was amazed at the physical beauty of the country, with its grainy Black Sea beaches, its stunning mountain ranges, and its forested river valleys. He admired the secluded serenity that drew pilgrims to the Rila Monastery. Bulgaria was struggling to emerge into the modern world, but the tranquility and sanctity of places like Rila made him feel, in many ways, that Bulgaria was a land where time stood still.

And finally, he had learned about Bulgaria's golden Thracian history and the wondrous artifacts that revealed the country's glorious past. This newfound knowledge he attributed totally to Sophia, who had captivated him with her colorful explanations and cultural anecdotes. The university lecturer had devoted quite a bit of her free time to helping him search for Scott. She had voluntarily accompanied him on his journeys; nothing was too much of a burden for her.

He had strong feelings for Sophia, and they were feelings of more than just gratitude and appreciation for everything she had done. He could recall the tingle that had run up his spine when she lightly touched his hand. She had awakened a side of him held dormant since his loss of Marcia, when he had also lost any desire to start anew with someone else. Even so, he was too old to be attracted to a woman, and this was quite ridiculous, actually. There was no chance that Sophia reciprocated his feelings in any way. He was leaving the country in the morning; he would never see her again. He dismissed these unexpected thoughts, disturbed that they kept racing through his mind and confusing him.

How could he ever repay her? Simon wondered. Sophia had volunteered to drive him to the airport, and he contemplated how he would bid her farewell. Should he buy her a gift? What was the appropriate Bulgarian custom for thanking someone as kind as her?

He was exhausted. When he got back to Chicago, he would need to rest for a number of days to fully recuperate from his adventures in Bulgaria.

He was about to shut his laptop when he took one last look at his Skype contacts. An English professor he knew at Oxford was online, as was a former colleague who now taught in Michigan. Daniel had already gone offline. Simon's tired eyes continued down the list until he reached the bottom entry.

WildScott1984. His grandson, Scott. The icon next to Scott's name was lit up in green. Scott was online.

Part Two: Prisoner of the Balkans

CHAPTER 24

The snow falls silently, heavily, constantly, and I am drawn again and again to the window, eyes opened wide. Flakes of different sizes, each one unique in its temporal shape, drop in irregular patterns from the heavens, accumulating in drifts that shift with the capricious wind and compound into accumulations of icy moisture. The naked branches of a nearby tree bend under the weight of the downfall before releasing it in sudden bursts to the ground. A lonesome bird shakes the snow off its wings before taking flight. It is cold outside, bitter cold, but I find that the sheer whiteness of the winter scenery fills me with unexpected warmth. I am protected here and pleased with what I see.

What attracts me to the snow? Maybe it's that snow is so foreign, so unlike anything I was familiar with while growing up. My earliest winter experiences were visiting my grandparents in Chicago, either for Thanksgiving weekend or on the rare occasions when I would fly there on my own for Christmas vacation. I really enjoyed those trips, especially when Grandpa would take me to a park not far from his house and send me soaring down what seemed at the time to be the steepest of slopes, wearing my blue parka and strapped to a tiny wooden sled. But there was no way to take the snow back home to Los Angeles, and those happy days quickly melted into fond childhood memories.

It is strange that I can recall those long-ago scenes down to their most minute detail, lacking only the names to go with the faces I picture, when everything else from my past is a mystery to me, lost in the darkness that clouds my mind.

They say the Eskimos have plenty of words for snow, but I heard once that it's just an urban legend. On the other hand, and I think this is true, there are some forty different words for snow in Finnish. Some of them actually refer to other types of frozen precipitation, like slush and frozen dew. But still, forty words! And whoever told me this, perhaps back in college, also mentioned that in Finnish there is actually no verb for "to snow". How could that be? Apparently, the only way to report this particular weather condition in Finland would be to say that "there is snow outside" or alternatively, "it is raining snow."

In Bulgarian, there is only one word for snow, and it's actually quite difficult to pronounce. Snow in Bulgarian is сняг, a strange combination of Cyrillic letters that spit off your tongue in a three-syllable sort of way: "snee-ya-k," with the accent on the "ya," and the "k" at the end drawn out toward infinity. Bulgarians say the word with a sneer, as if this regular winter phenomenon is an unwanted gift from a distant relative up north in Russia. But there's no way to avoid it. Bulgarians must deal with their snowbound homeland for weeks on end.

Snow! It is so perfect, so simple and natural. The silence is comforting, the beauty of winter surreal. I clearly have a lot of time on my hands, allowing me to stare out the window for hours on end to watch the snowfall caress the forests and whiten the meadows. The drifts pile up higher and higher, engulfing the slopes and creating a winter wonderland. Even the small vegetable garden just outside my bedroom is no longer in view, cloaked instead in its wintry coat.

I calmly watch the snowfall and wait for Katya to make her way up the path and bring me food and supplies.

It is warm in the cabin. Outside, the temperatures dip well below freezing, and it doesn't matter if you do your calculations in Fahrenheit or centigrade. Here in the Bulgarian mountains, the thermometers drop below freezing at the beginning of winter and don't bother to climb higher for months. Even when the snow temporarily stops and the Balkan sun emerges to prove it still commands the sky, it is very, very cold.

But inside the cabin, I am content. Content and safe. It is quiet and warm, and there is no one who can harm me. *Cabin* is my word for this small building up in the mountains, far from all signs of civilization. It's a stone house, actually, with a sloping red-tiled roof. The roaring fire in the fireplace keeps me warm, and there is enough chopped firewood to last through the winter. I wear a lightweight long-sleeved sweater and jeans, but at night, when I slip under the thick down blankets, I strip down to my underwear and don't feel the cold at all.

There is one definite drawback to living up here. The cabin has an outhouse, which is, in fact, just that—out of the house. It is a mere hole in the ground, surrounded by a wooden shack, and that's where I have to go to relieve myself. Even when it's not snowing, you can literally freeze your butt off out there. Because of the bone-rattling cold, I refrain from visiting the outhouse more than absolutely necessary.

I stare at the copse of trees at the foot of the meadow, watching the snow cover them completely from top branch all the way down to their roots. And then I see the small figure in the distance, trudging up the path slowly, one snow-covered boot at a time.

She is wearing an oversized brown parka, making her appear much bigger than she actually is. With her bulk and slow movements, she looks like a Bulgarian mountain bear. Her winter wear is not streamlined to be adaptable to the ski slopes but rather is practical for handling winter walking. She navigates her way around the drifts.

I see she is carrying two heavy packages. I should run down the path and help her, but by the time I could get bundled up, she'd already be at the front door. She is a saint, that woman, caring for me as she does. I don't know how she is capable of making her way up this path every few days in the worst weather. She's been doing it for some time now, and she never complains. She apparently doesn't care at all whether it's sunny or snowing.

It takes her some time to trek up the path. Finally she climbs the wooden steps and swings open the door. A blast of winter fills the room; snow and ice and the outdoor chill enter my sanctuary uninvited. She slams the door shut behind her and begins the slow process of unthawing. Layer by layer she removes her heavy clothing. Her parka, wool hat, ski gloves, and ski boots all end up in wet puddles on the wooden floor. She shakes the last flakes out of her curly, brownish hair and turns to me.

"*Kak si?*" she asks.

"*Dobre*," I reply. We talk in basic Bulgarian—so different from my native English—and sometimes a smile forms on my lips as I carefully pronounce words in the Slavic tongue.

"There's a lot of snow out there," I say, stating the obvious as I help her unpack the groceries.

"Have you kept yourself busy?" she asks. She tenderly strokes my forehead, the touch of her fingers temporarily distracting me.

"Yes," I lie to her. I force a smile, gazing at her pretty face. Then I look away.

I haven't done anything all day. The English novels gather dust on the shelves, and I don't think I could concentrate enough to read them anyway. Of course there's no electricity or Internet access up here in the mountains, so there's not a lot to occupy my time. Most of what I do, day after day, is stand at the window and watch the snow fall from the sky.

And try to remember.

The mind works in mysterious ways, and no one, not the most famous physician or the most learned scientist anywhere in the world, really understands it. I certainly don't, and I've had plenty of time to sit and contemplate my condition. The problem is I don't recall what happened to me. In fact, I don't remember much at all. Some days all that I can picture in my mind are events from long ago, from my childhood, while my time in Bulgaria is completely fogged out. At other times, I can't recall what I had for breakfast just a few hours before, or if I even ate breakfast at all.

That is why I'm so grateful to Katya. She cares for me, brings me food and clean linens. She washes the dishes, which I promise to handle myself but always leave piled up in the sink. She gathers the garbage bags to take them back to the village for disposal. I am not an invalid, I tell her over and over, but she just smiles and goes about her errands as if her role as my housekeeper was not up for discussion.

I turn to Katya, to express my gratitude for her help, but she is already gone. In fact, it is dark in the cabin. The daylight disappears so quickly and without warning during the winter months. I don't remember Katya leaving, but this is yet another time my mind has played a trick on me.

The pain in the side of my head is intensifying again, so I swallow two painkillers and lie down, fully dressed, on my cot. I will get up soon and fix myself dinner, I think, but my eyes grow heavy. I try to do some mind exercises, to force the gears inside my head into action, to recall the past, but I'm too tired. I find myself drifting into a sleep that's as silent and undisturbed as the snow falling outside the cabin.

CHAPTER 25

It's starting to get dark on a spring night as I walk along the street to the home of my host parents, where I've been staying for the past two weeks. I was just hanging out with Lance and some of my other buddies at a neighborhood pub. We got pretty wasted while making jokes that none of the locals even bothered to try to understand. Somehow our sense of humor doesn't carry over into Bulgarian. Doesn't matter. We had a good laugh!

In my backpack I'm carrying the language textbook and my notes, but the grammar we learned today has totally escaped me. I couldn't concentrate as the teacher spurted out a stream of conjunctions, verb cases, and rules of gender. Lance is adapting better to these foreign surroundings than I ever will. He has an ear for new languages, and his simple Bulgarian is free of the American accent that I can't banish from my tongue. I think he's in love with everything Bulgarian, especially the women. And for their part, the women here seem enthralled by the sight of a handsome African-American male in their midst. None of them show the slightest interest in me. Maybe they would notice me if I was capable of conducting a simple conversation in their language. In order to become a Peace Corps volunteer, I must pass my Bulgarian tests. I doubt if I'll ever master the material I'm taught in class.

I hurry toward the house, eager for strong, black espresso. I swagger a bit, not only because of my fuzzy head, but also because the sidewalks here—like the sidewalks all over this undeveloped country—are broken, and no one bothers to fix them. I find it difficult deciding where to plant my feet. I'll be okay, I tell myself. Just need to get to the house and drink that coffee.

And that's when I nearly collide into Boris.

I hadn't noticed his dark shape standing near the fence. He is smoking a cigarette, the tip sizzling red with each vigorous puff of the strong tobacco. Boris is not happy to see me. He shoves me, and his sheer strength nearly knocks me to the pavement. I try to steady myself and shrug off what he just did. I smile at my host father and mutter one of the only expressions in Bulgarian that I know.

"*Kak si?*" I ask, laughing to myself at the sound of the word "kak".

Boris is in no mood for pleasantries. In fact, he hisses at me, upset that I disturbed him, that I interrupted his waiting. He didn't want anyone to see him; that is apparent to me now.

I attempt to say the word for "sorry" but all I can mouth is, "*Suh-zha...*" I can't remember what comes next.

His breath stinks from alcohol even more than my own, which I've cleaned up a bit by having popped five Tic Tacs into my mouth. The grin on my face vanishes as Boris steps forward to shove me again. My knees are weak, and I stagger backwards.

Boris starts cursing. A wild flow of quick Bulgarian comes spitting in my face. What have I done to upset him? I step off the broken sidewalk to avoid his reach.

And then an old pickup truck makes its way slowly up the street, its front lights off and its engine sputtering in the dark. I move away quietly until I'm on the far side of the road, hoping that Boris won't come after me. Luckily, he's distracted with the pickup's arrival. When it stops in front of the house, he steps forward, exchanges a few words with the driver, and then goes around to the back and opens the tailgate.

As I stand unnoticed in the shadows, Boris and the driver unload several big cardboard boxes and carry them to the cellar door at the side of Boris's house. I hear them descending the creaky wooden stairs to a room I've never entered but where I know Boris makes his super-strength homemade *rakia* and where Ralitsa stores her pickled preserves. The men make repeated trips until the pickup is fully unloaded.

Boris slaps the driver on the shoulder, and the other man gets into his truck, fiddles with the key until the engine catches, and drives off. Boris stands near the gate to his house for several minutes, puffing on another cigarette. He has forgotten all about me. Then he turns and goes inside. A few minutes later, my head totally cleared, I follow him.

I take off my shoes in the hallway, slip into my house slippers and walk as quietly as possible on the wood floor to the kitchen. It's quite late, but Ralitsa has saved dinner for me. She is standing next to the stove, stirring something aromatic in a steamy pot. I apologize in broken Bulgarian for missing the meal and ask for the black coffee I crave. I thank Ralitsa profusely when she hands me a cup of the strong, dark liquid.

Over the next few days, I continue my routine of attending Bulgarian classes, hanging out with Lance and the other recruits, trying to impress the local Bulgarian girls, and eating Ralitsa's tasty cooking. Her freshly baked *banitsa* in the mornings is enough to keep me going for hours, and there's always something just as delicious waiting for me at lunchtime. In the afternoons, when I have time and patience, I help Rado, my host-family brother, practice his English. I pointedly ignore his insistence on learning curse words. My job in this country will be to teach the English language, but I doubt if swearing will be included in the curriculum.

I rarely see Boris. He is usually still asleep when I leave the house in the mornings, and he sometimes returns for dinner after I've already eaten. I prefer to avoid him whenever possible. I haven't given a second thought to the recent nighttime incident when I bumped into him and his anger.

Late one afternoon, Ralitsa gives me the key to the cellar and asks me to bring her a jar of pickled cauliflower. She is in the kitchen preparing dinner, and I'm sure the entire neighborhood can smell her fried fish. Boris hasn't yet returned from his construction job, and Rado is at a neighbor's house watching dubbed American-television sitcoms.

I go outside and breathe the fresh spring air, noticing that the sun is still high in the sky. The days are getting longer with promises of warmer weather. I wonder how hot it will be in the summer and whether Lance and I will get a chance to travel to the Black Sea. I'm dying to check out the beaches. I've heard that Bulgarian women are very liberal and don't mind topless sunbathing.

I walk around to the side of the house and unlock the cellar door. The rank odor from beneath the house stings my eyes, and I hesitate momentarily. The homemade *rakia* must be in an advanced stage of fermentation, I assume. I bravely descend the narrow wooden stairs, searching for the wall switch.

The cellar is a tightly packed storage area, with wooden shelves along the outer walls bearing the weight of Ralitsa's preserves. The *rakia* is contained in huge wooden barrels at the far side of the room, and I don't want to get any closer. The center of the cellar floor is an open space filled with the cardboard boxes I saw Boris and the driver unloading from the pickup truck the other night.

I approach the nearest shelf and search for pickled cauliflower. Jars of various fruit preserves are lined up in rows, with undecipherable labels declaring their contents. Apparently my host mother specializes in making jam. The quantity of what's stored in the cellar is overwhelming.

My eyes return to what's stacked on the concrete floor. What's in these boxes? I wonder. My curiosity gets the better of me, and I fiddle with one of the cartons. If I lift the side slightly, I will be able to glance at its contents without leaving a mark that the box has been opened.

I'm shocked at what I see inside the box. The carton is filled with dozens, if not hundreds, of small packages containing designer watches. I see labels for Rolex, Seiko, and Swatch. I open one of the packages, and sure enough, there is a timepiece positioned fashionably against its cardboard backing. Without thinking, I lift the side of another carton, and inside I see the Casio and Tag Heuer logos. Another carton is full of Nautica and Omega watches.

There is no way for me to know if these are actual brand-name items or counterfeits, but they certainly look like the real thing. I can't fathom the total value of all these watches. This is a huge shipment, I realize, and it's sitting in my host family's cellar!

I smooth down the flaps of the boxes, hiding any indications that I had peeked inside. I return to my original mission of selecting a jar of pickled cauliflower and head back to the cellar steps.

And that is when I see Boris at the top of the stairwell, peering down at me with his stern face framed by the light of the late-afternoon sky.

"Ralitsa asked me to get this," I say, holding up the heavy jar as I begin climbing the stairs. It's only after I reach the top that I realize I've spoken to Boris in English, which he obviously doesn't understand.

As I emerge from the cellar, Boris pushes me, and I slam against the brick wall of the house. He shoves me again, and I drop the cauliflower, the jar fragmenting into slivers of glass and pickled vegetables as it hits the ground. Boris grabs me, securing me in place as he raises his fist. I close my eyes, preparing my body to absorb the shock it will suffer with the impending blow.

Ralitsa shouts at her husband, and the blow is not delivered. She approaches us, and Boris hesitates. Finally, after a long, breathless moment, he mutters something and lets me go. I straighten up but realize that my feet are wobbly, as shaky as if I had actually been punched.

They quarrel for several minutes before Boris slinks off. Ralitsa watches her husband depart with a frown on her face. Then she turns to me, puts her hand on my shoulder, and asks me if I'm okay.

I assure her I haven't been hurt and point to the ground to apologize for the shattered jar. She shakes her head and leads me into the house. I sit down at the kitchen table while she turns on the kettle to prepare me a cup of herbal tea.

I've had it, I tell myself. I will pack up my bags tonight and leave this hell hole in the middle of the Bulgarian countryside and head back to the States. Enough of trying to be a Peace Corps representative—I can't deal with the locals! My nerves are totally shot, and my hand is shaking as I sip the hot tea. I stare down at the table, barely feeling Ralitsa's hand as it tenderly caresses my shoulders and my head.

After I finish the tea, I withdraw to my room, slam the door, and light up a joint. I lie on my bed and close my eyes, waiting for the weed to do its magic. The earthy aroma fills my lungs, and immediately I feel its buzz right above the ears and in my forehead. The high comes on very quickly, confusing and bewildering me initially before settling in to relieve my stress. I hope the joint will unburden me from all worries. Then I remember I'm running low on my supply and will need to find some money to purchase more. I put that thought aside and take deep breaths. My mind is light; the weight has lifted.

What would I gain if I quit the program? I ask myself, surprised that some sane thoughts are filtering into my mind as I chill. I am not a quitter, I vouch. I don't want to return to America, a move that would be seen as a sign of failure by everyone. I can make this work. I can learn basic Bulgarian. I can figure out how to handle these unusual customs and traditions. I can avoid Boris and make sure not to get him angry. I can deal with this. I wonder if I will be able to convince myself to stay when I'm no longer stoned.

CHAPTER 26

In the spring, the only traces of lingering snow are on the distant peaks. The meadows are cloaked in tiny purple flowers, popping up seemingly overnight. Tree branches that were previously barren now flaunt their budding foliage as if it were expensive jewelry. The birds are noisy, flirting with each other as they soar high overhead. The air is fresh and heavenly, the purest of gifts delivered each day. It's still a bit chilly when I take my early-morning walks, thoroughly enjoying the exquisite beauty of undisturbed nature.

As beautiful as this wooded valley is, I long to leave my mountain cabin. I desperately search through the fragments of my mind for the clues that will allow me to reclaim my life.

I can't say how long I've been here. Time has no meaning for me; it is a casualty of my injuries. I can recall surviving the recent winter, but I cannot say if this was my first winter here or my third. It has been a long time, of that I'm certain, but I cannot quantify the period of my isolation. Time goes on, and I live a life of solitude as its captive.

Physically, I'm in pretty good shape. I have a set of weights inside the cabin, and every morning I exercise for almost thirty minutes before tiring. I lack any semblance of physical stamina; that is why my walks through the meadow are short and never lead me far away.

There is another reason I don't stray into the hills. Serbia is just over the ridge, I've been told. I don't want to cause an international incident by crossing the unmarked border.

The only part of my body that bears testimony to my injuries is my head. Luckily, the external sores have mostly healed, but I still suffer the most excruciating headaches. They are throbbing and intense like the fiercest migraines. I'm not sure what triggers them or how to prevent the pain. When the waves of darkness come, I fear that my eyes will pop out of my head. My hands and feet freeze up and my face becomes pale, as if I've been transformed into a living ghost.

The pains are unilateral, only occurring on the right side of my head where I was struck. The only thing that I can do during these attacks is to lie on my cot and wait for the anguish to subside. I pop two of the pills that Katya brings me, not even sure that they do anything to relieve the pain. I cover my face with a wet washcloth, and pray for sanity to return. Eventually the darkness recedes and vision returns. I remove the cloth from my forehead and regard my surroundings with hesitation, as if a monstrous being waits to come for me again. But I am always alone to deal with my injuries and headaches.

The most serious symptom of what I suffered is not the migraines, for as horrific as those are, they are temporary and eventually relief arrives like a long-lost friend. What worries me more is the damage inside my mind. My memories have abandoned me, leaving me without my identity. I am confused and afraid. I don't know if tomorrow I will remember what has happened today, and in most cases, this is a fear that actually comes true.

I know, instinctively, that I should go to the nearest American embassy and file a report as a lost, very confused citizen who can't find his passport. But I am as incapable of making this journey as I am of seeking medical attention on my own. Katya has warned me that if I leave the safety of my mountain cabin, those who caused my original injuries would seek to harm me again. Instead of reaching Sofia where I could get help, my battered body would wind up floating in the chilling waters of a Balkan stream.

When Katya arrives in the afternoon, I am glad to greet her. She has brought not only supplies for the week but my laptop as well. Due to the lack of electricity in the cabin, Katya has agreed to lug the laptop to the nearby village to recharge the battery so that I can enjoy three or so hours of computer usage before it again runs out of power. Once a week she takes the laptop to charge, and a day or two later she returns. While this is hardly the perfect solution, it's the only option I have to power up the computer.

Katya says there's a café in the village. I wonder if it has an Internet connection. Is that too much to hope for in rural Bulgaria—an establishment modern enough to have Wi-Fi? Every time I suggest accompanying Katya to the café, she reminds me that I'm not strong enough for the journey. She insists that I remain in the cabin and never complains about carrying the heavy laptop back and forth just so its battery can be charged with new life.

Lacking the Internet, playing solitaire on the laptop is one of the few options I have to keep busy and exercise my mind. There are a few different versions available, but I prefer spider, for some reason. To liven up the action, I change the color of the deck before each game. It's a pretty lame situation, but I can't concentrate on anything for any length of time.

I sit at the wood table and use the laptop pad to flip the cards. An ace appears, and then I get a red queen. Watching the cards fit into numerical order gives me a sense of accomplishment. I play only one or two games before powering down the laptop. I know that I must budget my computer time to save some battery life for the next day. The hours pass.

"Did you take your pills?" Katya asks me.

"I don't have a headache today," I reply, rubbing the sore side of my head.

"You need to take them every day," she insists.

I dutifully comply, swallowing two of the blue pills. Sure enough, as if to punish me for my hesitation, an ice-cold wave of pain descends on my temples a bit later. I can't determine what the hour is or how long ago Katya left. The only thing I can do is swallow two more pills and lie down in the dark to wait for my head to clear.

One late-spring day, someone knocks on the cabin door. During the harsh winter months, no one ventures into this area because these mountains are not suitable for skiing, but occasionally, when the weather is warmer, hikers trek along the highland paths. They avoid getting too near the Serbian border but from time to time approach my cabin with curiosity.

When I hear the knock, I immediately freeze in place. Has someone seen me through the windows? Luckily, there is no fire burning; no traces of smoke are rising from the brick chimney to provide evidence I'm inside. But has someone heard me clicking on the keyboard as I play my virtual card game?

A chill shoots up my spine, and I fear the worst. I am living in this isolated cabin for a reason. My life is in grave danger, and no one can know that I am here. The only person who is aware of my existence is Katya, and I trust her with my life not to reveal my location. If I open the door to what is probably just a friendly hiker, the whole world would soon know about me. Tales of the crazy, solitary American man with a head injury living in a mountain cabin would pass like wildfire from one hiker to the next, and soon enough the story would reach those who would seek me out and cause me real harm.

Another knock, but I cannot allow myself to answer the door. Hopefully this unexpected visitor will quickly give up and go away. I sit nervously at the table, hoping that no one will peer through the windows and see me. A long period of silence follows, and I wonder if I'm alone again at last. And then another pounding wave of darkness begins building in my head. I realize that I need to immediately go and lie down.

Trying to be as quiet as possible, I take cautious steps toward the bedroom. The floor boards creaks beneath my feet, and I hope these sounds do not carry outside. There hasn't been anyone knocking at the door for some time. My head is a jackhammer of riotous pain, and it will take time before the effect of the painkillers I swallowed kicks in. Things are starting to go black in my mind, and I fear that I will pass out before I reach the cot. I force myself forward, no longer caring if my steps are quiet.

At that moment, there is a loud crash. One of the cabin windows shatters with the projectile force of a large stone. Fragments of glass land in a sparkling array on the floor, glistening like diamonds. As I continue my slow progress toward the bedroom, I feel the sharp prick of a shard through my stockinged feet. Ignoring the pain, I reach the other room at last and collapse on the bed. And then everything goes dark.

CHAPTER 27

Things are tense between Boris and me. In the mornings, I pass him in the hallway on my way to the bathroom, and I fear that he is going to reach for my neck. His eyes watch me with a seething hatred that almost brings me to pack my bags on the spot to depart for our training headquarters in Vratsa. Just when I think Boris is about to explode, Ralitsa pops out of her bedroom, issues a stern warning to her husband, and he backs off.

I am seriously considering asking to switch to another family, but so far I've hesitated to move on this. Maybe I'm giving Boris a chance, believing that he is inherently a good person. Or perhaps I'm just too lazy to ask for a substitution.

But one evening, something happens that changes everything.

Ralitsa has gone out of her way to prepare a mouth-watering dinner. There are the usual *shopska* and *snezhanka* salads for starters, and then a warm and very agreeable monastery bean soup. This is followed by a *gyuveche* oven-baked casserole of cheese, meat, and vegetables. Even Rado, who is a fussy eater, can't help but ask for more. And Boris is in a relatively good mood, which makes things much more pleasant for everyone.

"Drink *rakia*," Boris says, mastering this short sentence in English. It's not a question, but more like a command, so I fill my small glass a third time with the potent liquid that he brewed in the cellar.

"*Nazdrave*!" I say, lifting my glass to his.

I've learned an important part about the custom of making a toast in Bulgaria. It's not enough to lift your glass and simply say "*Nazdrave*" One must also make full eye contact with each person you're toasting. So, as I raise my glass to Boris, I look him in the eye and find that, surprisingly, there is no hatred there. Quite the opposite is true. Boris is smiling and indicating that I am welcome in his home.

I clink my glass with Ralitsa's as well, and in her eyes, I see she is also a bit taken by Boris's change in mood. Rado lifts up a glass of Coca-Cola and knocks it against mine so roughly that it spills carbonated soda all over the table, spotting the red-and-white tablecloth and leaving drops of brown liquid on my plate.

"Rado!" Boris says strongly, reprimanding his son. But there is no anger in his voice when he turns to address me.

"What did he say?" I ask Ralitsa.

"He wants to talk to you about something after dinner," she says. "I'm not sure what it is, but it's something he can't discuss at the table."

"How will I understand him?" I ask, fearing that Ralitsa will leave me alone with her husband.

"His friend, Vladimir, is coming over tonight. Vlady, that's what we call him, knows English. He will translate."

"Okay," I say. If Boris wants to talk to me—and the subject matter does not concern any plans to kill me—I have no problem with meeting Vlady.

Then dessert is served. Just when I think I can't pop another morsel of food into my mouth, Ralitsa brings a platter of *baklava* to the table. The thin layers of cake are literally dripping with honey. This treat is so sweet and irresistible that I have not one, but two, big pieces. And then I am so full and my head is so quickly spinning from the *rakia* that I can barely get up from my chair.

"*Ela*," Boris says, insisting that I follow him to the living room.

We sit down and he lights up a cigarette, and this time I don't even mind the smoke.

There is a knock on the door, and a minute later I am introduced to Vlady, who lives not far from Boris and Ralitsa. I could be mistaken, but I think that this heavyset man is the same person who drove the pickup truck to their house that night, delivering the shipment of watches and helping store the boxes in the cellar.

"So, you are the American peace-lover?" Vlady says, shaking my hand vigorously. He has a round face with a mischievous grin. As friendly as he seems, I take an immediate strong disliking to the man.

"Not peace-lover. I'm a Peace Corps volunteer," I explain, correcting him and withdrawing my hand from his strong grip.

"Peace Corps, peace-lover, same thing," he says. He accepts both a bottle of beer and a cigarette from my host father. Nothing is offered to me, but I don't mind. Vlady sits down on the lumpy sofa, and I sit back in my chair, staring at the room's one framed painting, the one of the farmhouse covered in snow. I don't have a clue where this conversation is going.

For the longest time, Vlady stares at me, not saying a word. He puffs silently on his cigarette, smoking in unison with his neighbor. Finally, he turns to Boris and the two of them talk for a while, knowing that I can't understand a word they're saying.

"Okay, peace-lover," Vlady says to me at last, his words accompanied by a burp that originated from his now-gone beer. "We know all about you," he says.

"What do you mean?"

"We know about the drugs."

"What?"

"We know about the drugs you have stashed in your room. We know you smoke those, what you call them, joints. We know you meet with that no-good gypsy in the town center to purchase the drugs. We know everything."

Had they followed me? Even Lance didn't know where I got our pot. And I took care to hide my stash in one of my dirty socks so that Rado would never discover it. How did Vlady and Boris find out?

And more importantly, were they going to turn me in?

"Don't worry, your secret is our secret," Vlady says with a smirk. "We won't say a word to anyone…conditionally."

"Conditionally?" What did Vlady mean by that, and how did he even know that word?

"How you pay for your drugs?" Vlady asks, swiftly changing gears. "Where did you meet that gypsy? What do you pay him? Do you trust him? He is not honest; gypsies never are."

"What is this?" I ask, staring at him and Boris. "Is this some sort of police interrogation?"

"No, no police," Vlady says, and Boris laughs at the one word he recognizes. "We don't like police any more than you do. We want to know how you can afford the drugs. You have enough money?"

"This is none of your damn business!" I say, my voice cracking as I speak. My eyes are stinging from their cigarette smoke, and my throat is dry. I start to rise to my feet, fighting the lingering effects of the *rakia.*

"Sit, sit. We have a business for you," Vlady says, a mysterious grin lighting up his face. "We have something we want you to do. You have no worries, no worries for money. You can buy what you want, we don't care. Would you like that?"

"What are you talking about? Boris?"

But my host father doesn't answer me. Even if he knew English, I'm not sure he would care to respond. Vlady seems to have total control of this negotiation.

"Here's the deal. We want you to work with us, and we pay you. How you say it, we pay you handsome."

"*Handsomely*," I reply without thinking. "That is the appropriate word."

"Yes. What you say, peace-lover?"

"I don't think so," I say, slowing rising to my feet, and this time not letting the homemade alcohol affect my movements. "I'm not allowed to work for pay."

"I think so," Vlady replies with a firm voice. "If you don't help us, your little secret, which is none of our damn business, might accidentally find its way to your peace-lover friends. What would they say if they knew this about you?"

"Are you blackmailing me?"

"Blackmail, now, that is not very pleasant word."

There is nothing I can say. They have discovered my secret and have cornered me into accepting their offer. It is, unfortunately, an offer I can't afford to refuse. If I decline, they will report my drug use. I will be kicked out of the Peace Corps and sent back to the States. I apparently have no choice but to accept, but what the hell am I getting myself into?

This will be a one-time thing and then it will be over, I assure myself. My period of living with my host family in Montana is about to end. I will soon return to the training program in Vratsa, and then I will be assigned elsewhere in Bulgaria. I will help them out this time, do whatever they want so that I can safeguard my secret, and then I will be rid of them once and for all. Fortunately, I will never see Vlady and Boris again.

"Whatever," I say reluctantly, not realizing what will result from my stating this one word of acceptance.

CHAPTER 28

"We need your passport," Vlady says without hesitation. When I look at him to question what he means, his eyes light up with a sense of impending adventure. "We need you to drive our truck."

"Oh, no," I say, starting to protest but failing to find a suitable excuse.

"Oh, yes, peace-lover," Vlady insists. "You will drive our truck, and we will go together on a short trip. For you, this is much better than going on big trip back to America, no?"

"Where are we going?" I ask with extreme hesitation.

"We go to the border."

"Which border?" He doesn't respond. Are we driving to Greece? Turkey? No, those countries are too far from here. We must be going north, toward either Serbia or Romania, both of them not far from Montana.

And there it is—my choice. Either I serve as their driver on what appears to be a mission to deliver their smuggled watches or they will report my drug habit to the Peace Corps, and I will find myself on the next plane back to Los Angeles. I'm screwed if I agree to join their illicit activities, and I'm screwed if I don't.

They converse for some time, and then Vlady stands and prepares to leave.

"When are we going?" I ask, wary of the plan's details but realizing that the sooner I know them, the better.

"We will tell you," Vlady says, and then he is gone.

Boris remains in his chair, smiling at me. He is incapable of explaining anything further, so I get up and go to my room.

What have I done? I lie on my bed and stare at the ceiling, feeling sorry for myself. Tingles of tension shoot up my nerves. I fear I'm getting mixed up in something that can only land me in trouble—a load of trouble. Phrasing it that way when I am about to drive a load of stolen goods to the border makes it all seem too humorous to be real. But this is no laughing matter. I am going to do something undeniably illegal. I fidget as I sense this looming danger approach. Bad things are ahead.

Then I realize that the only way I can calm down is to get high. I reach under the bed and pull out the pair of wool socks lying on the floor. How did Boris and Vlady know about my stash? Had they come into my room and looked through my dirty laundry? They have cornered me, and now I am at their mercy, about to commit a crime that is a thousand times worse than smoking marijuana while serving in a Peace Corps training program.

A few minutes later a pleasant haze settles over me, and I begin to relax. It won't be so bad, I tell myself. I will drive their truck to the border. I will help them with this job. They will pay me, and that will be that. It'll be okay, I convince myself before falling asleep with a tired smile on my face.

In the morning, I set off for Bulgarian classes as if nothing had happened. I join Boris at lunchtime for the spinach *burek* Ralitsa has prepared for us, but he doesn't say a word. It's as if our negotiations the previous night never took place. I return to the school for the afternoon lessons and do my best to concentrate on the grammar. Lance notices that something's bothering me, but I shrug him off, refusing to tell him anything about what's going on between my host father and me.

In the evening, I join Rado at the schoolyard, and we shoot baskets for a while. Rado insists that he'll be Bulgaria's first international basketball star with a long career in the NBA. My heart is not in the game, and I miss most of my shots.

Ralitsa helps me with my homework in the evening, complimenting me on a composition that describes her house and lists details of the tasty meals she has been cooking for me as her guest.

Boris goes off to a neighborhood pub, and I decide to call it an early night, but I can't fall asleep. I'm full of worries about what my host father and his neighbor have planned. Maybe none of this will happen after all. Time is running out; my days in Montana are numbered. Perhaps I'll return to Vratsa without having to do this dirty job of theirs.

I finally drift off well after midnight and sink into a cycle of disturbing dreams. I can't figure out what they mean, but I find myself struggling to break away, to escape a dark force that is getting closer by the minute, threatening to engulf me and carry me away to places unknown.

"Scott!" Someone is saying my name, shaking me.

"What?" I have a hard time opening my eyes. It is dark in the room and at first I can't see anything. But then I recognize the fruity aftershave that Boris often sprays on himself to hide his alcoholic breath.

"*Haide*, *haide*," he urges.

I know that word. It means to hurry up, to come on. He stands in my room until I get out of bed, and only when I prove to him that I'm getting dressed does he leave me alone.

It is pitch black outside. I don't have a clue what time it is, but I'm guessing it's something like five in the morning. Vlady is already there but doesn't greet me. The two men drink from paper cups. I refuse their offer of bitter coffee, knowing that it will just upset my otherwise empty stomach.

The Bulgarians don't say anything, but the moment they finish their coffee I realize that it's time to get going. I'm the one who goes down the creaky cellar stairs to take out the cartons. I hand them one by one to Boris at the top of the stairs, who delivers them to Vlady, who stacks them on the open back of the pickup. The boxes aren't that heavy, but there are a lot of them. We work silently, efficiently. In a very short time, the cellar is empty and the truck is loaded. Boris locks the cellar door, and we're ready to leave.

Vlady starts the ignition, and I sit between the two men. They both smell like shit. Boris's aftershave has fallen victim to his predawn efforts. When I look at him, I see he hasn't shaved in days. I've grown accustomed to my host father's rustic looks and ungodly odor, but I've never sat this close to him before. I hold my breath, feeling uncomfortable yet eager to get on our way so that all of this will be behind me.

"So, where are we going?" I ask pleasantly, trying to make light of the situation.

"Romania," Vlady answers, and though I should have known that something like this would be the reply, it still hits me with brutal force, as if I'd been punched in the stomach. "You have passport?" he asks, our entire journey contingent on my response.

"Yes."

"Good. We go."

And we are off. Vlady navigates through the quiet, dark streets and sets our course for the highway outside the town. Soon we are on the northbound road leading to Vidin.

I have studied the Bulgarian map and know the country is bordered by Romania to the north and that the Danube River separates the two. But I also know that the only bridge spanning this mighty European river between the countries is located far to the east, connecting the city of Ruse in Bulgaria to Giurgiu in Romania. Shouldn't we be driving east? I wonder.

We continue heading directly north. After driving for just five minutes, Vlady swears under his breath, and Boris straightens up, fully alert. I look ahead on the highway and see what has disturbed the two men. Not far in the distance are the flashing blue lights of a police car, pulled over to the side. And then I see the patrolman standing in the center of the road, signaling for us to stop.

I can't believe this is happening. We're transporting contraband from Bulgaria to Romania and the police have already stopped us, just a short way into our journey. We'll be arrested for sure! This is far worse than getting caught smoking some weed. I don't know what I fear more—serving a sentence in a cold, dank Bulgarian jail cell or being deported back to the States with a dishonorable discharge that will stain me for life. In any case, we're totally fucked.

Vlady pulls the truck over and rolls down his window. The policeman approaches and eyes our truck with suspicion. His tone is not threatening, but it certainly doesn't sound like neighborly pleasantries either. Vlady shrugs a lot, trying to convince the officer that we are innocent merchants transporting our goods to market. I'm not sure if he is successful in presenting our case.

The policeman looks at the boxes in the back, and a knot forms in my stomach. Any second now he'll discover that we're transporting a shipment of stolen watches. He'll take our papers, confiscate my American passport, and I'll be on my way to jail. I wonder if I get a free phone call. I wonder who I'll call.

Vlady gets out of the truck and follows the policeman around back. I watch them through the rearview mirror, which is positioned just in front of me. The two men argue a bit, but neither one is looking at the boxes we're carrying. Boris sits in his seat, not moving, his eyes fixed on the far horizon.

Finally, after five minutes that seem to stretch out much longer, Vlady returns to the cab and the policeman goes back to his car. Vlady switches on the ignition, mutters something to Boris, and we're on our way.

"What happened? What did you do?" I ask, wondering what he had done to set us free.

"We negotiated the price," Vlady says, a smile returning to his face.

"The price?"

"Yes. Only one hundred leva. Very cheap, I think." He stares ahead while I watch the police car getting steadily smaller in the rearview mirror.

Vidin is situated on the shores of the Danube River, and I know little about the town. We continue about five kilometers farther north, where I see a sign stating that we've reached the International Dock, whatever that is. We get into a line of traffic heading down to the river.

"Is there a bridge here?" I ask.

"Bridge?" Vlady says, somewhat amused at my question. "One day there will be big bridge, from Vidin to Romania. Now, no bridge. We go with ferry."

And then we switch places. This apparently is their big plan. They want me, an American, to drive their truck onto the ferry. They think that if an American citizen is the one driving there will be little chance of a customs inspection. In truth, though, they don't have too much to worry about. As we've learned in our general introduction courses, both Romania and Bulgaria have recently joined the European Union, and there is mostly free trade between the two countries and the rest of Europe.

And this is indeed the case. The border policeman inspects my driver's license and my passport, as well as forged documents produced by Vlady and Boris. The customs inspectors at this border crossing seem indifferent to what we're transporting in the truck. We pay the fee, and I drive the truck onto the ferry.

I don't recognize the boat as a ferry. I guess it could be described more as a motorized raft. But it's a big motorized raft. There is room for a number of container trucks, passenger cars, and medium-sized vehicles such as our pickup. I get out of the cabin as we pull away from the Bulgaria dock. The early morning brings with it a light drizzle, and I wipe the rain from my face as we begin to cross the mighty Danube.

Somehow I never pictured the famous river as being an unexciting expanse of murky water with the distant Romanian shoreline partially hidden in fog. My thoughts of the Danube were more romantic, based on its association with Vienna and Budapest. The phrase "Danube Waltz" comes to mind, as do brief memories of studying the music of Johann Strauss sometime in my past. The Danube is Europe's second-largest river, I recall, and its most important international waterway as well. Here it serves as Bulgaria's northern border. In any case, it's a much wider body of water than I expected, and it takes about twenty drizzly minutes to reach the Romanian side.

After the hurried actions of our predawn departure, the tension I felt when we were stopped by the police, and the fear of having a customs inspection on one side of the Danube or the other, our delivery of the watches to Vlady's Romanian counterpart is a bit of a letdown. It's an anticlimax to our morning's adventures, and I wonder why this journey got me so worried in the first place.

We park the truck on the outskirts of Calafat, flash our lights at another vehicle parked farther along the road, and within minutes we're transferring the boxes to a short flatbed truck. Without exchanging more than a few words with the Romanian driver, we're done with the task. We drive back the way we came, arrive at the dock, and wait for the next hourly ferry to cross the river and return us to Bulgaria.

We did it, I think, as we journey south on the other side. My debt to Vlady and Boris for their secrecy has been paid. I have no further obligations to these small-time smugglers. Now I can turn my attention in earnest to the Bulgarian lessons and prepare for the next stage of my training.

"That went well," I remark to Vlady as we near Montana.

"Not bad," he admits. "Now we plan next job."

CHAPTER 29

I am not expecting the bagpipe. The troupe of entertainers strikes up its Balkan beat with enthusiasm. One musician plays an accordion, another pounds rhythmically on a shoulder-strung *tupan* drum, and an older man pipes out simple sounds on his *kaval* flute. But it's the bagpipe that surprises me, as I would normally associate this animal-skinned bag instrument with the Scottish highlands.

"It's called a *gaida*," one of the Peace Corps instructors explains to me. "It's quite common all over Europe, actually."

It is strange to hear the long, whiny notes emerging from the bag being carried under the arms of the mustached band member. To produce this protracted sound, he puffs into the blowpipe at the top, squeezing the bag to force air through the reeds of the pipes, and a mesmerizing Balkan drone fills the hall.

"You know a lot about bagpipes!" I joke with the instructor.

"Oh, not really, but I do know one thing," he says, laughing. "When you finish playing your *gaida* each night, you pour a glass of *rakia* into the bag."

"You must be kidding me!"

"No, it's true. *Rakia* acts as an antiseptic within the bag to keep it from rotting. It's apparently also quite common to rub hand lotion on the exterior of the *gaida* bag. A well-kept *gaida* can last for some thirty years!"

I stand and watch, entranced by the music that has been advertised as coming straight from the Rhodopes Mountains. Then I join Lance at the open bar. He hands me an ice-cold Shumensko and helps himself to a handful of pistachio nuts.

"Great party," he comments, "but not enough girls."

"Why do you keep insisting that Bulgarian women are so beautiful?" I say, clinking my beer bottle against the one held by my friend.

"They just are," he responds lightly. "They're so thin, with jet-black hair, pointed noses, tight asses. Their legs stretch for miles, and their skin is so white! Take a look around at our fellow American inductees. All the girls from the States are pudgy, short, and entirely unattractive. Hold me back if you find me trying to elope with that lovely Ivanka we met at the pub the other night."

I laugh, not knowing if he's serious or if he's gotten a head start with Bulgarian beer consumption for the night.

The party is quite lively, a fitting tribute to our having completed the pre-service training. We are now officially Peace Corps volunteers, serving as ambassadors of the United States and qualified to give Bulgarians a better command of the English language and an appreciation of the American way of life. The party is in the Vratsa high school, where our final courses took place. I am proud of myself for completing the course. I am truly capable of accomplishing anything if I work at it hard enough, I tell myself.

By now, my command of Bulgarian is *gore-dolu*, or so-so, but it's enough to get along. The locals can understand me—grammar mistakes and all. I am ready for my initial volunteering assignment, wherever that will be. But first, it's time to get drunk and party!

The band members wear traditional Bulgarian attire. The men sport black pants, white shirts, and embroidered vests. A woman joins the ensemble, dressed in a plain black skirt with colorful embroidery at the lower edges. Over the skirt she has an orange-and-red plaid apron. She wears a white blouse with decorative embellishments and, over that, an open jacket with a neckline framed in more color. Her dark hair is garlanded by a large pink flower.

The woman takes the microphone and launches into a sorrowful Balkan melody. I don't understand the words, but by her expressions, I can determine that this is a heartfelt tale of lost love. The entire audience, Peace Corps inductees and local residents alike, stands still in respectful silence as the singer's woeful melody runs its course. We all clap appreciatively when she reaches the end.

And then the folk dancing begins.

I am not a dancer. Never was, never will be. It doesn't matter how much patience and encouragement go into efforts to get me to join in the frolicking, whether it's at a discotheque or at a party offering Bulgarian folk dances, I don't dance. I know that I will only end up making a fool of myself if I try.

Lance is enthusiastic about the opportunity to grab hold of one particular dark-haired girl. He circles the room with her to the beat of the complex rhythm. The name of the dance is the *horo*. The dancers start by moving to the right with a series of lift-steps, and then they move to the left. They cross the right foot in front of the left, transferring the weight onto the right foot while moving the left foot to the right. It all seems so complicated, but Lance picks up the moves effortlessly; they come as naturally to him as his successful attempts to pick up the local women.

The dancers circle around ever faster as the beat of the music picks up in intensity. Lance draws his partner as close as possible and almost trips over his feet as a result. I hold up my beer to salute him, but he doesn't notice me as he swirls around the room.

A man at the far end of the room is staring at me. With a sense of impending horror, I realize it is Vlady. I haven't seen him since our journey together to Romania. I made efforts to avoid Boris during my last days in Montana, and I certainly have no desire to see his accomplice. I figured I was through with these two crooks. What is Vlady doing here now?

I move back, trying to hide from Vlady's view, but it's no use. Before I have a chance to escape, he has slipped across the room and is standing at my side.

"We need to go," he says, his breath thick with alcohol.

"I'm at a party, can't you see that?"

"We go now," he says, leading me by the elbow out of the room.

Lance is too busy dancing to notice my departure, and there is no one else for me to tell that I'm being forced to leave. Before I fully comprehend what's happening, I am sitting in the pickup truck next to Vlady, and we are driving away from the school.

"Where are we going?"

"We go to the train," he says, not bothering to explain anything more than that.

A few minutes later, we are parked at Vratsa's train station, a sorry-looking building with few comforts to offer passengers bound for Sofia in the south. But I soon learn Sofia is not where we are headed.

Boris meets us outside the station and wordlessly climbs into the back of the truck. He lifts out a portable moving cart and hands it down to Vlady, and then he starts handing me some very large but surprisingly lightweight boxes.

More stolen watches, I assume. Soon we have all the cartons lowered to the ground, and we begin wheeling them into the station. It takes three trips, but finally we have the boxes stacked together in neat piles on the platform. Boris hurries to return the cart to the pickup and then returns to wait with us in the dark for the train to arrive.

"I should get back now," I say to Vlady, but he ignores my statement. I could just run, but they would probably chase me if I did. I still remember Boris's fist looming in front of my face, a pounding that was averted only at the very last second by Ralitsa's intervention.

"Train comes," Vlady says.

And then I hear it, long before it comes into view. It sounds like a very tired train, struggling along the tracks, reluctantly transporting its cargo on the journey north. A lonesome whistle sounds, spooking me even more. And then the headlight pops around the corner, shining a beam down the length of parallel iron rails until it lights up the concrete siding of the platform.

What the hell am I doing here?

The train pulls into the station as if it has just arrived from the 1950s. The cars are dirty and rust-colored, their graffiti-covered exteriors looking like they're from the Iron Curtain era. The passenger windows are small, as if added as an afterthought. As the whistle blows again, the train grinds to a halt alongside the concrete where we are standing.

We quickly get into action. Vlady jumps aboard one of the passenger cars, and Boris and I hand the cartons up to him. Shouldn't these be stored in the baggage compartment? I wonder, but there is no one to ask. When the last of the boxes is loaded, Boris pushes me ahead of him, and I am forced to climb the narrow metal steps onto the car itself.

Not too many passengers have boarded the train, and the three of us have an entire compartment to ourselves. The narrow sleeping bunks don't appear particularly accommodating. I ask Vlady a question to which I already know I don't want to hear an answer.

"Where are we going?"

"Belgrade," he says. "We'll get there tomorrow."

He talks in rapid Bulgarian with Boris while I stare out the window at the dark Balkan countryside. I am on a train to Serbia? This can't be happening! I've been kidnapped, I think, forced to travel on this train against my will. I stand up, ready to pull a lever and make the engines stop and end this nightmarish journey.

"Where you go?" Vlady asks.

Just then a conductor arrives and points at the cartons at the end of the corridor. Both Vlady and Boris argue with him for several minutes, and then Boris takes out his wallet and leads the conductor out of sight to negotiate the price of our travel. I'm not quite sure if a bribe is involved, but when Boris comes back to our cabin, he is whistling as if nothing had happened.

I'm hoping that's the last of our troubles. As the two of them chain smoke despite the no-smoking warnings, I climb up the thin metal rungs to an upper bunk and lie down, with my feet hanging partly in midair. The flickering florescent fixture just inches above my head swings back and forth like a pendulum, its movement partially hypnotic and strangely comforting. My eyes slowly adjust to the half light of the compartment, and I find myself totally relaxed. The rumble and creaking of the old train shake me back and forth, but despite my worries and troubles, it's as if I am being rocked in a cradle, and soon I'm fast asleep.

The train slows as we approach the Serbian border crossing, and I'm jerked awake. It's at this moment that a sudden thought pops into my mind. I don't have my passport with me!

I sit up quickly on the bunk and see Vlady pulling out documents from his travel bag. I see that he's holding three passports, and one of them is mine!

"Hey, where did you get that?" I ask, jumping down to the cabin floor.

"We knew you'd need it," Vlady replies.

I am about to grab the passport from him, but there is movement in the corridor. We all realize at the same time that a customs inspector has boarded the train and is about to discover the shipment we're transporting.

Vlady and Boris whisper to each other, and I sit down on the lower bunk opposite them. Boris again takes out his wallet and goes to talk to the inspector and negotiate our passage into Serbia.

This time, though, he is gone a long time. At one point I hear strange sounds from the distant end of the corridor, but I'm afraid to dwell on what this might mean. And then Boris returns, his eyes a bit glazed over as he sits down. Vlady avoids looking at his partner.

The train begins moving again, slowly, inching forward as it passes over the line on the map that designates the border between Bulgaria and Serbia. I wait for it to pick up speed, but it continues at this sluggish pace as if it has all night to reach Belgrade, which, of course, it does.

I stand up and move to leave the cabin.

"Where you go?" Vlady asks, reaching out to grab my arm.

"I need to go to the bathroom."

"No bathroom now," he says, and I drop to my seat.

Hours later, the ordeal of this night train is over. We pull into the Serbian station before the sun has risen. A sign declares that we've arrived in Beograd, but I realize that this is just the local spelling for Belgrade, the country's capital. There is a rough-looking man waiting for us on the platform, and we help bring the boxes to his van. Our delivery mission is completed with little fanfare, not even a word of thanks is exchanged. We return to the station to wait for the morning's train back to Bulgaria.

The next day, as I'm packing up my room to leave Vratsa, where I had completed the Peace Corps training, I log on to the Internet to check the English-language news from Sofia and the local weather forecast. A headline catches my eye, as if planted there specifically for me: "Customs Officer Dies During Search for Smuggled Cigarettes." I skim through the lines of the short article:

Passengers on the train traveling between Bulgaria and Serbia are said to have heard some kind of noise. The train crew was alerted but only discovered the body of the customs officer in one of the bathrooms when the train pulled into the Belgrade station. The case is under investigation. Trains traveling on this route are frequently used to smuggle cigarettes between the two countries.

CHAPTER 30

By the time I regain consciousness, whoever threw a stone through the cabin window is long gone. I don't know if anyone saw me lying on the cot with my foot bleeding from the broken glass. I limp around the room, avoiding the shards as I assess the damage. The front door has been jacked open, and someone has forced his way inside. My belongings are scattered. Shirts and sweaters have been thrown from their drawers, and my paperbacks are lying everywhere on the floor, their pages bent back and exposed. Smashed dishes clutter the sink. The garbage pail is overturned. Unbelievably, my laptop is where I left it on the kitchen table. I have no other valuables in my possession—no money or documents to steal—so I guess I have gotten off quite lucky.

I take in the mess for a few minutes and worry that the disorder will set off a debilitating migraine. I look for my bottle of pills but don't see it anywhere. I search under the cot, behind the table, in the entrance hall. When was the last time I took my painkillers? I am getting a bit edgy, fearful that my medicine may have been stolen by the intruder. Why would anyone take a bottle of prescription pills? How will I manage without it? I return to the bedroom and lie down, waiting for the waves of darkness to engulf me. Surprisingly, they never arrive. My head remains clear, and my thoughts remain focused.

I get up and begin sweeping up the shattered glass. Katya will know how to go about switching the window pane, I tell myself.

And that's when I began to think seriously about Katya—possibly for the first time. She has been caring for me for so long, coming to the cabin regularly from her home in the village, yet I know absolutely nothing about her. She must be in her mid-thirties. She's about my height, has a slim figure and curly brown hair. Her face is pleasant enough, not overly beautiful, but then again, she's the only woman I've seen in a long time. In other circumstances, I might have been attracted to Katya. Perhaps if my life in the cabin was a work of fiction, I would have fallen in love with her by now. But, in this real, very strange situation, I haven't had a sexual thought in months, maybe longer. I suspect that my libido was also damaged when I was struck in the head.

I continue to clean the cabin, surprised that the severe headache I'd been expecting does not arrive at all. My mind is sharp, refreshed. It's as if I've woken from a long slumber, and I'm re-energized. I return the books to the shelf, gather up my clothing, and remove the fragments of broken dishes from the sink. I set the garbage pail back in place and sweep up the last of the mess. By the time I finish, it is starting to get dark. I go outside to breathe in the pure mountain air, filling my lungs and feeling very light on my feet. It's quite chilly and I shiver.

I touch the silver chain strung around my neck. The chain and its Jewish symbols played an important role in my childhood; I am convinced of this. If only I could figure out the chain's meaning I would be able to fully piece together my past. I believe it's a vital clue to regaining my memory. The way I'm feeling now, with a lucid mind that's free of pain, I'm sure I'll be able to figure everything out very soon.

I stare up as the clear sky fills with more stars than could ever be imagined. A bitter cold is descending with the night, and I've never felt more alive. I'm fully confident that I can free myself from my addiction to the medication. How could I have been so blind to the fact that I'm perfectly capable of coping without the pills?

I look forward to sharing the good news with Katya. She'll be extremely happy to learn that I am recovering at last from my head injuries.

"What happened here?" Katya asks me the next day, coming inside with a big bag of groceries.

"Someone broke into the cabin," I tell her. "They threw a stone through the window and jimmied open the door."

"Are you all right? I see you're limping."

"It's nothing. I stepped on some broken glass."

"Let me take a look at your foot."

She sets down the groceries and kneels to examine my injury. My sock is bloodied, but my foot is no longer bleeding. Underneath the stained cotton we discover an insignificant cut, nothing serious. When Katya pushes the skin to the sides, searching for slivers of glass, it's quite painful, and I force myself to refrain from crying out.

"We'll replace that windowpane," she says, bandaging my foot. "Scott, other than the foot, how are you feeling? Did you take your medicine?"

"I didn't, but I feel just fine," I reply, eager to share this news with her.

"You must take the pills, especially after the trauma you've just been through with this break-in," she says. "Yes, I insist on it."

Before I have a chance to respond, I notice her staring at me with a strange look in her eyes. "Scott, do you know what day it is today?"

"No," I answer truthfully. I don't have a calendar, so there is no way for me to track time.

"I brought you a *martenitsa*!" she exclaims, rising to her feet.

"What's that?" The name sounds vaguely familiar, but I can't connect it to anything specific.

"Don't you remember? *Baba Marta*?"

Baba is the Bulgarian word for "grandmother" and *Mart* is the Bulgarian word for the month of March. Saying the two words together refers to a certain day of the year, but the meaning escapes me.

"Let me remind you about the holiday," Katya says patiently, tying red-and-white strings around my right wrist. "Baba Marta is a very moody woman, just like the month of March. When she is happy, the skies are blue, but when Baba Marta is angry, rains and winds sweep the countryside. On the first of March, this is how we welcome the arrival of spring."

The words bring back recollections of exchanging the traditional tassels. The colorful string ornaments are also pinned to lapels, I recall, and everyone has them. Perhaps they are worn as an amulet to ward off evil. I'm not sure.

"How long do I need to wear this?" I ask, regarding the string around my wrist.

"Until you see a stork or the first bud on a tree," Katya said, reminding me of how the custom plays out. "If you see a blossoming tree, you can take it off your hand and tie it on a branch."

"Well, the snow is gone, and, as you've seen, the first hiker of the year has visited the mountains, causing all this damage," I reply. "I'm sure spring will come early this year."

"You seem agitated. Let me get your pills," she says.

I hadn't noticed that a new supply of the drug was included with the other items in her delivery. Before I have a chance to refuse the offer, she is handing me two of the small blue tablets and insisting that I pop them one after another into my mouth.

I almost gag, nearly choking as I try to spit out the first pill. Don't swallow it, I tell myself, but then my resistance fades and my throat relaxes. Could it be that despite my realization that these pills are harmful to me I'm still addicted to them, and more importantly, to how they affect me?

I try to mumble some words to Katya, but I'm incapable of saying anything understandable. Soon the pounding in my head becomes unbearable. I make my way to the cot where I collapse, relapsing into the tortured condition from which I cannot escape.

When I awake, it is dark and Katya is gone. I wonder who tied the *martenitsa* around my wrist.

CHAPTER 31

We're at Sin City, our heads spinning from Red Bull and vodka, watching the Bulgarians bounce to the strange but hypnotic beat of their revered *chalga* music. I don't get it. How can this crass form of pop-folk, which I find both degrading and degenerate, appeal to otherwise seemingly mature adults? I see no value whatsoever in the pulsating beats, the blasts of high decibels that reverberate across the crowded dance floor. The spiky-haired deejay pumping the sound seems like a freak to me, only slightly more respectable than the female Bulgarian pop star clutching the microphone on the stage at the far end of the hall.

Our Bulgarian friends had invited Lance and me to attend Andriana's performance, and they were full of warm praise for this popular *chalga* singer. She certainly makes an impression, with her full mane of bleached, stone-white hair, her skintight black leather pants and jacket, and a low-cut dress revealing a massive pair of perfectly sculpted breasts. As for her voice, well, it is more throaty than sensuous. I don't understand what she's singing, but the lyrics probably relate how desperate she is to have someone ravish her—and at that very moment on the dance floor, if at all possible.

The air is thick with cigarette smoke, and the only sound I hear other than the disruptive music blasting from the loudspeakers is the clink of glasses. Alcohol is poured freely and consumed quickly, as if there is an imminent threat that prohibition will disturb the party. Lance says something to me, but I cannot hear his words even though he is nearly kissing my ears with his mouth. I grin in his direction. The hall is dark, interrupted by a roving spotlight that briefly illuminates clusters of *chalga* groupies as they drink, dance, and mingle.

As much as Lance and I have tried to fit in with the Bulgarian youth with whom we're working, both in the English-language classes we give and in the after-school group activities we've been organizing, I still feel quite out of place in this beat fest of Bulgarian pop culture. I find the music and the top-heavy singer tawdry and shocking; I'm surprised that the locals seem to love it. Andriana launches into yet another top-ten medley that the crowd immediately recognizes from the MTV-rip-off channels. The hall is too crowded to allow for real dancing, so all that the clubbers can do is stand and sway like a tin of tormented sardines.

The setting is foreign to me, almost as foreign as the Rhodope village in the south where Lance and I have been trying to help residents organize the building of a playground, which will be the first in their village. I smile to myself as I think of what Lance and I have been doing together on this project. The budget has already been approved, but before the order can be sent to the company that provides the lumber and parts, we need to make sure the villagers are aware of what lies ahead. Building the playground for their children is the end goal, of course, but doing it together, with everyone pitching in, is the real objective of our community mission. Not all the village residents realize that they'll have to participate in the physical labor. What do they expect—that Lance and I will do all the work for them?

After our latest stint of volunteering, Lance and I traveled to Sofia for the weekend to get some much needed rest and relaxation, except that clubbing is more important to Lance than actually catching up on lost sleep. I would have preferred to stay at the apartment, but Lance convinced me to tag along to Sin City. The place turned out to be a complex of clubs and venues, all under the one roof of an ultra-modern, red-walled building standing out in stark contrast to the run-down buildings of central Sofia. The security at the entrance was tight and selective. The broad-shouldered thugs on duty were there to weed out not only teenagers but also anyone deemed unworthy of entering such a high-level establishment. Luckily, Lance and I were easily identified as foreigners, respectable enough to get by with only a perfunctory inspection. The security guards feigned interest in my American passport picture but then waved us into the noisy club.

Standing in the mayhem, the vodka and Red Bull mix gives me a nice buzz, but I find that I need something more. I pull out a joint from my pocket and wave it at Lance, but he shakes his head to indicate that he's not interested. A tall, thin guy about our age grabs my hand and starts pulling me toward him. I immediately think it's someone wanting to share a puff of my weed, but it turns out he has a more powerful offer for me.

"You want to get really high?" he shouts in English, and I barely hear him in the commotion.

"Sure," I respond. What's he got? Blow? Freebase coke? Crack? I'm not particular to the exact name as long as it produces the desired effect.

I follow him into the men's bathroom, which is a glistening, mirror-filled corridor bordered by stainless-steel stalls and a row of urinals, each capped for some strange reason with a mound of glistening ice cubes. There's a couple in one of the stalls banging each other and shaking the dividers. I don't have a clue as to what sexes are involved. My head is spinning, and I feel like my feet aren't even touching the floor. It's only when the thin man pulls out the syringes and alcohol swabs from his pocket that I start getting nervous.

While I smoke weed recreationally—well, maybe excessively—and while I've been known to snort coke at parties and among friends, I've never shot heroin before. I don't know if I'm ready for this. I'm a bit reluctant to try this for the first time in the restroom of a flashy Bulgarian nightclub.

"Give me some cash, and I'll give you the ride of a lifetime," the guy says to me, and I notice in the florescent lights that his inner arms are scarred with the markings of heavy drug use. I immediately don't trust him at all. I should get back to Lance on the dance floor. What was I thinking?

"Try it," he insists, his voice soft and innocent. "This is the purest high you'll ever experience."

For a Balkan drug addict, he knows pretty good English, I think. "Thanks, but I'll pass," I reply, voicing my refusal and attempting to push past him.

The grunting in the stall continues, the couple oblivious to the deal being conducted nearby. "I thought you Americans liked the real stuff," the guy says, upset that his offer has been rejected. "This is the best powder, straight from Turkey. Come on and try it. You'll like it. You won't be sorry."

That's when two men burst into the bathroom. Oh, no, busted!

"It's not mine!" I cry out, distancing myself from the acne-faced man with the syringe in hand.

But it's not the Bulgarian narcotics squad. I almost smile when I recognize the unexpected visitors in the club bathroom.

"Thank God you're here," I greet them.

"You're coming with us," Vlady says. My host father Boris, never one for words, shoves the drug addict to the floor as easily if he were a thin piece of cardboard. "We've got work to do," Vlady adds.

As much as I hate hanging with these two crooks, these no-good smugglers and assumed murderers, I'm glad that they've arrived just in time to save me from making what could have been the biggest mistake of my life. We leave the bathroom just as an orgasmic cry signals satisfaction in the toilet stall.

CHAPTER 32

How did Vlady and Boris know to find me in the Sofia *chalga* nightclub? They know a lot more than they're telling me. The deviousness of their actions never ceases to amaze me. I resent the fact that I'm being held hostage to their whims, unable to escape and powerless of controlling what will happen next. I wonder if we're returning to the ferry in Vidin for another smuggling trip across the Danube to Romania. Or maybe we're going to board the night train to Serbia with an additional load of stolen cigarettes?

Without disclosing a word to me about our destination, they drive the pickup truck to Sofia's central bus station, which is located right next to the train station. We park near the glass-faced modern construction, and I follow them inside. It's just after midnight, and most of the platforms in the bus terminal are empty, with only a few odd-looking stragglers hanging around in apparent preparations for an overnight stay. It's not my first time in the station, but I've never visited the terminal when it's been this quiet. I've traveled on some of the local lines, and there are international connections here as well, with bus lines serving Barcelona, Belgrade, Bucharest, Budapest, and many other European destinations. But those buses depart during the daytime hours. What are we doing here at this late hour when it appears the station has shut down for the night?

"Here's your ticket," Vlady says, handing me a slip of paper as we approach a back door leading to a gray bus parked outside. "It departs in ten minutes, the last one to Varna until morning. Boris, give him the package."

I turn to my host father, who hasn't said a word since they picked me up at the club. He hands me a sealed cardboard box, about the size of a basketball. I hadn't noticed him carrying the box, mainly because Vlady's done all of the talking.

"What's this?" I ask innocently.

"That's not important for you to know," Vlady says, spinning me around to face him. "What is important is that you listen closely to the instructions I'm going to give you."

He speaks softly, articulating his words to ensure that I understand. He gives me the name of the person I'm supposed to meet, and then he tells me how to find him once I've arrived in Varna. Then he makes me repeat everything back to him, which I manage to do even though my head is still rolling from the effects of Red Bull and vodka.

He seems satisfied with my repetition of the information. "Go get on the bus there," he says, pointing to the door. "We'll talk to you when you get back to Sofia."

It's only after I board the bus and take my assigned seat toward the back that I realize I haven't been given any money for the return trip and I'll have to cover that expense myself.

What the hell am I doing? I think of Lance, still at the club and possibly wondering to where I've disappeared. He knows a bit about my dealings with Boris and Vlady, but he doesn't have a clue as to the stranglehold these two criminals have over my life. It all boils down to the fact that they're blackmailing me. I'm forced to do their small jobs to prevent being exposed and expelled from Bulgaria. I thought my debt to them had already been paid in full! If I hadn't been so wasted when they arrived at the nightclub, I would have protested this new mission they'd planned for me. Sitting in my seat on the bus, I am determined to deliver the package in the morning and get back to Sofia as quickly as possible. I can't help but think that I'm being forced into actions I will later regret.

The bus speeds east through the dark and forbidding Bulgarian night. The rhythm of the tires on the asphalt pavement soothes my worries, and I close my eyes, eager to forget the strange happenings that have led me to this unexpected journey. I fade into a pleasant dream and welcome my grandfather into my mind. It's my bar mitzvah again, as colorful and exciting as it was to me when I was thirteen years old. My grandparents are both with me, beaming with pride. My grandfather hands me a present, and I'm almost embarrassed to accept it.

"This is for you," he says.

I take the silver chain and regard the *chai* pendant attached to it. I'm about to say that necklaces are for girls, and that I will never wear such jewelry, but the pendant and its shiny Jewish symbol catch my eye. Of course I'll wear this, I assure him. I hug my grandfather with a loving embrace. He helps me secure the gift around my neck.

As the bus speeds toward Varna, I unconsciously finger the *chai* chain that is wrapped comfortably around my neck even now. It's a real-life link to my grandfather. I think about the emails I've sent to him describing my experiences in Bulgaria. I smile in my sleep, recalling when I taught him how to navigate the Internet, how to communicate using Skype. It's strange that people of my grandfather's generation simply can't pick up the technological innovations that make the world tick these days!

With these pleasant nocturnal thoughts keeping me company, I have no sense of the minutes that pass or the kilometers that the bus has driven. The night is a temporary distraction, and soon it is morning and we are pulling into the unassuming Varna station that is our announced destination. For me, however, this is not the final stop on my eastward journey. I still have this strange package to deliver.

I flag down a passing taxi, and the sullen driver transports me outside the city and drops me off at the Happy Sunshine Resort Hotel in Golden Sands. I pay the fare, realizing that this is another business expense for which I undoubtedly will not be reimbursed. I go inside the ritzy-looking building.

The person I'm supposed to meet has yet to arrive, so I sit down on one of the lumpy leather sofas in the lobby. I put the package at my feet and close my eyes. I haven't fully recuperated from the alcohol at the party or the overnight bus journey, and before I know it, I'm snoring loud enough to attract the angry stares of the housekeeping staff.

"The manager now see you," someone says to me in broken English, jolting me awake.

I am jolted into a state of consciousness and rub the sleep from my eyes. The security guard standing over me is immense, with wide shoulders and powerful muscles bulging out of his shirt sleeves. His head is bald, reflecting the light of an overhead chandelier. A flashy earring sparkles in one of his ears. He is so huge that he makes Boris seem like a weakling.

"The manager?" I ask, questioning this bulky man's message.

"You have something for Alexander Nikolov, no?"

"Yes," I reply, making sure to shake my head in the appropriate Bulgarian fashion.

"Come with me."

I pick up the package and follow the security guard up half a flight of stairs to the back office, a dark and shabby room that is totally unlike the lobby. A poster advertising the Black Sea coast hanging on the wall fails to make the place more appealing. Behind a large, cluttered desk sits a smartly attired man wearing a white shirt and tie—but that doesn't comfort me in any way. A head of greasy hair, combed back across a flaky scalp, and a pair of beady eyes complete the picture of an untrustworthy character.

Without waiting for a formal invitation, I sink into a deep-cushioned chair. I am ready to leave the package on his desk and hurry out the door, but my instructions state explicitly that I must wait for Nikolov to personally confirm its receipt.

"Who the hell are you?" the man behind the desk asks in English.

"I'm Scott Matthews. I brought this from Vlady and Boris," I say, pushing the package toward him.

He puffs for a minute on his cigarette, his smoke curling upward and clouding the room. "Do you have identification?" he asks.

"Sure," I say. I reach into my pocket and pull out my American passport.

He compares my university mug shot with what I look like after an all-night bus trip and then scans through the pages of visa stamps. I extend my hand, but he hesitates and doesn't return the passport.

"This better be what I've been waiting for," he says, turning his attention to the package on his desk.

He takes a pair of scissors and uses one of its blades to dissect the ribbons of masking tape around the box. I watch with full curiosity as he removes an object from the bubble wrap, uncovering an item of such startling beauty that I'm left speechless.

It's an ancient vase in shades of aquamarine, with colorful depictions of Greek-like people carrying sacrificial offers in a circular procession around its base. I am shocked at the incalculable value of the item I've been transporting across the country. It's obviously a collector's piece, something that is totally out of place in this dark office and that belongs in an archaeological museum.

Where did Vlady and Boris get this? More accurately, from where did they steal this? The audacity of those thugs startles me. Not only are they smugglers of stolen goods and presumed murderers of Serbian customs officials, they're also antiques traffickers. I'm sure that they're on Interpol's most-wanted list. I've got to finish this job and get the hell out of here.

I feel sure that Alexander Nikolov of the Happy Sunshine Resort Hotel will immediately confirm the authenticity of this Grecian artifact and release me of any further obligations. I start to get up from my deep-cushioned seat, ready to leave the room and rush back to the Varna station to catch the next Sofia-bound bus.

"This is not what was arranged," he says, dismissing the beauty of the ancient vase with a sneer as if it were a stray dog in a Sofia alley. "You brought the wrong piece."

"What?"

"You have delivered the wrong item," he says, his voice rising.

"I brought you what they gave me," I say, coughing up my excuse.

"It is unacceptable!" he says, nearly shouting now. "What kind of fool do they take me for? They send me a vase?"

He spits with disgust into a wastepaper basket at the foot of his desk. For a minute I fear that he will throw the ancient piece to the floor, shattering both it and any chance I have of getting out of here alive.

"You will go back to your friends and tell them to stop their little schemes," he says. "You will get from them the item I ordered—the real thing. Only then will you come back to me."

"I'm sorry, but it's not really my fault," I say, standing in front of him.

"It don't matter whose fault it is," he says. "Now, get out of here and get me what I asked for!"

I am totally confused, not sure why there has been such fucked-up miscommunication between Vlady and Boris back in Montana and their contact here in Varna. Why did I have to be the middleman in this argument? I'm not a party to their smuggling deals, and my involvement is just sinking me deeper into trouble.

Thinking of Nikolov's reaction when I made the delivery, I am aware that I am carrying out thankless tasks and no one ever appreciates my efforts. Enough is enough! I will not run any more errands for Vlady and Boris, I vow to myself as I return to the Varna bus station and approach the ticket window. I don't care what they might do to me. Let them tell the Peace Corps anything they want. I've had it with their games and schemes. I don't care anymore if I get kicked out and am forced to return to the States.

I will terminate my connection to these gangsters once and for all.

I board the bus and breathe a sigh of relief when the door slams shut. My Varna delivery trip is already just a bad memory. We depart the station, and the bus begins the long return journey to Sofia. Hours later, as we approach the Bulgarian capital, I reach into my pocket for my passport, but it isn't there. I sit up with alarm as I recall the last time I used it. I had handed the passport to Nikolov, to verify my identity as being the American I said I was.

Nikolov never returned my passport! I am totally up shit creek now.

CHAPTER 33

I am in the backyard of my host family's home, the territory as unfamiliar to me as if it were a foreign country. I am not alone. Boris and Vlady are here, and they're actually doing most of the work. Each of us is taking turns shoveling, but they've been doing the lion's share of it while I watch the dirt pile up alongside the long trench we're digging. Occasionally they argue with each other, but mostly they concentrate on the task at hand. The sun is beginning to set, and evening engulfs our excavation work in a surreal twilight. We've been working for over two hours, only stopping for occasional swigs of a foul-tasting liquor drunk straight from a wine bottle. I wonder if we'll continue to dig when it gets dark. And then with a dull clang, Boris's shovel hits something hard.

I think back, recalling the circumstances that brought me here. After my unsuccessful trip to Varna, I immediately contacted Vlady. His lack of sympathy for my missing passport didn't come as a complete surprise. I had hoped that he would have leverage over Nikolov and could arrange to have my passport shipped back to my current home in a Rhodopes village, or, if that wasn't possible, to a pickup spot in Sofia. Instead of offering assistance, Vlady insisted that I come to Montana for the weekend. He informed me that I'll be assigned a new task, one that will again send me to the Black Sea coast.

"Don't worry. It's all arranged," Vlady assured me over the phone, clearing his throat to indicate that he wasn't concerned in the least about the mission.

But that was what was worrying me. I didn't trust Vlady and Boris. Nothing good could possibly result from their smuggling schemes.

"I want out." I tried hard to make my voice sound forceful, but my hand was shaking as I clutched the phone to my ear. "Just help me get my passport back so that I don't have to involve the American embassy. I'm an American citizen, for God's sake!"

"The embassy staff isn't going to help you here, young mister peace-lover," Vlady replied smugly. "Now get your ass up to Montana so that we can prep you. Only by going back to Varna will you get your passport back."

As the week passed, I concentrated on my Peace Corps duties. I had to fake an illness to escape weekend responsibilities; only Lance knew that I was actually bound for Montana on personal business. I told him I was just going to visit my host family, but somehow he grasped that there was much more at stake. I wished I could confide in Lance and tell him everything. Is it fear of repercussions from Vlady and Boris that held me back? Or did I lack the courage to acknowledge my latest predicament, a complicated situation for which I was solely responsible?

"Spill the beans, Scott," my friend insisted. "I know you're in big trouble. I can help."

"What trouble?"

"I know you're up to something with your host father," he continued. "Just tell me what's going on."

I smiled at him but remained silent.

My talk with Lance seems like ages ago, even though it was just yesterday. Now, as I stand sullenly next to a pile of dirt, I'm anxious to see what Boris has upturned with his shovel. The yard behind the house is like a junkyard, with rusted relics from the family's past scattered on a gradual slope leading up to a fence-like thicket of trees.

Prominent in view is the skeleton of a Wartburg Knight, a popular Bulgarian car from the 1960s that I learned about in one of the Peace Corps sessions on local folklore and culture. The old vehicle is raised on a platform, with its tires missing and the interiors exposed to the elements due to the absence of glass in the windows. A broken tractor engine lying on the ground next to the car connects the family to its agricultural heritage, but the lack of care they gave to this small plot is somewhat disturbing.

In the fading light, Vlady chuckles loudly, indicating his excitement. What is buried in the trench? A long, rectangular shape becomes visible under the dirt, and I fear they are exhuming a corpse. Anything is possible. These guys have murdered a customs official on a Belgrade-bound train, so why couldn't they have dead bodies buried in their backyard? But how would the exhumation of a murder victim prepare me for a new trip to Varna and getting back my passport?

In the hole, I see a box of some kind, smaller than a coffin. There are no dead bodies here, I sigh with great relief. As more of the buried object becomes visible I realize that it's actually a metal trunk. Boris is careful not to damage the sides as he clears away the dirt. Finally, enough of it is exposed for him to reach around to get a handhold. Vlady jumps into the pit, and the two of them shift the box back and forth, freeing it from its encasement of soil. They bend down and begin to lift. Seconds later, I'm leaning over, helping them raise this strange metal container. It's not as heavy as I had assumed from their efforts. They climb up, and the three of us stand next to the pit, staring at what we've unearthed.

"What is it?" I ask, not expecting anyone to answer.

"This is what you need to deliver to Nikolov," Vlady replies.

In my mind I picture myself carrying this strange rectangular box as I board the Varna-bound bus. The thought sends shivers up my spine.

"Let's get it inside," Vlady says, and then he turns to bark instructions at Boris.

We set the box down on the kitchen table, oblivious to the dirt trail we've created. Ralitsa offers to make us coffee, but her husband snarls at her so harshly she seems to wilt as she withdraws from the room. Vlady is already working at the rusty latches on the box. I lean back against the humming refrigerator, afraid to interfere and fearful that Boris will send me out of the kitchen before I have a chance to see exactly what we've pulled from the earth.

Vlady carefully lifts the top of the box, exposing a wine-colored gym bag. I am immediately relieved at seeing the familiar Adidas logo, thinking this can't be so bad after all. Vlady unzips the bag and a mountain of bubble wrap is exposed, expanding rapidly with its exposure to air like a growing mound of freshly popped popcorn. The two Bulgarian men stand there, filled with awe at what they're about to reveal. Apparently Vlady cannot contain his own curiosity. He quickly reaches into the bag and removes a heavy, bubble wrap-encased item and places it on the table.

Setting the trunk on the floor, out of the way, Vlady begins to strip back the sheets of bubble wrap. Slowly, with delicate maneuvering, he continues to unwrap the package. Sections of silver shine in the kitchen light, growing in size and shape as more of this buried item comes into view. And then the last of the bubble wrap has been removed and discarded on the floor, fully revealing the amazing treasure it has protected.

I don't have a clue what I'm looking at. I don't know how to describe this item except that it's ancient—and it's absolutely stunning. It's some sort of old relic made entirely of silver, although the precious metal has tarnished due to prolonged burial beneath the earth. It is about half a meter long and seems quite delicate. There are tiny gems embedded at the ends, possibly pearls. The vessel is open at the top and capable of containing liquid. Is this a simple drinking cup? It seems a bit big for that.

Something at the lower part of the vessel catches my attention and makes my appreciation of it grow even more. At the bottom I see an intricately carved lion's head; there is no mistaking this majestic animal. The lion's mouth is open, forming an outlet for any liquid poured into the vessel from above. Now I'm convinced this is nothing ordinary. I'm guessing it was used by priests, who drank from it in ritual ceremonies, imbibing their sacred beverages and chanting in some long-lost tongue.

"I see you appreciate ancient art, mister peace-lover," Vlady says, smiling at me. "This is from the Bulgarians of old, maybe you've heard of them. They were called the Thracians."

I shake my head to indicate that I don't have a clue. Who were the Thracians? I thought the Romans ruled this country in ancient times. I remember visiting the old Roman amphitheater in Plovdiv on a free weekend during the training course.

I am not too knowledgeable about ancient history, and it doesn't particularly matter to me which ancient people created this amazing artifact. In any case, Vlady mistakes my head shaking as a positive reply. He doesn't bother to provide any additional information about the Thracians or their use of this ancient silver vessel.

"*Hubavo*," Vlady says, turning to Boris, and I recognize the Bulgarian word for *beautiful.*

Indeed! The vessel was obviously stolen, I realize, but apparently not recently. It had been buried behind Boris's house for some time; the discolored silver proved this. When and from where had Vlady and Boris stolen this? Had they broken into a museum somewhere—perhaps even the National Museum of Archaeology in Sofia—and walked away with this precious item of incalculable value? How had they accomplished that without getting caught?

It amazes me to think that my host family in Montana has hidden treasure in their backyard. Boris had buried the artifact among the clutter behind his house with the sole purpose of retrieving it at a later date. When stolen, it had probably been too hot to place on the market. Now, we have dug up this treasure and exposed it once again to the light of day, even though the last of the day's light is already gone and it has grown quite dark outside.

As the magnificent item rests on Ralitsa's kitchen table, the weight of what I'm expected to do hits me.

"Oh, no!" I say, backing away from the table and trying to distance myself from the upcoming trip to Varna.

"What is the matter, Mr. American peace-lover?" Vlady asks, and even Boris looks a bit concerned.

"You can't possibly expect me…" I begin, still reeling from what these thugs are planning. "This is an expensive item. It should be transported in a Brinks armored car or something!"

"What, and draw attention to it?" Vlady grins at me with that horrific sneer of his. "No, peace-lover. You will take this to Varna, to Nikolov. No one will suspect you of transporting the Rogozen Drinking Lion."

"Rogozen what?" I ask, but Vlady doesn't explain.

And then they start wrapping it up again, hiding the ancient silver from view under layers of protective bubbles. They ease the covered vessel back into the Adidas gym bag and zip up the zipper.

"You will take another bus trip," Vlady says, smiling at me.

"I can't take this by myself! What if the police stop me? Or someone tries to steal it?" I'm not thinking clearly, just stating the first concerns that come to my mind. "What do I say if I'm asked where I got this?"

"Hey, no police! Don't you worry. You will not travel by yourself."

Oh, great, I think. Vlady and Boris are coming with me on the long bus trip across Bulgaria. We'll have plenty to talk about, I say to myself sarcastically. These guys are really pleasant company.

When Vlady and Boris go into the living room to celebrate their excavation efforts with hard liquor and tobacco, I step outside, eager to breathe the fresh air of the cloudless night. I wish I had a joint with me. I need to get high, to ease my mind from the stress of my impending mission. I pull out my cell phone and dial the number of the one person I can talk to when I'm confused.

"Scott, what the hell are you doing up there?" Lance asks.

"Oh, just some family business," I reply, thinking that this is a family with whom one shouldn't do business.

"So, when are you coming back?"

"I need to go to Varna," I say, knowing that this will just make him more curious, and concerned about my plans.

"Varna?"

"Yes, it's just a short trip, and then I'll be back."

"Short? It's all the way across the country. Why the fuck do you need to go to Varna?"

"I have to deliver something," I say, but then I'm sorry this has slipped from my tongue. Anything I say can—and will—be used against me. I need to keep quiet about my activities.

"I'll go with you," Lance volunteers, surprising me with the offer.

"No, there's no need, really."

"Someone's got to cover your ass," he continues. "Tell me when you're going. Are you going by train or bus? I'll join you."

This is not something I can explain to Lance. He can't get involved with the criminal activities of Vlady and Boris. It's enough that I've fallen into their trap and have become a helpless pawn in their plans, one who must carry out their illegal delivery missions.

"Sorry, Lance. This is something I've got to do by myself," I say, hoping the nervousness in my voice will not betray my misgivings. "Just cover for me with the Corps."

"Sorry, buddy, that's not good enough for me," Lance insists. "I'll meet you in Varna. What time will you arrive there?"

I refuse to give my friend any details about the upcoming journey. One of the main reasons is that I don't have a clue as to how, and when, I'm going. Shortly after hanging up the phone, Vlady comes outside, and he's not alone. He approaches me with a woman at his side. I don't recognize her.

"You won't be going to Varna on your own," Vlady says, puffing on his cigarette. "This is Katya."

CHAPTER 34

"DO NOT take the pills!"

The message stares at me from the laptop screen. I have not seen this warning before and cannot fathom who has planted it on my computer. The only person who uses the laptop is me, and I didn't write these troubling words. Or did I?

I don't recall typing the note. I have no recollection of it at all, but if it was me, it must have been during my previous session on the laptop. When was that? The timing is not important. I need to focus on what I've just read.

How can I stop taking the pills? I swallow them frequently, yet it's true that I'm not getting better. I continue to suffer from the migraines. My mind is still a complete blank when I question how I came to Bulgaria, how I arrived at this cabin in the mountains. Is my memory loss because of the pills? Are they prolonging my symptoms?

Something tells me that I already know the answers to these questions and that I composed the message on the computer during a recent period of lucidity to warn myself against further consumption of the medicine.

I can't allow myself to overlook this self-written warning. I am drawn to the obvious care and premeditated planning that had guided my earlier actions. I cannot ignore what I am reading. I will stop taking the pills, I vow, wondering and hoping that this is the correct thing to do.

To clear my thoughts, I go for a short walk, not straying far. It feels good to stroll through the tranquil meadow and in the nearby woods, with the sunshine gently caressing my face. The days are wonderfully warm and not even the occasional summer rain can disturb the brilliance of nature in the mountains. Birds soar above on their aerial missions, butterflies frolic among the colorful flowers, and the mountain breeze refreshes my spirits. I think about the village that lies down the road, not too far from the cabin.

The more I walk, the better I feel. In fact, I've never felt more alive. I feel free, no longer captive to my drugged and cloudy state of mind. I realize that I'm retracing vital steps in my recuperation, and this thought comforts me. I am reaching the same conclusions—the ones that will lead to the end of the debilitating headaches and the restoration of my memory. The laptop warning has returned me to a previously taken path, one that I pray will ultimately lead to my full recovery.

I finger the silver chain that's wrapped around my neck, knowing intuitively that this thin piece of jewelry is one of the most important clues to my past. I hope that in the village, with its Internet hookup, I will gain access to the key that will unlock my memory, reveal my life, and restore my identity to me. That village is freedom. I am determined and strong enough to make the journey to get there.

Katya is due to arrive at the cabin soon to bring me new supplies. I cannot divulge to her that I am free from my narcotic addiction, especially since it's been Katya who insists that I swallow the pills during each visit. Why has she been forcing me to take them? What secret agenda does she have for me?

Could it be that Katya is intentionally drugging me, keeping me in a state of semi-conscious stupor? Why would she possibly be doing that? And why isn't she encouraging me to rediscover my past? She should be urging me to leave the cabin and accompany her to the village. She should be as eager as I am to discover my true identity and to reconnect with my family and friends.

Now I'm becoming paranoid! This must be another side effect of having been addicted to the painkillers for so long. I have grown so dependent on the pills that the moment I stop taking them, I am ready to accuse my caretaker of trying to drug me. No, Katya would never do something like that! She is too kind; she cares deeply about my well-being. I can't imagine that her intentions are anything but good. I try hard to dismiss these disloyal thoughts and head back to the cabin to await her arrival.

"I brought you two boxes of cornflakes," she says to me a short while later, unpacking the supplies.

"Thanks," I reply. And then, without thinking, I add, "Maybe next time I'll go with you to the village."

"I don't think that would be wise," she says, reprimanding me. "You're in no physical shape to handle such a walk."

"I feel great!" I say quite honestly. "What is the date today?"

"Why do you ask?"

"It's so beautiful outside. Let's go take a walk," I suggest.

"You need to save your strength," she says, dismissing the offer. She continues to unpack the sugar, jam, tea, and soap that she's brought.

Save my strength for what? I wonder. It's all a game for her, I realize. It's a mind game, this absolute control she has over me, but for what purpose? She's been pulling my strings for some time, like a mad puppeteer directing the actions of its spineless and mindless creation. Why is she doing this? What possibly could be the reason that she is keeping me isolated up here in a mountain cabin?

I need to find out!

"Katya, tell me again how we met," I say, toying with her.

"I've told you this many times," she says, not paying full attention to my question.

"Yes, but you know how I forget things."

"We met on a bus trip to Varna," she says, caution creeping into her voice. "We were traveling together. You had to deliver something to a hotel there, in Golden Sands. Do you really want me to tell you this?"

"Yes," I encourage her.

"We talked on the bus," she says, choosing her words carefully. "I went with you to the hotel, and I was with you when you were injured."

Without thinking, my fingers caress the indentation on the right side of my head. "Yes, but how did you come to care for me?" I ask her.

"What's with all these questions?" she asks, frowning at me. "Let me make you some tea."

Ignoring my attempts to discuss the events that brought us together, she goes about her duties, cleaning the cabin and preparing meals for the days when we will be apart. As evening approaches, she leaves the cabin, and I begin to make my own preparations, laying the blueprint for what I will do the next day.

That night, I toss and turn, my body aching and demanding the narcotic numbness provided by the painkillers, which, I now believe, are actually the source of all my pain. My mind keeps racing. I realize that sleeplessness is yet another sign of withdrawal from the powerful control those pills had over my life. I force myself to lie still, not to move a muscle, but the night seems endless.

In my restlessness, I begin to worry. What if I regain my memory only to discover that the person I am—or was—is not, by nature, a good person? I fear that perhaps my memory loss could be a gift, hiding secrets from my past that would be best left uncovered.

But no, I need to know who my family is and to understand what I'm doing at this isolated cabin. So much mystery surrounds my cloudy existence, and I really can't take it anymore. I am eager to set out tomorrow to regain my life.

As I lie there, twisting with discomfort on the bed, I touch the silver chain on my neck. Tomorrow I will understand its true meaning, I vow, just before falling asleep.

CHAPTER 35

Fog envelops the mountain valley at dawn, shrouding the copse of trees down the path in a cloak of mystery and foreboding, yet I regard the chilly day as one full of promise. This is the first day of the rest of my life, I tell myself, chuckling at how much of a cliché that is, yet it's a statement I hope to prove to be true.

It is midmorning when I set out, my laptop secure in the backpack on my shoulder. I take a bottle of water and two apples for snacks. It feels good to set out on this journey. The village and my soon-to-be manifested past can't be far down the path.

I hadn't previously paid much attention to the variety of colorful flowers brightening my mountain setting, but I find the meadow covered with them. They are of different sizes and shapes, but most impressive are their colors, which range from deep violet to pinks and whites. The fact that I don't know the name for any of the varieties proves that I wasn't a botanist in my former life, I think, chuckling to myself.

The meadow is buzzing, and at first I think that my mind is playing tricks on me. But it's true, for everywhere around me are flying insects—bees, butterflies, air-born grasshoppers, and other tiny creatures to which I can't put a name. Something like a dragonfly takes flight from a tall stem of wild grass. A cloud of bothersome gnats hovers over a fallen log. A fly buzzes close to my ear and then returns for a second annoying flyby.

I lean over to smell the heady fragrance of a white flower with narrow petals. It is at that exact moment that something alights on my neck. I feel a prick and instinctively swat at where I've just been stung by a bee. I don't think I'm allergic to bees, but I can't remember for sure. The attacking insect has disappeared, but its assault has left a small swollen spot that feels hot to the touch.

I take a long sip of water and resume my journey down the path as it wends its way through the woods. The first of the village houses is now in sight. I shift the laptop's weight and hurry forward.

I don't know the name of the village, but it seems as if time has forgotten this place. The houses are rustic, made of chipped stone or unpainted wood and are unkempt in their appearance. The tiled roofs are broken in parts, as if the owners are indifferent to rain or snow. Weeds grow high in the untended gardens. The paths are dirt—or spotted stretches of cobblestone at best. It is dead quiet in this forlorn village, as if it has been abandoned by its residents and left to the elements.

Then a cow's lowly moan breaks the silence, followed by another. As I walk down a path set between two clumsily constructed fences, a herd of cows comes my way, swaying back and forth as they approach a watering hole farther ahead. The word *herd* is a bit of an overstatement; it's only three black-and-white spotted animals, with steam rising from their flanks and a swarm of black flies playing tag with their heavy tails.

"*Haide*," shouts a villager, prodding the most reluctant of the animals with a long wooden stick.

I smile at the man, and he replies with a grunt that shows his indifference to strangers. He follows his cows to the trough at the side of the path. The man's dog, a cross between a German shepherd and a terrier, bounds up behind him and approaches me warily, barking and wagging its tail furiously at the same time. The man issues a strong warning to the dog, and the animal lowers its head and comes to sniff my pants. Then it bounds down the dirt path after the cows.

I stand back, allowing the animals to pass, and then I continue toward the village center. Here the houses are in better condition, their wooden sides recently painted and their stone fixtures firmly in place. Windows with colorful frames are open wide with thin curtains blowing outward as they catch the late-morning breeze. Flowers are abundant in these gardens and leafy vines climb the walls. It's a peaceful setting, with little need for signs of modernity.

Village residents are strolling about the plaza of the central square, most of them elderly and dressed in the simple clothing of the countryside. Some are waiting for the morning bus to Sofia; others are shopping at an outdoor fruits and vegetables stand. A pair of older women is sitting on a wooden bench, gossiping as they pass the time.

Just past the bus stop, I spot the village *mehana*, a traditional Bulgarian pub that serves local cuisine and hard liquor. I look around for signs of a café that would be a better candidate for Internet access, but the square offers nothing else. Eager to fulfill my mission of going online, I enter the *mehana* and hope for the best.

"*Dobro utro*," I say to the mustached man behind the counter, who is busy drying beer mugs with a checkered towel.

He grunts in return, and I wonder if people in this remote village even speak Bulgarian. "*Imate li…*" I begin, confident at first in my command of the language, but then suddenly at a loss for words. I turn to English, hoping that my request for an international commodity will be understood. "Do you have an Internet connection here?" I ask.

"Da," he replies. "Feel free to hook up. We have no password," he adds in English.

In moments, I'm setting up my laptop at a table near a window looking out onto the square. I plug in the cables, juicing up the battery. I order a cup of cappuccino, which mistakenly arrives as a small glass of bitter espresso, but I thank the man nonetheless. The laptop hums into power, and the opening screen with the Windows logo is like a door to civilization for me. Soon I'll be reading my email, renewing contact with my friends, re-establishing the ties with my family. As soon as I figure out who they all are.

After I see the sign indicating that I'm online, I double-click the Skype icon on my desktop. I've done this previously in the cabin, but obviously there I have only used the program in an offline state. Now I'm eager to have someone welcome me by name or offer a greeting that would place me in context of their lives.

The green icon at the bottom of my screen lights up as Skype whoops into operation and I'm automatically logged into my account. I see the list of my contacts and wonder which of the unfamiliar display names I should choose. Whom should I talk to? What will I say? I will select one person at random and start chatting. Surely the response will offer clues as to my identity.

And then I see one name that immediately brings a smile to my lips: Grandpa. The status icon next to it is green. My grandfather is online!

Without thinking, I touch the silver chain resting around my neck. Subconsciously, seeing my grandfather's name in the list of contacts makes me think of this Magen David pendant. Is there a connection?

As I finger the chain, I also feel the warm spot where the bee stung me when walking through the meadow. The wound is more swollen now, and the chain is pressing down on it. I reach around to the back of my neck and unhook the chain to remove it, relieving some of the pain from the bee sting. I place the chain on the table next to my computer and take a sip of the black coffee.

I am about to type a short message to my grandfather when some movement outside the window catches my attention. I look out at the square and see that a car has pulled up near the *mehana*. The driver, a woman, gets out and goes to the trunk, where she struggles for a few moments to remove something heavy. At first, I can't tell what it is. There are handles and a set of round rubber wheels. The woman sets this object on the ground and leans down to push it into shape. It's a wheelchair.

There is something familiar about the woman. I seem to

recognize her, with her thin face, long legs, and loose brown hair. A smile forms on my face, but I can't connect her with a name. Is she someone I know?

There is a man in the front passenger seat, and he is being helped into the wheelchair. I see the side of his face, and the sternness of his composure drives away my smile. He appears to be a powerful man, with bulky arm muscles protruding from his shirt sleeves, but he is confined to the wheelchair. He snaps at the woman as she eases him into his seat.

The chair is wheeled around, and the man's face comes into full view. I sit up straight in my seat and coil back with instant recognition. I know this man. He played an important part in my past, and more than that, I believe he may have had something to do with my injuries and my subsequent loss of memory. And then the man's name pops into my head.

Boris!

That man is evil, I think, looking around the *mehana* as if there is someone who can be sent to prevent this person from entering the establishment. Obviously Boris doesn't know that I'm inside, but if he comes in, he will recognize me and that can only cause me harm.

Before I have time to react to this fragment of my past coming to light, someone else gets out of the car from the backseat. It's another woman, and she, too, is very familiar. As she slams the back door, she turns, bringing her profile into full view. It is Katya!

I slam my laptop closed and stuff it into my bag. Abandoning the bitter coffee, I approach the proprietor and ask him where the toilets are. He points down the hallway, past the kitchen. As I go, I spot a door that leads to the yard, and I hurry outside. I don't look back as I run down the narrow alley leading away from the square.

As I dash up the path to the cabin in the upper valley, I realize a few things about my sudden departure from the *mehana.* I didn't pay for my coffee, and, in fact, I don't have any money at all. More painful than that is the thought that I left the silver chain with the Magen David pendant on the table with my unfinished beverage.

CHAPTER 36

She is in her mid-thirties, with a slender figure, curly brown hair, and a pleasant, friendly face. Her eyes are green, and they twinkle when she speaks to me. Her English is very good, with only the slightest traces of a Bulgarian accent. I find myself attracted to her, which surprises me due to our age difference.

Her name is Katya, and she is Boris's sister. She has been assigned the task of accompanying me on the bus trip to Varna in the guise of an innocent travel companion. The Adidas gym bag containing the precious treasure is on the seat between us, and we're sitting a few seats back from the driver. I find it easy to talk to Katya. Maybe this journey won't be so bad after all.

"I studied in Sofia," she tells me. "I majored in pharmacology at the Medical University."

"What's that?" I ask. Did she just say something about farms?

"Pharmacology. It's the medical field that explores the interactions between living organisms, for example human beings and the drugs they take. Chemicals affect the biological systems of people, and pharmacologists understand this and search for substances that improve functionality."

"So, basically it's the study of drugs," I say.

When she admits that this is true, I laugh to myself. Here I am, an addict who can't control his dope habits, and I'm stuck on a long bus ride with a woman scholar who majored in how drugs affect the human body.

"In my studies, I focused on chemical agents providing therapeutic value and their potential toxicity on biological systems."

"Toxicity?"

"Yes, that refers to the harmful or possible toxic effects of drugs."

"So, if I needed to poison someone, I would come to you," I joke.

"We were not taught to develop poisons," she responds, quite seriously. "We consider drug safety levels for human consumption, determining how stable potential new medicines would be in the human body, and what their best delivery form would be—for example, if they should come in tablet form."

"So, if you're an expert in all of that, what are you doing living in this remote part of Bulgaria?" I asked. "Montana seems a bit small for any practical use of pharmacology knowledge."

"My brother and his family live there. I live in a village not far from the town. That is where we are from, our family."

When she pauses, something funny comes to mind. If Ralitsa is my host mother, and Boris is my host father, what does that make Katya? Is she my host aunt?

"Surely you can't get work as a pharmacist in a small village," I say, hoping this came out politely.

"Pharmacologist, not pharmacist," she replies. "Everyone makes that mistake. I don't work in a pharmacy, dispensing medicines to patients bringing in their doctors' prescriptions. I am a pharmacologist, studying the effects of drugs. Even so, you are right. There isn't much work for a pharmacologist in the countryside."

Again she pauses, but after a few moments she continues without need for encouragement. "Our mother lives in the village, and she is quite ill. I moved back to the village to care for her, as she needs constant attention."

"Oh, I'm sorry to hear that." I think differently about Boris for a minute. Even petty criminals like him have mothers.

"Do you and Boris get along?" she asks me unexpectedly.

"Well, to tell you the truth, not really," I say, hopeful that I'm not hurting her feelings by saying this. "We don't talk that much, seeing as he doesn't speak English at all." I was hesitant about divulging any of my altercations with her brother. "I get along better with Ralitsa," I quickly added.

"He's not really a bad person," she says, touching my arm as if to force her point. "He does what he needs to do to care for his family," she adds.

I have an urge to discuss with her the things I've seen Boris do. The stolen goods in the cellar. The smuggling trips with Vlady. The possible murder of a customs official on the train to Belgrade. But Katya seems too kind, too protective of her brother. As Boris's sister, she would probably defend his actions and dismiss any suggestions of wrongdoing on his part.

"He's not a thief," she says, as if reading my mind.

"But that artifact that I'm delivering …," I say, thinking about the package stowed in the bus's storage compartment.

"Boris is just a middleman. What did you think? That he stole that? Sorry, you don't know Boris. He just takes on jobs, whatever he can get to make money. When an offer comes his way calling on him to deliver an art treasure, he takes it. He can't afford to turn down a proposition to make money."

"But it was buried in his backyard!" Something about what she's telling me just doesn't ring true.

"Sometimes there can be, how can I say it? Intervals. There was an interval between when that piece was delivered to Boris and when he was asked to deliver it to its final destination. It was in his backyard, safeguarded, for quite a while."

"Why can't Boris deliver it himself?"

"Boris has enemies," she says, her voice trailing off.

"And Vlady? What about him? Why am I mixed up with these guys and their little delivery jobs, as you call them?"

"What does any of this matter? Just deliver this bag in Varna and you'll be through with them, once and for all."

I wish I could believe her. I stare at her profile as she watches the passing scenery, again noting how attractive she is. If only I could accept what she's saying—that her brother is not a felon after all. That he's just a regular guy, someone making a buck by arranging deliveries, no matter if they're legal or not. It would be easier to come to terms with what I'm doing if I was convinced that my dealings with Boris and Vlady will conclude the minute I deliver their stolen goods. I fear that this will not be the case.

It is midday when the bus rolls into the Varna station. Passengers bump into each other in their hurry to disembark, but I wait until the aisle clears before getting off the bus. Katya flags down a taxi, and I slip into the backseat with her, the Adidas bag on my lap. As we travel through the narrow streets, aiming for the tourist district on the shore where I previously made a delivery, I remember what the most important part of this trip is for me. Delivering Boris's stolen treasure has provided me with an excuse to return to Varna, to see that bastard at the hotel again.

I must get my passport back!

Fortified by this determination, the first semblance of a plan begins forming in my mind. I resolve to stand firmly in the negotiations I will soon be conducting at the hotel. I will refuse to hand over the Adidas bag until Nikolov accedes to my demand. The treasure I'm transporting is my leverage. It's what Nikolov wants. Only after I have regained possession of the document will I deliver his ancient artifact.

It sounds so simple, but how can I arrange this? Especially with Katya breathing down my neck. And what about that security man who met me on my first visit to the hotel? He was huge! If I refuse to let go of the gym bag, Nikolov and his thuggish bodyguard will just pull it out of my hands. How can I fight them?

We arrive in Golden Sands. The taxi pulls up outside the Happy Sunshine Resort Hotel, and Katya pays the charges. I get out of the vehicle, adjusting the bag's strap on my shoulder as I squint in the bright sunlight. I wish the purpose of my visit was to check out the hotel's pool and to relax on the beach. I wish my friends were with me. As the taxi drives off, Katya surprises me with an unexpected announcement.

"I'm not going in," she says.

"What?"

"Nikolov knows me. He knows that I'm Boris's sister. Let's just say that he and Boris don't get along too well. You must meet him by yourself."

Suddenly I have cold feet. I've delivered a package to Nikolov in the past, but this time it's different. The bag I've brought from Montana is much more valuable, so valuable that Boris and Vlady refused to let me travel by myself. They insisted that Katya accompany me, to watch over both me and my precious cargo. And now, at the last moment, Katya is refusing to enter the hotel. I am somewhat nervous at the prospect of proceeding on this mission without her at my side.

Katya urges me forward, and I walk through the entrance doors into the gaudy lobby with the bag strapped lazily over my shoulder. Tourists and employees are milling about, but no one pays any attention as I stroll toward the back corridor leading to the manager's office. And then I see the guard, standing near the reception desk, and I stop in my tracks.

How can I possibly confront that guy? He looks like a Bulgarian weightlifter—and a very fit one at that. He could crush me with one hand tied behind his back. There's no way I can threaten him and Nikolov—or refuse to hand over the bag. They would laugh at any such attempts on my part. They'd grab the bag from me as easily as if they were taking candy from a baby.

And then, something in the corner of the lobby catches my attention. Someone is there. Someone is calling out to me, someone very familiar. I shove past a bellboy pushing a cart of suitcases and hurry over to a person I know very well.

CHAPTER 37

Clouds have appeared out of nowhere. The first drops of rain strike me as I approach the meadow at the edge of the woods. The darkened sky matches my mood, for my mission in the village was unsuccessful. Just as I was hooking up to the Internet, Boris and Katya had arrived, upsetting my plans. Instinctively I feared these people would harm me. If they discovered that I was sitting in the *mehana* going online in attempts to recover my identity, it would not end well at all. Lacking money and the knowledge of who I am, my only option is to retreat temporarily to the minimal safety offered by my isolated cabin.

And now it is raining. This is typical for a Bulgarian summer day. It can start out with a totally cloudless sky and end with a torrential downpour. Even now, the rumble of thunder is growing louder, echoing through the mountains like an approaching army. Lightning flashes, illuminating the pine trees and capturing them in its photographic lens.

I reposition the backpack on my shoulder, hoping that no rain will seep in to damage my laptop. I feel cheated and uncertain how to proceed. I need money, and I need to escape. But apparently today is not the day that will bring me the freedom I seek. My immediate mission is to get out of the rain.

It is coming down heavily. I make my way into the woodland alongside the muddy path in a desperate search for cover from the rainfall. A branch scrapes against my face, and I grimace as I brush it aside. The trees offer me their protection; the leaves above serve as a partial umbrella. I am out of breath and a bit hungry. I reach into my pack and take out one of my apples.

As I bite into the fruit, I hear a noise nearby. I spin around, afraid that I've been followed from the village. There is a rustling in the bushes. I look through the trees and am sure that something is moving through the undergrowth, pushing aside the scrub bushes. I wipe the dampness from my face and edge closer, curious as to what I've discovered in the mountain forest.

Steam is rising amidst the thick vegetation. Patches of dark brown fur are partially visible between the moist leaves. It's an animal of some kind, and it looks like quite a big one. As I part the bushes, more of this creature comes into view. It resembles an oversized shaggy rug, one that has been left out too long in the rain. The animal is sniffing and searching in the underbrush; heavy grunts mark its efforts.

I stand frozen in place when I realize fully what I'm seeing. It's a bear—a large, wild, and slightly damp brown bear. Vapors are rising from its matted fur like the heated fumes from a subway vent on a New York City street. There is an unpleasant smell—one that can only come from the wet coat of an enormous animal. The bear is on all fours, shifting and shaking its massive weight as it navigates its way through the weeds. Oversized paws crush and flatten everything that stands in its path. And it is coming in my direction.

The bear appears to be staring at me, even though its beady eyes are not truly focused on me at all. It snorts as it eases forward, its huge steamy mass wagging from side to side almost like an afterthought.

It's a large animal, bigger than anything I could have imagined. Who would have known that wild bears roam through the mountainous Balkan forests? Will it attack, even if I don't provoke it? I certainly don't want to test this creature's attitude. So as not to startle it, I slowly back away.

The bear stops in its tracks, and I stand still as well. It is amazingly quiet in the forest, with the patter of rain on tree leaves barely audible. There is a noticeable absence of bird calls, and even the bees have ceased their buzzing. We are alone here, the bear and me. Two creatures caught together in the moment, and each of us a bit surprised by the other's existence.

And then the bear shifts its weight to its hind legs. Its front half rises slowly and steadily from the ground. The animal appears to be grinning at me, its uneven mouth tilted and its eyes dark and deceptive. The bear opens its mouth wide and releases a deep, ominous growl. Drool drips from a range of jagged teeth. The animal's bad breath, smelled even from a distance, is quite appalling.

Before I realize what is happening, the bear lunges forward. It swipes at me with its huge paw. Sharp claws streak across my right leg, ripping my jeans and raising welts of red blood in their wake. I am unprepared for the sharp pain.

Shaken by the attack, I react with the only weapon I have. I throw my half-eaten apple at the bear, hitting it just above its hairy snout. The bear drops to the ground and sniffs at the fruity projectile. I reach into my pack and take out the second apple and throw this at the bear as well, striking it on its furry flank. And then I turn to run.

I don't look back as I push through the bushes, desperately trying to find my way to the path. The pain in my leg is throbbing. I glance down and see that my ripped jeans are plastered with blood. There's no time to stop and address the wounds. I must get away from the bear.

The animal doesn't chase me, and finally I reach the dirt trail, panting and bloody, but alive. I lean over to catch my breath, covering my mauled leg with my hand in attempts to stem the flow of blood. Can you get rabies from bears? I wonder. Or is that only if they bite you? I am lucky to have escaped!

The pain in my leg reaches deep inside me, shaking me to my core. It is not the bloody wounds on my leg that unsettle me but rather the memories erupting from within in the wake of the attack.

A cloud has lifted. The amnesia, caused by a physical blow to my head, has been shifted aside by an equally painful strike at my leg. The bear's assault, in addition to inflicting severe physical discomfort, has relieved me of my mental anguish. Suddenly, unexpectedly, I know who I am!

I am Scott. Everything is clear; everything is remembered. Growing up in Los Angeles, my mother and father—all this comes rushing back to me. My grandparents in Chicago, all those wonderful childhood memories—I remember them. And the bad things, too, they return to my consciousness, uninvited but part of my past nonetheless. My heavy drug use. Almost being kicked out of school. The horrific habits I had while addicted to drugs.

I recall exactly how I came to Bulgaria. Memories of my Peace Corps activities, hanging out with Lance in Sofia, and living with my host family in Montana—everything is known. There are no longer secrets.

Ralitsa! My host mother—that was her in the village square, I realize as I wipe the dampness from my face with my handkerchief. And the man in the wheelchair, the one I identified as Boris, instinctively fearing his intent to cause me harm—that was my host father! What was he doing in a wheelchair? His disability didn't match the images that were flashing back to me.

More bad things come to mind. The smuggling trip with Boris and Vlady to Romania. The train ride to Serbia. And the final journey to Varna. And that is when I remember Katya's role in everything.

I touch the permanent wound on my forehead, tracing the damaged flesh as I question what to do. Perhaps I should return to the village, where I've spotted Ralitsa. Ralitsa will help me; she's a good woman. But Boris is with her, and I don't want to confront that man. I'm not strong enough for that.

The pain in my leg is getting worse. I should clean and bandage the wound. I am starting to feel feverish and can't allow an infection to set in. I limp forward, reaching the muddy path just as a new burst of rain showers down from above. I am not far from the cabin; I will continue onward and then rest. I need to rest, to recuperate. I can return to the village—and to the civilization it offers—another day. But I cannot allow my newly regained memory to ever abandon me again.

CHAPTER 38

"Where's my package?"

Nikolov stares at me with a burning intensity, his eyes drilling into me like bullets going for the quick kill of an execution. He raises one hand as if to slap me but then retracts it to caress his greasy scalp instead. I am standing empty-handed next to his desk, trying to look as innocent as possible. Despite his seething anger, I'm determined to achieve my goal.

"Give me my passport, and I'll give you your package," I respond, my voice cracking and revealing my uncertainty at making this demand. Yet I know I cannot back down. This is my one chance to retrieve my passport.

Nikolov barks into his phone, and in a minute, the bulky security guard appears, as big and loathsome as ever. The two of them converse in words that are guttural and threatening. And then they turn to me.

"My dear American, I am giving you one last chance to comply with my request," Nikolov snarls, his mouth wide with flashes of gold-coated teeth. "I really believe you want to end our dealings on a pleasant note, do you not?"

I don't move a muscle. I hold out my hand to receive a passport that has not yet been produced nor offered to me.

Nikolov hisses a throaty command. Before I know what is happening, the guard is dragging me from the office and down a corridor, away from the crowded lobby and into the bowels of the hotel.

"Where are we going?" I ask, but the muscleman is silent. We go down a set of stairs, and then another, into a long, dark passageway. I hear machines rumbling in the nearby rooms. The basement walls are gray, smudged with the shadows of swinging lightbulbs. There is no one around to witness the spectacle of a confused and protesting American being led unwillingly into a subterranean realm of menace.

We pass the hotel laundry room. For a split second I see uniformed employees bent over the mouths of huge washing machines, half hidden behind the steam of industrial-size clothes presses. Should I call out for help? What would I say? How can I explain my predicament?

And then we arrive at an uninviting windowless room at the end of the corridor. A door slams shut behind us, and I am alone with the muscle-endowed guard. There are no furnishings in the room. I retreat to the corner and spin around to face him. What can I say to protest my innocence? How can I convince the guard if I haven't made my point with Nikolov? Surely it's clear to both of them that the moment they hand over my passport I will reveal to them the location of the bag.

I smile at the guard, as if none of this disturbs me in the least, but my legs are wobbly. My smile vanishes when I notice that he is wielding a thick, wooden stick. What is it called? A baton? Why am I thinking about the name of the weapon this guy is carrying when I should be concerned—very much concerned—for my life!

He swings the baton back and forth, slapping it lightly against his leg. His efforts to intimidate me are working. The message doesn't need to be stated in words. Either I tell him where the Adidas bag is, or I am going to be beaten to a pulp.

"You make no good with Nikolov," he snarls, enjoying his role of confronting someone who cannot fight back. "You do no good thing."

I am not one to stand up to threats, stated or implied, and I cave immediately. "It's in the lobby," I say, quite truthfully, but this anguish-filled statement clearly doesn't strike a chord with the guard.

He lifts the baton and smacks it hard against my shoulder. The last of my fortitude crumbles at the blow. My knees buckle. I feel myself begin to topple forward. Intense pain shoots through me.

"The lobby," I repeat, over and over, but each time my voice is getting weaker. The blows are coming faster now, one to the upper arm, another lands on the back of my hand.

It's in the lobby, I say, but I don't know if I am still capable of saying these words aloud.

A final blow, more powerful than the rest, strikes me on the right side of my head. Everything goes black.

CHAPTER 39

A rifle shot cracks the silence of the morning, reverberating between the trees and echoing back from the shadow-cloaked mountain slopes beyond. Another shot rings across the valley, and then another. They sound quite close.

I drop to my knees, taking cover behind an outcrop of rock. My breaths are labored. I wheeze as I fight to recoup my strength after a mad dash through the woods. I check to make sure that my backpack is strapped tightly to my shoulder. My precious laptop is my gateway to civilization, and I can't afford to damage it.

I hadn't expected to be hunted down like an animal on my escape from the cabin, just a few days after my encounter with the bear. Without knowing that I had been attacked, Katya informed me that a local farmer had been mauled by the beast, leading the villagers to launch a hunting party to track it down. My wounds from running into the bear have mostly healed. The parallel scars on my leg are still warm to the touch, but at least I no longer have a fever. I discarded the blood-stained jeans in the woods before Katya had a chance to see them. Compared to what I've gone through on my road to recovery, the bear attack was a minor distraction.

From my vantage point behind the rocks, I see the hunters approaching. There are three of them, tall, skinny men camouflaged in green and black and wearing caps with droopy ear flaps. Each of them bears a shotgun. I have no doubt that these men are trigger-happy, ready to fire at the slightest provocation. They advance steadily, regarding their surroundings with the fever of the hunt in their eyes.

After such a long time of living on my own in the mountains, I have no desire to confront villagers of any kind—and certainly not hunters—on my final departure from the cabin. I will have enough explaining to do when I reach the *mehana* and make contact with my family. Everyone will question where I've been all this time, how I've survived. I don't need to reveal this information to complete strangers as well.

I have no regrets leaving Katya without saying good-bye or offering an explanation. I will remain forever grateful for what she has done to save me. It was Katya who rescued my battered body at the hotel, who took me to a local doctor to treat my most serious wounds, and who transported me back across the country to the remote cabin in the mountains. Katya singlehandedly nursed me back to health, ensuring that my physical injuries would heal. If it wasn't for her, I wouldn't be alive today.

She has indeed been kind to me, but on the other hand, her actions have also prolonged my isolation and suffering.

Katya has kept me prisoner in the cabin all this time, under the spell of the addictive narcotics that she prepared specifically for this sinister purpose. She told me repeatedly that everything she did was for my own good, insisting that she was acting to protect me from the inherent dangers awaiting me if I left. Somehow I find this all quite hard to believe now that I have recovered my memory. Why did she act this way? Her motives remain a mystery to me, but I don't have the luxury of time to think about them.

Before the hunters have a chance to notice me, I dash into the woods, making my way through the bushes and overgrowth into darkened areas not visible from the path. I will wait here until I am sure the men are gone.

And then more shots ring out.

I hear excited shouts, not far from where I am standing. I fear they have spotted me, possibly mistaking me for the wayward bear. A muscle in my clawed leg is cramping; there is no way I can outrun these men. And these local hunters know the forest better than I do. I am about to give up, to raise my hands and reveal myself. But instead of announcing my presence, a survival instinct takes control over my actions, and I scurry deeper into the woods.

Finding a thick bed of tall wild grass, I ease myself to the ground. I lie down, partially hidden from view. Hopefully my horizontal position will not be visible if the hunters gaze in this direction from a distance. My heart beats loudly, a regular hammering that I fear will serve as a beacon to draw the men toward my hiding spot. After a few moments, my breathing eases into a slower, more relaxed pace. Lying prone on the moist mountain soil among the weeds, I await my fate.

One of the men comes close. I hear his steps, his heavy boots trampling on the ground cover with little regard for the twigs and vegetation crunching in his wake. His breathing is shallow and even. He stops suddenly, maybe just a meter or two from where I lie in the grass. With all the time in the world, he takes in his surroundings. There is no bear here, I whisper to myself, wishing that he would come to the same conclusion and leave me alone.

Then the man does something that, if nothing else, proves that he has absolutely no idea I'm lying in the brush near his feet. He unzip his pants and lets loose with a steady stream of urine that splatters on the ground, just inches from my head. I smell the acidic urine, which momentarily masks the reek of the hunter himself. The flow seems to go on forever, and then it slows to a tinkle until it stops altogether.

"*Haide*," one of the hunters calls from afar, and the man zips up his pants and leaves, trampling the weeds as he hurries to rejoin his friends.

I remain on the ground for many minutes, grateful for a summer breeze that whips through the pines and beats the wild grass into waves of submission. The hunters must be gone by now; I haven't heard their voices or movements for some time. Yet I fear that if I get up it will lead to my discovery, so I continue to hug the earth as if it alone can protect me.

The sun has crossed the sky and is beginning its descent behind the distant peaks when I finally rise, brush off my clothing, and head back toward the path. Luckily, I haven't strayed too far off course. Soon I am on the dirt trail leading to the village. Eager to reach the first signs of civilization before darkness falls, I quicken my pace.

The same mustached man is on duty behind the counter of the *mehana*. I order a coffee, knowing that I will have to budget my purchases with the limited money I've stolen from Katya's purse. I sit down at a table and take out my laptop, firing up its power to reconnect with my life.

The thick black coffee is served just as my Internet connection is established. Where do I start? There is email to check, family members to notify. The first thing is to just give a shout out that I'm alive. I need to provide my loved ones with an indication of my location, somewhere in the wilds of northwestern Bulgaria.

I launch Skype and search among my contacts to see who is online. My grandfather! His icon is green, indicating that he is available. He can help me. Even before I have a chance to type in a greeting, the chat box opens mysteriously on its own.

"Scott, are you there?"

I stare at these words and smile. My long ordeal is about to end.

Part Three: The Fortress

CHAPTER 40

"Scott?"

Again she called his name, but she knew he was gone. There was no laptop on the table, and the wardrobe doors were open, both signs that he had hastily packed his clothes. She ran to peek in the outhouse but only flies disturbed the foulness of that enclosed putrid hole. Back inside, she circled the two rooms repeatedly, as if it was possible to miss him in a corner or under the cot. The cabin was empty, drained of its inhabitant and its purpose.

On her last visit, she had had a premonition that he would leave, but she had failed to take any precautions to prevent it. At the time, she sensed that he had searched through her purse, and when she returned to her village, she realized she was missing some money. Now that piece fit into place as well.

For a moment, Katya didn't know what to think. It was as if someone had punched her in the stomach, sapping her strength. Her mission in life had vanished into thin air. After everything she had done for Scott, after the many months of unwavering devotion and the long nights of caring attention, he had departed without notice from the sanctuary she had created for him . He had left no farewell message, not even the simplest thank you. Scott was gone from the cabin, no longer under her protection.

And that is what frightened her. Again and again she had warned him that his life would be in danger if he left the cabin, and that warning reflected a true threat. She had done everything possible to protect him, and now he was on his own. If Boris or Vlady saw Scott, there was no telling what would happen. Vlady was a man who always got what he wanted. As for Boris, it didn't matter that her brother was confined to a wheelchair. He was powerful and cruel, and Scott stood no chance of resisting him.

How could he be gone? As thoughts of Scott's predicament filled her mind, she unconsciously drew her left hand toward her stomach, as if she had suffered a physical blow there. Slowly she moved her right hand on top of the other, and long fingernails sought the soft skin of her wrist. She dug in, tears forming in her eyes as the nails penetrated and drew their first blood.

Where would he go? Katya wondered, wincing at the self-inflicted pain. And how much did he know? She was sure that Scott must still be confused, not focused enough to make calculated decisions about what to do. The pills she had concocted and forced him to swallow on each of her visits were the type that would leave his mind in a cloudy state. She had selected the chemical composition carefully to ensure that the homemade medication would impair Scott's memory and his grasp of reality, with the accompanying severe headaches as their only perceivable side effect. Could there have been a mistake in the formula? No, she was too good a pharmacologist to err when choosing the ingredients for the drug she prepared. There was only one explanation for this, Katya realized. Scott had secretly stopped taking the pills. He was free of the narcotic addiction that had confined him to the cabin. And that meant he must already remember—and know—everything.

With a clear mind, Scott would recall transporting the Thracian artifact from Boris's backyard to the hotel in Varna, where Nikolov was to pay good money for its delivery. Katya had accompanied Scott on that fateful bus ride, yet had stupidly allowed him to enter the hotel on his own. She could still picture him lugging the Adidas gym bag into the lobby. She would never forget that image, as it was the last she had of Scott before he was injured.

Still unsolved was what had happened to the bag Scott was holding. The location of the precious object packaged within remained a mystery. Unless Nikolov was playing games with them, which seemed unlikely, he had never received the ancient artifact. Nikolov had threatened Boris and Vlady enough over the past few years to make it clear that the delivery mission had not been executed as planned. No, if Nikolov had obtained the artifact, it would have signaled a conclusion to their deal, with no need for the subsequent violence.

All this meant that Scott had hidden the bag somewhere before his fateful meeting with Nikolov, but the only place he had been out of her sight was in the hotel lobby. It didn't make sense. Now that Scott was free, his impaired memory restored, it was obvious to Katya that Scott would seek to recover the priceless treasure.

If this was clear to her, Vlady and Boris would realize it as well. And that was why Scott was in danger. If he was spotted, he would be harmed. Boris and his partner would torture Scott until he revealed the artifact's location. She had no way to warn Scott about what they were capable of doing.

Scott's recovery and escape from the cabin overwhelmed her. She couldn't search for him by herself; she needed assistance. There was only one person with whom Katya could share her concerns, but that meant breaking the realm of secrecy in which she had safeguarded Scott's existence. It was time to take that person into her confidence and come clean. That was the only way she could ensure Scott's safety.

Katya wiped the blood from her wrist, not sure when she had cut herself there. She left the cabin, standing outside and taking a long moment to regard the remote mountain valley that had served her well. She walked down the dirt path until she came to her car. She unlocked the door of the rusty Lada, squeezed into the front seat and sat behind the wheel. She pulled the ignition key out of her purse and prepared to start the motor. But before she did this, she inhaled deeply.

Yes, it was still there, lingering in the closed confinement as it had for years. The slight trace of a smell—tobacco mixed with Old Spice aftershave—tantalized her nostrils and awakened old memories. It was barely perceivable, but it was there. This scent was all that she had, all that was left. Trapped in the torn upholstery and stained dashboard, the scent was a poignant reminder of Hristo, her beloved husband.

Hristo had smoked as he drove and never bothered to empty the ashtrays afterward. This was a chore Katya took upon herself because she couldn't stand to see the ashes falling to the floorboard. Once, when they stopped for a quick roadside meal, Hristo dropped his lit cigarette onto the passenger-side cushion. When they returned to the vehicle, a small fire was ablaze on the front seat. Quickly doused, the flames led to uneasy laughter and unfulfilled promises from Hristo to be more careful in the future. The cushion cover was replaced, but the edge of the dashboard was still scarred as a memorial to Hristo's occasional carelessness.

They enjoyed taking long road trips in the Russian-made vehicle, with its light blue panels and tight cabin. They drove the width of Bulgaria, from the mountains in the northwest to the seacoast near Burgas. One weekend they camped on the rugged Black Sea shoreline, flicking stones into the surf at sunset and making love repeatedly on the uncomfortable backseat. They drove south to the Turkish border, stopping for a laughter-filled lunch of sea bass and chips in a tattered Sozopol fishermen's restaurant. They drove to the ancient city of Nessebar, its cobblestone streets and thirteenth-century churches helping grant it UNESCO recognition as an official World Heritage Site. And they drove along the coast to the resort hotels of Sunny Beach, they parked the rusty car outside a rented room while they concentrated on their lovemaking for hours.

They made frequent trips to Hristo's hometown of Stara Zagora in the center of the country. Hristo was a slow driver, never minding that his car was passed by speeding Mercedes and BMWs. For him, driving on the narrow roads was a pleasure, to be savored like a fine wine and not to be finished too quickly. In Katya's mind, she could see her husband pat the car's roof almost lovingly after it successfully delivered them to their destination. They were childless, to Katya's dismay, but for Hristo, the Lada was the third member of their family.

This car was Hristo, Katya thought. The faint odors of tobacco and Old Spice were all that she had left of him.

She sighed, putting aside her memories and trying to forget what had happened later, and started her drive to the village. She hoped to see Scott walking along the mountain path or resting in the village square, but realized that if he had secretly planned his escape from the cabin, he would be taking care not to be visible. Where would he go? She needed to find Scott before he was harmed.

Three men were walking along the path, heading towards the village. She steered the car around them, and as she passed, she noticed they were carrying rifles. She slowed to a stop and rolled down her window.

"*Zdravete*," she said.

"*Dobre den*," came a chorused reply.

"Were you hunting in the woods?" she asked as she turned off the motor.

"Yes, hunting!" one of the men responded, laughing.

"We were looking for a bear, a big bear," another said.

"But there were no bears," the third man said, spitting a wad of tobacco to the ground. "Perhaps we should do our hunting in the Sofia zoo."

"Did you happen to see a young American man? He's tall and thin, and speaks some Bulgarian."

"Was he hunting the bear as well?" The three of them laughed as if this was the funniest joke they had heard all day.

"He would have been carrying a backpack and a laptop."

"Ah, a laptop," the first man said. "There is good Internet connection in these woods."

The Internet! That would be the first thing Scott would want. His first destination in the village was clear to her now. Katya thanked the men and restarted the ignition.

The mustached bartender in the *mehana* was sharpening a kitchen knife, honing it repeatedly in alternating directions on a small whetstone. Slivers of lemon were piled on the counter, ready for someone to slip them into a cocktail. Except for the bartender, the pub was empty; its chairs were arranged at straight angles to each table so that they all lined up perfectly with the entranceway. Some of the tables bore the remnants of meals and drinks consumed by recent visitors. Cleanup duties weren't the bartender's strong point. Katya approached the man and coughed to catch his attention.

"Katya!" he exclaimed with recognition. "*Kak si*?"

"*Dobre sum*," she replied, a smile lighting up her face as she conversed with her primary-school classmate. "How are you, Ivaylo?"

"I'm also good. How's your mother doing?"

"Not so well," Katya replied truthfully. "She's bedridden and is pretty apathetic to my efforts to care for her."

"Your mother is a good woman. I remember when we were growing up together, how your mother always went out of her way to make sure I had enough food to eat, that I was dressed warmly. I'm sorry that she is ill."

"Getting old is part of life," Katya sighed.

"So, what can I get you?"

"Actually, I'm looking for someone, and I wonder if he might have come in here today."

"Yes?"

"An American man, in his mid-twenties. He's tall and thin, and he would have been carrying his laptop looking for an Internet connection."

"Yes?"

"So, did he come in here?"

"Why are you asking?" Ivaylo cast an inquisitive glance at her, wiping the bar counter as he spoke. "Is there something between you and this American?"

Enough already! Katya thought. She had gone to primary school with Ivaylo and was aware of his childhood crush on her. Ivaylo was a good friend of Boris, the two of them had been teammates on the school football team, but in his awkward teenage years, Ivaylo preferred to hang around her incessantly. Although she denied the definition, Ivaylo considered her his girlfriend and had naturally assumed that the two of them would end up together, even holding onto this fantasy when she left the village to pursue academic studies. Despite being married now, residing upstairs with a wife and children in a crowded apartment, Ivaylo constantly flirted with Katya whenever she popped into the pub. She didn't need that.

"He's a friend, and I think he might be lost," she replied, afraid to reveal too much information.

"There was a foreigner in here this afternoon, but I can't say for sure if he was an American. We spoke in English, but I'm not an expert in determining people's nationalities."

"That must be him. Did he have a computer?"

"Yes, he did."

"And?"

"And what?"

"You're not exactly a fountain of information, Ivaylo. Did your foreign visitor happen to mention which direction he was heading?"

"He asked me about bus schedules," the bartender admitted, not offended by Katya's curt remarks. "I told him about the morning bus that runs to Sofia. I told him it passes through Montana, and that seemed to interest him."

"Did he say where he's going to be staying tonight?"

"So many questions! No, he didn't say anything about tonight. You sure I can't get you something, a beer maybe?"

"I have to go now. My mother…" she said, her voice trailing off.

Katya turned to leave, staring for several seconds at the table near the far window, lit up by the last rays of the setting sun. A dirty coffee cup rested there, yet another sign of Ivaylo's lackluster regard for his duties. Katya wondered if Scott had sat at that very table, using the nearby electric socket to charge his laptop and the pub's wireless service to connect to the Internet. At least she knew where he was heading and the bus on which he would be traveling. She would carry through with her original plans and confide her secrets to the one person with whom she was willing to share the news of Scott's recovery.

Katya got into her car and waited patiently until the motor caught. Scott may be gone, away from her loving care, but it wouldn't be for long. Tomorrow morning, she told herself, she would board the bus in Montana to join Scott on his journey to Sofia. Everything would be all right, she thought, trying to convince herself that this was true.

A few moments after Katya left the *mehana*, Scott returned to the main hall of the pub. He had hurried to the bathroom when he spotted the rusty car pulling up outside. Hidden in the men's stall, he overheard the bartender and Katya conversing, afraid that his presence in the pub would be exposed at any moment. He heard them talking, but he couldn't make out what they were saying. Had the bartender even seen him enter the bathroom?

How stupid it had been to ask the man for information about bus service to Sofia! Although Scott planned to take the morning's southbound bus, he originally intended to disembark in Montana. That was where he had told his grandfather to meet him. He suspected that Katya had learned of his intentions and therefore he needed to make other arrangements.

"Oh, you're still here?" the bartender said, when he saw Scott setting up his laptop again on the table near the window. "Someone was just asking for you."

"I know. It's okay," Scott replied. He was nervous, anxious to connect to the Internet and leave the *mehana* as quickly as possible. He would just send a message to his grandfather, informing him of a change in plans.

CHAPTER 41

A foreign tourist is lost in the center of Sofia and approaches two Bulgarian policemen to ask them for directions. He first asks in English. The cops, who don't speak any foreign languages, fail to understand anything. The tourist then asks in French, in German, in Italian, in Spanish. Still nothing from the policemen. Frustrated, he walks on.

"We should really start studying foreign languages," says one of the Bulgarian policemen.

"No, we shouldn't. They are totally useless," the other officer replies. "Look at this guy! He knows so many, and they still got him nowhere..."

Sophia laughed along with her stiff-lipped colleagues. She found it strange that her fellow academicians, usually humorless to the point of boredom, were being reduced to giggling, joking commoners as they repeatedly raised their whiskey and beer glasses in a darkened corner of the pub. Sophia didn't know the name of this establishment. New bars were popping up frequently in the center of Sofia and few survived for long. Some of the pubs were trendy, chic, and ultra-modern, while others featured dark-wood fittings, quasi-Irish upholstery, and lavishly illustrated menus. Whatever the setup, she readily joined her peers from the university on their weekly pub visits to let off steam, gossip, talk politics, and tell jokes.

Dimitar, the chemistry lecturer with thick glasses and a perpetual frown in the classroom, was charming his associates with another joke, one from the endless supply he had memorized and reserved for drinking occasions like this.

An elderly Bulgarian man is having his annual medical checkup, and the doctor asks him how he is feeling. "I've never felt better!" the elderly man boasts. "I've got an eighteen-year-old bride. She's pregnant and having my child! What do you think about that?"

The doctor considers this for a moment and then says to the man, "I knew a guy up in the mountains who really enjoyed hunting, never missing an occasion to go out into the woods. But one day he left his home in a bit of a hurry, and he accidentally grabbed his umbrella instead of his rifle. He was walking in the woods when suddenly a black bear appeared in front of him, standing on its back paws and growling. The hunter aimed his umbrella and squeezed the handle."

"What happened?" the elderly man asks.

"The bear dropped dead in front of him!" the doctor says.

"That's impossible!" exclaims the old man. "There must have been someone else who shot that bear."

"Exactly," the doctor replies.

"Here, I have one," offered Stanislav, another lecturer, wiping the foam of beer from his lips.

A Bulgarian wife starts shouting at her husband at two in the morning: "I left two bottles of rakia in the fridge! Why is there one bottle left?!"

"Because I didn't see the second one," the husband replies.

"How many times have we heard that one before!" Sophia

protested, but she was laughing just as hard as the rest of them.

"So, you tell one," Rossi said, urging Sophia with a playful elbow.

"I can never remember any punch lines," Sophia said, raising her beer mug to the other female lecturer in their party.

"Well, here's one you probably don't know," Stansilav began, looking confidently at the others. "Georgi told it to me just last week."

As soon as he said this, Stanislav stopped, dropping his eyes to the table in embarrassment. How stupid it was of him to mention Sophia's ex-husband, when all of them knew how painful this would be to the lecturer of Thracian history.

"Sorry," he said, forcing a smile in Sophia's direction.

"It's okay, really," she replied.

But it wasn't okay. The mere mention of Georgi's name still stabbed sharply at her heart, even after all this time.

She stared solemnly at her beer, not hearing the words of Stanislav's joke nor joining the laughter that followed.

Sophia and Georgi had met during their first year of studies at St. Clement of Ohrid University in Sofia. Sophia had majored in Bulgarian history while Georgi enrolled in the faculty of education with the declared intention of becoming a primary-school teacher. The university was the oldest institution of higher education in Bulgaria, founded in 1888, just ten years after the liberation of the country. Sophia and Georgi enjoyed the fact that they were students in a historic, yet modern university situated in the very heart of their country's capital, far from the backward ways of their home villages and the familial duties required of them there.

Sophia was immediately attracted to Georgi's athletic build and handsome face. He seemed so much more mature, so much more self-confident than the slender, insecure youths of her village. She fell captive to his positive attitude, to his ability to set her heart beating just by staring at her with his deep brown eyes, and to the surprisingly soft touch of his lips.

They began to date, although their outings were scheduled around the demands of Sophia's studies. She spent long nights in the university libraries, never tiring of her reading requirements and thoroughly enjoying every minute of her research projects. Georgi, on the other hand, couldn't care less about his class work and studied in earnest only in last-minute efforts to pass his examinations. He tired quickly when reading and frequently turned to Sophia with requests that she summarize the long-worded texts on which his wandering mind couldn't concentrate. In the innocence of her youthful crush, Sophia readily complied, not noticing that the more time she spent helping Georgi, the less time she had to devote to her passion, the study of Bulgaria's Thracian past.

Georgi was not Sophia's first lover, but he was the most passionate man who had ever shared her bed. Initially, she was hesitant to allow their friendship to develop into a physical relationship, but after the first time, when he took care to ensure that she enjoyed herself as much as he did, she wondered why she had waited. He never tired of pleasuring her, even if that meant his making extra efforts to divert her from late-night study sessions. During those passion-filled weeks of their blooming romance, she found his attentiveness pleasing and felt grateful that someone could love her so much.

Swept along by the physical pleasures, she truly believed that she was experiencing love. While he never actually voiced the words, she felt that he was as much in love with her as she was with him. It seemed only logical that the next step would be for them to marry. When she hesitantly raised this possibility, he smiled, stating that he could vision no other future than one spent with her. They argued about whether they should wait until they finished their university studies. Most Bulgarians married late unless an unplanned pregnancy provided an excuse for an early marriage. In the end, Sophia convinced Georgi that there was no need to delay the official declaration of their devotion.

The ceremony took place on a bright Saturday afternoon in the Sveta Nedelya Church, right in the center of Sophia. The Eastern Orthodox structure, destroyed and rebuilt many times over the centuries, provided a perfect background for the occasion. Sophia's parents and brother, Georgi's parents and older sister, and a handful of other close relatives and friends were in attendance. The wedding gown Sophia wore had been in her family for years, and she couldn't remember if it was her grandmother or her great-grandmother who had originally sewn it. After an expensive celebratory family meal in a fancy restaurant, and a short but picturesque honeymoon in Venice, Sophia and Georgi returned their attentions to university studies.

The early weeks of married life were similar to those that preceded the ceremony. Sophia concentrated on her studies while Georgi made only the minimal exertions necessary to ensure that he passed his tests and completed his assignments.

Thinking back, Sophia wondered why she hadn't seen the warning signs. Those rose-colored days were too careless and frivolous to last forever. Love is not built solely on the tender caresses one enjoys when the lights go out at night. Why hadn't she realized that Georgi's lack of seriousness regarding his studies was just a prelude to the troubles that lay ahead—fierce arguments and accusations of disloyalty which would tear their marriage apart?

As she advanced her career, Sophia eagerly anticipated her weekend explorations of Thracian archaeological sites. She enjoyed the company of her colleagues and the academic banter that accompanied their car rides and meals. She relished the hands-on investigation of burial tombs and the hours spent filtering centuries-old piles of debris in search for the invaluable treasures they may conceal. She loved the aftermath of a day's work in the field, when she would type up her notes and compare them to the scholarly research of others. The keys to the mysteries of the past were in her hands. Each field trip promised to reveal more and to refine her knowledge. This was what it was all about.

And that meant spending less time with Georgi.

He had his own life, his own hobbies and activities. Yes, they shared a common circle of friends, but Sophia had less and less time to join them in pubs or at football matches. Weekdays were spent on their separate professions, and in the evenings they were rarely together. It was during the weekends that Georgi expected more of her, but she continued to concentrate solely on her career, disregarding any notion that this could affect their relationship.

Could she blame him for seeking alternative female companionship? She realized with a jolt that they seldom slept together. She couldn't remember the last time they had enjoyed consensual sexual relations. Mostly it had been a matter of surrendering to Georgi's physical needs in a state of semi-exhaustion. Sex was a side of their marriage that she had forsaken in the name of science. There were more important things in life, she felt, and her calling led her away from any sort of companionship with her husband.

Their marriage was a train wreck waiting to happen, and there was nothing that could prevent the inevitability of a painful separation. Even though years had passed since their divorce, Sophia couldn't help but cringe every time her colleagues mentioned their ongoing friendships with Georgi. She no longer had feelings for him and their marriage. The relationship was one that should remain buried in the past.

Sophia was shaken away from her painful memories when she heard a faint buzzing. Ignoring it at first, she laughed as Dimitar reached the punch line of a joke, but then she realized what she was hearing. She opened her purse and took out her cell phone. The number seemed familiar, but it wasn't labeled as one of her contacts.

"Hello?"

"Sophia, it's me, Simon."

"Who?" The phone held tightly to her ear couldn't shield her from the laughter and music in the pub.

"Simon Matthews," the man said, and then she recognized the voice of the American she had spent so much time with over the past few days.

"Hi, Simon," she said. He was probably calling to reconfirm her plans to take him to the airport the next morning. "Sorry, but there's a lot of noise here. You'll have to speak up."

"He's alive! I spoke to him!"

"What? Simon, I can't hear you."

"I spoke, well actually chatted online, with my grandson. He's alive, and I know where he is."

"Simon, there's a lot of interference. I thought you said you talked with your grandson."

"Yes, yes, that's exactly what I said."

Sophia sat up straight in her seat, the cloud of alcohol she had just consumed dissipating quickly from her head.

"Simon, let me go outside the pub and call you back."

"What?" Now he couldn't hear what she was saying.

She ended the connection and pushed past her companions at the table.

"Where are you going?" Stanislav asked. "We're just getting started."

"Sorry, I have an important call to make," she replied.

The news that Simon Matthews's grandson was alive was quite unexpected. And, for Sophia—just as much as for the American professor—this startling development changed everything.

CHAPTER 42

"I am certain that Scott is alive."

The statement shocked Katya. How could Ralitsa know this? Scott had been kept in total isolation, hidden out of sight in the secluded mountain retreat. No one had followed Katya on her trips to deliver food and supplies, and not a soul had visited the cabin. She never spoke about what she was doing, although the burden of caring for the injured American was often too much to bear. She had preserved the secret for three years; now it was time to open up and reveal all.

She had arrived at the family's Montana home late the previous evening, but with Boris encamped in the living room watching a televised football match, it had been impossible to have a private conversation with her sister-in-law. She had thanked them for their suggestion to stay the night, hoping to find time to be alone with Ralitsa the next day. Now, Rado was at school and there was no sign of Boris.

The two women sat at the kitchen table, barely touching their morning coffee. The bus to Sofia wouldn't arrive at the Montana station for at least an hour. There was time to talk and to tell Ralitsa everything. Except, Ralitsa seemed to know far more than Katya had expected.

Emboldened by the confirmation she saw on Katya's face, Ralitsa continued. "I suspected this for some time, ever since you came back from that trip to Varna long ago and reported that Scott was missing without providing an acceptable explanation as to what had happened. But only recently did I find evidence proving my suspicions.

"Do you remember when we went to the village together?" Ralitsa asked. "We were visiting Mother, but we stopped at the *mehana* first. Boris insisted on getting a beer. I guess he just wanted to chat with Ivaylo. You and I had coffee while the two of them discussed the latest football matches."

"Yes?"

"When you stood up for some reason, perhaps to get sugar from the bar counter, I noticed something shiny on the next table, near the window. There was a thin object there, reflecting the sunlight, so I got up to see. It was his chain! It was Scott's silver chain, the one he always wore."

"How do you know it was his?"

"There were symbols on it, Jewish symbols. Scott told me that the silver letters formed the Hebrew word for life."

Katya tried to think back and picture Scott. Yes, he had always worn jewelry around his neck.

"Did you place it there?" Ralitsa asked.

"No, of course not!"

"If you didn't put it on the table, Scott must have left it. Say, what are those scars on your wrist?"

Katya instinctively drew back her left hand, not bothering to answer Ralitsa's concern. She tried to think back to the last time she had seen Scott in the cabin. Had the chain been around his neck? She had visited him so frequently over the past years that she hadn't given a second thought as to whether he was wearing a chain.

"Don't you see? Scott must have been in the *mehana*," Ralitsa said, looking up from Katya's wrist, her eyes wide as she waited for confirmation of her assumption.

"He left the cabin and came to the village," Katya whispered, almost to herself. "For some reason he left the chain on the table. Or he forgot it there. Ralitsa, can I tell you something, something that I've never told anyone before?"

"Of course! You are like a sister to me."

"Where is Boris?" Katya asked, lowering her head and noting that the door to the bedroom was closed.

"He's sound asleep. That's what drinking does to him. You can talk to me, Katya."

And then she told Ralitsa everything. The protective wall she had built around herself safeguarding a deep secret crumbled, leaving her vulnerable and desperate for her sister-in-law's understanding and support. The words spilled slowly at first, but her voice grew more confident as the weight lifted from her shoulders. She spoke of the beating Scott received in Varna, how she transported him across the country to the west, and how aided his health in the isolated cabin. And she told Ralitsa of the fears she had for Scott's safety if he was discovered alive by those who wished to hurt him, hinting at Boris's involvement in this threat without saying his name aloud. The only thing she refrained from mentioning was Scott's dependence on drugs, their origin and purpose.

"You've been with Scott all this time!" Ralitsa said, but she wasn't angry at Katya. "I'm so relieved he's alive. You don't know how much it devastated me when he disappeared. When he went missing, it was like losing a son. I can't believe it. Scott is really, truly alive!"

Tears streamed down Ralitsa's thin cheeks, tears formed by three years of dealing with the uncertainty and pain of losing a family member reported missing and assumed to be dead. Katya realized she would never fully comprehend how her sister-in-law had managed to cope with the loss while living under the same roof as Boris, for whom Scott's absence was nothing more than a serious business setback. Her brother had grieved his lost opportunity to cash in on the sale of the artifact Scott was meant to deliver to Varna. The discovery that Scott was still alive was welcomed with immense relief and joy by Ralitsa while for Boris it would awaken an urgency for payback and revenge.

Boris had always been prone to getting into shady business deals, and this was something Hristo had warned her about long before. "He's up to no good," Hristo told Katya, when shortly after their marriage he was approached by her brother with an offer to join him in a marketing venture. "I don't know who he's dealing with, but I bet they aren't the most respectable citizens," Hristo said, indicating his dislike for Vlady, whom he had met through Boris.

Despite turning down Boris's proposal, Hristo became close buddies with him. The two of them would frequently go to Ivaylo's pub for drinks while Katya visited her mother. Hristo would return from these sessions reeking of alcohol and smoke, regaling her with tales of how Boris and Vlady had concocted infallible get-rich schemes and tried unsuccessfully to convince him to partner with them. Yet when he regained his sobriety, Hristo again made fun of Boris's initiatives and insisted that Katya's brother was nothing more than a provincial bumpkin.

Over time, Hristo and Boris began to share a wintertime activity. Leaving Katya alone in their cold city flat on weekends, Hristo would drive to the village to pick up Boris, who was already partially inebriated and anxious to get going. They would speed south on back roads covered with ice and marked by potholes nearly the size of their car. Bypassing Sofia, they continued on their journey until they reached the turnoff into the mountains. The Lada struggled to make the ascent, but eventually they reached their destination, a dilapidated winter resort in the town of Bansko. They rented a one-bedroom flat by the season and never considered that they would need to heat the place. After all, the moment Boris's head cleared, they were ready to hit the slopes.

Skis and equipment were readily available for rent at the lift station. Boris never dressed warmly enough, but Hristo came equipped with the appropriate apparel, from an insulated body-fitting jacket and waterproof, breathable pants, to durable ski gloves. While Boris brought along his regular sunglasses, Hristo sported a pair of reflective goggles that kept the mountain fog off his lenses and the chill out of his face. Boris was ready to rent the cheapest skis, but

Hristo insisted on procuring only the very best.

"When you ski, ski like a pro," he would say to Boris as he picked out a pair from the rack that were guaranteed to take the turns with security and grace, no matter the speed.

"What are you, some kind of Olympic perfectionist?" Boris asked him.

"Maybe I am," Hristo replied, checking the flexibility of the tapered ski poles he had just selected.

Hristo certainly took to the sport like a pro, Boris realized the first time they came down the mountain together. Leaving Boris far behind in his wake, Hristo mastered the wintery terrain as easily as if he had been born on the slopes. He flew downhill with unbridled energy and a passion for speed and form. No trail was too difficult for him, no change in weather conditions could serve as a deterrent. His body and his skis became one as he slalomed past other skiers as if he were racing for an Olympic medal. At the bottom, when Boris arrived panting and eager for a beer to calm his nerves, Hristo was ready to take the lift up the mountain again for another run.

Katya realized that she had become a winter widow. During the long, cold months when the Bulgarian mountains were cloaked under their snowy blanket, Hristo was out enjoying his sport. He invited her to join him for weekends in Bansko, and once, she waited nervously for hours in the unheated rented flat. In the end, however, she let him enjoy his winter hobby on his own. She stayed home, concentrated on her chemistry studies, and listened anxiously for the sound of their old car pulling in late on Sunday nights.

Now confined to his wheelchair, Boris was long past skiing, and Hristo had been gone for years. The past conjured many powerful memories and was filled with the pain of heartbreak and disaster. Now, things were swiftly changing, speeding out of control. Katya was no longer pulling the strings; Scott was no longer where she wanted him. Her anxiety at his being free, on his own, worried her to a great degree, although she realized that this development was welcomed by her sister-in-law, who naturally expected Katya to share in her excitement.

Aware that the American man she had loved like a son was actually alive, Ralitsa's face regained its healthy glow. Her tears were an outpouring of relief and joy. For Ralitsa, the fact that Scott was alive more than compensated for her agony of dealing with his extended absence.

Katya wiped the moisture from her sister-in-law's face but then thought of something. "Where's the chain now?" she asked.

"I don't have it," Ralitsa replied.

"Where is it? Does Boris have it?"

"No, of course not! I didn't mention it to him. I gave it to Scott's grandfather."

"What?"

"Scott's grandfather and a woman, a university lecturer, came here to ask about Scott. That was before I found his chain at the *mehana.* They were searching for Scott, even after all this time. When they came to the house, I told them how much we enjoyed hosting Scott and how he diligently studied Bulgarian during the time he stayed with us. Boris was quite mean to them, I recall. In any case, I don't think our talk provided them with any information that they didn't already know.

"But afterwards, when I discovered the chain, I wanted to give Scott's grandfather this vital sign indicating that his grandson was still alive, to allow him to share in this exciting news. I wanted to grant him renewed hope that he would soon find Scott and that his coming to Bulgaria was not in vain."

Ralitsa told her sister-in-law how she had traveled to Sofia and left a message for Scott's grandfather at the hotel where he was staying.

"The message I dictated to the hotel switchboard was: 'Meet me at the Sofia synagogue tomorrow morning for important info regarding your grandson.' I chose the synagogue because I knew that Scott was Jewish, and the synagogue would have deep meaning for his grandfather as well. I wanted to hand over the chain in person, but at the last moment, I couldn't face him. I didn't know what to say, nor could I offer any explanation as to how I happened to have found the chain. I just wanted to encourage him to continue his search for Scott.

"Scott is still alive, and that's the important thing," Ralitsa concluded. "We've got to find him."

"Yes, we've got to find him."

In the excitement of their conversation, neither of them had noticed Boris, sitting in his wheelchair in the bedroom doorway. "That's quite a story I've just heard from you two conspiring hens," he said, looking at his wife and sister in turn. "Two stories, actually. I don't know which of you is guiltier: Katya, for helping Scott all this time behind my back, or Ralitsa, for discovering that he's still alive and not mentioning this to me. As you've said, he's alive, and that's the important thing."

They looked at Boris, wondering if his words were masking a volcano of anger that would burst forth at any second. Boris had a horrific temper, and now he was facing two women, both of whom had betrayed him. Who would he lash out at first? What actions would he take, physical or verbal, to show his displeasure at being tricked by those who loved him most? They waited, but the expected outburst never came.

"We must make plans," Boris said, wheeling himself into the room. "We must find Scott right away."

Katya realized immediately what her brother was up to. Boris had no time now to deal with his rage toward her and Ralitsa. His bitter disappointment in their actions would provide its retribution later, at his time and choosing. And, despite her initial fears, Boris wasn't planning to search for Scott in order to kill him in response to the failed delivery mission. No, Boris had something else in mind, something far more urgent.

Boris knew that Scott held the key to the location of the missing artifact. If he could find Scott, he would be one step closer to recovering the priceless treasure. And this meant he had to get to Scott before Nikolov learned that the American was still alive.

"Call Vlady now," Boris instructed his wife. "The bus will be arriving soon, and we must meet Scott at the station."

CHAPTER 43

"Tell me more about ancient Thrace," Simon said pleasantly as they drove north.

"You really want to know?" Sophia asked, her gaze glued to the narrow highway.

"Sure. We've got a ways to go until we meet up with Scott," he said, glancing at the green fields bordering the road and the lofty mountain peaks in the distance, scenery familiar from their previous trip to the Peace Corps training center in Vratsa. Simon was so wound up with excitement about the upcoming reunion with his grandson that he sought some form of distraction to calm his nerves. He hoped an academic discussion between university professors would stimulate his mind, and also, he admitted to himself, he was fascinated with Sophia and longed to get to know her better.

"Where did the name Thrace come from?"

"We're talking about a civilization that rose to importance in the fourth century BC," Sophia began slowly. "The name Thrace was actually given to the region, and to its inhabitants, by the Greeks. In fact, the first reference to the Thracians is in the *Iliad*, which described them as allies of the Trojans. The Thracians included a distinct group of militant tribes that lived in this area, and they had their own language, kings, burial customs, and cultures. They fought against the ancient Greeks and Persians, were conquered by Philip of Macedonia and later by the Romans. Considered to be ruthless warriors, they were hired by their conquerors as mercenaries, and apparently they enjoyed the looting and pillaging that came in the wake of their battles. Oh, I'm sorry, now this is starting to sound like one of my lectures in the university!"

He laughed and reached down to massage a cramp in his left leg. "Tell me, Sophia, how did you become interested in all of this? I've told you about my academic career, but you haven't said too much about yours."

"Oh, it's really not that interesting. I would just bore you."

"No, of course you wouldn't!"

She was silent for a few minutes, her own eagerness at the impending meeting with Scott hidden by efforts to concentrate on the driving. How much should she tell Simon about her career? How much was she allowed to tell him? Revealing too much would jeopardize everything. She needed to be careful what she said.

She was on safe ground talking about her early days in academia. She recalled the thrill she felt when first learning of her country's glorious past and how she had been just as stimulated by library research as with participating in on-site explorations. She had reveled in the studies, welcoming her newly gained perspectives of those long-ago civilizations with heartfelt excitement as if they were monumental discoveries. More than anything, she remembered her heated confrontations with an esteemed Bulgarian archaeologist, public arguments that had established her as an expert in Thracian history and culture.

"The ancient Thracians were not barbarians—far from it," the lecturer informed the audience in the university auditorium. "They were skilled metal workers, adept at creating the finest jewelry and working with the most-valued metals. The Thracians were a highly militaristic tribal people, feared throughout the Balkans as they expanded their sphere of influence. Their wealth rivaled that of the surrounding countries of that age. Their sculptures were crafted with remarkable artisan skills and were often crowned with semiprecious stones. The Thracians were knowledgeable in the science of viniculture and engaged in elaborate drinking rituals. They believed in resurrection after death and buried their leaders in opulent tombs full of objects that would be used in the afterlife. In short, the Thracians who lived in our country should be regarded with the same esteem as the ancient Greeks and Romans, for they, too, were a people who raised civilization into the Modern Age," he concluded.

The audience rose to applaud the lecturer, with the ensuing snap of row after row of wooden seats announcing mass departure from the hall. Sophia, an eager student struggling with the demands of her thesis work, hurried toward the front to engage the speaker.

"Professor Smirnenski," Sophia said, calling to the man as he spoke to some of the university staff lingering around the podium. "May I have a word with you?"

"Ah, Sophia, the ascetic student of ancient Thrace," he replied with a wink of his eye. "Did you enjoy the lecture?"

"Yes, you really know the subject matter," she said. "But you didn't speak of your methodology."

"Methodology?" he asked, bidding farewell to a colleague and moving with Sophia to the side of the emptying hall.

"Your methods are quite controversial," she stated. "You have been highly criticized for sensationalizing Bulgarian archaeology because of the way you work. I had been hoping that you would discuss this in your lecture."

"Why would the audience be interested in methods, when the results are much more fascinating? And, you must admit, what we've found is so spectacular, so indicative of the power and knowledge and craftsmanship of the ancient Thracians, that it was worth everything we did."

Professor Todor Smirnenski, white-haired in a grandfatherly fashion, was an internationally acclaimed archaeologist who frequently lectured at the university. He was known throughout the world of archaeologists for his role in excavating some of the most magnificent Thracian burial tombs in central Bulgaria. Although many of the sepulchers had been looted in ancient times, the relics

Smirnenski discovered in untouched sites were sensational, and they changed how modern scholars regarded the Thracian people and their rulers.

"The audience might not be interested in your methods, but other scholars are. And your methods are destroying some of our most important archaeological ruins," Sophia said, challenging the lecturer.

"Did you come here to listen to my words or to argue with me?" Professors Smirnenski responded, the remains of a hesitant smile wavering on his lips.

"Is it not true that you've used bulldozers to open some of the burial mounds during excavations in the Valley of the Thracian Kings?" Sophia charged, continuing her line of questioning as if she were a prosecutor in a court of law. "Don't you know how much permanent damage that is doing to these historic sites?"

"Young lady, I don't believe that I have to defend myself against your impolite accusations," he said, the smile fading from his face. "Even so, let me just say this. You may believe that brushes and trowels are more appropriate for use in the tombs we've discovered—and normally I would agree with you. However, these are trying times. There are those who seek to profit from our finds, those who don't hesitate to loot and rob the ancient Thracian treasures we've unveiled. These unscrupulous individuals use the most modern means of extraction, with little regard for what they're extracting. We need to use bulldozers and other heavy machinery to win the race against profiteers who don't hesitate to employ high-tech gear and speedy off-road vehicles.

"The looters, they dig day and night. As a result, some of the greatest treasures have been stolen right out of our hands. Young lady, there are those who think that my methods are destroying the burial mounds. I pity these detractors because they are missing the bigger picture. Look at what my work has done for the Thracians and their role in history. Look at what my work has done for Bulgaria!"

Sophia was about to say that much more could be done for Bulgaria if excavations were conducted in a more controlled manner, but the archaeologist's hand was raised, his index finger held high with a sharp demand that she remain quiet.

"I think you have quite the nerve to attack me like this, charging that I am destroying our national heritage when I have done so much to preserve it," Smirnenski concluded, and then he walked away quickly without looking back.

When the professor slammed the door behind him, Sophia was left alone in the lecture hall. To her dismay, the lights were being switched off, section by section, leaving her standing at the front in near total darkness. She hurried toward the exit.

Her apartment in the center of Sofia was far from welcoming. She and Georgi lived a spartan life, unable to afford furnishings that were basic necessities for many. They didn't own a television; purchasing such a luxurious appliance would strain their already tight finances. As a result, Georgi spent most evenings drinking with friends at a neighborhood pub. This was just fine with her, giving her the freedom to study without distraction.

Georgi was employed as an instructor in the athletics department of a nearby primary school, while she devoted her time to completing her doctorate. Georgi took little interest in her subject matter, but she continued to be spellbound by the ancient peoples and cultures that lived in the region. She had completed her Thracian history studies with distinction, following that with a Masters in Ancient History. Now all that was left was to finish her doctoral thesis, with the chosen subject for her final paper to be *The Symbolism of Thracian Rhytons and Other Ritual Objects*.

The word *rhyton*, Sophia knew, derived from a Greek word that meant "to flow," and more commonly referred to the action of pouring. A *rhyton*, therefore, was a container from which liquids were poured, or from which fluids were intended for drinking, and which was used in ritual ceremonies, such as a libation offering to the gods. *Rhytons* usually featured a wide mouth at the top and a small hole at the bottom. One would scoop up a quantity of liquid, such as wine or water, from a storage container, while covering the hole at the bottom, and then one would hold the vessel in the air to allow the liquid to flow downward into the mouth.

Rhytons had been common in many of the ancient Middle Eastern and Near Eastern civilizations, from the Greeks to the Persians. Also known as drinking horns, *rhytons* were originally carved out of animal parts, such as the horns of bulls and goats, but archaeological excavations had failed to unearth specimens to prove this theory due to the decay of the items. Later, *rhytons* were sculpted out of clay or metal. The Bronze Age Minoans of Crete crowned their vessels with silver and gold bull heads bearing small openings permitting wine to be poured from their mouths. In Persia, *rhytons* were typically made of precious metals.

The writings of Xenophon, a Greek historian soldier who was a contemporary of Socrates, indicated that drinking horns were an integral part of the region's religious ceremonies *kata ton Thrakion nomon* ("after the Thracian fashion"). Sophia relished this information, digging repeatedly into the ancient texts to shed further light into the role *rhytons* played in Balkan life.

It was Professor Smirnenski who had discovered the Rogozen Drinking Lion in the village of Rogozen in northwestern Bulgaria in 1985. The Rogozen Drinking Lion was the largest, most magnificent *rhyton* ever discovered in Bulgaria. Almost half a meter in length and weighing nearly two kilograms, this unique Thracian vessel was completely silver, but covered at its ends with pearls, a sign that it had belonged to a royal family, possibly to King Seuthes himself.

As part of her studies, Sophia made several visits to the museum in Vratsa where the Rogozen Drinking Lion, along with other Thracian artifacts, was on display. No matter how many times she visited the museum, she was always awestruck by the ornate drinking vessel, its lower part a finely carved lion's head, with a mouth hole for drinking. As the item was housed in a glass display case, Sophia was unable to see the small letters carved on its inner rim, but she knew that the translation of this ancient Thracian script meant "Mother Earth."

Sophia couldn't help but fantasize about that long-ago gathering, with Thracian ruler Seuthes on one side surrounded by his wives, and across from them, reclining on silk cushions, the delegation from powerful Athens, including the visiting Greek soldier and his party.

"When they had poured libations and sang the paean, the Thracians rose up to begin the program and danced in armor to a flute accompaniment," Xenophon wrote of the encounter.

In his book *Anabasis,* in which he described his adventures and journeys, Xenophon wrote of the dancers leaping up in the air with their weapons brandished. At the climax of their dance, one would strike another with such a seemingly stunning blow that the audience thought the victim was dead. The scene was so vivid, and the description so real, that Sophia knew that Xenophon's writings would be permanently embedded in her mind. This was the scene that guided her studies and kept her focused on her subject matter.

Sophia would have continued on an unremarkable path to a doctorate followed by years of undistinguished academia if it had not been for her attending a press conference called by the university. Professor Smirnenski was due to announce a major new discovery, and the campus buzzed with anticipation of what this could mean. Sophia reserved a seat, just as eager as the others to learn what ancient wonder would be revealed by the eminent archaeologist.

The gathering took place in a spacious hall of the Sheraton Sofia Balkan Hotel in the center of the city. Reporters and photographers packed the room while a crew from Bulgarian National Television set up cameras at one side of the podium. In the rows of wooden fold-up chairs, many of Smirnenski's colleagues sat anxiously alongside students from the university and curious archaeology enthusiasts. Sophia took her place and fidgeted in the seat, waiting for the conference to begin.

"Ladies and gentlemen, may I have your attention?"

The murmurs of the audience dissipated when of one of the university's archaeology fellows took his place behind the podium and adjusted the height of the microphone. His welcoming remarks were long-winded and full of wordy biographical details, information that was basic not only to Sophia, but to many others in attendance as well.

"We know little about the language of the Thracians, and they had no alphabet of their own," the announcer said. "What we have learned about this magnificent people who inhabited our lands is from the stories and legends passed through the generations. However, in these modern days, we are determining the true prominence of the Thracians and their rulers. Only now have we become aware of their role in spreading wine culture, of their artistic craftsmanship, and of the significant part they played in our history.

"We can attribute much of our newfound awareness in the importance of Thracian history to the work of our famous archaeologist, Professor Todor Smirnenski. Single-handedly, Smirnenski has restored this ancient people to their proper standing in our region. He has ascertained the greatness of the mighty Thracians, and for that we will be forever grateful.

"Without further ado, I would like to present a scholar who needs no introduction. We are aware of his accomplishments, we take pride in his achievements, and we have frequently seen how his studies have bettered the lot of Bulgaria in the world. Allow me to present Professor Todor Smirnenski, who will announce to us the great news of his latest discovery."

As Smirnenski stood up and approached the podium, the hall erupted in a loud burst of applause. The cameras rolled and flashbulbs popped brightly as the professor shook hands with the announcer, and then the professor was left standing alone, waiting for his boisterous reception to calm down.

"Thank you, thank you," he began, smiling at the many students and colleagues he recognized. "Allow me to begin by saying that there are naysayers who slander the ancient Thracians by describing them as opportunistic barbarians, vulgar backward tribes that were incapable of national unity and civil habitation of the region. On the contrary, I stress that the Thracians played an even greater role in Balkan civilization than we could ever imagine. I am convinced that the greatest discoveries regarding this ancient people are yet ahead of us. I have dedicated my life's work to uncovering this glorious past and making it known to all of you. This I do for the purity of the science and for the betterment of all Bulgarians. I thank you for coming here today to learn more about the glory of ancient Thrace."

After these brief introductory words, Smirnenski launched into background details of his excavations at a burial tomb in central Bulgaria, near the town of Kazanlak. The professor and his team had excavated the site for three seasons and had already unearthed a wealth of Thracian pottery, ceramics, and sculptures, which they dated to the fourth century BC. But their greatest discovery was also one of their smallest. Smirnenski held up something in his hand to show the audience.

"Allow me to present this wonderful Thracian coin, dating to the reign of King Sitalk," Smirnenski said. As he spoke, an overhead projector hummed into life, and an image of the coin appeared on a white screen behind the podium. "Regard the face of Dionysos, the god we all know so well for his role in protecting the grape harvests and wine production of these regions. This is quite a common feature of coins from the period, and not what makes this specimen so remarkable. Let's consider its reverse side. Here is vivid proof that our beloved Thracians of old participated in the Olympic Games alongside their brethren in Athens and Crete."

The audience gazed with interest at the image on the screen. The backside of the coin was an engraving of a rower flexing his muscles. Depicted in miniature were the features of a sportsman, struggling to propel his small boat forward in a maritime competition. This coin, which once played a role in primeval commerce, clearly confirmed what Smirnenski was announcing. The Thracians had participated in the greatest athletic and cultural activity of that day and age. An invitation to join the powerful Greeks in the Olympics proved that the Thracians were considered their equals in the ancient world.

Sophia squirmed on her seat. Something about this announcement just didn't sit right with her. As Smirnenski elucidated the significance of his finding, with the audience held captive by his charisma and reputation, she searched through the libraries of knowledge in her mind, desperately seeking the cataloged fact that would reveal the fallacies and erroneous conclusions in the professor's statements. There was something wrong here—of that she was certain. What was it?

And then it came to her, as clearly as if it had been posted in modern Bulgarian on the auditorium walls.

"Excuse me!" Sophia interjected, an inner, previously unknown force propelling her from her seat and causing heads to turn. "How can you claim that this coin represents Thracian participation in an Olympic sport that did not exist at the time?" she challenged.

At first, Smirnenski took no notice of the doctoral student in the second row interrupting his emotional explanations of Thracian coinage. He pointedly ignored Sophia's pleas for attention, and members of the audience hushed her to be quiet. One gentleman tried to forcibly sit her down. A former classmate from her early years at the university whispered, "Sophia, don't embarrass yourself," but she gathered her courage and steadied her voice with carefully enunciated words. The crowd quieted, shocked at the untimely disturbance, yet listening attentively to what Sophia had to say.

"The ancient Olympic Games did not include rowing. Rowing was only added in modern times. Athletes from all the Greek city states were invited to participate in the games, as long as they were free men, spoke Greek, and adhered to the customs of the day. But the games never included water sports. Originally, there were only running races, but later boxing and wrestling and even chariot racing were added. But never rowing. Therefore, you offer no conclusive proof that the Thracians participated in the game."

She waited for a moment, letting the significance of her statement sink in. The archaeologist at the podium stared at her with murder in his eyes, while the audience exchanged whispered comments and regarded her as if she had fallen into their presence from another planet.

"How can you be so sure that your discovery was minted in the reign of King Sitalk, a period in which no local coins were minted?" she said, adding yet another argument to her contradictions of the professor's claims. "What possible proof do you have for that?"

At this point, two security guards appeared, as if from nowhere, and began pushing past the people seated in the second row, trying to get close to where Sophia was standing, her voice raised as she launched accusation after accusation.

"You have advanced the science of Bulgarian archaeology, it is true, but this announcement today is purposed to better your own personal standing. It is sensationalism for its own sake!" Sophia charged, her eyes wide as she shouted the words.

The famous professor ignored her, yet he paused from his speech as he waited impatiently for the disturbance in the hall to be quelled.

The guards reached Sophia and physically dragged her from her spot. Wooden chairs snapped, collapsing to the floor one by one like dominoes as the audience parted to allow the heckler to be escorted from their midst. Even after Sophia was removed from the hall, the commotion continued for several minutes. The professor stood behind the podium, seemingly unperturbed by what he had witnessed.

"So, you confronted one of Bulgaria's most famous archaeologists, challenging him about the authenticity of his discovery!" Simon said, staring with renewed appreciation at the Thracian expert who was driving the car. "You must have totally destroyed his career!"

"I didn't cause the slightest dent in his reputation, but that was never the point."

"What did it do to *your* career?" he asked her.

She smiled to herself, still amazed at her uninhibited attack on the archaeologist at that press conference. Initially she feared that she would be regarded by her academic superiors and colleagues as nothing more than a sensation-seeking rabble-rouser. She had acted based on her convictions; she had no regrets for the interruption.

"I couldn't allow him to state things that weren't true," Sophia said calmly. "I couldn't allow our magnificent treasures, discovered in the excavations and digs across our country, to be scandalously dated, labeled, and classified. Accuracy is a virtue, and I took it upon myself to make sure scientific expertise and professionalism would guide our knowledge of the past."

She couldn't tell him more than that—not now. She couldn't

reveal to Simon that in the aftermath of that press conference, and especially after receiving her doctorate, she had evolved into the leading expert in her field, a renowned specialist for identifying and dating the many artifacts being discovered in the country. She became recognized and esteemed as a purist who could easily discern the legitimacy of archaeological finds, determining which were authentic and which were mislabeled and erroneously presented to an uneducated public. She became known throughout Bulgaria as the foremost authority in verifying the authenticity of ancient Thracian treasures.

It was due to her expertise that she had been assigned her present mission. With the delicate nature of her undertaking, secrecy was of utmost importance, and therefore it was dangerous to reveal additional information to the visiting professor from America. Some things at this stage were best left unspoken. It was more important that Simon think that she was simply sharing in his excitement at reuniting with Scott. If details of her assignment were known to others, it would jeopardize what she needed to do.

CHAPTER 44

"I haven't been here since I was a child," Sophia said, as they approached their destination in northwestern Bulgaria after the long drive. "It's hard to forget such a place."

Simon's eyes darted back and forth between Sophia and the surreal scenery they were passing. The narrow road was flanked by bizarrely shaped rock formations, standing alert at odd angles, like sentinels protecting a king's treasure. Each turn in the ascent revealed new elements of limestone and rugged sandstone cliffs. Needle-like pinnacles of rock, uniquely shaped and colored in ranges of reddish browns to grayish yellows, vied to catch rays of sunlight in the narrow passage. Pillars with jagged edges and darkened crevices saluted their arrival.

Simon was reminded of Badlands National Park in South Dakota, which he had visited with Marcia on one of their westward treks. There, too, he had viewed a vast landscape of sharply eroded rock buttes, interspersed with triangular spires that seemed lifted from cathedral roofs. Here in Bulgaria, the formations ran alongside the paved road and into the town itself.

"This is Belogradchik," Sophia announced, as they drove past the welcome sign.

"I wonder where Scott will be waiting," Simon said. "Originally he told me to meet him in Montana, at the bus station. Then he came back online and sent me a short note stating that plans had changed, and that we should come to Belogradchik."

"That's strange because Montana is so much closer to Sofia. But we don't know which village Scott is coming from, so we can't be sure."

Soon he would be reunited with Scott, Simon thought, excited to see his grandson. He touched the scar tissue on his face, a souvenir of his fall at the Rila Monastery and a sign that he must be patient and not rush ahead with abandon. But this time it was different. He had actually chatted with Scott, and he knew Scott was keenly anticipating their reunion as well. Scott was really alive and waiting for him!

Simon thought back to his telephone conversation the previous night with Daniel, when he had finally managed to contact his son with the good news. At first, Daniel had been skeptical, but when Simon mentioned that Scott had chatted about his bar mitzvah ceremony as a way to prove his identity, Daniel had finally come around. By the end of the call, Daniel was ready to book the next flight to Sofia, but Simon persuaded him to wait until he could verify that Scott was actually in Bulgaria as his Skype chats indicated.

The final burst of text his grandson had transmitted stuck out in his mind. The message read: "Plans changed, going to Belogradchik. Meet me there." What had caused Scott to change his plans so suddenly? It really didn't matter. The important thing was that Simon was driving into the rugged Bulgarian town with Sophia at his side. They had arrived at last.

"Where do we start?" he asked, looking at the first houses and buildings they passed. There was nothing remarkable in the constructions, nothing that could provide a clue as to where they should begin their search.

"I think we should head for the town center, and ask around if anyone has seen Scott," Sophia suggested, not fully convinced that this was the best option. "We can start at the hotel. Maybe he booked a room last night," she said, trying to build up hope in the possibility.

They made their way up the winding road past modest homes,

occasional shops, and a brick-faced primary school. They passed an open-air market, crowded with shoppers seeking fresh produce and groceries, but elsewhere the town was quiet, the windows shuttered and the narrow roads empty.

"At the top of the hill is the *kaleto*, the fortress," Sophia told him. "Belogradchik is famous for its castle set among the rocks."

Belogradchik Fortress. There was something about the name that attracted Simon's interest almost like a magnet. Could that be where Scott was waiting?

They parked at what appeared to be the main square—a commercial area marked by banks, pharmacies, an optician's shop, grill restaurants, and an unappealing café. A modern building stood across the plaza, with a yogurt bar and beauty salon on its ground level. Proudly identifying itself as the three-star Belogradchik Hotel, the multistory construction overlooked the forested valley through which they had just driven. It was a view interspersed with the unique rock formations that had caught their breath during the ascent to town.

They crossed the street and entered the hotel. Inside the automatic doors they discovered an ultra-chic setting, complete with marble floors, a fully stocked tropical aquarium and over-sized metal sculptures. Stairs led to the doors of a souvenir store and a restaurant. There was a lack of seating in the lobby, but that didn't matter because there were no guests in sight.

"*Dobre den.* Can I help you?" the front-desk clerk asked them in Bulgarian when they approached.

Sophia talked to the clerk in her native language, explaining that she was accompanying the visiting American professor who was looking for his lost grandson. Then she switched to English to allow Simon to join the conversation.

"We have reason to believe that he might be here. His name is Scott Matthews," she said.

"I have a picture," Simon offered, reaching into his side bag.

"I'm sorry, but I can't give out information about our guests," the clerk responded politely by rote.

Simon was despondent, about to turn to leave, but Sophia grabbed his forearm and whispered something in his ear.

"Maybe this will refresh your memory," Simon said, pulling a bill out of his wallet and handing it to the clerk.

"Ah," the clerk sighed. "Let me take a look."

Seconds later, the clerk nodded his head with recognition. "Yes, I believe this man was our guest last night. He checked out early this morning, didn't even have breakfast."

"Did he say where he was going?" Simon asked eagerly.

"Not exactly, but he did ask for directions to the fortress."

"The fortress!" Simon exclaimed. "Thank you very much."

"No problem," the hotel clerk replied. Then, as they began to walk out of the lobby, he called out after them. "You know, someone else also came here asking about your grandson."

"What? Who was looking for Scott?"

Sophia conversed with the clerk in Bulgarian for a few seconds and then turned to Simon with a worried look.

"We need to hurry," she said, with a note of urgency in her voice that surprised him. She clicked through her cell phone's list of contacts to make a quick call, whispering into the instrument as she walked. She ignored Simon's puzzled look as they left the lobby, giving no clues about what she had learned or whom she had called.

CHAPTER 45

Katya opened the car window to take in some fresh air and to try to clear her head. It wasn't the thick cigarette smoke that was bothering her. There was something about the way Boris and Vlady were whispering in the front seat. Their short, half-finished sentences carried a conspiratorial tone, and the fact that they never included Ralitsa or her in their secretive discussions suggested that their scheme was well-advanced and soon to be implemented. If she only knew what her brother and his friend were really planning!

Their car was parked at the entrance of the Belogradchik Fortress complex. The parking lot was nearly empty now. A busload of noisy schoolchildren had just pulled away, the absence of laughter almost palatable in its wake. Near the gateway to the site were three rickety tourist stands with displays of trinkets and locally produced honey. Bored-looking merchants sat on wooden stools drinking small glasses of muddy coffee. Their only customers were the ubiquitous flies. High above, the mid-day sun was bright against a cloudless sky.

"Maybe he's already inside," Ralitsa suggested from her seat in the back next to Katya.

"Yeah, and maybe he's in Montana after all," Vlady grunted.

"The hotel clerk said he was asking about the fortress," Ralitsa said. "Didn't he tell you that?"

"Yes, but who knows if that was true," Vlady mused.

They had waited at the Montana bus station earlier that morning, anxious for the bus from the village to arrive. They stood side by side like a local welcome delegation, three of them erect and one of them leaning forward in his wheelchair, but there had been no one to greet. The bus pulled into its berth on time, allowing for some passengers to disembark and others to store their luggage and board. A cloud of feathers descended from the open bus door when one passenger emerged carrying two very agitated chickens. Katya and Vlady climbed the steps and pushed past the puzzled driver. They shoved their way up the aisle, acting with implied importance as if they were ticket collectors on official business, sidestepping the noisy travelers until they reached the back of the bus, but Scott wasn't aboard. They returned to the front, and Vlady spoke briefly with the driver. In the end, convinced that their mission was unsuccessful, Katya and Vlady rejoined Raltisa and Boris on the platform as the bus swerved around to begin the next leg of its journey to Sofia.

"He was never planning to take this bus," Boris hissed at his sister.

"But he asked about the bus schedule!" Katya protested.

"What other buses are there from the village?" Vlady asked.

"He could have taken the northbound one."

"Where does that go?"

"It goes through Belogradchik to Vidin."

"I think he was purposely trying to throw us off his tracks," Boris said, as his wife wheeled him back to their car. "He asked about the bus to Sofia so that we would think he had headed to the south. I bet he went to Belogradchik to spend the night."

And that is when they decided to drive to the northwestern town. Ralitsa suggested that they start their search at the hotel off the main square, and this hunch had proven correct. Scott had spent the night there and then left after asking the hotel clerk for information about the *kaleto*. They were sure to find him at the famous fortress.

"Let's go inside," Ralitsa said from the backseat of their parked car. "Why should we stay here when he's probably waiting inside, expecting someone to come meet him?"

"She's right," Boris said. "We need to find him before anyone else arrives. Who knows who he has called? Maybe Americans will come from the embassy."

"It would take quite some time for Americans to arrive from Sofia," Vlady said. "I'll go in and look for him."

"I'll come with you," Katya said, opening her car door.

"No, if he sees you, he'll run," Boris said, twisting around in his seat to cast a stern glance at his sister. "After all, you had him for what, three years, and he ran from you."

"Ralitsa will come with me," Vlady said decisively. "The two of you will remain here. Call me if you spot him, or if you notice any officials arriving."

Two car doors opened and two car doors slammed shut, and then only brother and sister were left in the vehicle. Boris sat in the front passenger seat, staring through the windshield at the path leading up to the fortress, while Katya remained in the back, staring at nothing more than the back of her brother's hairy neck.

Boris said something quietly, but she couldn't hear what it was. "What are you mumbling about?"

"If you want to talk to me, come into the front seat," her brother replied, flicking some ash from his cigarette out the open car window.

Katya unbuckled her seatbelt and got out of her seat. She went around and opened the driver's door and squeezed in behind the steering wheel. For a moment she regarded the dashboard as if it, too, was to partner in the conversation, but when the silence became overbearing, she turned to her brother.

"You must be furious with me," she said, offering him an opening that could result in a painful backlash, yet one that was necessary to get past.

"Katya, I'm angry with you, I can't deny that, but you've also given me hope."

"What do you mean?"

He sat there, dragging on his cheap cigarette until it became a stub too short for his fat fingers to hold. He flicked this out the window. She thought she spotted a tear in his left eye.

"Look at me," he said, staring down at his shattered, unmoving legs, manually positioned in front of him. "I'm not much of a man anymore. Sometimes I don't want to open my eyes in the morning because it hurts too much, but I can accept who—and what—I am. What you've done, as unfaithful and secretive as it was, has given me hope—hope that someday I can repay them for making me a cripple."

Katya knew what her brother was talking about because she had been there with him on that fateful day. She had seen the worst of it, and she still cringed when she thought about what had happened. She couldn't help but feel responsible for allowing Boris to reach this state.

It had been shortly after she had surreptitiously brought Scott to the cabin in the woods, not far from the village where her mother lived. Katya split her time, spending her days caring for her aging mother and heading into the woods once or twice each week to bring Scott supplies and the drugs that kept his mind blank and her control complete. Her mother was an old-fashioned country woman, a peasant whose clothing and habits were simple and her beliefs in time-honored traditions strong. There was nothing modern about Katya's mother, for like many who lived in the countryside, her life remained captured in the past. She still owned the same furniture and dishware that had graced her home since the days when her Serbian-born husband, Katya's father, had been alive. Her only nods to modernity were a noisy and often erratic refrigerator and an oversized radio that barely received the static-filled transmissions of a distant Sofia news station. The home could have come straight out of a previous century—or at least a previous generation.

Katya's mother maintained a vegetable garden in the backyard, and this was her pride and joy. For hours each morning, despite her age and frail health, and with little regard for the weather, she would bend her back to hoe, weed, or plant, her long, plain skirt dragging in the mud. Each tomato bush and every pepper plant in the garden received her delicate attention; every cucumber was personally groomed ahead of pickling. There was nothing tastier than the long, homegrown sweet red peppers she stuffed with rice and *sirene* cheese. Katya frequently returned from visits to the village with a basketful of her mother's crops and containers stuffed with home-cooked dishes.

One day the old woman fell to the earth, damaging—if not breaking—the bones of her right hip, and she was unable to rise from the furrows of her plot. She lay there, biting her lip against the pain as the summer sun bore down relentlessly, draining her strength and threatening to snatch away her final breath. The twilight and then the star-filled night renewed her grasp on life, the coolness relieving some of the pain but not quenching her growing fear.

The next morning, following an overnight trip to Sofia to pick up additional narcotics for her cabin-confined patient, Katya discovered her mother sprawled atop the prized pepper plants. Scattered pulpy remains of the red vegetables bore her mother's tiny teeth marks. She carried the frail woman into the house and laid her on the sofa, where her mother remained wordlessly during the doctor's visit and for nearly a week until she regained some of her strength.

Boris, whose visits to the village to see his mother were becoming less and less frequent, obliged to his sister's tearful request to show some concern. He drove up with Ralitsa one morning a few days after the old woman's fall to make a token appearance. Sitting with Katya and his wife in the living room while gazing at his mother's diminutive wrinkled body on the sofa, he remained quiet, offering few words of encouragement or sympathy. The entire time his mind was focused on escaping to the *mehana* for drinks and discussion of the latest football matches with Ivaylo.

Boris hadn't realized that he had been followed on his drive from Montana. As he sat with his family, his wife and sister engaging his mother in meaningless conversation, two black utility vehicles pulled up outside the house. Hearing the car doors, Boris glanced out the window, and his eyes opened wide in alarm. Four men, dressed in black and looking more sinister than agents of the long-disbanded *Darzhavna Sigurnost* secret service, were approaching. It was too late to run.

"Boris Kotsev!" they called, pounding on the front door.

"Who is it?" Katya's mother whispered, looking back and forth between her daughter and daughter-in-law for some explanation.

"I better open the door," Boris said, rising from his seat in slow motion.

"We are here on behalf of Alexander Nikolov," the first man announced, as if this wasn't already clear to Boris. The man had a huge shaven head that bulged out from a black shirt that seemed two sizes too small. He sported stud earrings and a sinister smile, as if missions of intimidation were his bread and butter. "Mr. Nikolov believes that you have not provided him with the services to which you were contracted," he continued, articulating his words. "A delivery did not arrive at its destination as was agreed. Perhaps you have this article here with you at this time?"

Unconsciously, a smile appeared on Katya's lips at this strange and somewhat formal language. She was fully aware of the reason these despicable men had come to visit. They were thugs associated with Nikolov and his crooked dealings, and this was not a courtesy call.

It happened very fast. Boris was dragged forcibly from the house, unable to fight off the overwhelming combined muscle power of four men who were trained—and probably had experience—in handling the protests of people who had done Nikolov wrong. Katya and Ralitsa attacked the men with their bare hands; they kicked at them for good measure. Neither their shouts nor an attempt by Ralitsa to bite one man's hand could prevent them from stuffing an overpowered Boris into the front car. Car doors slammed, and the two vehicles sped off down the alley toward the village center.

"I'm going after them," Katya said, pulling her car keys out of her purse.

"They'll kill you, too!" Ralitsa screamed.

"Stay with my mother," Katya commanded, and she hurried to her car.

She drove blindly, not knowing which way the cars had gone. Were they heading south to Sofia, or perhaps north toward the border? Katya feared that Nikolov was waiting for Boris somewhere, ready to kill him on sight if Boris didn't provide him with the Thracian treasure. But Nikolov's real dealings had been with Vlady as well. Where was Vlady now? Had Nikolov's thugs already gotten to him? All of this was because Scott had not delivered the goods in Varna. Everything that was happening was entirely her fault! She felt extremely guilty about letting the American out of her sight when he entered the hotel lobby. Scott had been beaten as a result, and now the violence was about to reach Boris as well. She had to save him!

Far ahead on the winding country road, a flash of black caught her eye, and she realized that it was one of the two utility vehicles. Of all the routes leading out of the village into the surrounding hills, thank God she had found their track! She pressed down hard on the gas pedal, pleading for the old Lada to pick up speed.

The road twisted its way through a forested mountain valley, with a bubbling stream to its left. The countryside here, close to the Serbian border, was quiet except for the water cascading over sharp rocks and the roaring engines of the racing cars. Katya pushed her car to its limits. Her mind raced as she tried to recall where this rural road led. Afraid that she wouldn't be able to make the next curve, she braked quickly.

She almost missed them. Just as she realized that the road would eventually veer back in a circular pattern to reach the eastern outskirts of the village, she saw the black cars off to the side, at the start of a dirt path leading into the pine forest. The vehicles were empty; there was no sign of the four thugs or Boris. She parked and switched off the motor.

And then she heard the sound. At first she thought it was a bird's call, perhaps an eagle signaling to its mate while circling above the mountain peaks on the horizon. It was somewhat unworldly, as if defying identification. But with a sinking feeling, Katya realized she was hearing the expressions of her brother's excruciating pain. Wincing as his screams pierced the morning's silence, she got out of the car, determined to stop this. She sprinted through the woods, resolved to save her brother's life.

A mosquito landed on her neck, and she slapped at it blindly as she forged ahead. A gnat buzzed in her ear. She dodged prickly bushes and overhanging branches that scraped her face. She followed a trail of half-trampled bushes and disturbed ground cover, using the fallen vegetation to guide her forward. The forest floor was thick with thorny weeds that slowed her pace. A fallen tree trunk threatened to trip her; she raced around it while fighting to maintain her direction. The sound was getting louder.

Finally she reached the clearing, an open, oval-shaped meadow surrounded by dark pines and carpeted with colorful flowers. It was so peaceful looking that she stopped in her tracks, trying to catch her bearings and seek out the source of the spine-tingling shrieks. And then she spotted the men.

Boris was propped upright, his back clamped against the trunk of a large tree at one side of the clearing. His head drooped downward, so she couldn't see whether his eyes were open. He was standing there, half conscious, possibly half dead. His face was bruised, marked with trails of blood. All sense of strength was visibly deleted from his being. His arms were pulled back tightly, tied behind him in an obviously painful manner. If they had been extended outwards, Katya would have found herself staring at a crucified image of her brother.

"Where is it?" the bald-headed leader of the gang shouted, but Boris was oblivious to the questions. Another thug swung a large bat at Boris's left kneecap, cracking bone and ligaments as if they were twigs. Another question, another swing of the bat. Boris was barely conscious, unable to protest and no longer responding to the repeated blows to his legs.

"Stop! Stop this!" Katya cried, running toward the circle of men assaulting her brother.

"Stay away," the bald man warned Katya, raising an arm that could signal the others to instantly attack her as if they were obedient attack dogs.

"He doesn't know anything," she protested, trying to block the thug from raising the bat again.

"Maybe he doesn't know anything," one of the men repeated, turning to the leader.

"Oh, he knows something," the bald man responded with a snarl. "We just don't know yet what he knows."

Two of the men seized Katya's hands and held her back, barely containing her as the beating continued. The bat swung repeatedly, targeting kneecap and then thigh, and then striking lower leg flesh as well. The bones in Boris's legs shattered to fragments; there was nothing left to crush. Boris remained upright and silent, bound by the thick ropes that were carving rivers of blood into his arms.

It was too much for Katya to witness, and she passed out. When she regained consciousness, the men were gone. Boris was still bound to the tree, all color drained from his face and his very existence hanging by the thinnest of threads. Katya struggled to her feet and moved to help her brother.

"I think I know why you did it," Boris said quietly, his hands folded on his flaccid legs as he sat next to her in the parked car.

"What? What are you talking about?" Katya asked, her eyes misty from painful recollections of the past.

"Caring for Scott all this time all by yourself. You think I can't see through you and your motives?"

Katya waited for him to continue, for proof that he understood her agenda. Could her brother possibly know the reason she had kept the American isolated in the remote cabin, nursing him back to health and a state of mind that was totally under her control? Could he accept her for what she had done after years of deception and secrecy? Growing up, they had never been close, they had never shared secrets. Now Katya didn't feel the need to explain her actions to Boris anymore than she expected him to expand on his statement suggesting that he understood them.

Suddenly Boris's cell phone rang, and he snapped it open. He barked a few words in reply to what he heard, and then the call disconnected.

"They've spotted Scott," he reported, and she sat up straight, ready to get out of the car at his command. "But there's a slight problem," Boris added.

CHAPTER 46

Simon was having a hard time with the ascent. His limp was becoming more pronounced and his breathing indicated that he was finding it difficult to continue up the path. She paused to wait for him and turned to take in the scenic view.

Set against a natural wall of spectacular rock massifs were the outer fortifications of the ancient garrison. This fortified outpost, built atop a windy remote peak, was assigned the task of guarding the roads crisscrossing the region that led to the plains along the Danube River. Only two walls were needed to secure the post, to the northwest and to the southeast. The other sides were naturally protected by inaccessibly steep rock cliffs that provided an impenetrable defensive barrier.

The view ahead could have been lifted straight from a Disney fantasy cartoon. Even seeing it repeatedly couldn't depreciate the stunning sight of a fortress wall with a slightly arched stone gate at its center, crowned by a backdrop of rocky red pinnacles stretching dozens of meters into the cloudless sky and carpeted halfway up with green brush. Looking closely, one could see that some of these needle-like protrusions were connected by a stone wall. The unique feature of Belogradchik Fortress was the fact that it had been built as a combination of human efforts and natural elements. She marveled at the wonders of this historic site and was inwardly pleased that their quest had brought them here.

"What is this, Roman or Turkish?" he asked, arriving at her side.

He readily accepted the bottle of water she offered him but momentarily found it difficult to swallow.

She gave him a concerned look for a moment before replying. "Belogradchik was originally built by the Romans. The Byzantines also fortified this hill. Much later it was an important fortress in the fourteenth century under Tsar Ivan Strasimir, who ruled out of Vidin on the Danube. The Ottomans eventually captured Belogradchik and refortified it."

"So these walls date back to the fourteenth century?" Simon asked.

"No, most of these walls are from the 1800s, when the Ottomans used this fortress as part of their efforts to put down our revolts and attempts to gain independence. The fortress was called, and is still known by many, as the *Kaleto*, which is a Turkish word."

"I've never heard of this place," Simon said, his breathing more regular now. "There don't seem to be too many tourists here."

"It's pretty much off the beaten path, like most of Bulgaria," Sophia admitted. "But we're campaigning to get Belogradchik recognized as one of the New Seven Wonders of the World."

In the distance a lone man was setting up a tripod, angling his camera for the best perspective of the sun-tinged rocks above the fortress. Except for this photographer and a pair of large-winged raptors soaring high above, they seemed to be quite alone.

"Where could Scott be?" Simon asked, quickly bringing them back to the purpose of their visit. "And why would he be hiding here?"

Sophia was wondering the same thing. But in addition to Simon's questions, she added one, one that she did not express to the visiting professor. Sophia wanted to know if Scott was looking for something, something in particular, hidden among the rocks of this cultural monument.

"We should continue," Sophia said, scanning the path ahead.

"Scott is probably waiting for us at the top somewhere."

Simon nodded his head in agreement. They continued through the next gate, reaching the foot of the reddened massif. To his dismay, the trail ended at a set of steep stone steps, inclining toward a gated entranceway set purposely into the cliff walls high above them. Beads of perspiration dotted his forehead just under the rim of his baseball cap, and his breath was coming in short, almost asthmatic gasps. But it was a different part of his body that was threatening to betray him.

"My legs," he said, as if she didn't realize what the problem was. "I don't think I can go any farther," he added, resigned to the fact that he was unable to complete his quest.

"Should I continue on my own?" Sophia asked. "I know what Scott looks like."

"He might be injured or frightened, or I don't know what," Simon said. He plopped down on a large rock at the side of the steps and urged her forward.

Without the professor in tow, Sophia was able to make quick progress, surprising herself with both the energy and excitement that propelled her to the next level. The steps curled around the rock walls, winding to the gate leading through a pillared passageway to an inner courtyard. This upper section of the medieval stronghold offered the perfect fortified enclosure. The cliffs provided natural defenses, but modern additions such as black iron fences had been added to prevent visitors from falling to the abyss of the rocky canyon below.

The panorama visible from atop the Belogradchik Fortress was absolutely breathtaking. Sophia looked out at the carpeted forest, spotted with the protruding rocky buttes, each topped with the illusion of sculpted heads and statuesque figures. Held spellbound by the beauty of the weathered pillars and the rock vista rising from the Danubian plain, Sophia recalled the oft-repeated story she had learned about their formation when she was just a child.

Long ago there was a stone-walled nunnery built among the scenic Belogradchik Rocks. Inside this monastery lived a young nun named Vitinia, envied by fellow nuns for her stunning beauty. The hood of her habit couldn't hide Vitinia's good looks—rumors of her beauty spread throughout the empire. The nunnery's mother superior reminded Vitinia not to forget that even though she was young and pretty, she had taken the veil and was betrothed only to God.

One year, during the midsummer St. Peter's Day celebration, a handsome aristocrat named Antonio rode up to the nunnery on his white horse in search of the well-known beauty. As soon as Vitinia saw him, she recognized that this was the man she longed for in her innermost dreams. Vitinia could not resist the callings of her heart and secretly met with Antonio.

The beautiful nun and the handsome aristocrat hid their love from the other nuns for some time. However, the illicit love affair was discovered through the cries of Vitinia's newborn baby. Mother superior decided to severely punish the wayward nun by all possible means. She cursed Vitinia repeatedly and turned to the monks from the nearby monastery to pass judgment on the girl.

It took a long time for the white-bearded monks to determine the appropriate punishment, but at last they decided to expel Vitinia and her child from the priory. The monks ruled that she should be treated like a leper and no one should dare talk to her, let alone give her shelter or food. Vitinia preferred to die rather than be turned out of the nunnery to a life worse than death itself. As heartbreaking as her sincere plea for mercy was, it did not move the monks to change their ruling.

As Vitinia and her child were exiting the nunnery's gates for the last time, an unexpected storm turned day into night, and thunder shook the land. Stones and boulders rained down from above, completely destroying the nunnery and the nearby monastery. The power of the storm was great, and all the judgmental monks fled from the chasms forming at their feet. Vitinia, holding her newborn in a pose reminiscent of the Madonna, and even Antonio, the horseman riding to his beloved on his white stallion, were turned instantly to stone.

To this day, the monks, the Madonna, and the horseman stand guard at the Belogradchik Rocks to welcome visitors to the site of an ancient love affair.

She navigated her way through the passageway and came to a steep black-metal ladder, leading to an even higher level of man-made fortress combined with natural wonder. Sophia looked back, but Simon was out of sight, somewhere far below. There was no one around, no indication whether climbing the ladder would bring her any closer to Scott or to fulfilling the true reason that she had accompanied Simon on his quest to find the missing American.

She began climbing, looking neither to the ledge high above her nor at the ground below, growing more distant from her feet. She concentrated on the black bars, repeating to herself the simple command to lift her legs, one at the time, rung by rung. Thank God Simon had stayed behind, she thought to herself. He would never have been able to ascend this sharply vertical ladder. She was amazed that she was capable of doing this herself. Don't look down! A few more rungs to go! And then she reached the top.

Here, too, remnants of ancient fortifications were set against the rocky massif of the mountain, but more prominent were the scenic lookout points, fenced off for protection but offering the most spectacular views. Sophia forced herself to ignore the panorama and instead concentrate on her mission. If Scott was anywhere on this peak, he had to be here. There was no higher level than this, she assumed.

Sophia heard a noise somewhere above her. It sounded like something moving, pushing aside branches. Perhaps she was mistaken and it was just the wind, breathing its existence on this lofty peak. Curious and eager to investigate, Sophia carefully lifted her leg and stepped into a natural foothold in the side of a large boulder. Shifting her weight, and grabbing onto the cool rock for support, she eased herself higher. Soon she was standing on the boulder itself, with the lookout point far below her. She turned around, crossing a weed-filled plateau until she came to a spot overlooking the red-tiled roofs of the town spread out across the valley. And then she heard the noise again, and it was coming from behind a leafy bush.

"Scott, is that you?" she called out, first in Bulgarian, then in

English.

CHAPTER 47

Before Boris could protest, Katya was out of the car and running toward the fortress. She bypassed the ticket taker at the entrance gate and entered the complex, eager to reconnect with the person who had—up until recently—been under her sole guardianship. She needed to see him, to talk to him, to reassure him that she had acted solely out of genuine concern for his welfare. The confinement, the pills, everything was for a good cause. She had only been trying to help him, to help him recover. He shouldn't have run away!

But in her mind's eye, Katya was not running to meet Scott at all. It was not a need to see the American that was propelling her forward. There was someone else just ahead, someone standing somewhere out of view at the foot of the sharp rock cliffs. In an alternative reality, he was there, expecting her to join him on the citadel grounds. He was waiting for her. This was the man that Katya truly sought, and he appeared to her in a vision so strong that it had to be real.

Hristo, her beloved Hristo, was on the mountain, and it was up to her to rescue him and bring him home.

She could picture her husband leaving their apartment early one Saturday morning long before, anxious to pick up Boris and head for the ski slopes. Again Katya would be alone in Sofia for the weekend, something she normally wouldn't mind if she was busy with her studies. This weekend, though, she and Hristo had been invited to a friend's apartment for a Saturday-evening barbecue, and she was eager for the opportunity to socialize with their acquaintances.

"Can't you stay home this time?" she pleaded with him, even as he was buckling his parka with his winter gear already packed and ready by the front door.

"I don't want to miss the slopes," he replied matter-of-factly. "Spring is coming soon, and I doubt we'll see any additional snowfalls this season. You remember that I'm planning on flying to Italy next week with my friends."

"How could I forget? You're always off skiing with your friends," she complained.

"Today I'm skiing with your brother," he said, checking himself in the hallway mirror. "You're not jealous of the time I spend with Boris, are you?"

"I'm not happy with the fact that you're on the slopes every free moment you have."

"Then you must be thankful that skiing is only a winter pastime," he joked, refusing to let her mood upset his plans.

It did bother her, to a greater degree than she would admit, that Hristo seemed to care more for his outdoor winter activities than he did for spending time with her. When he was home, Hristo was demonstratively affectionate, making extra efforts to entertain her and keep her happy. But even when they spent quality time together, she would often catch a whimsical look in his eyes, and she knew that he was secretly making plans for another ski vacation. One weekend he would head south to Bansko, and then the following weekend he would hook up with friends to hit the slopes at Pamporovo in the Rhodope Mountains. He seemed to prefer Pamporovo, with its ski tracks of all difficulty ranges. Hristo was becoming very adept at the sport. He worshipped his gear as if the slender skis were a pair of extended limbs.

Katya was resigned to the fact that she couldn't dissuade her husband from his winter outings, but there was something in their relationship that bothered her even more. Katya wanted to start a family, an unreciprocated desire that resulted in frequent arguments with Hristo.

"We're too young for that," her husband insisted. "You're still studying at the university. When do you have time to be a mother?"

Katya had many things she could say in response. Approaching her thirties, she was most definitely not too young to start a family. Quite the opposite. She felt that she would soon be too old to raise children. Her biological clock was ticking. Any further delay would be detrimental to her physically, she feared, leaving her no opportunity to achieve motherhood. She couldn't shake off these motherly instincts. Children should come when their parents are young enough to care for them and when they can fully enjoy them. She thought of her own mother, who had been in her mid-forties when she and Boris had been born. That was an unacceptably late age to bring children into the world. If she didn't start a family soon, Katya realized, her mother would never take pleasure in being a grandparent.

With her inclination to look at everything scientifically, Katya considered Bulgaria's low birth rate and the lack of desire among newly married couples to raise many children. The average family unit in Bulgaria was small; she knew this from observing society around her and from consulting the statistics. The country's typical household was 2.6 members, and this low figure didn't vary between city residents and village dwellers. Bulgaria's birthrate was one of the lowest in Europe. The country's population was dropping, thanks also to the emigration of many of her countrymen to the richer industrial countries of Western Europe.

How could she convince Hristo that they should bring a child into the world? With rational thinking taking precedence over emotion in her scientific mind, Katya began organizing the debate points and imagining the possible objections Hristo would raise to counter her arguments. She launched into her own internal debate, preparing her reasoning for starting a family in modern-day Bulgaria. Bulgaria was now a free country, unshackled from the oppression of its former communist rulers. Bulgaria was a democracy, where anyone and everyone could speak his own mind, read editorials criticizing the government in the free press, and travel wherever they want. There were no longer restrictions on their lives. One day soon Bulgaria would join the European Union, opening up its borders to its European neighbors and emerging from its third-world status. Fences and walls would tumble down, giving them unprecedented freedoms of which previously they could only dream.

What better time than now to bring a child into the world?

Oh yes, she could state these fact-proven arguments—that was the scientist within her speaking. This was how her mind worked. First, take into consideration all rational and logical aspects of a problem, and then determine a scientifically acceptable resolution. But there was also the emotional side. The yearning to raise a child was rising from the depths of her being and calling out to her. She longed for someone to love and nurture, someone to shower with affection. The call of future motherhood within her was nearly overwhelming. She desperately needed a child.

Why couldn't Hristo understand this? Why couldn't he consider anything other than how to satisfy his own physical needs? With a sigh, Katya realized that this was why he went skiing so frequently. He needed the energetic rush of slaloming down the slopes, breathing the thin air at the extreme elevations, and feeling the biting chill of the wind on his cheeks. Only this physical exertion could satisfy Hristo. He totally lacked the inner desires that were so powerfully calling out to her.

Nonetheless, she was determined to bring this up again with Hristo, to explain the logical reasons for starting a family. If need be, she would explain the emotional side as well. Having a family would be good for him as well. He would understand.

She would talk to Hristo as soon as he got back from Pamporovo.

"You wouldn't believe how wonderful it was!" Hristo said, whispering in her ear on his return.

She had waited up for him, even after he called from Plovdiv to inform her that he was stopping there to meet friends on the way home from the ski resort. A few drinks and they would be on the road, he promised. She lay down on the lumpy sofa, watched a dated Russian film on the television, drank a cup of coffee for the caffeine punch, and even puffed a few cigarettes as she waited nervously in their living room. Anything to stay awake, to prepare herself for the confrontation that could no longer be delayed. But in the end, her eyes had drooped and her mind had tired. She told herself that she would just lie down on the bed for a short while, but the minute her head hit the pillow, she was fast asleep.

In the morning, she woke to find that Hristo had already left the apartment. He had to attend to his job's demands, while a morning lecture was on her schedule at the university. There was no note from him waiting on the kitchen table. Only a pile of wet ski pants and boots in the corner served as a sign of his weekend absence. She would talk to him that night.

But dinner talk centered on financial problems at the company where Hristo was employed, difficulties in cash flow that threatened to necessitate staff cutbacks. Katya could see that this was not the appropriate time to bring up the possibility of expanding their family. Afterward, Hristo sat wide-eyed while smoking in front of the television, engrossed in the latest local political scandal. He watched both the nightly BNT newscast and the follow-up discussion panel. No, tonight was not the night to talk about this.

In the morning, Hristo was again out of the apartment before she opened her eyes, and that evening he went out to a pub with some of his colleagues. The opportunity to talk with him about what was on her mind was postponed, time after time, until Katya realized that she would need to force the subject—to compel him to listen to her arguments, to her logic and emotions, and to accept her reasoning. To manage this, she would need to schedule a time for this important discussion, but unfortunately, that would have to wait until his return from the ski trip to Italy.

She was going to be on her own again in the cold Sofia flat, and she wondered what she would do to keep busy. The demands of her studies were not overwhelming, and she had nearly completed her thesis as graduation approached. She could go up north to visit her mother, but a rainy forecast kept her close to home. Perhaps she should take the tram to the center to look for shopping bargains. Maybe there would be a good film on television. There was that novel she had picked up a few times, only to lose interest after the first chapter. She would be quite bored this weekend, she realized.

Hristo called her from the resort in northern Italy shortly after his arrival with his ski buddies. The snow cover was great, he assured her, and yes, he would take plenty of pictures to show her the beauty of the Alps. The resort was very nice, the food was good, the excitement of hitting the slopes the following day was great, but now Hristo and his friends were planning nothing more than to get totally wasted in the local bar.

Saturday morning showed Sofia at its worst. The rain came down incessantly, in slanted sleets of moisture unleashed furiously from bitter Balkan skies. There was a strong, biting wind, which shrieked around corners and into her apartment even though all the windows were closed. The cobblestone streets and rundown neighborhood buildings were as gray and foreboding as the skies above. Unable to sit still in the cold and dark, Katya dressed warmly and went for a walk, struggling to keep her umbrella upright as she walked past the shuttered fruits and vegetables stand, the tiny barbershop where Hristo got his hair cut at a ridiculously cheap price, the flower stand where nothing attractive was ever blooming, and the small booth where one of her neighbors sold huge quantities of alcohol and cigarettes no matter what the weather. The downpour and the emptiness on the streets depressed her, and she quickly returned to the apartment without having accomplished a thing.

The phone call came at four in the afternoon. When she heard the ringing, Katya wondered if it was her friends inviting them to another dinner party—one Hristo would undoubtedly find excuses not to attend. Maybe it was Boris calling, or his wife, Ralitsa, for whom Katya had developed a growing fondness. Maybe it was even her mother, but no, her mother typically called around dinnertime.

Hristo had told her he would phone her late that night, so she certainly wasn't expecting him. Katya picked up the receiver to answer the phone call that would change her life forever.

The call was from Italy, but it wasn't Hristo on the line. There was static, and at first Katya couldn't identify the voice, or what the man was saying in short bursts of excited words.

"Who is this?"

"It's Aleks," he replied, and then he hesitated.

"Aleks?"

"Hristo's friend."

"Ah, Aleks. Wait, aren't you in Italy with Hristo?'

"Yes."

And then silence.

"Are you there?" she asked, shaking the receiver as if it would clear the static.

"Yes, Katya, I'm here. I have something to tell you."

"What? I can barely hear you."

"It's about Hristo."

"Hristo? Put him on the phone."

"Katya …"

"I want to talk to Hristo."

"Katya," he repeated.

And then he told her. It didn't matter if there was static on the line because the words were just not sinking in. There had been an accident. A skiing accident. On one of the steeper slopes. Aleks had warned Hristo that it was a difficult descent. Hristo had shrugged off the warnings. "I can do it," he insisted. "You're not up to that level," Aleks said to him, attempting to dissuade him from tackling the steep run. Hristo was set on trying it and urged Aleks and the others to accompany him to the lift.

"We couldn't stop him," Aleks told Katya, his voice fading as he choked back the difficult words. "He came down fast, too fast I guess, and missed a turn. There was a tree, and well," he said, not completing the sentence.

With the phone secured between her head and shoulder, Katya

pulled her left hand in toward her stomach and her right hand grasped it tightly. Unconsciously, her fingernails began clawing at the soft skin of her left wrist. With each word she heard from Aleks, the nails dug deeper. Blood began to trickle from the puncture wounds, and she bit her lip at the sharp, unexpected pain. "Where is Hristo? Is he okay?"

"Katya, he didn't make it," was the sorrowful reply.

And that was it. Aleks kept talking, mentioning a rescue team, a doctor, and transportation of the body. Katya ignored the throbbing in her wrist and held the phone to her ear, but she wasn't listening. It didn't make sense. Hristo would be back first-thing Monday morning. He had promised. She would talk to him again about her desire to start a family. Surely he would listen to her this time. She needed a child. She needed a baby to care for. She needed Hristo.

He was on the mountain; he just had to be. He had been tragically injured, it was true, but hadn't she done everything she could to nurse him back to health? She had tenderly cared for him as he recovered, making sure that he had everything he needed in the isolated cabin. She had protected him, kept his mind free of painful memories. With her tender and loving care, no one could ever harm him. Her beloved Hristo.

Soon they would be reunited. He was on the mountain, and she ran into the fortress complex to find him.

CHAPTER 48

The pain in his left leg was intensifying. He sat on a rock at the side of the path and massaged his sore muscles in a circular motion—not that it was helping to ease the tension he felt. He shifted his weight, adjusted the baseball cap on his forehead to ward off the warm rays of sunlight, and waited anxiously for Sophia to return from the higher levels of the fortress. She would not be coming back alone, he told himself, repeating these words with inner optimism as if they were his mantra. He hoped and he prayed that Sophia would arrive at any minute, leading Scott down from the mountain. It just had to be. His lips again mouthed the words: *I will find him.*

In his mind, he hummed a refrain that could have been lifted straight from a 1970s Paul Simon single. *The grandfather and child reunion is only a moment away*. It would be great, no, it would be absolutely amazing, to reunite with Scott after all this time. It was a dream come true. It was even more than that. It was beating insurmountable odds and proving all the naysayers wrong. It was seeing the pits of hell and coming out alive to tell the tale. It was being reborn. It was a happy ending to a tragic story. It was getting back his beloved grandson. Ha, it was a miracle!

I will find him.

And then, as if his innermost prayer had risen directly to the heavens for instantaneous fulfillment, Sophia appeared atop the steep set of stairs. She rested in the stone gateway, squinting at the strong sunlight that momentarily blinded her vision. And, to complete the consummation of the moment, to reward his trip to Bulgaria and fully compensate for three years of hopes and prayers, Sophia was not alone. His grandson, slightly thinner than he remembered, followed the Thracian lecturer through the gate and began to descend the steps. The silent call of Simon's mantra had been answered.

Simon stood up, his arms wide and his heart beating in boundless elation. And then Scott jumped down the last of the steps to hug him excitedly. Simon's cap fell to the ground as he repeatedly kissed his grandson's unshaven cheeks. The pain in his leg was quickly forgotten as years of longing exploded into a prolonged, excited embrace.

"Scott, I'm so happy to see you!"

"I can't believe you're here, Grandpa!"

"I came to find you, to bring you home."

"Grandpa," Scott cried.

Tears poured down Simon's cheeks as well, and after another long embrace, he suddenly remembered that they were not alone.

"Oh, I see you've met Sophia."

"No, actually, I have no idea who she is," Scott said, wiping his face.

"I've been helping your grandfather as he searched for you all over Bulgaria," Sophia said, extending her hand.

"All over Bulgaria? This is totally unreal. What happened to you, Grandpa? Why is your face all scarred?"

"Don't worry about me," Simon said, dismissing the fall at the Rila Monastery as if it had never happened. "Are you okay? Your parents are dying to hear from you, to know that you're okay. Are you all right? What's this horrific wound on your head? Does it hurt?"

"It's okay," Scott replied, shaking off his grandfather's hand. "I'm fine, really I am. I've been through some rough times, but I think that's all behind me now."

"What were you doing here, on top of this mountain? What's the name of this place again?" Simon asked, still clinging to his grandson as he turned to Sophia.

"Belogradchik," she reminded him.

"Right. Belogradchik. What are you doing here?"

"I was looking for something," Scott replied, hesitating and wondering whether now was the appropriate time to continue. "It's a long story, a really long story."

"We have plenty of catching up to do," Simon said. "We need to get you back to Sofia and then on a plane to the States. Your parents will be thrilled, and that's putting it mildly. We'll call them right away and let them hear your voice. Scott, I can't believe it!"

"There are things I need to do," Scott said, without further explanation, adjusting the strap of his backpack.

"I have to give you something," Simon began, his voice choking with emotion.

"What?"

"I believe this is yours," Simon said, pulling the thin silver chain from the side pocket of his travel bag.

"How the hell did you get my chain?"

"I guess we both have things to tell each other."

"Let me help with that," Sophia said, stepping forward to fasten the chain around Scott's neck.

"This is the second time you've given this to me," Scott said, fingering the Hebrew-lettered pendant.

"It's a symbol of life." Simon embraced Scott again, clasping him tightly, afraid to let him go.

They began walking down the path, away from the citadel set among the ruddy rocks. Sophia led the way, with Simon's eyes fixed on his grandson as they went by the fortified barrier walls. Scott shut his eyes tight and then blinked them open rapidly, amazed that this was reality and he was here, free of the horrors that had engulfed him for years. He took in the surroundings in total wonderment, as if he didn't fully recall having come to this strange and scenic place. And then he noticed the Bulgarian couple trailing them.

He recognized them immediately. A smile lit his face initially when he saw Ralitsa. Ralitsa, who had warmly welcomed him into her home and who had patiently helped him with his Bulgarian homework—what was she doing here? He wanted to run to her, to hug her and prove that he was okay even after his extended absence.

His initial warmth faded abruptly when he identified the man who stood next to Ralitsa. Vlady, the foul-smelling man who had repeatedly addressed him as his "young American friend" stared at him with a threatening gaze. His presence was bad, very bad news.

"Let's hurry," Scott urged his grandfather, and then without waiting for a reply, he rushed ahead on the descent to the parking lot.

"Wait up," Simon called, unable to keep pace. "Why is he running?" he asked Sophia.

"I don't know." Sophia looked around nervously and spotted the Bulgarian couple farther back on the trail. The man was holding a cell phone to his ear and pointing excitedly at Scott. When Scott started to run, the couple hurried forward as well. "Let's get to the car," Sophia urged Simon.

"Stop!"

At the sound of the familiar voice, Scott stopped in his tracks just inside the entrance gate. Ahead of him was another person from his past, but this woman was even more evil than the man who had forced him to join the smuggling excursions. It was Katya, who had imprisoned him in the remote cabin, lying to him about his family and identity. It was Katya, who, in the guise of helping him recover after his head injury, had in fact been doping him with strong narcotics to prolong his amnesia and intensify his migraines. It was Katya, who had caused him so much pain, and now she, too, had mysteriously appeared to confront him at this mountain fortress. Her arrival with Vlady was a manifestation of his worst nightmares.

"Stay away from me," Scott said sharply, and then he repeated the words in Bulgarian.

"I'm so glad you're all right," Katya replied calmly. "I'm relieved that I found you. I am here to care for you. I've missed you so much. Everything will be okay."

"Stay back," Scott said, raising his hand to ward off her approach.

"You need not fear a thing," she continued. She reached out to touch him, but he pulled away, unwilling to come into physical contact with her.

Simon and Sophia joined them. "Who is this woman?" Simon wheezed, laboring to catch his breath.

"It doesn't matter who this is, we have to leave right now," Scott said, pleading for his grandfather to follow him as he passed through the gate to the parking lot.

Katya screamed after him one more time, but it was not Scott's name she called. Her anguished cry fell on deaf ears.

A few minutes later, they were sitting inside Sophia's car, with the three Bulgarians staring at them from the complex's gate. Sophia fiddled with her key, afraid that the engine would not kick into life.

Seated in the backseat, Scott glanced around the parking lot, at the bored trinket sellers manning the rickety tourist stands and at the other cars. One vehicle was parked parallel to Sophia's. A man was seated in the passenger seat, and as Scott stared at him, his features became clearer and more familiar until full recognition set in with a jolt.

It was Boris! His host father had showed up as well!

Why had everyone suddenly converged at Belogradchik? The answer was clear to Scott, as frightening as it was to accept. They were all here because he alone held the key to the treasure they were seeking. Not that he fully understood, or remembered, how to decipher that key. They were coming after him, and they wouldn't stop until the mystery was solved. No, he couldn't let them get hold of this knowledge; he couldn't surrender the secret to them. Having failed in his delivery mission, he realized that it was now payback time, and Scott feared for his life. It was crucial to escape. Thankfully, this was now possible with the miraculous and timely arrival of his grandfather. He needed to get away.

"Let's go, please let's go," he pleaded to Sophia as she finally started the car and executed a careful reverse.

Simon glanced back at the medieval stone gate where the three

Bulgarians were standing. Beyond them in the distance, he saw the fortifications and the stunning red rock pillars of the mountain fortress. And then Simon glanced at the man sitting in the car next to theirs. It was Scott's host father from the town of Montana. He was here, too! Simon recalled that despite being confined to a wheelchair, the burly man had issued a severe threat, one which Sophia had hesitated to translate. Only reluctantly had Sophia revealed the meaning of those heated words: *When I see Scott again, I will kill him!*

What did these people want from Scott? How had they determined he was still alive after his mysterious disappearance and absence these past three years? What did Scott know that had caused them to follow him to Belogradchik Fortress? Even though his grandson was sitting safely in the backseat, Simon was more worried than ever for Scott's well-being. He had to get Scott out of Bulgaria as quickly as possible.

They pulled out of the lot, and the fortress walls disappeared from view. Sophia shifted into second gear, and the car picked up speed as it descended the winding streets toward the town.

"We need to go after him," Katya said to her companions at the gate, her eyes misty with emotion.

"We'll get him, don't worry about that," Vlady said. "But only when he leads us to what he failed to deliver in the past."

Two shiny black utility vehicles pulled into the parking lot and screeched to a stop where the three of them stood. Four men dressed in identical dark suits jumped out to confront Vlady, Ralitsa, and Katya. Angry words passed back and forth until the men got back into their vehicles and raced off in hot pursuit of the car that had pulled out moments before their arrival.

Part Four: Festival of Roses

CHAPTER 49

At first, Simon hesitated to order the *tarator* soup. The thought of a concoction of yogurt, cucumbers, garlic, and dill didn't appeal to him, and he couldn't imagine that it would soothe his appetite. In general, he was not a fan of cold soups; it was only out of politeness that he would partake of the tomato-based gazpacho offered to him at summertime functions at the university. There was something about the unconsummated expectation of a soup's warmth that bothered him when he took a spoonful of coldish red liquid. Now, sitting in the hotel restaurant for dinner, the white *tarator* that Sophia insisted he try as part of her ongoing introduction to Bulgarian cuisine surprised him with its coolness. It had a calming effect and helped to refresh him after the day's heated excitement. After trying just one spoonful, he nodded in appreciation to Sophia for her suggestion.

Scott would have preferred to head down the street for a Big Mac at the yellow-arched restaurant that symbolized everything American he had lost over the past few years. On the drive back to Sofia that afternoon, he had demonstrated an insatiable appetite when they stopped for lunch, ordering a second portion of *kebap* and finishing—without the slightest trace of embarrassment—Simon's untouched skewer of grilled chicken. Following their lunch, as Simon and Sophia drank herbal tea, they watched Scott fork down two large portions of baklava, and now, at dinnertime, he was again hungry, finishing his meatball soup quickly and then attacking a few slices of black bread while he waited for them to finish their first course.

Scott was quiet as he ate, having spilled most of his story during the journey from Belogradchik. He had started by telling of his relations with the host family in Montana, how he had not gotten along at first with Boris but later joined him on strange—and quite obviously illegal—delivery jobs. Without the slightest hesitation, Scott admitted that he accompanied Boris and Vlady, his neighbor, on their smuggling missions in order to finance a drug habit he couldn't control, and to keep its existence under wraps. If Scott was remorseful for his actions, it was hard to tell.

"I'm clean now," Scott told Simon and Sophia proudly, leaning forward from the back-seat of the car to rub his grandfather's shoulder. "I'm not pleased with what I did, but that's all behind me at last."

Scott spoke of being sent on one final delivery mission, when he was required to bring a priceless item to a contact at the Golden Sands hotel.

"I don't know how to describe it. It was quite old, probably Greek or Roman. Made of silver and covered with decorations. And there was a lion's head at the bottom. I had never seen anything like it."

"That sounds like something we saw at the museum," Simon said, turning to Sophia to confirm the comment.

"Yes, it does sound like a Thracian artifact," Sophia responded. Up until that point she had remained silent, concentrating on every word in Scott's story and eager for him to reveal more of his ordeal. The appearance of the four Bulgarians at the fortress—people who obviously knew Scott and wanted him to accompany them for some reason—troubled her, but she didn't voice her suspicions.

Sophia slowed the car, easing into a lower gear as they fell behind a large truck on the highway.

"You mentioned something with a lion," Simon said, trying hard to recall the museum exhibits he had seen in Vratsa. "There was one item that had been stolen. Didn't it have a lion's head?"

"Yes." Sophia picked up speed to pass the truck.

Scott continued his story, telling about the bus trip to Varna and how a woman had accompanied him to the hotel.

"Katya is Boris's sister, and she was my guardian on the mission. But I fooled her; I fooled everybody, although with disastrous results."

"What do you mean?" Simon asked.

"The hotel manager had my passport," Scott said, not that this information explained anything at all.

"What do you mean he had your passport?" Simon said, turning around to face his grandson.

"I had been there before when I, unfortunately, allowed that man to hold onto my passport in his office. It was being held, almost as ransom, until I delivered that old treasure to him."

"And I thought, the police thought, that the manager found your passport at the hotel after you disappeared!"

"No, he had it and refused to release it." Scott stopped for a minute, regarded a horse and farmer's wagon ambling down the highway as if there were no worries in the world, and then continued. "I decided to pull a trick on him, anything I could do to get my passport back. I refused to hand over the package until he gave me back the passport."

"How could that work? That hotel manager had a mean-looking security guard working for him," Simon remembered from his visit. "Surely they would have just grabbed the package out of your hands?"

"Yeah, for sure. That's why I didn't bring it to his office," Scott said.

"What?"

Sophia looked up at the rearview mirror. Scott's story was filling with details that would be important to recall afterward. She couldn't afford to focus her attention on the black asphalt.

"Let's stop for lunch," she suggested, pulling off the highway. "I know a good *mehana* in this village."

They veered onto a forested side road. Moments after they disappeared from sight among the trees, two black utility vehicles raced down the highway they had just left, speeding toward Sofia farther south.

Seated on the wooden benches inside the rustic pub with its crude smell of alcohol, they ordered lunch and then Scott continued his story.

"I had a friend in the Peace Corps," Scott began. "His name was Lance. Perhaps I told you about him?" he asked his grandfather.

"Yes, of course. I wrote to Lance a few times over these past three years."

"Yes, Lance," Scott said, a sorrowful look in his eyes. "We were working on a community project together, and we hung out a lot. I didn't realize at the time how good a friend Lance was, how much he cared for me. Even though I told him not to, he followed me to Varna when I undertook that delivery. He came to the resort in Golden Sands. He knew I was up to something, that I was doing something dangerous. He only came to protect me, to make sure I was okay."

"What happened?" This time it was Sophia who asked the question.

"When I entered the hotel lobby, Lance was there. It didn't make sense; it just couldn't be. But he was there, waiting for me, willing to do anything to help. Without thinking, I gave him the Adidas gym bag. I told him that I was going in to see the hotel manager. I said I would be right out but made him promise one thing."

"What was that?" Simon asked.

"I made him promise to safeguard that bag with his life should anything happen to me."

"And then you went to the manager?" Simon said, trying to imagine the most likely conclusion of Scott's story. "And he got angry you didn't have the delivery for him?"

"Right. But I never had a chance to get back to Lance in the lobby. One of Nikolov's goons—Nikolov was the manager's name, by the way—one of his security guards took me away and beat me up. That's where I got this," he said, indicating the dented wound on his head.

"What happened to Lance and the gym bag?" Sophia asked, eager for the story to continue.

"What happened to Scott is what I want to know," Simon said, regarding her curiously as if she had missed the whole point of Scott's revelations.

Their lunch was served, and Scott downed a whole bottle of frosty Zagorka beer in one go. He wiped the suds from his lips and attacked his meal with fervor.

It was only over dessert that the rest of Scott's ordeal was revealed. He spoke of his loss of memory, of being transported across the width of Bulgaria by Katya, Boris's sister, and how she had cared for him in a remote cabin in the mountains. Scott spoke of the pain he had suffered but did not mention what Katya had done to prolong his amnesia and his misery. That was something for another time, when all of this was behind him.

"I finally built up my strength and, despite her protests, I made my way from the cabin to Belogradchik," Scott said in conclusion.

"And what's with that gym bag?" Simon asked.

"I've tried to imagine where Lance took it," Scott said. "It's clear that Nikolov didn't get it, nor was it recovered by Boris and Vlady. Otherwise they wouldn't have come looking for me."

"We can just ask Lance!" Simon said. "We'll call him the minute we get back to Sofia."

"There's a problem," Scott said. "One of the first things I did when I went online after leaving the cabin was to check my email. I had hundreds, no, literally thousands of unread messages. I guess my disappearance really caused people to take an interest in me because some of them kept writing to my account. Anyway, I sorted the messages by name and looked for the ones written by Lance. There were a number of emails, but only the first and the last are of interest to us now."

"What are you talking about?" Simon asked.

"The first one was written just a few days after the incident in Varna," Scott explained. "Lance had returned to Sofia, and he didn't have a clue where I had gone. I guess that along with everyone else in the Peace Corps, he assumed that after ditching him at that resort hotel, I had just taken a few days off from my assignments. He was sure I would turn up. No one knew, no one could even imagine, that I had been beaten and nearly killed, and that I had lost my memory and didn't have a clue where or who I was. I still don't fully understand the meaning of Lance's email. Maybe he was pulling my leg, giving me clues as if this were just a game to him."

I have taken the item and hidden it well. It is safe at one of our favorite places. You know where that is.

"What does that mean?" Simon asked, turning to Sophia, but she just shrugged her shoulders.

"I've thought about that a lot over these past few days. *One of our favorite places.* I can only imagine that Lance was referring to a place we went to together in Bulgaria. We toured the country quite a bit, Lance and me. We visited the mountains, the monasteries, and the seacoast. We had quite a number of favorite places, and the first place that came to mind was Belogradchik. One weekend while training in Vratsa, Lance and I visited the fortress. We were accompanied by two young Bulgarians from the town. I fell in love with the place, with its rustic scenery and medieval fortifications. I know Lance enjoyed the fort as well. That was why I assumed he had hidden the gym bag at Belogradchik Fortress."

"So, that's why you went to the fort," Sophia spoke up. "You were looking for the artifact."

"Yes," Scott replied. "But I couldn't find it anywhere. I mean, come on, where in the hell would he hide it? I didn't have a clue where to look."

"So, we'll just ask Lance," Simon suggested for the second time. "Why should this remain a mystery? We'll call him and solve this once and for all, and then we can get you back to the States."

"There was another email," Scott continued quietly. "It was sent only a short while ago. It came from Lance's account, but it wasn't written by him. It was from Lance's mother, writing to all of his friends. She informed us that Lance had been in an automobile accident in Denver. He never had a chance, she wrote. He was driving, and another car, with a drunk driver at its wheel, plowed into him at an intersection. It happened so fast that Lance didn't feel any pain. At least, that was what his mother wrote. I quickly responded with a few words of sympathy. I didn't know what else to write. What can one say in such a case?"

"Lance is dead?" Sophia asked.

"Maybe he took the bag back to the States," Simon said. "We could ask his mother."

"His earlier email, written three years ago while he was in Bulgaria, said that he had hidden it well, and I can only assume that means it's still in the country."

"Well, as interesting as this sounds, we have to get you back to your parents. You've been through quite enough," Simon said.

"No, Grandpa. You don't understand. I'm not going back to the States until I get to the bottom of this. I need to know where Lance hid that bag."

"We'll talk about that later. Let's finish our lunch and get back on the road."

At dinner that evening, Sophia excused herself to go the ladies room to freshen up. Scott gulped down the last of his meal, and Simon sat back to consider his options. There was no question in his mind what he had to do. On the phone earlier, Daniel was thrilled at speaking to his son but insistent that they get on the next flight out of Sofia. Susan was tearful, so emotional that her words were hard to understand, but their meaning was crystal clear. She was overjoyed at reconnecting with Scott in the trans-Atlantic call but could hardly wait to see him in person. "It's a miracle," she kept repeating. Neither Scott nor Simon mentioned the missing artifact or Scott's plans to recover it before he left Bulgaria.

There was also one bureaucratic errand they had to handle before their journey home. Scott didn't have a valid passport. His old one, discovered at the Black Sea hotel, had expired. They needed to visit the embassy to fill out the necessary paperwork for a new one before finalizing flight arrangements. The Americans would be curious about Scott's whereabouts over the past years. Simon hoped there wouldn't be too much time-consuming red tape in the process.

He didn't care about the missing Thracian treasure. Why did finding it matter to Scott so much? Why couldn't the boy forget about it and just hurry back to his parents? Simon saw that he had a serious impediment ahead of him. He wasn't sure how he could convince his headstrong grandson to accept his family's demand that he board the first flight home.

"We have to leave now!"

Simon and Scott looked up in surprise as Sophia approached the table quickly, her eyes wide and serious.

"What's going on?" Simon asked her.

"There are men in the lobby looking for you!"

"Maybe they're from the embassy?"

"No, these are not that kind of men. Come on!"

Simon slapped a few Bulgarian bills down on the table and rose to his feet. Hearing the urgency in Sophia's plea, he followed his grandson and her to the restaurant's back door without another word. They slipped out to the patio and the city park beyond just as the men in dark suits entered the restaurant and began to scrutinize the faces of the diners sitting at the tables.

CHAPTER 50

"So, let me get this straight. You're being pursued by strange, well-dressed men without knowing the reason why, and you're not interested in our protection? Somehow, none of this makes sense."

Simon smiled again at Thompson, the deputy consul at the embassy. How could he explain what was going on, without revealing what was actually going on?

"Maybe I've made it all seem too dramatic," he said, trying to backtrack from his earlier statements. "The important thing is to arrange Scott's new passport so that we'll be able to book our flights."

Simon smiled at his grandson, sitting next to him at the table in the brightly lit office. He was eager to wrap up the bureaucratic paperwork and leave the embassy. There were so many phone calls he wanted to make before they left. All of them would relay the happy news of his having found his grandson. He just worried that he had told Thompson too much and that this would prolong the procedures.

They had arrived at the embassy after having spent the night at Sophia's apartment in the center of the city. There had been no time to check out of the hotel or to retrieve his personal belongings, so they stopped in at a neighborhood pharmacy to purchase toothbrushes and a few other essentials. Simon planned to stop by the Hilton afterward to settle his bill, and hopefully they would be able to book a flight and leave right away.

At first, Thompson couldn't believe it when a clerk informed him that Simon was waiting to meet him and was accompanied by his grandson Scott, whose disappearance three years before had been written off as an unsolved mystery. The deputy consul walked into the room with an incredulous look on his face, eager to see if what he had heard was true.

"We looked everywhere for Scott, and now after you've been here for just a short time, you've managed to find him," Thompson said. "I can't imagine how happy you must be. Your whole family must be ecstatic. Scott, are you sure you're all right? That wound on your head looks pretty bad. How exactly were you injured?"

"I must have fallen," Scott said, searching for the words. "I suffered a bad case of amnesia, so I'm not really sure what happened."

"Your passport was discovered at a resort hotel in Golden Sands. Do you have any recollection of visiting there?"

"That part of my past is completely blank, a total mystery to me." Scott shrugged his shoulders. No need to tell the American official anything more than what was absolutely necessary.

But of course Simon had recently blurted out a report of the incident at the hotel restaurant the previous night. This resulted in Scott casting a stern glance at his grandfather and renewed interest by the American official.

"Why would they be looking for you?" Thompson asked again. "It's obvious that the two of you are in need of our protection. I can arrange for you to stay in a safe house until your flight back to the States."

"We are staying in a safe house," Simon replied quickly, causing Scott to frown at him. "I mean, we're staying with friends. No need for the embassy to worry about us. I'm sure I was mistaken. Those men weren't really looking for us, nor did they mean us any harm. Sorry if I sounded like an alarmist. Please, can we have Scott's new passport so that we can go?"

Thompson cleared his throat and shuffled a pile of papers on the table. "There are some formalities we need to handle," he began. "Forms have to be sent to the States, official documents must be cleared. It's not every day that someone comes back from being presumed dead and requests a new passport. I believe we can have it ready for Scott, let's see, by Tuesday."

"Tuesday!" Simon exclaimed. "We were planning to leave before the weekend."

"I will have to consult with our legal department. Unfortunately, I doubt we can move this through the pipeline any quicker than Tuesday."

"No, that is unacceptable," Simon said, rising from his seat. "It is unacceptable that you can't arrange for us to be on the next flight out of Sofia."

"Grandpa, it's okay," Scott whispered.

"There's something I must explain, Scott," Thompson said, clearing his throat again. "Without a passport, you are basically in Bulgaria without permission. You have overstayed your visa, and the local authorities will not agree to your being here without our official intervention on your behalf. Therefore I must insist that you stay put in Sofia. Again, I strongly suggest that you stay in our safe house. On behalf of the American government, I assure you that we will do our utmost to protect you."

A short time later they were on the street, waiting to hail a taxi. Simon was glad to get out of the embassy yet upset that Thompson had not been more helpful. In the distance, the imposing mass of Vitosha—the mountain massif visible from nearly every part of Sofia—was brightly lit by the morning sunlight.

"They do their utmost to protect you," he said sarcastically. "Where were they for the past three years when you were missing?"

"Grandpa, leave it," Scott said. "They're just doing their jobs. The important thing is that soon I'll get a new passport. We can book our flights for Tuesday afternoon. Don't worry, Grandpa. I'm going home."

Sophia had gone to the university that morning to attend to some of the workload left untouched while she escorted Simon on his journey to Belogradchik. When she returned to her apartment in the late afternoon, she found Simon and Scott already there after having checked out of the Hilton and retrieving Simon's belongings.

"Are you sure it's no problem if we stay here?" Simon asked her again as she set about making them tea.

"No problem at all. I insist," she told them. "What have the two of you come up with? Scott, did you read through all of Lance's emails? Did he leave any other clues as to where he had taken the gym bag?"

"No additional clues," Scott said, sinking deeply into the lumpy brown sofa that took up much of Sophia's modest living room. "I read through all of my old emails, from Lance and from everyone else. It was strange to see that many of my old friends kept writing long after I was presumed dead. Touching, in fact. Anyway, I read all of my old email from Lance, and besides that puzzling message stating that the bag was well-hidden in one of our favorite spots, there was nothing else."

"So, what are we going to do?" Simon wondered.

"It's obvious," Sophia said, serving him his tea and then holding an empty cup out to Scott, who shook his head in refusal of the offer. "We start visiting Scott's favorite places in Bulgaria until we find where Lance hid the bag."

Scott immediately perked up at the suggestion, but Simon looked dismayed. "Why are you suggesting that?" he asked her. "The embassy insisted that we stay in Sofia. Scott doesn't have a visa to be in Bulgaria. And what are our chances of finding this bag?"

"Don't worry about the authorities," Sophia argued. "The two of you will be with me. It'll be okay."

"What about your responsibilities at the university?"

"I arranged everything this morning."

Simon sipped at his tea, which was unsweetened and strong, as he preferred. How was Sophia able to take off so much time from her work to be with them? While he appreciated her willingness to transport him around the country, he couldn't help but wonder why Sophia had taken such a personal interest in their activities. Could it be that she was as eager as Scott to recover the ancient Thracian artifact ?

CHAPTER 51

Rows of proud sunflowers flanked both sides of the road, their bright, eager faces tilted toward the morning sun. From a distance, these fertile fields appeared as patches of brilliant yellow on a green hillside carpet; from up close, it was stunning to see their fiery blooms, golden florets, hairy stems, and large, rough leaves. Katya couldn't remember where she read it, but she had learned that second to corn, sunflowers grown for the oil they provided were Bulgaria's most important summer crop. The sunflower's hardiness and its tolerance for dryness make it suitable to the country's climate, she recalled reading. Planting areas were restricted, though, due to the sunflower's susceptibility to disease and pests. The article, she now remembered clearly, stated that while demand for Bulgarian sunflower oil output was increasing across Europe, local farmers were not always following recommended practices of crop rotation, and this was resulting in decreased output. Advisors from the American Foreign Agricultural Service were helping farmers improve their crop yields. She applauded herself for recalling the main arguments of that scientific essay.

Katya shook her head, chasing away numbers and dry facts to focus on the pure beauty of the flowered scenery as they headed toward the rising sun. Eastward they went, past the villages of

Bulgarski Izvor, Sopot, and Mikre she noted, catching the names on the signposts. Farther east they drove, past the turnoff to Lovech and the exit to Troyan with its famous monastery to the south. The further they drove, the more their destination was a mystery to her. She turned to question Vlady, but her companion concentrated on the road—and specifically on the car ahead of them that they were following surreptitiously.

It was just the two of them on this journey. This was decided following a vociferous argument the previous night, when shouted accusations of culpability for their troubles increased in volume at a direct ratio to the quantity of alcohol consumed. The American, who held the key to the location of the valuable Thracian relic, had stood before them at the *kaleto,* and they allowed him to walk away. Not one of them would take responsibility for letting this happen.

"What did you think, that he would voluntarily return to that cabin in the woods?" Boris shouted, lashing out at his sister for the first time.

"What was I to do?"

"Perhaps she thought he would just blurt out where he hid our package the moment he saw her," Vlady added, swigging back another shot of strong whiskey. "Oh, hello, Miss Katya, the package is on the big bus," he taunted her in broken English.

"I can't believe it," Boris said, his words slurred and spiteful. "You had so many chances to wrench the secret out of him. What a waste! How could you do this to me?"

"He had amnesia," Katya protested. "He didn't remember a thing. I was trying to help him, to assist him in regaining his memory," she said, not revealing the true nature of her actions. "He would have revealed the secret sooner or later if he hadn't escaped."

"Three years!" Boris said, slapping his hand down hard on the wheelchair's armrest. "And yet you let him escape. That's not good enough, my sister."

Then Boris directed his fury at his partner. "What did you expect to happen at the fortress? That wasn't the smartest planning, Vlady. We need to do something more. Otherwise, we'll lose any chance of recovering the treasure. It'll fall into Nikolov's hands for sure. That treasure's ours. We have a right to reclaim it!"

"Oh, we'll get it back," Vlady stated with a confidence that was his alone. He wiped his lips with a cloth handkerchief. "We'll do something, and Katya here will help us. This time we'll do it correctly."

"What do you mean?" Katya asked, apprehensive at what his next words would demand of her.

"You know so much about drugs. You drugged the American for three years. Well, I say we drug the boy again," Vlady started. "We drug him, get him to come with us, get him to talk. He'll confess what we need to know. Surely you have drugs like that in your arsenal."

"I don't know," Katya replied, her mind racing through the implications of what Vlady was suggesting. How did he know that she had forced Scott to take the narcotics? What did he expect her to do now? She turned to her sister-in-law for support. "Ralitsa?"

"This shouldn't have happened," Ralitsa said softly. She didn't expand on what she was thinking.

"We go tomorrow," Vlady said, rising from his seat.

"Where do we go?" Boris asked.

"No, just me and Katya. It will simplify things, make us quicker. Luckily, while the rest of you were standing in the parking lot, openmouthed and frozen to the spot, I was smart enough to write down the license plate of the car in which the American was traveling. As soon as my contact at the police calls me with the address of the owner, we'll find Scott. This time we'll drug him and take him with us. That's the plan."

"Another one of your stupid schemes!" Boris sighed.

"This one will work," Vlady assured him, rubbing the wheelchair-bound man on the shoulder. "Trust me."

The problem was that Katya didn't trust Vlady. She hadn't trusted him for a long time, not since that foggy night, years before, when he had corrupted her beloved husband. It had been before Hristo's ski accident; her husband had been alive but vulnerable. She blamed herself for failing to prevent him from participating in that fateful, illegal nighttime escapade.

Hristo had known for some time that Vlady and Boris were up to no good. But once, Katya recalled, Vlady had been insistent that Hristo's presence on a "fail-safe job" was absolutely necessary. Vlady refused to provide more details of where they would be going or what they would be doing. Katya's misgivings increased when Vlady showed up unannounced at her apartment with Boris to pick up her husband.

"Tell me something, Katya," Vlady said, half serious as he waited for Hristo to get ready. "Is it not true that a person will lose consciousness if he inhales chloroform gas?"

"Yes, everyone knows that. You always see this in the movies."

"And how quickly would a man be knocked out after breathing chloroform?"

"Within a very short while. Why are you asking these questions?"

"Oh, just to improve my knowledge of the sciences," Vlady replied, winking at her.

"*Haide*, Hristo. Let's go," Boris said.

"Just a minute," Hristo called from the other room.

The wire cutters sticking out of her brother's back pocket made Katya nervous. And when Hristo came into the room carrying a ski mask, she felt as if she had just been stabbed.

"Don't worry, sister," Boris said. "We'll make sure Hristo doesn't get into any trouble," he said, but there was a trace of uncertainty in his voice.

Chloroform? A ski mask? Where were the three of them going? What were they planning to do? Why had Hristo agreed to accompany them?

Nothing good would come of this, Katya knew, but she was as incapable of keeping her husband at home now as she was of preventing him from spending the winter season on the slopes. The three men walked out into the fog, leaving Katya alone with her reservations.

Katya tossed and turned, her mind racing with worries about

Vlady's nocturnal schemes and their potentially dangerous consequences. The hands on her bedside clock refused to move. The ticking of its internal mechanism sounded louder than life as the minutes stretched into hours, and the hours became an eternity of sleepless fidgeting. Yet somehow she managed to drift off, because when Hristo stretched out on the bed beside her, she didn't perceive the nervous twitches of his troubled limbs.

If Boris didn't have such a loose tongue, she may never have learned what the three men had done on that foggy night. But a short time later, while enjoying a festive dinner of roasted lamb prepared by Ralitsa to celebrate Palm Sunday, her brother joked with Hristo about how successful their nighttime escapade had been.

"We were in Vratsa, sister," Boris said with a mouthful of food. "Don't worry about your faithful Hristo. He wasn't hanging around with loose women; I can vouch for that."

"What did you do in Vratsa?"

"Maybe you shouldn't be asking this," Ralitsa said quietly.

"No, I want to know. I demand to know."

"We visited a museum," Boris said, laughing.

"Boris!" Hristo said sharply.

"A museum? Wait a minute. I heard on the radio this week that there was a break-in at the regional museum in Vratsa."

"Really?" Boris said, a strange tone in his voice.

"What did you guys do?" Katya asked, turning from her husband to her brother and back again.

Neither of them would supply her with answers. Katya stormed away from the table and went to stand at the kitchen sink.

Ralitsa put down the blue ceramic serving dish she was rinsing and turned to her sister-in-law. "Don't fret about this, Katya."

"Vlady made them do it," Katya said, not bothering to keep her voice low. The fact that she had been unable to prevent her husband from joining the criminal scheme was burning her from the inside.

"I know," Ralitsa whispered back. "And to think that he's forcing Boris to keep it here."

"What are you talking about?" Ralitsa seemed to know a lot more than she did.

"It's in the basement now—the item they stole from the museum. Vlady insisted that Boris safeguard it. Katya, I'm worried. It's stolen property. What if the police came and found it? Boris would be arrested, and I would be an accessory to the crime!"

"What are you women gossiping about?" Boris asked, opening the refrigerator to retrieve two more beers. "Ralitsa, there's nothing to worry about. As for you, my dear sister, stop sticking your nose where it doesn't belong."

It was only later that night, when Katya was alone with her husband, that Hristo confessed to what he had done with Vlady and Boris.

"I thought they were joking," he said, sitting in his armchair and refusing to look his wife in the eyes. "Vlady said there was a huge demand for silver artifacts. We could get a fortune selling the museum pieces, he said. All our financial problems would be solved, and no one would ever know. Vlady had connections with the night security guard. He assured us that the guard could easily be bribed to look the other way, and, well, we had a bottle of chloroform to make sure he wouldn't interfere.

"Everything went according to plan, well, according to Vlady's plan that is," Hristo continued. "Boris cut the wires of the alarm system, we broke the lock on the back entrance, and Vlady used a rag soaked with that gas to knock out the guard. The valuable items in the museum were like candy for the taking. We could have taken so much, but Vlady steered us to the back room, where the Thracian treasures were on display. Those were our real targets, he explained. We would get good money for them, he assured us."

"So, how much did you take?" Katya asked, her voice almost too soft to be heard above her beating heart.

"That's what was strange. I thought we would take everything in sight, as much as we could carry. After all, there was so much silver there, so much gold. But Vlady led us to one specific piece. He was keen and single-minded. It was clear to me that this was not a random robbery. He knew what he was looking for. He knew which piece he wanted."

"And which one was that?"

"The featured item on display was something called the Rogozen Drinking Lion. It was an intricately sculpted piece of silver. It's famous. I think I actually heard about it when that famous professor discovered it a number of years ago. What was his name?"

"Smirnenski."

"Yes, that's the one."

"You stole the Rogozen Drinking Lion!" She was stunned at this news.

"Vlady stole it. Well, him and Boris. I was just there with them, Katya, providing them with cover. I didn't actually touch anything or take anything," Hristo said, proclaiming his innocence.

"Ralitsa said that it's in her basement," Katya said, remembering their interrupted conversation. "What are you going to do with it?"

"What am I going to do with it? Nothing! I'm through with those guys. I'm sorry I ever went with them. I shouldn't have done it, but now it's in the past."

"But that museum piece! It's just sitting in Ralitsa and Boris's house?"

"It's a hot item, too hot to market. When we took it, when Vlady took it, I assumed he already had a buyer lined up. But I guess that deal fell through. Now he needs to keep it out of sight. He said he might bury it, literally, until he can market it safely."

Years had passed since that foggy night when her husband had joined Vlady and Boris on their museum heist, and now Hristo was long gone, victim of a freak tragedy in the Italian Alps. She remembered when Vlady informed Boris that he had finally found a buyer for the Thracian artifact, which led to its being dug up from its hiding place in the family's backyard. Scott, who had been called on to deliver the item to the buyer in Varna, had somehow pulled a fast one on all of them. In the three years of being held as her captive in the mountains, the American had never divulged what he had done with that precious bag.

It was all her fault! She cringed as she recalled Boris's harsh words accusing her of doing this intentionally to harm him. She gingerly touched the scar wounds on her wrist, the visible self-inflicted result of her failure to learn where the bag was located. There was only one way to redeem herself, she realized, and that was by assisting Vlady now. They needed to capture and drug Scott until he spilled the secret of the treasure's location. Sitting in the front seat of Vlady's car, she touched the medicine kit that was resting on the floor between her legs, reassuring herself that she was ready with the necessary supplies.

A short while back they had passed the road signs announcing Sevlievo and Gabrovo, yet they continued eastward. They had been traveling for hours, both of them tired and restless after long stretches of open highway with little traffic. Occasionally Katya glanced at Vlady, as if to ask him if what they were doing was right. He offered nothing to reassure her, no excuses or further explanations. His silence stated clearly that there was no turning back.

The car ahead of them was exiting the highway, and Vlady slowed down to match its speed.

CHAPTER 52

As Sophia drove the car toward their destination, she realized that she didn't recognize the road at all. The villages and towns of the countryside were strangely unfamiliar, and her American passengers certainly couldn't provide any sort of guidance. They passed the turnoffs to Sevlievo and Gabrovo, but her mind went blank at the names. She felt as if she were driving on autopilot with the vehicle steering itself, leaving her no control over gears or brakes. Even though they had determined their destination before leaving, she held the steering wheel tightly in her hands, captive to its whims. Only the full blast of sunlight in her face gave clue to the fact that they were traveling east. Instead of concentrating on the road and the task at hand, Sophia was thinking of other things, other times.

Her thoughts drifted to the Thracian sites of her country, for she knew the tombs and treasures of this ancient people like the back of her hand. She had led university field trips to the Tomb of Sveshtari in northeastern Bulgaria and joined colleagues on the ascent to the acropolis at Peperikon. Her participation on these expeditions was frequently requested due to her vast knowledge of Thracian funeral and burial customs and her particular expertise in Thracian etymology. Her ability to precisely identify and date the relics of this ancient people was in high demand.

Recently she had been called upon to authenticate an inscription discovered at a burial site in the Valley of the Thracian Kings. On a tiny stone slab, at about two centimeters in height and carefully inscribed, a series of Greek characters formed a long word that was apparently not from that language.

"Is this ancient Thracian?" asked the archaeologist in charge of the excavations.

"Let me see," she replied, looking closely.

What was known about the language of the Thracians? Although spoken throughout the Balkans and in Turkey before the rise of the Greeks, the common belief among linguistic scholars was that the Thracians did not enjoy a high literacy rate, and this would account for a lack of written texts in their language. A significant number of Thracians were Hellenized, and the few words that could be attributed to them were transcribed in Greek or Latin letters.

Remarkably, only four Thracian inscriptions of any length had been found in modern times, the most significant of them being a gold ring discovered in the village of Ezerovo in1912. Dated to the fifth century BC, the Greek letters on this ring formed words that bore no resemblance to any known language.

In her studies, Sophia learned that there were more than twenty conjectured translations for the text carved onto the tiny Ezerovo ring, but none of them was universally accepted. The reading of the letters was not difficult—even Sophia was able to decipher them, but their division into words, and what those words meant, was uncertain. As the ring was found alongside a miniature golden spoon, a round bronze mirror, and a broken bronze bracelet, the widely accepted assumption was that it had belonged to a rich, noble Thracian.

Another ancient Thracian inscription, known as the Kjolmen inscription, was discovered in 1965 on a stone plate above a grave in the northeastern village of that name. This inscription, consisting of fifty-six letters, was a bidirectional text known as a *bustrophedon*, in that one line ran from left to right, while the next line contained reversed letters running right to left. According to the translation offered by a prominent linguist, this inscription read:

Ebar (son) of Seza(s) of 58 years lived here. Do not damage this (grave)! Do not desecrate this deceased, for this (the same) will be done to you!

Most of the ancient Thracian texts discovered so far related to their funerary customs. Knowing a few words of the defunct language had been a required part of her studies, although this hadn't been a particularly difficult task as there wasn't much material to consider. Some scholars claimed that a total of only twenty some words could be accurately ascribed to the ancient Thracians, while others argued that the recognized glossary actually consisted of more than a thousand words, however, many of these were personal names or geographical locations. All that modern science knew about the Thracian tongue was based on inscriptions discovered at the burial sites and the few words that had made their way into Greek texts.

"Let me examine the lettering," Sophia said to the archaeologist at the Valley of the Thracian Kings burial site. She examined the stone, carefully wiping away the centuries-old dust. "It reads *Muka-kakaes*, which is a two-component name," she explained. "It means 'man of the clan', or alternatively, it could be translated as 'son of the clan.'"

"Fascinating! So the person buried here was most definitely a member of a Thracian tribe."

She recognized the Thracian origin of the letters and shook her head to confirm this conclusion. Discovered at a burial site that had been partially ransacked during antiquity, the letters were all that bore testimony to the clan that lived in this land more than two millennia before. No additional words were available to shed further light on the ancient tribesman, his people, or their customs. The language of the Thracians, like the Thracians themselves, had vanished from the face of the earth.

"Veliko Tarnovo."

"What?" Sophia asked, jutted out of her Thracian thoughts.

"The sign said Veliko Tarnovo," Simon said, pointing out the car window as they neared the central Bulgarian town predetermined as the day's destination.

"Oh, yes," Sophia replied. She snapped to attention and steered the vehicle toward the exit she had almost missed. Thoughts of the vital undertaking ahead, which would challenge her vast knowledge and expertise, intensified with the urgent necessity of finding the ancient artifact. As she left the highway, she barely glanced at the rearview mirror and its reflection of the car pulling off the road behind them.

CHAPTER 53

Unable to keep up with his grandson's eager pace, Simon stopped to catch his breath and take in the scenery from the drawbridge. A lion captured in relief above the city's shield on a stone pillar marked the beginning of the passage, which led through a series of gates. Ahead was the citadel hill, capped by a domed structure set alongside a singular tower, possibly a church's belfry. The historic site was protected by low fortress walls, and the valleys to its sides were deep. Red-roofed structures perched precariously on the distant slopes above the twisting course of a dark river far below.

"This is the fortress of Tsarevets," Sophia explained when they got out of the car in the center of Veliko Tarnovo. "It served as our capital during the Second Bulgarian Empire of the thirteenth and fourteenth centuries."

"I remember visiting here," Scott noted, impatient to cross the bridge and begin the ascent to the citadel. The stone-walled fortress was very familiar and certainly had been one of the highlights of his travels in the country. "I have a feeling this could have been what Lance was referring to when he wrote that he hid the gym bag at one of our favorite places."

Resting on the drawbridge as his grandson forged ahead with Sophia, Simon recalled his latest phone conversation with Daniel. His son's words continued to damper the excitement of reuniting with Scott. Daniel was clearly upset with how his father was handling things. He argued that Simon wasn't doing enough to get past the bureaucratic red tape at the embassy. When he learned that Scott's return to the States was being delayed, Daniel stated emphatically that he had already started pulling strings. The last thing Daniel told his father was that he had contacted his congressman, extracting a promise to speed up the passport process.

Simon sighed, wary of Scott's insistence at conducting this futile search for a long-lost parcel, far from the relative safety of the Bulgarian capital. Ahead, Scott and Sophia joined ranks with a tour group making its way through the second gate. Surely something would trigger Scott's memory, cluing him in as to why he and Lance considered the historic site to be one of their favorites. And certainly this sign from the past would guide them to the exact spot where Lance had hidden the bag.

Simon walked through the first unimpressive stone gate and continued toward the next one. He adjusted his baseball cap and leaned down to caress an aching leg muscle. His throat was dry, and he was sorry that he hadn't accepted Sophia's suggestion that he carry his own water bottle. He approached the second gate where a flash of fabric caught his eye.

"Welcome to the ancient stronghold of Tsarevets, home of Kaloyan, tsar of the Second Bulgarian Kingdom between the years 1197 and 1207. It was Kaloyan who conquered many lands of both the Ottomans and the Hungarians. It was Kaloyan who captured Baldwin, emperor of the Crusaders' Latin Empire who ruled from Constantinople. Kaloyan extended the political power of the Bulgarians and is considered one of our greatest emperors."

The lines were chanted in singsong fashion by an elaborately costumed marionette, almost life-size, sitting on a cardboard throne alongside three other similarly dressed puppets propped up against the shadowed inner wall of the gate. The bearded puppet, whose lips moved in synchrony with the recorded words, wore a gold-plated shield over his long red robe, and a round silver-foil crown rested atop his black hair. To the side, temporarily at rest from the demands of string and wire, was a female marionette, quite obviously the queen, regally gowned and crowned with jewel-like plastic beads. Her heavily made up face was stiff and expressionless.

A man stationed behind a black box to the side pulled the strings, controlling his actors and playing their scripts in turn. The man winked at Simon, instinctively knowing to play the tape in English.

Simon took comfort in the shade and smiled at the man and his costumed wooden charges.

"I will relate the tale of Baldwin and the Bulgarian queen. While being held captive at Tsarevets Fortress, in the tower just yonder that still bears his name, Baldwin fell under the charm of our queen and tried to seduce her. When Tsar Kaloyan discovered this, he put the Latin Emperor to death and turned his skull into a drinking cup. Kaloyan defended the queen's honor; yes, he defended the honor of all Bulgaria."

Simon dropped a few coins into the puppeteer's upturned hat and continued through the gate. He walked past an artist's rendition of what the famous fortress had looked like when it served as capital of the Bulgarian kingdom. The path continued to ascend, snaking back and forth toward the hill's summit. He lost sight of Scott and Sophia but assumed they were heading to the top, to the most strategic place in the fortress. Logic determined that the crest of the hill was the best place to scout out the entire site.

Simon realized that despite the pressure he was feeling in his legs, not exactly painful yet noticeable just the same, he would need to hurry to follow them. He couldn't afford to let this mystery be solved without him. He needed to see what Scott would see, to understand the purpose of this quest. He continued toward the summit, concentrating on nothing more than putting one foot ahead of the other.

"Grandpa, I can't believe you made it!" Scott exclaimed when he saw his grandfather arrive at the white steps leading to the church's entrance. "I thought you would have waited for us at the bottom."

Simon didn't reply for a minute. He thanked Sophia for her offer of water and drank vigorously before speaking. "What are those for?" he asked in a short breath, pointing at three enormous bells set in wooden frames at the side of the path.

"There's a sound and light show here every night," Sophia replied. "It uses lasers, dramatic lights, and music—and those bells as well—to tell the story of Veliko Tarnovo's fall to the Ottomans. It's really quite a fascinating show. We could see it tonight if you want."

Scott looked around nervously, searching for the clue that would redeem their visit to the medieval fortress. He took a sip of water from his own bottle and paced back and forth across the plaza.

"There's not too much here," Simon noted, impressed at the scenery but finding it strangely lacking. He wasn't sure if he could put his finger on what was missing.

"That's true," Sophia said. "Most of the grandeur of Tsarevets Fortress has been destroyed. This church, the Patriarchal Cathedral of the Holy Ascension of God, is actually quite new, constructed in the 1970s and '80s on the site of a fourteenth-century church."

"I'm not seeing anything," Scott said. "Nothing that can shed light on the past."

"Think of what you did here with Lance," Simon suggested, as he screwed the cap back onto the plastic water bottle.

"My mind is blank."

"Maybe from the tower you'll see something," Sophia said. "At least from up there you'll have a view over everything."

"Something is bound to help you remember," Simon agreed.

They left the plaza and circled round to the back of the cathedral. The bell tower, a rarity among Balkan churches, according to Sophia, jutted prominently into the bright blue sky. High above, a row of colorful pennant flags fluttered in the breeze. Only the shrill call of a solitary lofty hawk disturbed the silence of the citadel's summit.

"Let's go up," Scott said, continuing toward the wooden door at the tower's base.

"I'll stay below," Simon replied. "I can't make that sort of climb."

"Simon, there's a lift that goes to the top," Sophia said, extending her hand to assist him.

The elevator was operated by a short, stubby man sitting inside it on a wooden stool. He welcomed them with an outstretched hand and a toothy grin. Sophia spoke to him, and Simon immediately understood that there was a demand for payment.

"How much?"

"Three leva a person," Sophia replied.

Simon paid the money, and they squeezed inside the cramped elevator as its operator shut the door. A motor jerked into operation and then settled into a low drone as it lifted them from the ground to the tower's pinnacle three floors above the plaza.

Sweat broke out on Simon's forehead. The closeness inside the cage left him standing almost on top of Scott. He was embarrassed that his arm was leaning into Sophia, and he moved backward, trying to give her more space. The elevator operator hummed to himself—or was that the motor? Simon shifted his weight from one leg to the other; the action resulted in a nervous ting, causing him more discomfort. There was little air in the lift, making it hard to breathe. The upward journey went on and on, and the claustrophobic sensation was getting worse. Something caught in his throat; his eyes began to tear. With a shutter, the elevator's climb came to a halt, and the operator swung a large metal lever. The door creaked open to a stream of welcome daylight.

"Wow, look at the view!" Scott exclaimed, bolting forward to a gap in the tower's crenellations.

Simon leaned back against the elevator door at the side of the narrow platform. His breath came in short gasps, and he felt lightheaded. He couldn't find the strength to join his grandson at the battlement wall.

"Scott, I'm going back down," he wheezed. He stepped back into the safety of the small box, to the surprise of its operator.

"Simon, are you okay?" Sophia asked with concern.

"I'll wait for you at the bottom," Simon stammered, and then the elevator doors banged shut.

Going down was better than going up. Alone with the operator, Simon had more space, allowing him to stand comfortably. It was still an ordeal, however, and he closed his eyes, silently counting the seconds until they reached the plaza level.

The purr of the motor eased off, and with a bump, the elevator stopped its descent. The operator reached for the lever and pulled it slowly. The door opened.

Before Simon had a chance to step out to the plaza, he was pushed backward with brute force. Two very impatient people couldn't wait for him to emerge from the lift. They shoved him repeatedly, elbows bumping into his and limbs colliding. Simon felt a sharp pain in his knee and someone stepped down sharply on his foot.

"Excuse me!" he cried out, reaching out to protect himself. His baseball cap fell from his head and came to rest on one of the lift's levers. The operator sat motionless on his stool, doing nothing to help Simon leave the elevator.

One of the intruders was a woman. Her curly hair brushed against his face, an almost pleasant sensation despite the circumstances. In the split second that they made eye contact, he witnessed a crazed madness unlike anything he had ever seen. It was as if she could see him and see through him—and as if she didn't see him at all. He didn't have time to consider this strange impression, because to his horror, he noticed the woman's hand held high. She wielded a long syringe in a menacing manner. Her mouth opened, and she cried something unintelligible as she moved forward to strike.

CHAPTER 54

From atop the belfry tower, Scott took in his surroundings, trying to envision them in the mind's eye of the past. The quaint wooden houses of Veliko Tarnovo, perched precariously on the sides of the hills, seemed poised to leap down to the dark waters of the Yantra River, snaking through the valley. At the center of the panorama was the Cathedral of Sveta Bogodoroditsa, rising majestically above the other historic buildings. The town was famous to Bulgarians not only for its medieval fortress, but also because it had hosted the drafting of the country's first constitution in 1879. In Suedinenie Square, the National Revival and Constituent Assembly Museum was a popular tourist attraction. Other colorful buildings stood out in the dramatic view, all calling out for attention.

In another direction, Scott spotted an oversized Bulgarian flag flapping noisily in the wind above a reconstructed fortress building. The horizontal bands of white, green, and red competed for dominance against the cloudless blue sky.

"There's nothing here," he said dejectedly, gazing at the distant town from his vantage point in a crenel of the tower's outer wall. His memories, clouded by an extended period of drug-induced amnesia and headaches, were unable to offer any clues as to what he might have seen back then. Something from the past was key to discovering where Lance had hidden the artifact, but he couldn't figure out what it was.

"I can't imagine what we were thinking when we came here. I can't remember a thing."

"Let me try to help your memory," Sophia said, standing to his side. "We'll do word associations. I'll say a word, and you'll reply with the first thing that comes to your mind."

"I'm not in the mood for games."

"This is not a game. We're trying to force your mind to make connections, to figure out what you can't get to consciously. Are you willing to try?"

With his grandfather having descended to the plaza, Scott nodded his agreement to Sophia's suggestion with hesitation.

"Sofia," she said, as they began to stroll around the platform again, the views no longer capturing their attention.

"Sofia?"

"Yes, Sofia. You know? The capital of our country?"

"Sofia?"

"Yes."

"I think of you."

"What?"

"Sofia. Sophia. The names are so similar."

"Come on, Scott. Be serious. We are doing this for a reason."

"Okay, sorry."

"Sofia," she repeated.

"Pubs," he responded quickly.

"Pubs?"

"Yes, sorry, but that's the word that pops into my mind."

"Varna."

"Beaches."

"Burgas."

"Burgas? I never went there," he said.

"Really? You should. Burgas is very nice."

"Maybe, someday. Should we go down?" he asked, completing their circuit of the platform. He pushed the elevator button.

"Plovdiv," Sophia continued.

"Paintings."

"Paintings?"

"Yeah," Scott said, trying to think how exactly this word was connected to the second largest city in Bulgaria. "Oh, I know. We took a walk through Old Town Plovdiv, you know, the old, colorful houses on the hill. I was with Lance and some others from the Peace Corps. We stopped in at a few of the house museums—those old houses from the last century that became museums, telling the story of your country's revolution or something. Some of them were art galleries, and I recall seeing many paintings on the walls. So, when you say Plovdiv, I think of paintings."

"Okay, Scott, that's nice," she said. "But could you think of using the word 'favorite' and Plovdiv in the same sentence?"

"No, I don't think so. This isn't really working, is it?"

"The elevator is so slow."

"I wonder if the operator fell asleep," Scott said, laughing. "It's kind of funny to need an operator for such a small elevator. I guess that's just another example of Bulgaria providing jobs for its citizens."

"Your grandfather didn't look so well."

"He probably had a claustrophobic reaction to being confined in such a small space. I'm a bit worried about him."

Scott went over to the platform's parapet wall and stuck his head through one of the gaps. He realized he was on the far side of the tower, so he walked around to the opposite section. Again he stretched forward.

"I can't see him. I can't see anyone in the plaza." Scott looked at her nervously and then leaned out again. "I wonder where he went. Grandpa!" he called, his voice catching in the breeze but bringing no response from below.

"Maybe he's resting in the shade. Should we continue our word associations?"

"No, I don't think so."

Scott circled the platform, looking through different vantage points at the plaza below. Sophia pressed the elevator button repeatedly.

"I hope the lift's not broken."

"Do you think it's stuck?" Scott asked her. "Wait, isn't that the elevator operator?"

The short, stubby man who had pulled the lever to close the lift's doors and set the motor into action could be seen running across the plaza toward the path that led to the church.

"Something happened. We need to get down there to help Grandpa."

"Hey!" Sophia called out, but the elevator operator didn't hear, or didn't care to answer. What had happened to Simon? His breathing had been shallow and forced when he emerged from the elevator. Had he suffered a heart attack? Was the operator running to get medical assistance?

Sophia punched a number into her cell phone and spoke quietly before frowning at the reply she heard. She joined Scott as he overlooked the plaza. What she saw next deeply disturbed her.

Four men dressed in dark black suits were striding across the pavement, heading toward the door at the foot of the tower. Intent on their unstated purpose, the men didn't glance sideways or up at the tower. This was not a team from Veliko Tarnovo's ambulance service. Instinctively, Sophia knew who—and what—they were seeking.

Three stories below, Simon slumped on the floor of the tiny elevator cage, unable to move. The weight of the unconscious stranger sprawled on Simon's legs was painful, but he couldn't shift his muscles to gain relief. The woman's wailing didn't ease his concerns, and she ignored his pleas for assistance. The operator had run off across the plaza, and there was no way to contact Scott and Sophia. How had he ended up trapped like this?

The struggle at the elevator's door had been sudden and unexpected. Out of the corner of his eye, Simon perceived the syringe wielded by the woman, and he raised his arm to guard against the threat. At the same time, he struggled with the man, who shoved him back against the cold hardness of the lift. He couldn't fight them both off; he couldn't escape their reach. He tried to shout, but his voice—like his strength—was totally sapped by the brutal assault.

And then the syringe plunged down, connecting with flesh and releasing its potent liquid content.

There was no pain because there had been no prick of a needle. Instead of burrowing into Simon's flesh, the syringe punctured the shoulder of the male assailant. The Bulgarian let out a cry and a string of irate curses.

The woman backed out of the elevator, and the man fumbled with his cell phone, frantically stabbing the buttons. Simon found breathing space as the pair eased back from the confrontation, but this freedom was not to last. The man completed his call and stared at Simon with unfocused eyes. Before Simon could do anything to prevent it, the man's weighty frame collapsed on top of him, constraining him on the elevator floor.

"Get my grandson and Sophia!" he pleaded, trying to indicate with hand motions the fact that they were atop the tower. "Help!" he called out, but the word barely escaped his dry throat. He couldn't move. He felt his leg falling asleep from trapped nerve endings. "Scott! Sophia!"

The woman sat outside on the steps, sobbing uncontrollably.

Katya grasped her left wrist tightly, the sharp pain from where she had just pierced into the flesh with her long fingernails only partially the reason she was crying. It wasn't supposed to have happened like this. Everything had gone wrong, and it was all her fault!

She had accompanied Vlady to Tsarevets, prepared to carry out their plan to drug Scott and bring him back for the questioning that would force him to divulge his secret. She had chosen propofol, a short-acting hypnotic agent used to induce a state of total unconsciousness prior to the administration of an inhaled general anesthesia in operating rooms. The drug was also used in procedures for sedation and would be sufficient to knock Scott out for a short time—or at least inhibit his ability to resist them. Vlady was strong enough to drag Scott back to the car on his own; she would assist if necessary. She didn't foresee any problem administering the drug. All that she needed was to get close enough to inject it.

They had trailed Scott and his companions through the fortress complex all the way up to the church tower at the summit. She had seen Scott go into the elevator with two other people, and she was ready for his return to the plaza. When the elevator door opened, she had the syringe out and primed, prepared to use it before Scott realized what was happening.

The next moments were very confusing. As Vlady forced his way into the elevator, she tried to position herself near Scott's arm. Vlady pushed forward, but someone inside the elevator was resisting, muttering in English. She barely noticed the lift's operator sitting frozen on his stool as she lifted her arm, ready to strike at Scott with the syringe. With all the commotion, she couldn't precisely spot her target.

Everything happened as if in slow motion. There was Scott, surprised at the assault, but it wasn't really Scott. No, it was someone else, not the person she sought, not the individual whose existence she needed to reclaim. She blinked, her vision adjusting to the reality of the tight elevator cage, and her eyes widening with a mental picture that only she could see. She needed to act, to rescue the person dearest to her. She would do anything for him, anything to save him.

"Hristo," she gasped.

Just as she plunged the syringe into flesh, releasing its liquid into an expanse of someone's shoulder, she realized with a jolt that the person in the elevator was neither Scott nor her beloved husband. But it was too late. The drug had already begun to work its wonders.

"What the hell?"

Vlady regarded her with a far-off look in his eyes. He shouted at her, cursing as he nursed the inflamed spot where he had been stabbed by the needle. His pupils lost their focus, growing smaller by the second. He stuck his free hand into his pocket to retrieve a cell phone. Wobbling on his feet, Vlady juggled the instrument, twisting it around to see the illuminated display. He punched only one button, but it was enough to establish a speed-dial connection. He barked some words into the phone and then fell backward, slowly, as if he had all the time in the world, until he finally collapsed on the older American man inside the cage. And then he lost consciousness.

She sat on the steps sobbing, a sense of total failure overwhelming her. Tears poured from her eyes as she realized that she was incapable of handling even the simplest tasks. Her efforts to give Scott back his health had failed, and now she had missed her one chance at redemption. The damage she had caused was irreparable, and she wondered how Boris would react to yet another betrayal. Ignoring the mumbling of the elderly American man inside the elevator, she wiped the blood from her injured wrist, her body shivering despite the warm sunlight.

And that is where Nikolov's men found her.

CHAPTER 55

"Get out of our way!" one of the four sharply dressed men barked at her.

"What are you doing here?"

"Where's the boy?" the man continued impatiently. He had yet to notice Vlady's slumped form inside the open elevator.

"The boy? What boy?" she said, rising slowly to her feet.

"We know he's here. We were informed."

"No, I don't know."

"Move aside, we're going up to the tower."

And that was when they became aware of the two bodies inside the elevator, one of them unconscious and the other one calling for help.

"Is he dead?"

"Of course not. It was a mistake! I never meant to inject him with the drug."

"Lady, I don't know what the hell you're talking about."

The men took no notice of the American's pleas for assistance as they dragged Vlady's limp, heavy body out of the elevator and carried him down the steps to the shade at the far side of the plaza. One man checked Vlady's pulse and another held a hand over Vlady's mouth and nose, searching for signs of life. It was obvious the men had no medical training.

"Leave him alone!" Katya screamed, but in fact she was relieved that they had arrived to care for Vlady. Since mistakenly striking him with the syringe, she had fallen to pieces. She knew she wouldn't be able to deal with Vlady's fury when he regained consciousness; he was sure to lash out at her. And when he realized that he was dealing with Nikolov's men, he would become hysterical. It was all her fault, she thought. The sharp edges of her fingernails dug even deeper into the flesh of her left wrist. She winced at the pain.

"Who are you people?" The American struggled to his feet at the elevator doors. He seemed almost a cripple, with one of his legs dragging behind him and a lack of balance making his efforts clumsy and ineffectual. He called out to them again but was ignored.

Katya's breathing returned to normal as the men doused Vlady's face with cold water. But as she began to calm down, new worries emerged. It was obvious that Nikolov's men had followed them as they searched for Scott, first to Belogradchik and now here to Tsarevets. She assumed that Vlady had tried to lose the tail, but within a few short minutes after his collapse, they had arrived unexpectedly. Their sudden appearance raised many questions, and she struggled to comprehend what was happening.

Who had Vlady called after she injected him with the propofol? Had he tried to call for an ambulance as he became faint? Or had he warned someone of his predicament? Her mind raced, ready to reach conclusions but fearful of the consequences of what she was thinking. No, that was too inconceivable, she concluded. She shook her head, forcing herself to dismiss such disloyalty from her head.

The efforts to assist Vlady were interrupted by the arrival of two more men. Unlike the four who preceded them, these arrivals were dressed in white. They were paramedics, carrying medicine kits and equipment. Immediately they launched into action, not waiting for Katya or anyone else to explain the situation. They leaned over Vlady's body and gave him their undivided professional attention. Moments later, a stretcher was readied, and Nikolov's men offered to assist in moving Vlady's body. The medics snubbed them and carried

Vlady's weight by themselves.

Without giving another thought to the American man who had emerged from the elevator, or to the original point of her visit to the Tsarevets Fortress, Katya followed the medics and Nikolov's men down the path to the ambulance.

Simon stepped out of the elevator, and the door snapped shut behind him. He was alone on the plaza, stunned that he had survived the strange assault. His surroundings bewildered him; he couldn't remember exactly when and where he had separated from his grandson and Sophia. But then they emerged from the elevator to comfort him after his traumatic ordeal.

"I feel much better now," Simon said, trying to reassure Sophia and Scott as they drove out of Veliko Tarnovo a short while later. "Why didn't you call the police to report this incident? It was quite serious. That woman's eyes were crazed, and I thought she was actually going to kill me."

"You have to realize that not every matter in this country is one that needs police involvement," Sophia said, her eyes fixed on the road.

"Calling the police would have meant involving the American embassy," Scott offered from the backseat. "Don't forget, I don't have official permission to be traveling around."

Simon closed his eyes, stressed at his growing difficulties handling these Bulgarian escapades. First, there had been the unpleasant incident of fainting in Sophia's apartment. Then the painful fall at the Rila Monastery; the bruises from that were still clearly visible on his face. All the walking was resulting in leg pains that just weren't going away. And now the strange sensation of claustrophobia in the tight quarters of the elevator and the frightful attack by a lunatic, syringe-wielding woman. His nerves couldn't take any more surprises. The search for Scott and the subsequent wild-goose chase on which they had embarked demanded more than his tired body had in it.

Daniel was right. It was time to go home. Simon had come to Bulgaria to find Scott, and he had been successful in this mission—more successful than anyone, even he, could have imagined. It was time to cut the sightseeing short and return to the States. He had no patience for Scott's attempts to find something that had been lost at the time of his disappearance, and which held no value for Simon. What chances did they have of finding this bag anyway? Why had Scott's friend bothered to hide it? None of this made sense, and understanding the answers was not important to him. He was drained from so many mixed emotions. He needed to take Scott home to his parents. He was tired, so tired of everything.

When Simon began to snore, Sophia turned from the steering wheel to gaze at the wrinkles of worry forming on his brow. As she drove south, she was engulfed with her own inner turmoil. She was troubled by what she had seen in the plaza on the citadel hill. The black-suited men's arrival was an ominous sign. Even though the men had walked off with Simon's assailant, Sophia knew they had come for Scott. They had followed him to Tsarevets, and, just by chance, they had been called off the pursuit at the last moment.

She checked her mirrors but didn't spot any suspicious cars on the highway. But she knew they were there. Somewhere they were watching them, following them. How else did those men happen to appear at Tsarevets? And how else had they trailed them to Belogradchik before that? Every move Sophia and her companions took was being observed. There was only a slim chance that they had made their departure from Veliko Tarnovo undetected. She needed to take precautions, to stage some sort of diversion. That was why she had decided to drive south instead of directly back to the capital. She hoped the detoured route would rid them of those who sought Scott's secret as much as she did.

It was clear that everyone was after the treasure that Scott's friend had hidden somewhere in the country. What could she do to get Scott to divulge more than he had already disclosed? She had tried word associations; she had suggested possible sites to visit. Scott had undergone quite an ordeal over the past three years, but now that he had recovered and his mind was lucid, there had to be a way to get him to remember!

Time was running out, she knew. In just a few days, Scott and his grandfather would leave for the States. The mystery of where the Thracian artifact was located would remain just that—a mystery. The priceless piece, described so vividly by Scott, and so familiar to her from her studies and many visits to the museum in Vratsa where it had been displayed, was something that demanded recovery. It was the leading Bulgarian treasure, the silver item that tied her country to the glorious days of its ancient past. It was the essence of everything she had studied and was symbolic of her entire academic career.

It wasn't just her professional, academic interest in the artifact's historic value or her charitable concern for Simon and his grandson that propelled her forward. Her aim in this journey was not solely to make sure Simon had a happy ending to his visit. She had other motives in mind, of which her American travel partners had absolutely no knowledge. There were objectives for her actions that she couldn't disclose. She needed to discover where the lion-headed *rhyton* was hidden. She needed to find it! It was imperative that she succeed in this mission.

"You know, maybe those word associations could help after all," Scott said, surprising her with the suggestion.

She looked at him in the rearview mirror. With her own eagerness to locate the artifact, she had forgotten that Scott wanted to resolve the mystery as well. This time, instead of naming Bulgarian cities, she decided to try objects that were unique or special to the country.

"*Shopska*."

"Salad!" he replied, laughing. He moved forward slightly to check the passenger in the front seat, but his grandfather's sleep was undisturbed by the laughter.

"*Rakia*," Sophia offered.

"Ah, *rakia*! The Bulgarian national drink."

"Did you drink any?"

"Of course! When I first stayed with Ralitsa and Boris, they introduced me to homemade *rakia*, which he concocted in large plastic barrels in their cellar. Boy, that was strong! Boris and his friend Vlady made me drink glass after glass of the stuff before we went out on their smuggling missions."

"Did you like *rakia*?"

"Not really. It was like drinking pure alcohol. I'll stick with beer, vodka, and gin."

"So, what word comes to your mind when I say *rakia*?"

"Bagpipes," he replied.

"What?" She regarded him through the mirror with a curious look. "What are you talking about?"

"Bulgarian bagpipes are cleaned with *rakia*. Didn't you know that? Lance and I learned about it during our Peace Corps days," he said, laughing.

"Really?" Could that possibly be true? She tried additional words in succession, hoping to force Scott's memory. *Horo*, snow, *banitsa*, sunflowers, cherries. Nothing she said brought meaningful responses. She was about to give up when she tried the name of another flower, not expecting that it would result in a significant reply.

"Roses," she said.

"Roses!" Scott sat up straight in his seat. The word conjured up more than he had imagined. It brought to mind a specific town in the center of the country, one to which he had traveled with Lance three years before. The festival, the girls, the beers, the costumes, the roses. There was a small café, where he sat with Lance enjoying the sounds and sights of the festivities. It was a small town, as quaint as any they had visited. The people were simple, the enjoyment complete. Lance remarked that they had come to one of his favorite places in all of Bulgaria.

Roses! Scott now knew where they should go.

"How far is it to Kazanlak?" he asked Sophia, causing her to look up at the rearview mirror and stare at him with growing understanding.

CHAPTER 56

In central Bulgaria, lying between the Balkan Range and the Sredna Gora mountains is a long fertile plain known as the Valley of Roses. Due to the high quality of its roses, mastered over centuries of dedicated cultivation, Bulgaria is one of the world's largest exporters of rose oil, used in the production of perfumes, beauty creams, chocolates, liquors, and jams. There is even toothpaste made from roses.

An enormous quantity of rosebuds is required to produce a minuscule amount of the valuable fluid. To extract one kilogram of this precious liquid, three thousand kilograms of rose petals are needed. Because of this, rose oil is three times more expensive than gold.

"We saw them harvesting the roses in the early-morning hours," Scott told them as they drove down from the mountain pass into the valley. "Mostly Roma were doing the work. Grandpa, do you know who the Roma are?"

"The gypsies?" he asked.

"Yes, there are quite a lot of them in Bulgaria. They get up before dawn to pick the petals at exactly the right time. It's quite a fascinating sight to see the moist flowers sparkling in the first rays of the rising sun. They need to be picked very early in the day because the oil evaporates in the sunlight. The bushes are head-high; you should see them! Young women pick the buds, drop them into these huge baskets, and then they're carried away on donkey back to distilleries. It's very picturesque, all that manual work, almost like a scene out of another century. And they have this festival every year to celebrate the harvest. It's in the town we're going to, Kazanlak."

"The annual festival is taking place now," Sophia added for Simon's benefit.

"I'm absolutely sure that Kazanlak is where we need to go," Scott said again. "Kazanlak is the place that Lance referred to as being our favorite."

"It's getting late," Simon said. His argument suggesting an immediate return to Sofia had already fallen on deaf ears. Sophia said there was no chance they'd be able to get back to the capital before dark, and Scott was anxious to get to the town where he was sure Lance had hidden the gym bag. Simon was tired, from both the physical exertions required by this journey and from dealing with his grandson's exuberance at solving this mystery. "Where will we stay?" he asked.

"My cousin lives in Kazanlak," Sophia replied. "He'll be happy to put us up for the night."

And that was how they found themselves, two hours later, sitting at a wooden table behind Sophia's cousin's home, their appetites growing as mouthwatering aromas rose from a brick barbecue. The son of Sophia's uncle on her father's side, Ivan Petrov was a jovial man with a large potbelly who enjoyed entertaining as much as he enjoyed eating. And he apparently ate a lot. He welcomed Simon and Scott into his home with open arms and greeted his cousin with a warm embrace that lasted a bit longer than Sophia appreciated. More than anything else, Ivan was excited to have a chance to practice his rudimentary knowledge of English.

"You come, eat," he said, waving them into his tree-lined backyard. "I make good food on fire, see?"

"Thank you for your kind hospitality," Simon responded.

"Hospital? No, no hospital," Ivan said with a frown.

Sophia explained what Simon had meant, and this caused Ivan's face to light up with understanding.

"I grill good food. You like pork? I make good pork."

"My grandfather doesn't eat pork," Scott said.

"Actually, I don't mind," Simon said, embarrassed that his grandson was reminding him about Jewish dietary laws.

Scott looked at his grandfather curiously, but Simon didn't think this was the appropriate time or place to explain himself. He smiled at Ivan, and it was clear to him that their host's mind was at work, searching for a solution that would please his guests.

"I grill good chicken? You like chicken?"

"Yes, that will be fine," Simon said.

As they waited for the meal to cook, Scott sat at the table next to a large bowl of cherries, popping one after another into his mouth. "You've got to try them, Grandpa," he said. "They're delicious."

"I don't particularly like cherries. There's too much work involved, spitting out the pits and all."

"Come on, Grandpa. Don't be such a sourpuss. If you've never tried a Bulgarian cherry, you don't know what the fruit is all about."

Reluctantly, Simon reached into the bowl of ripe, red fruit—some of them nearly the size of golf balls—and picked out a cherry still attached to its tiny stem. He took a bite, and a burst of sweetness brought sudden, intense pleasure to his mouth. The cherry was so meaty, so full of sugary charm that he couldn't help but take another one.

"I told you," Scott said, laughing. "There's nothing like the cherries in this country. And They're addictive. You just can't stop eating them."

Sophia was standing next to the grill talking with her cousin, so Simon took the opportunity to raise a touchy subject with his grandson.

"Listen, Scott, there's something I've been meaning to say to you," Simon began, hopeful his grandson wouldn't think he was lecturing him. "It's time for you to go home, especially after the ordeal you've been through. Your father doesn't have a clue what we're doing here in central Bulgaria, what we're looking for. And if he knew, he certainly wouldn't approve."

"I'm not asking for his approval."

"Scott, don't you realize this is all a terrible waste of time? Seriously! It's been three years since you handed that bag to Lance, and now that we've learned he was killed in a car accident, we'll never know where he hid it."

"Grandpa, we're already in Kazanlak, the favorite place to which Lance was referring. Tomorrow we'll continue and complete the search."

"That message, about hiding it in your favorite place, it doesn't offer much help. Face it, even if he hid the gym bag in this town, you don't have a single clue where to start looking. It wouldn't be hidden in plain sight. It must be buried somewhere or stored in some safe location. Scott, admit it. You're looking for a needle in a haystack."

"Grandpa, I'm sure we'll find it. Trust me. There was a bit more to Lance's message than just stating it was hidden in our favorite place. I never informed you or Sophia about the rest of what he wrote to me."

"What? You mean you know more than what you've been telling us?"

"I didn't want to get you too worried," Scott said, lowering his head so that Sophia and her cousin wouldn't overhear their conversation. "Trust me. I just know that we'll figure this all out tomorrow."

"I'm not so sure."

"Grandpa, I've changed a lot over these past three years. I doubt my parents will even recognize me. When I came to Bulgaria, and even during my stint in the Peace Corps, I really wasn't me. Face it, I was addicted. I was a drug addict. But going through this ordeal, I've totally changed. Grandpa, I suffered a lot. This gaping dent on my forehead is a constant reminder of what I went through. All that time of not knowing, not remembering, it was horrible. But I came through it. I survived, and I'm a better person for it."

Scott rubbed his grandfather's arm for a moment before

continuing. "Hold on just a little bit longer. We'll find the gym bag tomorrow, head back to Sofia, and then fly home. It'll all be okay."

"Dinner food is served!" Ivan announced proudly, bringing a huge platter of barbecued chicken to the table. His wife, a pleasant woman who didn't understand a word of English, spread before them a variety of salads in colorful Bulgarian ceramic dishes. Ivan snapped open several bottles of beer. "How you say in English, dig up!"

"Dig in," Scott corrected him.

"So, how you like Bulgaria?" Ivan asked Simon after a huge amount of food was consumed, and they sat completely satiated around a table cluttered with chicken bones and dirty plates.

"You have a beautiful country," Simon replied. "We've encountered some interesting people here," he said, thinking about what had happened to him at Tsarevets Fortress.

"We have good people," Ivan admitted.

"Simon, you need to understand something," Sophia said, searching for words. "Just like every country, Bulgaria has its good people and its bad people. Don't take your attackers at Tsarevets as examples of what we're like. We're similar to every nation. We have our ups and downs. And we're playing a huge game of catch up with the world. Look at how far we've come. We only became a democracy less than twenty years ago."

"I understand all that," Simon replied. "Don't worry. I'm not making rash judgments based on a few bad apples. On the whole I've found Bulgarians to be very friendly, open to visitors, and proud of their country. I hadn't planned to do this much sightseeing, but I'm not upset at all. What I've seen is absolutely beautiful. I'm surprised you don't get more tourists."

"Tourists, yes!" Ivan said, leaning forward as if to make a point. "We have many tourists now. Kazanlak, our festival. *Praznik na rozata.* You come here at good time. You'll see!"

Ivan and his wife began to clear away the dishes, and Scott stood up to help them, unleashing strong protests from his hosts. Scott wouldn't take no for an answer, and he joked with Ivan in broken

Bulgarian, demonstrating a good mood for the first time since reuniting with his grandfather. Laughter filled the kitchen as the dishes were washed, leaving Simon alone with Sophia at the backyard table. High above, the Balkan night sky was filled with a canopy of stars—stars seemingly as numerous as the rosebuds of the valley.

"Sophia, there's something I've been meaning to ask you."

"Yes?"

"I need to know why you've taken such an interest in my visit. You've gone out of your way to guide me as I looked for Scott. And now that I've found him, I'm surprised that you didn't want to get us back to Sofia as quickly as possible."

"It was no problem at all, really. I told you, there are good people in Bulgaria."

"I can't help but think that there may be something more," he said, not sure how to express his thoughts.

"What? Oh, no," she said, touching his arm gently. "I don't want you to get the wrong impression. I've enjoyed every minute being with you, Simon, but it's not like I was looking for any sort of companionship other than what we've had. You're a very nice man, Simon, and I really like you. You didn't think…"

"No, of course not. I'm not exactly a spring chicken."

"Simon, I suffered through a horrible divorce. I never mentioned that before because, well, it's not important. Let's just say that I'm not one for commitments. I've always been more attracted to my work, to my studies, and my profession. I guess I found that you had a sympathetic ear, one ready to take in a bit of Bulgaria's history and culture. I never meant to give any other impression. I hope I haven't misled you."

"No, not at all," he replied. Could he have been so vain to think that there had been anything more than simple friendship in their relationship? At his age, how could he have allowed himself to be carried away with such fantasies?

They were interrupted by the shrill ringtone of Sophia's cell phone, and she stood up to take the call. As she turned to face the smoldering coals of the grill, she covered the receiver with her hand, not that Simon would be able to understand any of her conversation.

A sudden thought popped up in Simon's mind, disturbing him and confusing him even more. Who was Sophia talking to? She had also made a mysterious call when they left the hotel in Belogradchik. It was as if Sophia was reporting not only her own whereabouts but where Simon and Scott were as well.

No, that was ridiculous, he thought, trying to dismiss his reservations about her actions. Yet he kept wondering if her interest in the missing Thracian artifact was more than academic. At times, he thought that Sophia was keener on retrieving the item than his grandson.

He hoped he could take Sophia's words at face value. More than anything, he wanted to trust her—to know that she was, in fact, one of the good people.

CHAPTER 57

She could yet make amends. Previous failures weighed heavily on her mind, but she could more than compensate for them today. All she needed to do was get close enough to ensure that this time there would be no mistakes.

She wasn't doing this for Vlady. Between swigs of beer at the *mehana* the previous night, the heavyset villager had forced her to repeat his dictated instructions until she knew them by heart. Vlady had quickly recovered from the short-acting hypnotic drug. By the time he regained consciousness in the clinic, Nikolov's men had already gone, so their sudden appearance had not been a cause for his concern. Instead of punishing her for the mishap, all that interested Vlady was renewed planning of how to abduct the American. They couldn't waste a minute in their efforts to learn where the artifact was hidden, he persisted, and he concentrated on setting their trap.

She wasn't doing this for her brother. Boris had called the previous night to get an update on what had transpired at Veliko Tarnovo. He chuckled when he learned that Vlady had accidentally been struck with the needle. "That's probably the only way to knock him out," were Boris's words. But then he turned dead serious, lecturing his sister on the importance of what she was doing, insisting there was no room for additional failure. The American had been followed to Kazanlak; that's where they would recover the artifact, Boris insisted with a confidence that Katya failed to share.

No, she wasn't doing this for either of them. She had her own reasons—reasons of far more importance for participating in this strange little scheme. She had lost the person dearest to her, and his memory still called out to her every day. The latest scars disfiguring her wrist showed how much she held herself accountable for allowing him to get away, but today she could take steps to bring him back. With every breath she inhaled she was reminded of him, every thought in her mind was turned to him. There was only one way to regain the closeness they had enjoyed, and that was by bringing him back to the confinement offered by the remote mountain cabin. She longed to care for him as before, when he knew nothing other than a life framed by her visits. The item that mattered to Vlady and Boris didn't interest her in the least. All that she desired was to bring her beloved back to the place where he would be hers alone.

Katya reached into her purse, and a huge sense of relief swept over her when she felt the coolness of the thin hypodermic syringe, wrapped in a small cloth and ready for action. The needle was protected, embedded in a small cork, but this could be instantly removed when she prepared to strike.

This time, she would make certain to identify her target before she made her move. With one prick of the needle, it would all be over. Vlady would be waiting nearby, ready to step in and handle everything else. Katya adjusted the strap of her purse and followed the crowd, which was growing in number as it converged on the festivities in the center of the town.

A few streets away, Simon walked with Sophia and Scott in the same direction. He enjoyed the slow pace, the warm day's stroll alongside typical Bulgarian families. Young children perched on their fathers' shoulders. Mothers pushed baby carriages, some of them especially built for twins lying side by side in tandem. Older residents ambled ahead with the aid of canes. Teenagers pushed forward wearing colorful T-shirts. Faded blue jeans appeared to be very popular with all ages.

As they walked, Simon could hear the discordant sounds of what sounded like a marching band—a slightly out-of-tune one at that. They passed storefronts with cardboard signs bearing the word "Sale" written in colorful letters in English. A poster advertised King-brand cigarettes. Another shop window was decorated with the familiar Coca-Cola logo. There were clothing stores and a restaurant. A vendor's arm was tied to a huge bouquet of helium-filled balloons. A stand offered trinkets and bead jewelry next to carts selling cotton candy and popcorn. Men drank beer from plastic cups, the foam spilling over to the pavement. A pack of battery-operated puppy dogs barked and danced in a circle on the sidewalk. Overhead, a huge banner strung across the street announced something in large Cyrillic letters.

"The parade starts at noon," Sophia explained to Simon. "They crowned the Rose Queen yesterday, and she'll be leading the marchers."

"Where do we go?" Simon asked Scott.

Scott's eyes were wide as he stared up and down the street, trying to see a familiar sight that would jerk his memory and provide him with the final clue. "Lance and I were here," was all he said to his grandfather.

The street ended at the town's central square, a large cement plaza surrounding a simple fountain. People hurried across the pavement to stand on the sidewalk alongside the bleachers set out for the town's dignitaries. A string cord roped off the street itself. The crowd swelled on both sides, waiting anxiously for the parade to begin. The music grew louder, blaring out of speakers strung from the light poles. People jostled for position, everyone straining for a better view.

Simon followed Sophia to a corner where the crowd was thinner. He looked around and suddenly realized that it was just the two of them.

"Scott's not here," he said, pulling Sophia's sleeve.

"I'm sure he's all right," she replied, tilting her head slightly as she gazed up the street.

Abruptly the music stopped and was replaced by the screeching of someone fiddling with the controls of an amplifier. Somewhere, out of sight, a man tapped a microphone to test the volume and began to address the crowd. His opening remarks were met by a loud round of cheering.

"That's the president of Bulgaria," Sophia explained to Simon proudly. "He's welcoming everyone to the Festival of Roses."

The speech went on for several minutes, interrupted occasionally by additional waves of applause. The crowd seemed restless. Young babies began to cry, and their mothers rocked strollers back and forth in efforts to calm them. Two boys bumped into an older woman as they hurried past on their skateboards, leading to a sharp heated exchange. The boys apologized and continued to skate behind the throngs standing on the street. The speech continued, the president apparently unconcerned with his audience's short attention span.

Scott was nowhere in sight, and Simon was starting to worry. What would happen if he had come this far only to lose his grandson again at the very last minute? What if Scott was following a clue toward the missing treasure and hadn't bothered to inform him or Sophia? What if someone was trying to harm Scott, attacking as unexpectedly as the assault at the fortress?

And then the parade began.

Farther up the street, Scott pushed his way through the crowds lining the sidewalk. He briefly glanced at the teenage girls leading the procession, their slim figures adorned with formal evening gowns and their coiffed hair topped with wreaths of flowers. The girls carried large bouquets of bright-colored roses, and sashes declaring the names of their hometowns draped over their shoulders. Taking their steps carefully, the pageant beauties waved at their cheering audience. Whistles and catcalls of appreciation hailed their passage.

A large contingent of young children marched by behind a street-wide banner announcing their school, but Scott turned his attention to the buildings on the far side of the street. Surely he would recognize one of the unpretentious two-story structures as having played a meaningful role in his past. A store? A restaurant? A hotel?

His eyes sought anything familiar that would connect everything together.

He thought back to the words of Lance's final email message. *It is safe at one of our favorite places. You know where that is. Remember when we were so tired?*

As he'd said to his grandfather and Sophia, Scott was convinced that Kazanlak was their favorite place in Bulgaria. But he had never shared the additional phrase in Lance's message. *Remember when we were so tired?* It didn't make sense on its own, but in the context of the other words, it must be connected to being in Kazanlak. The final piece of the mystery was almost within his reach, nearly tangible and visible, but he had yet to grasp what it was.

A large procession of adults made its way up the street, all of them attired in traditional Bulgarian outfits symbolic of their region in the center of the country. The men's clothing was simple, as if their outfits were geared for work on their farms, but large red sashes wrapped around their waists, and small black hats on their heads gave them a festive appearance. The women of the group wore fancier garments. Long streamers of yellow ribbon were tied to flowery headdresses, their blouses were of that bright color as well, and their lavish skirts were wide, swishing as they walked. Two men swaggering behind the group pounded on large drums, providing a beat to guide the marchers.

Pushing past the onlookers, Katya spotted the man she was looking for. He was not far ahead of her, on her side of the street. The man was not gazing at the participants in the parade but rather at the buildings beyond the crowd. Katya excused herself repeatedly as she made her way past the spectators, inching closer to him with each step. She clutched her purse tightly to her side, ready to withdraw the item that lay in readiness within. There were just too many people here, she thought. On the other hand, no one would notice her actions when she made her move.

The man she sought eased forward to the curb, staring at something across from him. As Katya approached, she saw the man's eyes suddenly light up with excitement. He stepped around the protective cord and into the street itself, nearly colliding with a baton-twirling girl costumed in festive red. The girl sidestepped him, and he shielded his eyes from the sun, taking another long glance at whatever had caught his interest.

Katya called out, expecting him to turn with recognition of her voice. He would remember everything and readily join her. There would be no need for the drug she had brought after all. It had been so long. She had missed him so much.

The man turned his back to the parade and began to shove past the people on the sidewalk. Suddenly, he looked up and noticed Katya. She smiled and opened her arms wide to embrace him.

He saw her, and the expression on his face changed instantly to one of alarm. It's me, she motioned to him, but he backed away. She inched forward, knocking into people and drawing angry looks and remarks in her wake. He moved back farther still, into the street itself.

"Stop!" she called out, but her voice couldn't be heard above the blaring music. She made her way to the pavement's edge. She reached out, and her hand briefly touched his arm.

With one last glance in her direction, he turned to run. He bounded up the middle of the street, knocking one of the marching girls to her knees and causing her baton to crash down with a tubular resonance on the concrete. He ran through the marchers, disrupting their movements and upsetting their efforts to conduct a precisely timed exercise. The girls cried out in panic and spun around to flee the intruder in their midst. Red-sequined caps fell to the ground in a flurry of scattering marching boots and short skirts.

As the crowd began to voice its alarm, Katya bolted into the street as well, pushing past the panic-stricken young girls in pursuit of the man that had interfered with their group. She nearly tripped over the fallen baton as she hurried forward, fearful that he would get away.

"Where is he?"

Katya turned to find Vlady at her side. She pointed, and they both spotted Scott racing through the marching groups, disrupting everything in his path.

"We can't let him get away," Vlady said, and then he ran after Scott, his heavy frame rushing forth like a bull in a china shop.

The marching music continued to blast from the loudspeakers, but the procession no longer paraded up the main street of Kazanlak. Instead, straight lines of an organized march morphed into chaotic disorder. Costumed marchers scattered as if being pursued by a stampede of frightened animals. Crowds on the sidewalk fled in panic, seeking safety in the narrow roads and alleys surrounding the square. Police whistles shrieked repeatedly. Someone barked orders through a megaphone. Infants cried out. Young children screamed as they ran for the protection of their parents. A small mechanized float, one of the few that had been part of the procession, careened into a roadside trinket stand, the impact resulting in a cascade of glass beads and shattered ornaments. In the commotion, a horse bolted, causing the wagon it was pulling to overturn.

Over everything, a massive cloud of pink rose petals lifted with the breeze and caught in the air, drifting back and forth to darken the sky.

CHAPTER 58

An unearthly apparition charged at Simon, startling him with animal-like features and an enormous fur-covered headdress topped with sharp, protruding horns. The blackened face of this frightening creature was angular and hairy; its eyes were demonic and dark. Simon was caught off-guard by what he saw racing toward him. It took a second to register that he was viewing a man dressed in an elaborate costume and wearing a bizarre shaggy mask. A string of cowbells around the man's waist clanged noisily with each approaching step. On his legs were knee-high white stockings, and leather thongs were tied to his shoes. A banshee-like cry escaped from beneath the mask as the man ran wildly toward the curb.

"What the hell?"

Leaping onto the sidewalk to escape the tumult of the disturbed parade, the masked man catapulted into Simon. The rim of an animal-skin drum jolted into Simon's thigh as the man passed. Within a moment, he had melted into the crowd, a fleeing spirit that may very well have been imagined.

"It's a *kukeri*," Sophia shouted, pulling Simon close. "The bells on their belts chase away the evil spirits."

Simon barely heard the explanation of the costumed merrymaker's origins. He was pushed back repeatedly by the rapidly dispersing crowd. He tried to stand in place and search through the crazy scene for his grandson. He reached out to Sophia for support, but she, too, was finding it difficult to remain on the street corner. Something had happened to disrupt the festivities, and it wasn't clear what it was.

"Grandpa, we've got to go." It was Scott, and he was panting for breath. "I know where it is. We have to hurry though because they're here, trying to follow us."

Scott pulled his grandfather along as they hurried down the narrow street toward Sophia's parked car. Music no longer played through the loudspeakers; instead, instructions were issued repeatedly, calling on everyone to remain calm. The tranquil scene of Bulgarian families enjoying the Festival of Roses celebrations was a distant memory to Simon; now all he saw were panicked citizens fleeing what appeared to be a major incident.

"Where to?" Sophia asked, glancing at Scott in the rearview mirror after she had started the motor.

"Do you know the Thracian Tomb of Kazanlak?"

"Of course. Is that where Lance hid the gym bag?"

Scott nodded, and Simon turned around to face his grandson. "Slow down, Scott. You need to explain what the hell is going on. Did something happen to you at the parade? We've already been to a number of places. How can you be sure that this is where we need to go now?"

"We don't have time for lengthy explanations," Scott said. "We're being followed by people who want what we want. We need to get to the tomb before them."

"No, that won't do," Simon said, angry at what he was hearing. "Sophia, stop the car. Really, stop!"

Sophia reluctantly pulled to the side of the road. Scott began to speak quickly, the words pouring out of his mouth, but Simon ordered him to slow down. As she listened, Sophia pulled her cell phone out of her purse and punched in a text message, but her attention was also focused on what Scott was saying.

"Okay, it's like this," Scott began. "I told my grandfather that there was more in Lance's message than just mentioning he had hid the bag in our favorite place in Bulgaria. He also said, 'remember when we were so tired.' I didn't know what that meant. I just assumed that if I remembered the place, I would also know how to decipher 'remember when we were so tired.'

"I told you yesterday that I had become convinced that Kazanlak was our favorite place in Bulgaria. I clearly remember sitting with Lance at a pub not far from the square we just visited. We were drinking beer and ogling the Bulgarian girls. Lance definitely said those words, that this was our 'favorite place.' But he wasn't exactly referring to the town of Kazanlak itself. Except when it's hosting the rose festival, Kazanlak is quite a lackluster place."

"What was he referring to?" Simon asked, unbuckling his seat belt so that he could face Scott directly.

"I didn't know for sure at first," Scott said. "It wasn't until the parade began that the final piece fit into place. I was standing on the street, looking for a clue, for anything, really, that would stir up a memory from my previous visit. And then I saw it. The pub where Lance and I were sitting. We had hiked all the way into town, and we were physically beat. That's why we enjoyed sitting down for cold beers. Lance's words, remember when we were so tired,' referred to the end of that hike when we sat at the pub."

"I don't get it," Simon said, looking to Sophia to see if she understood. She shook her head to signal that she was as confused as he was.

"The pub," Scott said, as if the answer was obvious. "The name of the pub then, as it still is today when I spotted it from across the street, is Thracian Glory."

"Thracian Glory?"

"I don't know what it's called in Bulgarian, but that's its name in English. Don't you understand? The town of Kazanlak is surrounded by many, many Thracian tombs."

"In addition to being known as the Valley of Roses, this area is also called the Valley of the Thracian Kings," Sophia confirmed. "There is a large Thracian necropolis near Kazanlak and countless burial tombs."

"Remembering our stopover at that pub, I understood the true meaning of our 'favorite place.' When we came to Kazanlak, Lance and I visited the famous tomb. Lance and I were both amazed at the colorful murals inside, depicting majestic horses and their riders. We were so spellbound by what we saw that they had to literally drag us out. It was the tomb of Kazanlak, not the town, that was our favorite place in all of Bulgaria."

Scott took a breath, and then continued his tale. "There was something else that Lance wrote in his message that I didn't mention to you before. He stated that he opened the Adidas gym bag. He saw the silver artifact … what was it called again? Oh yes, a *rhyton*, and he knew that it had been taken from an ancient Thracian burial tomb. He planned to hide it appropriately at our favorite place, and I now know this meant he intended to conceal it in the Kazanlak tomb."

"Are you sure?" Simon asked, not entirely convinced by the story.

"For us, the highlight of our Bulgarian adventure was experienced here, in the Valley of the Thracian Kings. That is why we enjoyed our visit to Kazanlak so much. We felt that we were able to touch upon that ancient time, those ancient people, and the real glory of Bulgaria's past. Everything came back to me in a flash when I saw the pub where we drank beer. Thracian Glory. I'm absolutely sure we need to go to the tomb!"

"It sounds plausible," Sophia admitted. "Simon, I think we should go and check."

"Let's just go back to Sofia now and leave all this drama to the police."

"No, Grandpa! We're almost there. We want to get there before anyone realizes where we're heading. I am convinced that this is where Lance went. Come on, please!"

The Kazanlak tomb was located just a short drive outside the town, and within a few minutes, they were there. As they walked from the car, Sophia explained the tomb's history and significance.

"It was unearthed by chance in 1944, when the army was digging an air-defense observation post," she said. "Unique to all the tombs in Bulgaria, it has a totally preserved ancient mural, quite a masterpiece of Thracian art. Because of this, the tomb was recognized by UNESCO and is included on its World Heritage List."

"Yeah, they told us all that when we came here on the tour. Let's go inside," Scott said impatiently, urging them toward the park's entrance.

A large sign at the side of the pathway announced, with a very noticeable spelling mistake, "*Vizit the Valley of the Roses and the Thracian Kings.*"

"Visiting hours are nearly over," Simon noted, reading the details listed.

"We have enough time," Scott replied.

They paid the three-leva entrance fee and entered the burial-mound grounds. The tomb was located on a hill set in a lush expanse of spacious green lawns and flowerbeds, pathways, and stairs. The first building they came to was marked with a prominent sign announcing that it enclosed the famous tomb. Built entirely out of reddish brick, the structure welcomed them with heavily barred windows and an entrance door secured in metal. Access to the ancient wonders inside was off limits.

"We can't get in!" Simon exclaimed. The tomb was locked, and they had come all this way for nothing.

CHAPTER 59

"Visitors aren't allowed inside the Kazanlak tomb," Sophia explained. "It's too delicate an ancient site for tourists. There's a copy, quite authentic, just ahead. Scott, which one did you visit when you were here?"

Not bothering to reply, Scott hurried up the path.

A copy of a tomb? This didn't make sense to Simon. He turned to Sophia and was surprised to see that she was whispering into her cell phone. Who was she talking to? What's with all these phone calls?

By the time they reached the entrance to the tomb's duplicate, the one open for regular visits, Sophia had finished her call and returned to her role as their tour guide.

"This duplicate of the tomb allows visitors to observe the beauty of the well-preserved frescoes dating back to the third century BC without causing any damage. I've been in the original tomb, and it's quite impressive, but it's not particularly visitor friendly. Setting up this duplicate was vital for the tomb's preservation. Otherwise, there would be nothing left of the unique structure."

Sophia explained that the Kazanlak tomb was of the beehive type, also known as a *tholos* tomb. This meant that it was a burial structure characterized by an internal false dome created by the superimposition of successively smaller layers of stones, creating a beehive effect. The outsides of such tombs were typically covered so that from a distance they appeared like small raised hills, or mounds.

"This tomb consists of three chambers, as is customary of all Thracian burial sites," Sophia continued. "There is a chamber for the ruler's horses, a corridor that included the material goods needed by the ruler in the afterlife, and a burial chamber for the body itself. What is particularly unique about the Kazanlak tomb, what makes it special, are its murals—perfectly preserved examples of Thracian art."

They stood in the dimly lit hallway, gazing up at horsemen and their steeds. The horses, portrayed in a variety of colors, were elaborately adorned with silver-gilt harness ornaments. The riders stood to the side, not dressed for battle or conquest, but rendered instead in simple white tunics. Sophia explained that they were viewing a typical Thracian gathering at a ritual funeral feast. It didn't matter that this was just a reproduction of what was discovered a short distance away. It was an awesome mural even if it was but a copy.

With closing time approaching, the last of the other visitors left the building, and they were alone, admiring the mural high above their heads. The chambers were dank and shadowy, the air stagnant and slightly unpleasant. It was as if they were visiting a centuries-old subterranean cavern and not something built for visitors in the past decade.

Scott moved to one side, toward the back of the main chamber. He began touching the walls, constructed in modern times in the fashion of the ancient Thracians. He had been here before, he recalled. He and Lance had been fooling around, pretending that they were the dead Thracian ruler's ghost come to life and ready to haunt anyone who disturbed his eternal resting place. They had chased each other around the central chamber, not particularly paying attention to the Thracian artwork above their heads. And that is when Lance had discovered the stone in the side wall that could be eased out of place.

And now, Scott found that exact spot. With a sigh of pleasure, he slipped his fingers into the tiny crack, moving the stone back and forth slightly, loosening it from its setting in the wall.

"What are you doing?" Simon asked, coming up to his grandson and ready to reprimand him for disturbing this tomb, even if it was only a replica of the ancient original.

Sophia looked on with fascination, holding her cell phone in her hand as if she wanted to photograph Scott's strange actions.

The stone came loose, and Scott slowly removed it from the wall. Exposed to view was a deep cavity, the same hole in the wall that he and Lance had discovered more than three years before. But unlike then, this time the hole was not empty. There was something inside, and Scott stretched his hands in to bring it out.

Scott withdrew the wine-colored sports bag with the Adidas logo and lowered it to the cement floor of the chamber. Without bothering to glance at his companions, he bent down to unzip the bag.

"Wait," Simon said, almost speechless.

"What is there to wait for?" Scott asked, looking up at both Simon and Sophia triumphantly. The zipper caught at first, but then eased down its track. Scott peeled back the fabric sides of the bag. Inside was an undefined object enwrapped in bubble paper, and he handled this package with extreme care.

Scott slowly removed the wrapping, exposing a half-meter-long silver ornament. Simon held his breath as he watched his grandson finish this delicate task. The chamber was deadly quiet as the ancient wonder was revealed. Scott held up the heavy *rhyton,* angling it so that it would be visible in the beam of an overhead spotlight.

The tarnished silver, untouched and unpolished for many years, was still magnificent to see. There was no denying the object's grandeur and appeal.

"That's quite amazing," Simon commented, staring in wonder at the grooved drinking horn used in mysterious ceremonies and rituals more than two thousand years before. The finely carved lion's head at its bottom was a stunning display of craftsmanship. "So that's what a *rhyton* looks like. I couldn't exactly picture it."

"Allow me to just check something," Sophia said. "May I?" she asked, reaching for the artifact.

"Sure," Scott said, preparing to hand her the heavy object.

A strange thought popped into Simon's head with no advance warning. Scott had rediscovered the ancient treasure, hidden as he had guessed in a Thracian tomb. It was a priceless piece, and the fact that Scott had located it was quite unbelievable. As inconceivable as all this was turning out to be, what disturbed Simon was a sudden and unexplained hesitation about allowing his grandson to hand over the valuable object to Sophia.

Should the artifact be given so freely to the woman? Simon wondered about all the strange phone calls she had been making, including a conversation conducted the minute they arrived at the Kazanlak tomb. With whom was she talking? Was she reporting on their trip, on their activities? Was she alerting someone, giving out precise directions how to find them? Had she instructed Scott's host parents to meet them in Belogradchik? Had she been in contact with the pair that had attacked Simon in Veliko Tarnovo?

His suspicion regarding his travel guide made him wonder if Sophia was really the specialist in Thracian history that she said she was. Was she really on their side?

"No, don't!" he said suddenly, holding back Scott and preventing him from handing the *rhyton* to Sophia.

"What are you doing, Grandpa?"

"Simon, what's the matter?"

"I think we should call the police immediately, and tell them what you've found. It's the safest procedure," he said, still firmly grasping Scott's arm.

"Grandpa, what's gotten into you? We finally found it. Our quest was successful. We can go home now."

"Simon, I just want to check that this is the original artifact, the one that's been missing from the museum all these years," Sophia said calmly. "I need to authenticate it. That's my job."

"Your job?" Simon asked. "What do you mean, your job?"

"Hand it over, please."

These words echoed in the enclosed chamber, but they weren't coming from Sophia. It was a male voice, authoritative and demanding. They turned in unison toward the corridor leading from the tomb's entrance and saw a large man standing there, menacingly aiming a pistol at them.

"Hand it over, mister peace-lover," he repeated, indicating the *rhyton* with a wave of his gun.

There was a woman to his side, and with a burst of recognition, Scott blurted out, "It's Vlady and Katya!"

"The couple who attacked me in the elevator!" Simon added with alarm.

"For the last time, I say, hand it over," Vlady said as he clicked back the safety of his revolver and placed his finger on the trigger.

CHAPTER 60

In all the years she had known him, Katya had never seen Vlady brandish a gun. Boris's partner was the mastermind of their illicit activities, capable of organizing petty thefts and cross-border smuggling missions. He had planned the museum heist, as well as a string of other robberies and break-ins. Vlady never stopped scheming, dreaming of how he would make the ultimate hit that would eventually allow him to live the life of a rich man and leave his life of crime. It was due to Vlady's efforts that Boris had likewise become involved in illegal adventures. Deep inside, she realized that she reviled Vlady. The man was short-tempered, impatient with his many failures At times, Vlady could turn violent, physically injuring those he distrusted or any who had slighted him. But she had never before seen him hold a gun. Where did that come from?

Vlady pointed his gun at Scott, signaling him to hand over the Thracian treasure. He ignored the two others in the chamber. They were insignificant bystanders, expendable if necessary. Right now, he demanded possession of the artifact.

Scott's expression was one of shock, not at being threatened with a weapon but rather by again seeing the woman who had incarcerated him for so long. His eyes burned with disgust, something that Katya could not begin to understand. She wondered why he had rejected her advances in Belogradchik, dismissed her attempts to get close. How could he ignore her then—or now—when she had done so much to care for him? Was he not thankful for her efforts?

The older American man took a step backward, holding up his hands and pleading softly for Vlady not to fire. The woman, though, stepped forward boldly and addressed Vlady and Katya in Bulgarian.

"I would put down the gun, if I was you," the woman said. "The authorities will be here any minute."

"Nice try," Vlady chuckled, his throaty laughter echoing in the chamber. "Nobody's coming to rescue you, and this park has already closed to visitors. Your only hope is to hand over the artifact without making problems. It's mine, and you'd be wise to give it to me before I use this weapon."

"The item doesn't belong to you at all," the woman argued, taking another hesitant step toward him. "This artifact is a national treasure. It belongs to all the people of Bulgaria, not to thieves and antiques smugglers. It's my job to make sure it's the real thing and to return it to its rightful place in a museum where everyone can enjoy it."

"What a nice little story," Vlady said, raising the gun and aiming it directly at Sophia. "It's too bad that none of you will see the day when this treasure will again be on display."

There were footsteps in the corridor, getting steadily louder as a group of people approached. Simon heard them coming, hoping and praying that it was the Bulgarian police. Perhaps that was whom Sophia had called after all. She had stepped forward to protect them against this gun-wielding couple, so she must be okay. He had been wrong to doubt her motives.

Four men in dark suits entered the chamber, adjusting their eyes to the dim light. One of them, a bald-headed man with gold-stud earrings and a huge physique, seemed slightly familiar. Another man was obviously the group's leader. With barely a glance at Simon and Scott, he went directly to Vlady and held out his hand for the gun.

"You've done your job very nicely, my friend," Alexander Nikolov said in Bulgarian to Vlady. "Thank you very much for leading me to the package that you promised to deliver so long ago."

Nikolov's arrival was enough for Katya to realize that she had been right to distrust Vlady. It was clear now that Vlady had been in constant contact with the antiques dealer, updating him regularly about their progress in recovering the Thracian artifact. Vlady must have been in cahoots with Nikolov and his gang from the very beginning. Boris had innocently served as Vlady's accomplice in crime, while in reality, Vlady had sold Boris out.

Crippled and confined to a wheelchair for the rest of his life, her brother was left with nothing, while Vlady, unscathed and aligned with the country's most-wanted criminal, would undoubtedly be paid well for his services after finally delivering the goods. She couldn't shake the fact that Vlady had betrayed her brother!

"You idiot!" Katya screamed, leaping at Vlady. With a ferocity that took him by surprise, she attacked his face with her sharp fingernails. Clawing him like a wild mountain bear, she drew blood in deep parallel gashes as he held up his free hand in ineffectual efforts to hold her off. Striking out with her nails was something Katya usually reserved for self-punishment, penance for her many failures. Now her nails served as agents of revenge for Vlady's betrayal of her brother and how he had ultimately deceived her as well.

Caught off-guard and shocked at the assault, Vlady lifted the pistol high over his head to keep the weapon away from his partner's sister. Ignoring the pain of his facial wounds, he held her off while the others looked on in stunned silence. Katya turned her focus to Vlady's weapon. She tried to reach up and seize the gun.

A single shot was fired and reverberated in the tight quarters of the burial chamber. Striking the ceiling, it caused a plaster shower from above. Katya stepped back, her anger spent. As shocked as the rest of them, Vlady held one hand to his bloodied face and forked over the revolver to Nikolov's bald-headed associate. Everyone remained silent, as silent as the long-dead Thracian ruler to whose memory an ancient artist had painted such a colorful mural in tribute.

"It's you," Scott said in English, staring at Nikolov with growing recognition and hatred. "You stole my passport and had your muscleman guard beat me. I lost three years of my life because of you!" He was furious, but unlike Katya, he did not leap forward to attack the person who had caused him so much pain. While it was the bald man who had actually inflicted his wounds, Scott's anger was directed solely at Nikolov, who had given the orders that resulted in his beating.

"You're the hotel manager from Golden Sands," Simon said, also recognizing the man. "I talked to you when I was in Varna. You barely gave me the time of day when I was trying to determine Scott's whereabouts."

"Ah, yes," Nikolov said in English, turning to acknowledge the foreigners. "You came to me in search of your missing grandson, and now, here he is. He is holding the very item that caused his disappearance. I am pleased that he has seen fit to find it for my benefit. Now, my young American friend, if you would kindly hand over that item, we can finish with all this unpleasantness and everyone can go their merry way."

Hearing the authoritative tone in Nikolov's voice, and realizing that the men in the black suits were armed with weapons much more powerful than Vlady's old revolver, Scott stepped forward and handed him the silver artifact. Nikolov took it without a word of thanks and swung it carelessly, as if it was just a scrap of old metal.

"A wise move," he said, nodding at Scott.

Nikolov muttered something in Bulgarian to his men. While neither Simon nor Scott understood the directive, Sophia immediately realized the explicit danger of this whispered command. Nikolov had instructed his men to "clean up."

Nikolov's henchmen quickly moved into action. One of them grabbed Sophia's wrists as she tried unsuccessfully to escape his grip. The bald-headed goon approached Simon, causing Scott to jump forward and stand between the huge man and his grandfather. Simon took a deep breath, not fully understanding what was happening.

"Not so fast, Nikolov!"

Due to the commotion caused first by Katya's attack on Vlady, and then by the sudden moves of the dark-suited men, none of them had noticed the sound of additional footsteps approaching in the corridor. Suddenly, the lights in the chamber switched on to their brightest intensity and the hall was filled with people and noise, a definite demonstration of authority. Scott noticed at least three armed policemen and two other men, one of whom stepped forward to approach Simon.

"Aren't you from the American embassy?" Simon asked, amazed at whom he was seeing. Strangers were appearing in this burial tomb at an incredible rate, and, surprisingly, he was recognizing them one by one.

"Yes, we've met a few times already," answered Brett Thompson, the embassy's deputy consul.

One of the new arrivals retrieved the precious Thracian artifact, and another officer snapped Nikolov's hands into cuffs. Nikolov's team was disarmed, and the officers prepared to lead them, as well as Katya and Vlady, out from the tomb.

As she was being dragged away, Katya mouthed one word repeatedly, a name. She took one last look at Scott, the man to whom she had devoted three years of her life. She had cared for him, acted as his nurse, brought him groceries, and delivered him the narcotics that were required by his condition. She had done so much for him, keeping him warm and safe in the mountain cabin, yet there were no words of thanks, no appreciation was expressed on the occasion of this final good-bye. Tears streamed down her cheeks as she realized she would probably never see him again. The loss was overwhelming; it shook her deeply. She mouthed his name, over and over, willing him to look at her, to come to her, to comfort her. The name she said silently, so that only she could hear it in her innermost soul, was the name of her long-lost husband.

"Hristo," Katya whispered, one last time, and then she was escorted from the chamber.

Only Thompson and the older man who had entered the tomb with him were left standing with Simon, Scott, and Sophia.

A big smile lit up on Thompson's face as he spoke to the American professor. "I want to thank you for your unwavering belief that your grandson was still alive all this time. You had the guts to continue the search for him three years after we closed his file, his disappearance unsolved.

"Thanks to your perseverance, not only has Scott Matthews been found, but we have also managed to recover the priceless Rogozen Drinking Lion. And that is due, in part, to the assistance of Sophia Ivanova, your lovely travel companion."

"Sophia?"

Ignoring Simon's questioning look, the American official continued to speak. "And finally, I want to thank both of you, Professor Matthews and Scott, for leading us, with irrefutable proof at last, to the capture of Alexander Nikolov, the notorious dealer of stolen Bulgarian antiques, who has evaded the police for so many years. Rest assured that the authorities will stage a fair judicial process for that man. Those other two, those villagers, are petty lawbreakers—not worth getting excited about. But Alexander Nikolov, he's the real thing."

"So, do we have confirmation?" asked the unidentified, gray-haired man, looking anxiously at Sophia.

"I haven't had a chance to examine the *rhyton* yet," Sophia replied. And then she turned to Scott, who had taken the artifact back from one of the officers when Nikolov was arrested. "May I look at it now?"

This time Simon didn't have a reason to object. Sophia tenderly clasped the silver drinking horn, turned it slightly, handling it with both professionalism and tenderness. She switched on a small flashlight and focused it on the drinking horn's inner lip. There she saw the ancient Thracian inscription, written in tiny Greek letters. She read them, one by one, her lips moving silently as she formed the words.

"Ah, yes," she sighed. "This is it. The inscription reads simply, 'Mother Earth.' This is the authentic item, the famous Rogozen Drinking Lion."

"Thank you, my dear," the older man said. "I had no doubt that this was the genuine item. I recognized it immediately."

"Excuse me for asking, but who are you?" Simon asked.

"Pardon me for not introducing myself. I am Professor Todor Smirnenski, chairman of the Bulgarian Academy of Science. I was one of Sophia Ivanova's lecturers in her student days. We didn't actually get along too well at that time, did we, my dear? In any case, in my later years I have led a campaign to help recover Bulgaria's most-valuable stolen treasures. Thanks to Sophia's great work, and assistance from the American embassy, we have now recovered the priceless Rogozen Drinking Lion."

"Professor Smirnenski discovered the Rogozen Drinking Lion in 1985," Sophia pointed out. "He asked me, due to my academic thesis on the subject of Thracian *rhytons* and my knowledge of the archaic Thracian language, to be the one to identify and authenticate this treasure whenever it was recovered."

"Yes, Sophia is the expert in these fields. What can I say? In this case, the student has managed to far outshine her old teacher."

"Shall we?" Thompson said, indicating with his hand that they should leave the artificial burial tomb and return to the very real sunlight of the June afternoon.

CHAPTER 61

"So, let me get this straight," Simon said, looking seriously at his hostess. "Nothing was by chance? Not even our meeting in the bar at the Hilton?"

They were sitting in Sophia's living room, sipping tea and eating bite-sized chocolate cookies while Scott took a shower. In another hour, Sophia would call for a taxi to transport the two Americans to the airport. Thanks to Brett Thompson from the embassy, all the red tape of issuing Scott a new passport had been removed. Flights out of the country were booked with no problems; they would reunite with Daniel and Susan in Chicago. The end of their stay in Bulgaria had arrived.

"That, I must admit, was arranged," Sophia said. "I don't know how well Thompson explained the situation, but while Nikolov and his antiques smuggling have been the focus of an international police investigation for years, they never were able to catch him in the act. Interpol was involved, and I think the FBI was also on alert. It was known that Vlady and his partner were mixed up in some of the smuggling, but they were small fry. The goal was to catch Nikolov, the big fish. It was Nikolov who contracted the museum robbery and the delivery of the *rhyton* to him to Varna. The cold trail created by the years-long burial of the stolen item didn't result in decreased interest by the authorities. Surveillance continued all the time. Even while Scott was trapped in that remote cabin, the police were still on the lookout, waiting for Nikolov or his agents to make their move."

"So how does that connect to your meeting me in the hotel bar?"

"The Americans knew that your grandson was involved, but they had concluded that Nikolov and his thugs had murdered Scott in Golden Sands. How else could his passport have turned up at that resort hotel? It was a logical conclusion, but Scott's body was never found. When you came to Bulgaria and met with Thompson at the embassy, the Americans decided to have you followed, to see if you would learn anything new about where Scott was or what he had done. Maybe, if they got lucky, you would discover where he had hidden the *rhyton*. This would benefit everyone."

"That still doesn't explain how you became involved."

"I don't know how much I've told you about my past, but I've assisted the police and Interpol before. I'm considered a local expert on Thracian artifacts. They asked me to tag along on your journeys, to authenticate the *rhyton* if you found it."

"And here I thought that you volunteered to accompany me due to my charm."

Sophia laughed and lightly touched his shoulder. "Simon, you are a very charming man, and I've enjoyed every minute of our travels, but as I told you, I'm not looking to form that kind of relationship."

"So, you purposely found me at the hotel bar, and then you also arranged to meet me, seemingly by chance, at Starbucks?"

"Yes, that's true. I hope that doesn't offend you."

"No, not really, because the main goal of my visit to Bulgaria was achieved. I came to find my lost grandson, and in my goal, I was hugely successful. It was only later that Scott forced me to join him on the Bulgarian treasure hunt."

"You know, I was almost certain we would see Scott at the Rila Monastery. You got that phone call suggesting he was there."

"Yes. I should really call Dave Harris from Varna to tell him of our success. Tell me, did you call Thompson when we arrived in Kazanlak, and later, when we went to the tomb?"

"Yes, he was informed every step of the way. I'm sorry, Simon, if I've deceived you. But in the end, we both got what we were looking for."

"It's okay, really."

"How is your son taking all this, I mean, besides the excitement of learning that Scott is alive? Didn't he argue with you all along against your coming to Bulgaria?"

"Yes, he was quite adamant in his opposition to my trip. In addition, Daniel became very angry when Scott and I extended our stay here while we searched for the Thracian artifact. But that's all behind us now. I spoke with Daniel, and he regrets doubting me, doubting my mission. While he didn't say outright that he's sorry, I could hear the apology in his voice. He promised me that the two of us will talk—really talk—when we get together in Chicago. I have a feeling we'll be able to sort out our differences. I look forward to talking to my son."

"There's one other question that sticks in my mind," she said, holding up the plate to offer him another cookie.

"What's that?"

"What did Scott actually plan to do with the *rhyton* when he found it? I mean, if Nikolov and the police hadn't come along?"

"I don't think Scott ever thought that through to the end," Simon said. "I guess he realized that leaving the Thracian treasure in the place where Lance hid it was not really appropriate. It's far better for it to be on display in a museum, where everyone can see it. That's where it truly belongs."

"Well, that's for sure," she agreed.

"I'm eager to get back to the States already. This has been quite an unplanned and eventful adventure. You know, I feel like this is the second time I'm leaving. When I packed up originally at the Hilton, I was sure that it was my last night in Sofia. I said my farewell to the country at that time. We had already visited Vratsa and Montana in the north, and the Rila Monastery in the south. I thought the adventure had come to its end. Little did I know that the biggest thrills of my visit were yet ahead."

"Maybe you'll come back one day to Bulgaria, to see the rest of the country at a leisurely pace."

"I hope so. Someday," he sighed, gently touching the bruise on his cheek.

Scott walked into the living room, his hair still wet from the shower. He adjusted the silver chain strung around his neck, its symbol of life glittering momentarily as it caught in the light. "Did you call the taxi?" he asked.

"It'll only take a few minutes for it to arrive, so we have time," Sophia replied. "I'm sorry I won't be able to take you, but as I told your grandfather, I'm meeting with some of my colleagues this evening. I've taken a lot of time off from my duties at the university and now, to my dismay, I must return to my work."

"Thank you for everything you've done—for me, and especially for caring for my grandfather," Scott said, reaching to shake her hand.

"Oh, come now. Don't be so formal," she said, standing up to hug him. "Maybe we should have a toast, to wish you a safe journey. How about a glass of *rakia*?"

"No!" Simon and Scott said in unison.

A few minutes later, Scott stuffed his laptop into his backpack and dragged Simon's suitcase to the door. Sophia called the taxi company, and they waited for the callback announcing a cab's arrival.

"How do you say good-bye in Bulgarian?" Simon asked.

"*Dovizhdane*," Sophia replied.

"Dovizh-da-what? That's almost impossible to say!"

"We could just say 'see you soon,'" Sophia suggested. "That's a bit easier. *Do skoro*," she said.

"*Do skoro*," Simon repeated. "I like that, and I'll try to remember it."

Sophia's cell phone beeped, and she stood up to hug Simon. He pushed down hard on the sofa and rose to his feet. As he stood, his face puckered up strangely and then unexpectedly he issued a noisy sneeze.

"*Nazdrave*," she said, wishing him good health.

"*Do skoro*," he replied with a smile. And then he embraced her and all that he had learned about Bulgaria.

Acknowledgements

Bulgaria is an amazing country, still mostly undiscovered by Western tourists. My wife and I had the opportunity to live in Sofia for two years and we utilized that time to travel around the country, to meet its people, explore its villages and parks, and to learn the country's story. Every effort was made in this book to portray Bulgaria's towns and cities, history, culture, customs, language, and stunning scenery as accurately as possible.

Bulgarians are warm and hospitable, and speaking from my own experience, they are very open to accepting foreigners into their homes and lives. The Bulgarians who play roles in this book are fictitious characters and in no way represent real people living in the country.

I have huge respect for the Peace Corps, and especially for the contribution it has made to Bulgaria since the first volunteers arrived in the country in 1991. The characters I described in this book in no way represent actual Peace Corps volunteers who have done so much to help Bulgarians learn English, build communities, and improve their lives.

I would like to thank Philip W. Rudy, Director of Programming and Training at Peace Corps Bulgaria, for his willingness to answer questions about the training program in the country. Thanks are also extended to Valerie Goode who served in the Peace Corps in Bulgaria for nearly 2 1/2 years and was very willing to answer my questions about her experiences.

As part of my research into the ancient customs of the Thracians who lived in the region I turned to linguistics expert Keith Massey, Ph.D. who confirmed many of my assumptions, including the fact that we know next to nothing about the language spoken by the Thracians. Some of the Thracian artifacts described in this book are quite real, while others, including the Rogozen Drinking Lion, are fictional.

Scott's amnesiac state, as portrayed in the book, was partially based on the article "Psychology Q&A: Dissociative Amnesia After a Trauma?" by Carolyn Kaufman, PsyD, however, I took certain liberties in expanding the symptoms due to the fact that Scott was being intentionally drugged by the woman who cared for him.

I am very grateful to Amber Barry Jones, who edited the manuscript of this novel. Amber not only improved the grammar, punctuation, and sentence structure of my narrative, but she also raised many pertinent questions that helped me focus my message and descriptions. I take full responsibility for any errors and/or typos remaining in the book.

My sincere thanks to Shiran Waldman, a former colleague, for designing the cover of this book, based on a photograph I took on one of my journeys in Bulgaria.

I would also like to thank the many family members, friends, and Internet acquaintances who offered comments and suggestions after reading initial paragraphs, chapters, and sections of the book. Thanks are due to my good friend, Ranen Omer-Sherman, who helped guide both the narrative and grammar, even though he never visited me in Bulgaria.

And finally, to my wonderful wife, Jodie, my sincere thanks for not only helping me improve this book, but for also being at my side during the two years of our Bulgarian adventure. I couldn't have done this without you!

About the Author

Ellis Shuman was born in Sioux City, Iowa, and immigrated to Israel as a teenager. He completed high school in Jerusalem and served for three years in the Israeli army's Nahal branch. Along with his wife, Jodie, he was a founding member of Kibbutz Yahel in the Arava Valley in Israel's south. On the kibbutz he worked in agriculture, industry, tourism, the dairy barn, and served as the kibbutz's general secretary.

After moving with his wife and three young children to Moshav Neve Ilan in the Judean Hills, Ellis received formal training in the hotel industry. He worked in a variety of positions at the Neve Ilan Hotel and later was Food and Beverage Controller at the Jerusalem Hilton. He served as the moshav's general secretary during a period in which the community underwent major social changes.

As a hobby, Ellis began writing on the Internet. He wrote extensively about life in Israel in his position as the Israeli Culture Guide at About.com. He designed and maintained websites for the Neve Ilan Hotel and for Indic—Independent Israeli Cinema. For two years he was webmaster for Yazam, an international financial firm that provided support for technological start-ups.

Ellis served for three years as Editor in Chief of Israel Insider, an online daily newsmagazine that developed new technologies as it posted the latest news and views, from and about Israel.

Starting in 2004, Ellis began working in a marketing company servicing the online gaming industry. In the years 2009 - 2010, his job was relocated to Sofia, Bulgaria. During those years, Ellis and Jodie traveled extensively in Bulgaria as well as in the countries of the region. Today Ellis continues working at this job, based in Ramat Gan.

Ellis's first book was *The Virtual Kibbutz*, originally published in 2003 and released in a revised digital version in December, 2012. *The Virtual Kibbutz* is a collection of short stories dealing with the changing society of the kibbutz, Israel's unique communal society. *The Virtual Kibbutz* is available at Amazon, Barnes & Noble, and at other online retailers.

Read about Ellis and Jodie's Bulgarian Adventure at their blog:
http://shumansinbulgaria.blogspot.com/
Visit Ellis at his writing blog, which he updates regularly:
http://ellisshuman.blogspot.com

Made in the USA
Middletown, DE
09 September 2023

38245288R00199